After a passionless marriage under the scrutiny of high society, Avery Stowe is taking back her life. All she wants is a little privacy and a quiet place to raise her autistic daughter, Hailey. Redwood Ridge, Oregon, seems to offer all the right ingredients. Except for the problem of the local sexy veterinarian. The last thing she needs in her life is to fall for his irresistible allure, even if he is a nice guy who keeps doing her favors. But the well-meaning patrons of her new hometown have other ideas, and it appears playing Cupid is one of them.

Cade O'Grady has never met a woman he couldn't handle, but when Avery Stowe walks into his office late one night cradling an injured puppy, he's struck stupid. Which might explain her total lack of interest in him. But now that she's working for his family's clinic, he doesn't have to lust from a distance. He might just have a chance at convincing Avery—and her too-guarded heart—that falling for the right man isn't a mistake . . .

D0932706

Books by Kelly Moran

Redwood Ridge
Puppy Love

Published by Kensington Publishing Corporation

Puppy Love

Redwood Ridge

Kelly Moran

LYRICAL PRESS
Kensington Publishing Corp.
www.kensingtonbooks.com

First Electronic Edition: February 2017
eISBN-13: 978-1-5161-0273-0
eISBN-10: 1-5161-0273-8

First Print Edition: February 2017
ISBN-13: 978-1-5161-0276-1
ISBN-10: 1-5161-0276-2

Printed in the United States of America

This book is whole-heartedly dedicated to my writing group, The Floozies. Vonnie, Alison, Angel, Auria, Sarah, Dixie, AJ, Mac, Amy & Arial...I couldn't do this without you.

A very special note to my nephew Connor, who lives with Autism and teaches me strength, humor and resolve continually.

Acknowledgements

A big thank you to the team at Brentwood Animal Hospital, especially Lynn, who made sure I got the veterinarian thing down right. Any errors are my own. And a gracious thanks to my street team member, Raquel, for answering aviary questions and sharing stories.

Chapter 1

Avery Stowe squinted and leaned closer to the steering wheel, trying to see past the fat white snowflakes blanketing a dark, quiet Redwood Ridge. They sure didn't make storms like this in San Francisco. She supposed her mom's insight on trading in her Camry for a SUV before the move had been the right call. Her sedan never would've gotten them through an Oregon winter. Even her flighty mother had to be right once and awhile. Once, being the operative word.

Grateful to almost be at their destination after two days of travel, Avery chanced a peek at Hailey in the backseat and breathed a sigh. Assured her daughter was still asleep in her booster, she directed her attention to the road.

Four inches had already fallen since they hit the state border. It was insane. Pretty, but insane. Having never been outside of warm, sunny California, this was a culture shock. But…new year, new start. Both she and Hailey needed this.

Even if the new town did look like *Silent Hill*. She checked for creepy zombie things, but found none.

The sidewalks had been rolled up for the night, the only illumination coming from the old world lampposts lining the two-lane cobblestone street. Avery thought her mom had fallen out of the crazy tree—and hit every branch on the way down—when she moved here ten years ago after inheriting a string of cabins from an aunt they never knew existed. Her mom had been happy, though, and figured Avery and Hailey would be, too.

It sure seemed ideal on paper. "Not *Silent Hill*, not *Silent Hill*." Seriously. Where was everybody?

Pocketed between the coast and the foothills of the Klamath Mountains, Redwood Ridge was both a tourist hotspot and a charming small town of fifteen hundred residents. It had to have merit if it was able to hold her mother's attention this long. Row after row of small, independent shops lined both sides of the street. It was like stepping back in time to simpler, sweeter days. If only it had people.

Ten minutes later, the snow was dwindling and they were on a private road cocooned by cypress, pine, and redwood. It was pretty freakin' amazing, but she'd have to appreciate it more later. In daylight. Right now it looked like the set for *Friday the 13th*.

Maybe she should stop watching horror movies altogether.

They passed a few larger homes still decorated for Christmas and, five miles down, made the turnoff to the rentals. She pulled up to the first cabin and parked, eying her surroundings. *Not Friday the 13th.*

That was a yes to no more scary movies. Definitely.

There were five log cabins in total, evenly spaced and single story, dusted with snow. Cookie cutter in design, each had a small porch and an A-frame slant roof. The first had a warm, yellow glow illuminating the windows and smoke billowing from the chimney. Her mother's car was parked off to the side.

For the first time in what seemed like ten years, Avery breathed and closed her eyes. No sirens or horns. No conversation or rush. No ex or in-laws to fight. Just…peace.

Until Jason arrives in his white hockey mask…

Okay, that's it. Nothing but comedy movies from now on.

It would take some getting used to, but the move would be worth it for Hailey. With her daughter's condition, too much stimulation equaled tantrums and fits. The city life wasn't for them. Maybe Hailey would excel better in this environment. Having her mother close by was a bonus, too. During her childhood, Avery often felt more like the parent in their two-person family as her mother was always off in la-la land. She never lacked for love, though, and right now, she desperately needed support.

It had been so long since she had someone to lean on.

Avery glanced in the backseat and reached around to tap Hailey's knee. "Hey, sweetie. We're here."

Like a switch, her daughter's dark eyelashes flickered to reveal blue eyes the same color as her dad's. All her other traits had come from Avery. Thick, brown hair and a curvy, lithe frame. Even at seven years old, Hailey was the spitting image of her.

Hailey took in her surroundings in the seemingly distracted manner Avery had grown used to since her daughter's Autism diagnosis. Her gaze darted everywhere at once, never landing on one spot for more than a millisecond. After a moment, she squealed and flapped her hands. *Well done, Mother,* Avery imagined her saying.

Since Hailey was a nonverbal Autistic, at least so far, Avery often choreographed her own dialogue in her head. It had helped her cope.

She smiled, pleased Hailey liked what she saw. "Grandma's inside waiting for us. Would you like to check out our new home?" At least it would be home until Avery could find them an apartment or small house to rent. Perhaps *not* next to Camp Crystal Lake.

Hailey squealed again and fumbled with the seatbelt, clumsily getting it undone. Avery quickly climbed out of the car and met her daughter by the rear passenger door before she could take off. Deciding to wait until after they saw the place, she left their bags in the car and directed Hailey up the porch steps, careful not to touch her more than necessary.

The door swung inward before they could knock, and the sight of her mother standing there had tears clogging Avery's throat. Justine Berry might be capricious and unpredictable, but she'd always been there. After everything her and her daughter had been through, Avery just needed...her mom.

"I'm so excited you're here!" She bent down at eye level with Hailey, bursting at the seams to hug her granddaughter.

It went against her mother's instincts not to smother, but Avery knew Hailey's limitations. She had warned her a million times before the drive, just in case she forgot. Her mother and memory lapses were BFFs.

Hailey nudged her grandmother aside and rushed into the cabin. *Outta the way, G-ma. Better things to do.*

Avery shrugged. "She's excited. That's a good thing."

In the next instant, she was wrapped in her mom's arms and squeezed until breathing became impossible. The familiar scent of patchouli filled her nose. She bit back the tears threatening to fall and smiled. "Hi, Mom."

"At least I can still hug you." Mom stepped back and patted her wild, shoulder-length brown hair. She preferred the natural approach to everything, so it probably hadn't seen conditioner or product. In decades. The fine lines around her mouth and eyes had grown deeper in the year since she'd last visited Avery in San Fran, which only added to her mother's charm. She was a woman who laughed often and loved hard. Four ex-husbands were proof. "How were the roads?"

Avery closed the door behind her. "A little slick, but not too bad. Wow, Mom. This place is great."

Not B horror movie at all.

The whole cabin was natural wood and stone and glass. Shiny, clean, and rustic. A floor to ceiling redbrick fireplace created warmth from a corner. Plaid print couches were nestled over the bare wood floor with scarred pine tables. The living room was spacious and separated from the kitchen by an island. Large picture windows encased the back of the open room, where moonlight caught the water trickling in a thin riverbed.

Hailey disappeared down a short hallway and squealed. Avery went to follow, but her mom stopped her with a hand on her arm.

"There's no exit back there and nothing to get into. These cabins are rentals, so they're pretty bare. I did stock the kitchen for you, though." She smiled and hugged her again. "I'm so glad you're here. Ten years and you just now get to see my town."

Avery pushed down the guilt and nodded. The past couldn't be helped. "You did a lot of work on the property, I remember you saying. This is lovely."

Mom sighed. "Good contractors and money left in the will took care of it. We're pretty busy year round. I live above my shop in town, but I'll stay with you tonight, if that's all right?"

Her mother owned a secondhand clothing store she'd named "Thrifty" in addition to the rental cabins. As far as Avery was aware, she had someone else manage the businesses. Finance was not her mother's strong suit. She had idealistic dreams and ideas aplenty, but the numbers and details she wisely delegated to others.

"I'd love it if you stayed the night. It's getting late, anyway."

And speaking of, Hailey had been pretty quiet the past few minutes. Worry and suspicion mounting, Avery made her way down the hall and found her daughter asleep in one of the twin beds, curled in a ball with her hat and coat still on.

Affection and love so deep it hurt punched her chest. Carefully, she unzipped Hailey's coat, leaving it on so she didn't wake her. Removing her hat, Avery ran her fingers through her daughter's dark hair. The only time she got to openly touch Hailey was when she was asleep, otherwise contact bothered Hailey to the point she screamed. But she had these few quiet moments of the early evening to watch her and stroke her perfect little pale cheeks.

Bone tired, Avery barely took stock of the bare wood furniture or bay window before finding her mom in the kitchen stirring a pot at the stove. Stunned still, she waited in the doorway.

Mom turned and grinned. "I made hot chocolate. Go have a seat in the living room. Take a load off. You look wiped out. I'll bring you a cup."

"Is it...edible?"

Mom shook her head, then said, "I think so."

"Remember that time—"

"One fire. That was one fire, Avery!"

Too exhausted to argue, she grinned, settled in a chair, and closed her eyes, amazed it was so comfortable. The crackling fire and scent of chocolate soothed her, allowing her to sink a bit deeper into her head. Darkness pulled heavy at her consciousness.

The next thing she knew she was shivering and a cooling cup of cocoa was next to her on the end table. There were mysterious chunks floating in it. Blinking, she straightened. Her mother was asleep in the chair beside her. Wow. How long had they been out?

Taking a moment to stretch before checking on Hailey, she stood and glanced across the room to make sure her mother had turned off the stove. It wouldn't be the first time she'd gotten distracted and forgot. Assured it was off, Avery tried to find the source of the draft circling the room and froze when she spotted the open back door.

No. God, no.

"Mom!" Avery screamed, already halfway down the hall. Her heart hammered in sickening panic.

Hailey's bed was empty.

No, no, no, no, no...

Bolting back into the living room, she slammed into her mother and quickly moved around her.

"What is it?"

Avery shoved her feet into boots and grabbed her coat. "Hailey's gone. We fell asleep. I didn't secure the door." A mistake she knew better than to make. Hailey took off way too often. Not to run away, but because she lived inside her head and had no concept of danger.

Oh, God. Her daughter was out there in the cold, in the middle of nowhere, at night. The region had mountain lions not to mention...

"Call the police."

She ran for the back door and rounded the house, but Hailey wasn't in the car or on the porch. Avery circled back around, fear clawing her throat as she slammed into her mom again.

"There's footprints." Mom tied a scarf around her neck. "She went straight into the woods."

Avery looked down. A small set of tracks her daughter's size led away from the cabin and deeper into the dense trees. She took off, following the tracks. Cold air rasped her lungs, and her fingers were numb by the time they reached the copse of pine.

Hailey was so small. She wouldn't make it long exposed to these temperatures. It had to be in the twenties. Hailey couldn't talk, either. If she needed help, she couldn't ask for it. Avery had done her research before the move. She knew the vegetation and wildlife, knew her daughter was at risk for an animal attack and from what animals. Black bears, mountain lions, and bobcats sprang to mind. Hailey wouldn't know how to defend herself.

Tears blurred her eyes. She quickened her pace to a sprint, kicking up snow in her wake.

Be okay, sweetie. Be okay.

The footprints made a hard right and, as they rounded a bend, the breath left her lungs in a *whoosh.*

Hailey was sitting on a stump, her back to them. Her pink coat was still on, but she didn't have her hat. The relief was dizzying.

"Hailey." Avery circled the stump and squatted. "We talked about this, sweetie. You cannot go running off—"

There was blood. Lots of blood. At Hailey's feet. On the front of her coat.

"Where are you hurt? Where are you hurt, sweetie?" She ran her trembling, frozen fingers over Hailey's head, down her neck, to her chest, and stopped.

A furry, warm head poked out of Hailey's partially opened coat.

A scream wedged in Avery's throat until she realized it was a dog. No, a puppy. A little, tan-colored fluffy thing. Hailey was rocking it, stroking its head, and jerking her gaze around.

Recognizing the motions as nervous and scared, Avery kept her voice quiet. Hailey would never hurt a living thing, so she had to have found the animal out here. "You found a doggy. It's okay, Hailey. Is the doggy hurt? Is that where the blood is coming from? Can Mommy see?"

Gently, she lifted the trembling ball of fur from her daughter's grasp and the poor thing yelped. Surprised by the noise in the quiet night, she fell back on her butt in the snow. It couldn't have been more than six weeks old. Seven pounds, max. Sad, scared brown eyes looked into hers and Avery melted.

"Well, crap on a cracker. You're adorable."

"Avery…its leg." Mom jerked her chin toward the dog and shoved her hands into her pockets.

Avery's gaze swept over the animal in the moonlight and eyed what her mother was talking about. The lower half of one of its front legs was severed clean. Blood saturated the fur. Her stomach churned. What could've happened to it?

Nausea swirled in her gut. "You poor thing."

Hailey began rocking in earnest.

Avery reached over and clasped a hand on her daughter's arm. "It's going to be okay, sweetie."

She looked at her mom, at a loss. She'd never had a pet before. It was freezing outside and who knew how long the little guy had been hurt out in the woods or how much blood it had lost. By all the red marring the snow, it seemed like a lot for such a small thing. It didn't have tags or a collar. It was doing little more than whimpering and trembling. She needed to get Hailey out of the elements, too.

Her mom unwrapped the scarf from her neck and passed it to her. "I'll call the O'Gradys. They own the vet clinic in town. Go. I'll take Hailey back to the cabin—"

Hailey shot to her feet and grabbed Avery's jacket, a sound of duress escaping her throat even as her gaze darted elsewhere.

"She wants to come." She looked at her mom. "Zip her coat, would you? Call the vet. We need to go. This little guy doesn't have long."

* * * *

Cade O'Grady stared at the tiny gray kitten as it sucked milk from the bottle he held. The furball was small enough to fit in one of his hands. Anger surged again, so he blew out a breath and glanced around the small confines of his clinic office.

It was late, and he'd decided to stay to catch up on some charts. That was two hours ago, and said charts were still in need of dictations. Good thing he'd stayed or the tiny kitten in his hand would've died, just like its mother and siblings.

What the hell kind of person left a box of kittens outside a clinic door in the snow? Cade had no idea how long they'd been in the elements— someone had dropped them by the kennels outside the back door—but the kitten he was currently feeding was the only survivor. He gnashed his teeth, mad enough to kill the SOB if he ever found him.

Luckily, the kitten, which looked like a Brazilian Shorthair, was made of strong stuff. She'd taken to feeding right away and didn't need an IV. In his exam, the temp and BP had been good, all things considered, and he found no outward signs of trouble.

Closing his eyes, he listened to the answering machine kick on from the reception desk outside his office. If it were an emergency, he'd be paged, since it was his week on call. Animal Instincts was a small clinic, started by his father forty years ago and run by Cade and his two brothers since the old man had passed away. Almost nine years now. Hard to believe.

The bottle empty, he set it on his desk and eyed the kitten. "You are a cute little bugger."

It mewed in agreement.

He laughed for the first time all day and rubbed its head. "Modest, too. I think I shall call you Cutin. Get it? Combining cute and kitten? Cutin."

Mew.

"You're right. They should take my man card on the spot."

Paws kneading, it settled into the crook of his arm and fell asleep.

"I'll take that as a yes. Can I get you anything else? A beer perhaps?"

It didn't respond. She. *She* didn't respond. He should stop calling her it. Shaking his head, he pulled a chart closer. His pager went off. He cursed. Just as he reached for it in his scrubs pocket, a pounding rattled the front door.

He glanced at the kitten. "Today sucked."

She mewed sleepily to second the thought. *Word! Try having my day.*

Rising, he settled Cutin on a pillow in a box on an office chair and checked the pager as he walked to the front door. The banging intensified. He didn't recognize the number, but the woman standing outside the clinic was Justine something-or-other, who owned a resale shop down the street.

He unlocked the door and held it open. At least the snow had stopped. "Was it you who paged me?"

She rushed inside, followed by a woman he didn't know, and a little girl about eight. "Yes, I paged." Justine pushed dark, windblown hair out of her face.

He closed and relocked the door against the biting airstream coming down off the mountain.

The other woman held out her arms. Inside a knit scarf was a puppy.

Cade looked down at all the blood on the girl's pink coat. Shit. Kicked into action, he motioned for them to follow. "This way."

"I'm going to wait out here in the lobby," Justine said, her face a suspicious shade of green. "All that medical stuff… I'll be good out here." She sat down hard to emphasize her point.

Inside an exam room, he donned gloves, turned, and reached for the animal. "What happened?"

"I'm not sure. Hailey found it in the snow about thirty minutes ago." Her voice was hurried, but calm, not showing any signs she was unnerved by all the blood.

Gingerly, he set the puppy on the table and unwrapped the scarf, taking stock of the situation. Yellow lab. Male. Eyes barely open. Lethargic.

Underweight. About five or six weeks old. Trembling. Leg severed below the knee. Wound clotting and not actively bleeding.

Son of a bitch.

Biting the inside of his cheek, he forced himself to look at the woman. "Come over here and stand by the table while I get supplies please."

Dark, cocoa eyes widened at his harsh tone. She turned to the girl. "Can you sit in the chair, sweetie? I'm going to be right over here."

The girl didn't answer, instead fidgeting and avoiding eye contact. After a moment, she settled into a corner chair. She was probably in shock, too.

When the woman sidled up to the exam table, Cade moved away, grabbing a saline IV bag and heating it in the microwave. Pulling out a warming blanket, he plugged it in and slid it under the puppy, then wrapped it around his back. Snatching an otoscope from his pocket, he leaned over to look in the dog's ears.

"How long was he outside?"

She shifted on her feet, and the scent of something fruity wafted in the space between them. Berries of some kind. "I don't know. We—"

"You don't know," he repeated dully and checked the puppy's mouth. Gums were pale, but the teeth were fine.

He inserted a thermometer for a rectal temp and eyed the woman. Though he didn't know everyone in Redwood Ridge, she certainly wasn't familiar. She had a pretty, chubby face, and wavy brown hair that trailed to her shoulders under a knit hat. They were close in age, perhaps late twenties if he had to guess. She was biting her red lips to the point of swelling.

Good. She should feel guilty. Leaving a new pet outside, unattended, was reprehensible. Plus, the puppy showed signs of neglect. By the look of his leg, he had probably been caught in a bear trap. Since they'd come in with Justine, he could only assume she was an idiot tourist renting one of the cabins who didn't know how dangerous the mountain—or what wildlife that came down the mountain—could be.

"Is he up to date on shots? Any other conditions?"

"I'm not sure. It's not—"

"Is there anything you *do* know?" he barked.

She closed her mouth and turned her head to check on her daughter, who was now staring at the ceiling.

Guilt for his tone rose in his gut but, dammit, neglecting a dog was lower than pond scum. He'd seen it so many damn times. People got a pet because it was adorable or they were lonely and had no idea how much responsibility went into having one. Then they'd go abandoned or to a shelter, forgotten.

He was sick of tourists, too. One of the clinic pets was a result of an idiot tourist who didn't bother to return to pick up their one-year-old Great Dane after he'd broken a leg.

People really sucked.

As the youngest of the three O'Grady men, Cade was the affable one. He was generally good with pet owners and could laugh himself out of a bad mood. Today, not so much. He'd had to euthanize old man Kiser's hound dog, the first client he ever had as a vet, lost a two-year-old retriever to a bowel obstruction, and found a box of dead kittens by the back door. Well, all dead but one.

So today? Today blew. He had no patience left in reserve, especially not for a woman who probably just broke her daughter's heart by putting their pet at risk.

Removing the thermometer, he noted the temp was low, but not nearly as down as he'd figured. He shoved the buds of his stethoscope in his ears and listened to his heart, lungs and abdomen. Nothing worrisome. BP was good, too. The little guy lifted his head and whimpered when he tried to better examine the leg.

"I know, little guy. It hurts, huh? I'll getcha something for that in a moment."

The wound had clotted, and though it didn't look infected, the puppy would need surgery to amputate the rest of the leg at the hip joint. First, he had to make sure the animal stayed stable to get an IV into him for fluids and antibiotics.

Straightening, Cade crossed his arms and faced the woman. "He's in decent condition for now, which is shocking. Vitals are a little low, but good. If he's doing this well in a couple hours, we'll do surgery to remove the rest of the leg. He'll need to stay a few nights for monitoring."

Cade paused, waiting for her to say something. When she just stared at him with a cross between worry and confusion, he shook his head. "This is going to be expensive, ma'am."

Not that he cared. If she walked out and left the dog, he'd still do what he could to save him. He'd eat the cost. Once the puppy was well again, Cade would try to adopt him out or they'd keep him for a clinic pet. Either way, he wasn't euthanizing an animal just because the leg was shot. Not unless there was no other choice.

She rubbed her forehead. "Can he live with three legs? Get around, I mean? I don't know much about—"

He ground his teeth. "People manage just fine with one or both legs amputated, don't they? He's young. He'll adjust. Yes or no, ma'am?"

Startled, her gaze whipped to his. She'd be a stunner with her huge eyes, pouty mouth, and button nose if he hadn't disliked her on the spot. "I… I'm not sure I know what you're asking."

He briefly closed his eyes and prayed for patience. "There's a healing period involved. Money to pay for his care. Are you going to be up for that? Because if not, just leave. Either he's your dog or he's not."

"He's…" Her brown gaze drifted to the exam table. Surprise flitted in her eyes. She covered her mouth with her hand as tears welled.

Narrowing his eyes, he turned.

The little girl stroked the puppy's head, her face pressed to the fur on his neck. She didn't say anything, nor did she appear upset, but the puppy sure liked what she was doing. His tail limply thumped the table and his trusting eyes were watching her. They seemed to have a bond already in place, which would make it even crappier if the woman walked out and never came back.

Turning to face her, he raised his brows in question, but she paid him no mind. She watched the girl and the puppy with a tentative smile and shock clearly evident. Why the shock? Kids loved animals. This was their dog, after all. It stood to reason the girl would be upset the little guy got hurt.

Even though she seemed to be having some kind of moment, it was getting late. He needed to get going on an IV. "Ma'am?"

She flinched and looked between him and the table. After a second, she collected herself and wiped her eyes. "Yes. He's our dog. Do whatever you need to do to help him." Her gaze softened once more as she stepped closer to the table and tapped the girl on the shoulder. "Time to go, sweetie. The doctor here is going to help…him. We'll come check on him tomorrow, okay?"

How odd she didn't try to comfort the child. Put her arm around her or offer a hug. Something. The girl had blood down the front of her and had been, no doubt, traumatized by seeing her pet injured. Yet the woman stood there as if she didn't have a heart beating or a compassionate bone in her body.

This was why he preferred animals to people. "What's the dog's name?"

"Oh. Um…"

He sighed. "Let me guess. You don't know."

A sliver of irritation flicked in her eyes before it was masked and she looked to her daughter once more. "His name is…" She tilted her head, chocolate eyes glazing over. "Seraph. His name is Seraph."

"Seraph?" It was rare someone surprised him anymore. He would've guessed Lucky or Champ or some other cliché.

"It's another name for angel—"

"I know." Still, she just got bonus points. "Head home. I'll get your info from Justine in the morning. You can come visit during clinic hours." She nodded and kneeled next to her daughter. "Come on, sweetie. We'll come see him tomorrow."

After they'd gone, Cade inserted an IV filled with warm saline to bring the dog's temperature up a little and started antibiotics. He drew some blood and ran a CBC to check platelets, then did vitals again. The little guy took it in stride. Pleased the puppy was doing well, he yanked a chair up to the exam table and pulled out his cell.

Drake was going to be pissed, but this couldn't wait until morning. The dog needed surgery, and his oldest brother was their clinic surgeon. Cade could do it himself, but he didn't want to call in a tech and Drake was better.

"I'm not on call."

Cade grinned. "Maybe I just missed you."

There was a lengthy pause. "What do you want? And by that, I mean you better be up to your ass in greyhounds needing my cutting expertise. It's almost midnight."

"Got a yellow lab puppy requiring an amputation. Does that qualify?"

Drake groaned. "Is it stable?"

Cade bit back the string of insults he wanted to let loose. It wasn't as if he wasn't used to being underestimated. "I'm not an idiot, you know. I have a degree and everything. I'm even sure I can spell veterinarian if I try real hard—"

"I'll be there in ten. Prep the room."

Cade pocketed his phone and rubbed the puppy behind his ears, earning two thumps of a tail.

"Seraph." He shook his head. "Your owner is really something. Kinda pretty, too. She gave you a great name, even if she did leave you out in the snow, the big meanie."

Two more tail thumps.

"I have to go prepare the surgery room for my ornery brother, but I'll be right back. You just hang out here for a minute." He stroked the puppy's back. "I promise we'll get you fixed up. You'll be good as new soon."

Thump, thump.

Chapter 2

After two anal gland appointments and a lethargic guinea pig rounding out his patients for the morning, Cade walked up to the front desk and eyed his aunt, who was baby talking their clinic dog, Thor. The Great Dane hid under the desk, cowering from She-rah, their evil cat. And evil she was. Charts teetered precariously from the long counter. At least the lobby was empty. It had been a damn crazy morning.

Squawk. "You spin me right round." Gossip, the cockatoo—yet another abandoned animal—bobbed his head. One of these days, Cade would have to teach him to say something other than song titles or lyrics. As it was, that's all the bird did thanks to his former owner. That, and tease the cat.

Cade scratched his jaw. "Am I good to go for lunch?"

Aunt Rosa sighed dramatically. Everything was dramatic with Rosa from her red spiky hair to her cheetah print shirt. "Will you look at this?" She narrowed her eyes at Thor. "Grow a pair and come out of there. It's just a cat."

She-rah licked her paw and meowed from the top of the printer, bored by the events. *I bet I can get the dog to lose his bladder. Wanna see?*

Thor didn't move.

Shaking his head, Cade picked up She-rah, much to her disdain—*put me down you insolent peasant*—and set her in the back room. Returning to the lobby, he called for Thor. The hundred and ten pound dog commando crawled from under the desk and hid behind Rosa's chair.

Cade lifted his brows. "Now may I go to lunch?"

Not that Rosa was their boss or anything, but he and his brothers knew not to rock the boat. For twenty years, their aunt had managed the clinic and acted as receptionist. Poorly, but beggars couldn't be choosers. Rosa was their mother's sister and one of what Cade liked to refer to as The Battleaxes. Their mother, Gayle, Aunt Rosa, and other sister, Marie—also town mayor—ruled Redwood Ridge with an iron fist and oatmeal cookies. They were crazy, meddling women who he loved and feared. Mostly feared.

"Have you found my replacement yet?"

He bit back a groan. Rosa had announced six weeks ago she wanted to retire to do...whatever it was the Battleaxes did. Eat small children, update Redwood Ridge's Twitter page with town gossip, matchmaking... He batted his eyelashes. "How could we ever replace you, Aunt Rosa?"

"Can the cuteness. Save it for the ladies."

Right. "No, we haven't replaced you yet." He'd have to get an ad in the paper, which would bring out all the crazies or every single woman in a thirty-mile radius. Damn it. He should make Flynn handle the hiring. As the middle brother, he was the most organized. Except he was their traveling vet and wasn't in the office much. "I'll get on it right away."

She narrowed her hazel eyes and tilted her head, her unnaturally red hair not moving with all the shellac she'd sprayed on it. "You said that more than a month ago."

Well, how was he to know she was serious? It was hard to tell with her. "I mean it this time. Now can I go to lunch? Pretty please?" There were only three people on earth he'd bust out the "pretty please" for, and one of them was right in front of him.

"Brent's already at lunch. Go ahead." She smacked his ass and waved him off.

Brent being his vet tech. Why didn't Rosa smack *his* ass? Brent would enjoy it. "It's really pervy when you do that."

She feigned innocence. "Love tap your rear end? It's a nice one."

He bit back a sigh. "You're relation. It's pervy." He was two steps from freedom when he remembered something. "Can you get a hold of Justine from that clothing store down the way? She came in with a tourist who had the injured lab—"

"You mean Avery Stowe? She's not a tourist. She's Justine's daughter. Just moved to town with her daughter. Bad divorce. They're staying up at one of Justine's rentals until they can find a place."

Perhaps he should've been nicer to her, but she'd caught him at the tail end of a crappy day and the fact remained, she hadn't taken very good care of her pet. Even without the injury, the puppy was malnourished.

Pulling on his coat, he reached for the door. "Can you get a number for her and let her know Seraph is recuperating nicely?" Not that she seemed to care. She hadn't visited the puppy.

"No need. Avery called three times this morning to say she'd be in after lunch. Apparently, there was a problem with their moving truck getting lost. Poor woman. No good luck. Plus, the daughter, Hailey, was pretty upset over finding the stray, so it took Avery awhile to calm her down after they left here. They slept in."

Cade locked in on one word in that whole rant. "What do you mean, *stray*? It's their dog, isn't it?"

She offered him her classical *duh* look. "It is now, but not when they found it. Can you imagine that poor little girl coming across a scene like that?"

He called to mind the exhaustion edging the woman's chocolate eyes, the way the daughter never spoke, and the way he'd all but jumped down her throat. He'd assumed the worst, which wasn't like him. The woman—Avery?—had rescued Seraph from bleeding out into the snow, alone and scared.

And he'd been curt with her for doing the right thing.

Shit. He was an asshole.

* * * *

Avery wiped her hands on a dish towel and went to answer the incessant knocking. Hoping it was the moving van, she pulled the door open to find Seraph's vet. "Oh." She took a step back and blinked. "It's you."

The Jerk, she'd begun to call him in her head.

Looking just as attractive as he had the night before, sans the irritation, his hands framed the doorway as he leaned into them, taking up the whole space. Sandy blond hair, a little on the longish side, curled around his ears and nape. Blue eyes damn near the color of the Pacific in June warily stared at her. A little gray mixed in to keep them from being too potent. His jaw had a day's worth of scruff and the man rocked a set of powder blue scrubs under an open leather coat.

God. He was an eye-gasm if she ever saw one.

When he didn't say anything, her heart started to pound. "Oh, no. Is… Seraph all right?" She turned to peek at Hailey, who was doing a numbers app game on the iPad at the kitchen table.

"He's doing fine. Recuperating very well."

His voice had her pausing, just like the night before, but today it wasn't as angry. It wasn't quite coarse or too deep, but there was a melodic rhythm when he spoke. Great. So his voice was an ear-gasm on top of his too handsome looks. Crap on a cracker.

She caught herself wrapping the towel around her hand in nervousness and stopped. "Then why are you here?"

Pushing off the frame, he towered over her five-six height to what had to be six feet. "I came to apologize. May I come in?"

"Um, sure." She held the door open wider and glanced at Hailey. If he got upset again or had a naturally loud voice, it could upset her. "Sweetie, why don't you do that in your bedroom for a few minutes? I'll be in soon."

Hailey grabbed her device and headed down the hall.

"She doesn't talk much, does she? For a girl, I mean. Thought they were all chatter boxes." He laughed uncomfortably and rubbed his neck.

The guy had adorable charm in spades.

His nervousness calmed her a bit. "She's a nonverbal autistic. Pretty high functioning in other areas, though."

He stilled and pinned her with round eyes. "I'm fu...mucking this up."

She smiled, more at ease with this version of him. Pretty sweet how he'd caught himself upright before cursing. "You didn't know. It's okay."

Gazing heavenward, he crossed his arms. His leather jacket strained against his muscles and movement. "Look, about last night, I'm sorry. I was rude. I thought you were a negligent owner. I'd had a bad day and took it out on you."

At the risk of sounding like a parrot, she said the only thing that came to mind. "It's okay. You didn't know."

The flutter in her belly hadn't happened in so long, she was unnerved. Plus, people didn't often apologize to her, and she'd spent so long in the shadow of her ex-husband that she didn't know what to do with Cade's intense stare.

One corner of his mouth quirked. Too cute to be sexy, but head-tripping just the same. "You never corrected me. You could've put me in my rightful place in the exam room. Why didn't you?"

She glanced at the hallway and back to him. He was still staring as if trying to figure her out. "Hailey gets nervous around raised voices. I figured we'd sort it out later."

He nodded slowly, a wrinkle forming between his brows. "Did I upset her?" He took a step forward and paused as if wanting to reach for her and thinking better of it. He seemed genuinely concerned about Hailey, the look in his eyes sincere.

"I don't believe so. She was worried about the dog, but I think she filtered everything else out." They stood awkwardly for a beat. Now what? "Can I get you something to drink?"

"No. I have to get back to the clinic, but thanks. I wanted to catch you before you came in so I could eat crow." One shoulder lifted.

God. The female species must flock to him. He didn't have a wedding band.

She tried for upbeat to put them on even footing. "Without witnesses? It's like the apology never happened."

His face grew a little impish, which made her laugh. Been awhile since she did that, too. "You haven't met my brothers yet. Or my aunt. She runs the front desk. For now. I'd never live it down if they got to see me removing my foot from my mouth."

It was a nice mouth, too. Full lips, firm. She shook herself just before a tremble could tear through her body.

He turned for the door. "I'll see you when you come visit Seraph. He really is doing great. Nipped my stethoscope this morning trying to play."

Relief settled deep. "Okay. I'll be in soon. I had...stuff come up this morning." Like the moving van not following her directions and getting lost on the wrong side of the Klamath. They claimed it would be a few days before they arrived.

They reached for the doorknob at the same time. Their fingers brushed, and it seemed so intimate, she froze. He had big hands. Warm. Then she caught a whiff of something...gastric emanating from him.

She must've wrinkled her nose or something because he laughed nervously. "Hazard of the job. That's Ode de Anal Gland you smell."

She pressed her lips together to hide a grin.

He closed his eyes and shook his head. "I just keep sticking my foot..." He sighed. "I'll see you soon."

She waited until his car was gone before turning toward the hall. The muscles of her cheeks ached and she realized she was smiling. When was the last time that happened?

After getting Hailey ready, they drove to the clinic. Hailey was a bundle of excited energy bouncing in her seat. Avery had never thought about getting a pet. Her ex, Richard, wouldn't have allowed one in the pristine house anyway, but Hailey had really seemed to connect with Seraph. They'd have to stop by a store to pick up supplies on the way back. What did a puppy need?

She opened the door to Animal Instincts and found...utter chaos. Unlike the night before, people filled the waiting room with varying breeds of dogs and cats. And...a snake? Yes, a big, big...

She chanced a peek at Hailey to see if the loud ruckus bothered her. It was hard sometimes to find her triggers. Car horns and loud music upset her the most. Shouting or raised voices, too. She seemed unfazed by the barking now.

The clinic was more spacious than it looked from the outside. To the left, the waiting room walls were painted in one giant mural of animals doing human things like cooking or reading. Two large windows flanked both sides to allow light inside. Slate tile was laid throughout, creating a natural feel to the place. She remembered from the night before that the hallway leading to the patient rooms had another mural of dogs walking their owners or cats petting their humans in a cute role reversal.

"Can I help you?"

Avery turned to the front desk. The middle-aged receptionist had unusually red hair and her penciled-in eyebrows pinged to her hairline. Her short, round frame leaned over to better see them.

"Um… We're here to visit our dog. We brought him in last night."

The receptionist's demeanor changed from irritated inquisitiveness to cajoling so fast Avery got whiplash. "I'm Rosa. I'm the O'Grady boys' aunt. You must be Avery. Your mom and I are good friends. It's so nice to finally meet you." She came around the desk. "And you must be Hailey." She squatted in front of her, but Hailey's attention was elsewhere.

Avery didn't like walking around telling people why her daughter was seemingly so rude. In fact, she hated putting a label on her at all, but the only way for others to understand was to explain. Before she could open her mouth, Rosa stood.

"The rec center has a few other autistic kids, too. Miles and Anya run the place. You'll have to check it out." Glancing at Hailey, she spoke to her again. "You'll like it there, hon. Plenty to do. Make new friends."

Sadly, Hailey didn't have any old friends. After her diagnosis at age two, their lives had been a steady stream of therapists.

Rosa waved her hand and assessed Avery as if plotting. Eyes narrowed, she nodded her head in approval. "I'll get Cade to take you back to see Seraph."

Avery eyed the waiting room. "You guys are busy. Can we maybe just visit on our own or we can come back…?"

"Nah. We're pretty slow today."

Slow? Patients were packed like sardines. She hated to see what busy looked like. A cat hissed behind them and batted its paw at a poodle wearing a red bow and an incredulous expression. Two dogs were vying for butt-sniffing rights while two others cowered under chairs. The snake had slowly wound itself around its owner's arm and was climbing the wall near a framed picture of dogs playing poker.

She shuddered and turned back, but Rosa was already behind the desk and Cade was walking toward them. He'd changed into a darker set of blue scrubs. God. Just…he was all masculine grace as he ate up the distance. Sinewy muscle, wide shoulders, narrow waist. Avery bit her tongue so she didn't swallow it.

He grinned and, damn, there went her air. "Come on back." He glanced at the waiting room and did a double take. "George, get that reptile in a cage." Wordlessly, they followed him down a long hall and into a back room where crates lined the wall with recovering animals. Yips and feral cries echoed off the walls.

"This is where we board."

She nodded. The twelve-by-twelve room smelled like wet fur and antiseptic. The walls had a continuation mural of grassy fields and blue sky. Several red fire hydrants were painted among the landscape. Pretty clever.

Hailey took off and knelt by one of the crates.

Before Avery could correct her, Cade strode over and squatted beside her. "Hold on, squirt. I'll get him out for you." After opening the cage, he reached in and removed Seraph, nuzzling the puppy to his broad chest. A cone had been placed around the dog's neck, but Seraph nudged Cade's hand for petting. "Who's a good boy?"

Oh. Oh, swoon.

She hadn't had so much as a flicker of attraction in so long she almost forgot the sensation. Her cheeks heated and her belly quivered. A flare of jealousy sparked when Seraph licked Cade's face. The rumble of Cade's laugh had her biting back a moan.

"Hey, squirt. Can you sit on the floor? Your little buddy might not be up to running yet."

As usual, Hailey took a few seconds to process his words, then dutifully sat on the tile floor. Even her daughter seemed smitten. She squealed and flapped her hands. *Yes, cute doctor man. Whatever you say.*

Cade gently set Seraph in her lap and, keeping one hand on the puppy, he lifted the other to Hailey. "I'm going to show you how to pet him." He took her hand and used it to stroke the dog's back. "Just like that," he said as if coaxing calm. "Good. Just stay away from the ouchie on his leg, yeah?"

Avery made a conscious effort to shut her mouth. Good with animals *and* kids. Not just kids, but disabled ones. He'd told Hailey what he was going to do before doing it and used a soothing voice for both her and Seraph.

Double swoon.

Cade grinned as Hailey giggled, and then he looked at Avery. "Best friends already."

"Yeah," she whispered. Was she drooling? She cleared her throat and stepped closer. Her heart swelled at Hailey's complete adoration of the dog. "When can we take him home?"

"Tomorrow, if he's still looking good."

"At the risk of you getting upset, I need to know what he requires. I've never had a pet before."

A flash of irritation lit his eyes before he blinked it away. He stood and dusted fur from his pants. "I'm sorry about last night. How I behaved wasn't me. Don't be afraid to ask me questions." As if in afterthought, he added, "I won't bite."

What. A. Shame. *Bad, Avery*!

Staring at her with intense, unwavering eyes, he sighed. "You'll need a leash until you can train him to mind commands. A couple of dog bowls for food and water. Toys, especially ones he can chew on until…" He rubbed the back of his neck. "Know what? I'll take you out to the supply place and steer you in the right direction."

Her jaw dropped. Again. "You don't have to do that. If you just make a list—"

"How's seven tonight? We close at six. That'll give me time to shower." Though his tone was genial, it brooked no argument. He held her gaze, patiently waiting for an answer. When she didn't say anything—because how long had it been since someone offered to go out of their way to help?—he jerked a thumb at the door. "I've got to get back to the patients, but meet me here at seven, yeah? I'll send Rosa in to help Seraph back into the kennel when you're done."

With that, he strode out, all alpha-male goodness.

The move and pressure he'd put on her reminded her of Richard. But Cade wasn't like her ex. Where Richard was controlling and cold, Cade was confident and warm. His mood today was a vast cry from the brash guy she'd met last night. She wondered which version was the real man, and then remembered the self-depreciating humor and the way he'd smiled with even his eyes.

Rosa opened the door and the barking started anew. "Hush," she called and went right to Hailey. "Time to put him back, but you get to take him home tomorrow. How exciting."

Hailey jerked her gaze around the room, upset.

Avery patted her arm through the coat. "They'll take good care of Seraph, sweetie. We'll see him tomorrow."

Rosa eyed Avery skeptically. She got the suspicion she was being dissected again, but had no clue why. "How are you settling in? Redwood Ridge is quite the difference from a big city."

Avery nodded. "It is, but it's very pretty. It'll just take some getting used to."

"Have you found a job yet? Your mom said you were looking."

Shifting her gaze from Hailey—who walked past the kennels—to Rosa, she shrugged. "I haven't had a chance yet." She'd been out of the workforce so long she didn't think she'd be hirable. Her savings would only stretch so far. "Do you have a medical clinic in town?"

Rosa pursed her lips. "We've got Dr. Brad Crest at the edge of town. Otherwise you'd have to travel forty miles north. Why?"

"Well, I've been a stay at home mom since Hailey was born, but before that I managed a cardiology practice." In fact, Richard had insisted she resign to remain at his beck and call for fundraisers or business dinners. He'd just used Hailey as an excuse to isolate her even more from society.

She squared her shoulders. Richard was a jerk of epic proportions, but she couldn't lay all the blame on him. She hadn't stood up to him or challenged his orders. But she'd gotten Hailey because of the sham of a marriage, and they were starting fresh. No sense dwelling on the past.

"Dr. Crest has a nurse and receptionist, so you're out of luck there." Rosa raked her gaze over Avery and nodded. "You'll do. You're hired."

"What?"

Rosa shrugged as if she hadn't just knocked Avery on her ass. "I'm retiring. Cade's been dragging his heels finding a replacement, and you have experience."

She rubbed her forehead. "I have experience in healthcare, not veterinary medicine. You haven't even checked my references."

"Don't need to. You're Justine's daughter, which is good enough for me. Besides, you're not going to be treating the animals, just running the office."

"True, but—"

"When can you start?"

Avery opened and closed her mouth several times. She did need a job and, though she hadn't been employed in a long time, it was work she could handle. It seemed a little too good to be true. She glanced at Hailey as she sat in front of Seraph's crate. Avery needed to get her enrolled at the elementary first, plus find someone for after school care.

"Um, Monday?" She looked at Rosa, who was grinning like a Cheshire cat. "What about my hours or salary or insurance?"

"We're open from eight to six, Monday through Friday, and eight to noon on Saturdays. The office is closed on Sundays. You'd have Saturdays off, as that's just an emergency day for on-call. We'll get you enrolled in insurance right away, but you'll have to wait sixty days for it to be active. What are your salary requirements?"

Head spinning, she tried to recall what she made at the cardiology practice and quoted that number. "Are you sure about this? It's awfully fast and you just met me."

Rosa slapped her shoulder. Avery nearly toppled with the force. "Welcome to Redwood Ridge. Small town life is different than where you came from. We look out for each other around here. Word of mouth is grail and everyone knows your business."

Right. Right, okay. Wow. She had a job.

"Come on. I'll show you around and introduce you to everybody."

Avery called for Hailey and followed Rosa to the front desk. Charts were piled on every available surface, the phone rang off the hook, the waiting room spilled with patients, and a giant dog was cowering under the desk.

A white bird with pretty yellow feathers standing straight up on its head ruffled its feathers from a stoop near the window. *Squawk.* "Welcome to the jungle."

Chapter 3

Cade stood next to Flynn in his brother's office in front of the lightbox, staring at the x-ray for a Yorkie who'd eaten a ball of yarn. "Crazy, yeah?" His hands moved quickly to sign the words.

Flynn nodded. *"Wrapped completely in the intestinal track, Drake's got another surgery on his hands."*

Cade turned at the knock on the door. Because Flynn was deaf, most people didn't bother knocking. Aunt Rosa walked in, followed by Avery and Hailey.

"Meet Avery Stowe, your new office manager. She starts Monday, so consider this my notice."

Cade's gaze darted between Avery and his meddling aunt. Avery shuffled her feet, her cheeks pink as she stared at the floor. He and Flynn exchanged a look. Cade signed, "She's the one who found the stray last night."

Flynn grinned, the asshole. *"The one that had you bumbling like a hormonal teenager? Nice. You're right. She's pretty."*

He sighed. This is what he got for talking to his brother. About anything. "Shut up."

Avery cleared her throat, then she…well, shit. She signed and spoke simultaneously. "You're deaf?"

Flynn nodded as Cade reared. Not a lot of people knew sign language. Flynn could read lips if he was facing the person, which was how he typically got around the language barrier in the practice.

"You can sign?" Which meant she'd understood the brief exchange between him and his brother. Wonderful. He just kept shooting himself in the foot.

"Yes. I learned how to communicate with Hailey, since she's nonverbal. Sometimes she signs when she needs to say something."

Cade was floored she was courteous enough to sign and speak at the same time for Flynn's benefit. And then he processed what she was doing here. "You hired someone without asking?"

Rosa crossed her arms. "You weren't gonna do it."

Flynn was more amused than Cade. "*Does she have any experience?*"

"I worked in a medical practice before staying home with Hailey. I'm a quick study." She was biting that pouty lower lip of hers. Her dark eyes bespoke more than simple nervousness, though. Like she had something to prove.

Flynn nodded. "*Good enough for me. Welcome.*" He offered Cade a raised brow that said, *this should be fun.*

Cade returned it with his own *shut-up-or-die* scowl. He scratched his jaw, knowing he had no say in the matter, anyway. It wasn't as if he was against hiring Avery, but it would've been nice to be consulted.

Rosa turned for the door. "I'm going back up front. Take her to meet Drake, would you?"

Though spoken as a question, Cade took it for the order it was intended. What in the hell was his aunt up to? Before he could comment, his tech, Brent, strode in. Hell, now it was a party. He pinched the bridge of his nose.

"You are all caught up." Brent sized up Avery with the kind of flare only an openly gay man could pull off. "And who is this?"

"Avery, meet Brent, my tech. Brent, Avery is our new office manager. Apparently."

Brent's eyes lit up. "Fresh meat. Hurray. Have you met Gabby yet? She's the other tech. You'll love her!" He took Avery's hand and started to drag her from the room.

Avery laughed and dug her heels in. "I have my daughter with me. Hold on."

That laugh made Cade's gut do something twisty. "I can watch Hailey for a couple minutes." Her *are-you-serious* expression matched his internal *what-the-fuck*. Like he knew anything about kids. Still, he nodded. "Drake's in surgery, so Hailey can't go back there. Gabby's assisting."

Brent, as if just noticing the tiny human in the room, clapped his hands and knelt in front of Hailey near the corner. "Hello. Aren't you a cutie pie? Gorgeous hair, too."

The only sign of acknowledgement Hailey offered was a half wave as she stared at the ceiling. It was more than Cade got.

More hot as hell lip chewing from Avery. "Maybe I should just wait until Monday to meet everyone else."

Hell, she'd only be gone a few minutes. How much damage could he do to Hailey's little psyche in that time? "Brent says I'm caught up, so go ahead." He looked at his tech. "Tell Drake about the Yorkie. He needs surgery." Then he thought it over and decided to tell Drake himself. The case was complicated.

Flynn, as if sensing the thought, tapped his shoulder. *"Go ahead. I got the kid."*

"Are you sure?" Avery eyed Flynn as if begging him to change his mind, giving Cade the impression she didn't leave Hailey in others' hands often.

"I promise to not let her play with syringes."

Avery laughed, which was twice now, and he hadn't recovered from the first. She told Hailey she'd be back in a minute and allowed Brent to take her by the arm down the hall. Cade followed.

Brent gave her a mask. "Just hold this over your face and don't touch anything. And no matter what Dr. Drake says, he's happy to have you working here." He leaned in conspiratorially. "He's broody."

"Got it." Amusement lit her dark eyes and, for the first time, Cade noticed the small hazel flecks mixed in with all that chocolate.

Brent knocked once and strode in with a flourish. "Dr. Drake, Gabby, this lovely doll is Avery, our new office manager. Gabby, we must do drinks tonight."

Gabby didn't look up. "Can't. Got plans with my cousin. And I told you I'm never drinking with you again."

"Never say never."

"I mean, *never.*" She peeked over her mask. "I still can't eat nachos."

Avery's hand shook where she held the mask. Her olive skin tone had lost some of its hue. As office staff, she probably wasn't used to seeing an open operation and had a weak stomach for blood. His aunt was the same way. Cade hoped she didn't yak all over the room.

Cade held the mask over his mouth and leaned on the doorframe. It looked like Drake was ready to close up on the Bullmastiff who had a tumor.

Drake never lifted his dark head from his task. "I'm in surgery. Go away."

Brent sighed. "Translation: Avery, it's nice to meet you."

"That's what I said."

Gabby's blue eyes slid to Avery, a smile in them. "Hey there. We're almost done. Are you new to...? Damn. Cade, she's gonna—"

Pass out cold on the floor. Down went Avery in a heap. *Shit.*

Brent blinked in awe. "How southern belle of her."

Drake growled. "Damn it, Cade. Get her out of here."

As if he was the one who'd brought her in the first place, but he was already at her side and cradling her head. Silky brown hair spilled over his hand and her berry scent rose up over the antiseptic. He lifted her in his arms. "Get the door, Brent."

Carrying her down the hall to his office, he tried to ignore the softness of her body against the hard planes of his. Dark lashes fluttered and lifted. He set her on the couch and asked Brent to get a cool cloth, never taking his eyes from her.

He lifted a strand of hair from her face as her eyes cleared of confusion. "Hey. Lie still for just a second. You fainted."

She gasped. "I did not."

He fought a grin. "Afraid you did."

She tried to sit up and he let her, removing his hand from her shoulder. Glancing around the confines of his cluttered office, she winced. "How humiliating."

Brent strode in and offered her a wet cloth. "Personally, I thought it was entertaining. I mean, swoosh. Like a feather, you fluttered down. Don't like blood then, doll?"

She dropped her head in her hands and sighed. "I guess not. I don't have much experience with it. I'm so embarrassed. I was fine last night with Seraph, but I guess I was too panicked to notice."

Cade looked at Brent. "Tell Flynn we'll be a few more minutes."

"Oh God. Hailey—" She tried to stand.

"Uh-uh." With his hands around her wrists, he coaxed her butt back on the couch. "She's fine. Sit for a few." He used his soothing tone reserved for cray-cray animals because her eyes were wide and the pulse in her throat beat double time. He casually pressed two fingers to her inner wrist and took her pulse.

When he looked up, satisfied her heart rhythm was normal, her round cheeks were infused with red and she avoided his gaze like he was the second coming of the bubonic plague. He kept his hands where they were, in hers, rubbing his thumbs over her palms. Her skin was soft in comparison to his rough calluses. His own heart rate sped at the contact.

"Does your head hurt at all? I don't think you bumped it."

She shook her head, looking at her lap. Not shy, but obviously mortified. He got the impression she hated—or was unused to—attention. With great regret, he let her go and stood as he was only adding to her embarrassment. "I'll get you some juice. Stand by."

He poked his head in Flynn's office. Hailey was sitting cross-legged on the floor, arranging his brother's paperclips into neat rows.

Flynn looked up from next to her. "*I think we need to hire her, too. Great attention to detail.*"

Cade laughed. "You can send her back to my office. Cover my patients for a few, would you?"

He strode to the break room, snatched a small bottle of OJ, and went back into his office. Avery had zipped Hailey into her coat and was tying a scarf around her neck.

He handed her the juice. "Take a few sips before driving."

She nodded and uncapped the bottle, obliging him. The column of her throat worked a swallow and his gaze landed there. He wondered if she'd tasted as good as she smelled. Strawberries or melon. Something summery.

Recapping the bottle, she finally met his eyes. "Thank you. I'm sorry about..." She waved her hand.

"Happens to everyone. Now we know not to put you in surgery."

She tapped Hailey's shoulder. "Let's go, sweetie." Her gaze landed on his and away, so unlike the confident woman he'd met at the cabin today. "I'll see you on Monday."

"Tonight." At her raised brows, he elaborated. "Pet supplies. Instead of meeting here, I'll pick you up. Still seven?"

"Yes, that's fine. Thank you."

From his position in the doorway, he could just make out her retreating form as she passed the front desk.

Squawk. "Pretty woman."

Indeed. She wasn't a sultry bombshell and not quite the girl next door, either. A conundrum. One minute she was all mama bear, the next she was tender, watching others with her kid. She had a sense of humor, displayed confidence, and yet he sensed a vulnerability she'd probably deny. Fascinating.

Flynn walked by and slapped a chart against Cade's chest. "*My Precious is acting 'off,' room five. Brent's in surgery with Drake. Gabby and I are hitting the road.*"

Cade nodded. Flynn and Gabby traveled most of the day to local farms or elsewhere on home visits. They were getting a late start today.

He eyed the chart. Owners who brought in animals claiming to be "off" was code for: single woman alert. They only booked an appointment and used their pets as an excuse to make a play for the vet. He was used to it. A piece of meat. Ten grand said there was a plate of cookies or a casserole up front waiting for him. Just about every available female—and some unavailable—seemed to think the way to his heart was through his blood sugar levels.

Drake had been a widow for almost four years now and, once most women figured out the broody façade wasn't, in fact, a façade, they moved on. With Flynn being deaf, a lot of potential dates passed him by because some people were just that damn shallow. Cade wasn't vapid enough to deny he and his brothers were attractive, or so Redwood Ridge's Twitter profile claimed, but it was Cade that got the most attention.

The funny one. The easy guy.

The good time.

Scrubbing his hands over his face, he sighed. Eying room five, he strode down the hall. *Slab of beef, coming right up.*

* * * *

After Avery got Hailey registered for second grade and talked with the special needs teacher on staff, she drove across town to her mom's clothing store to figure out after school care. Back in San Francisco, Hailey attended classes in the mornings and had therapists come to the house in the afternoons. Avery was always there. The only babysitter her daughter ever knew was a nanny they'd used when they'd had to attend a function for Richard.

She rubbed her forehead. This was a lot of change for Hailey all at once. New town, new home, new school, and now Avery wouldn't be with her as often as she was accustomed. For the longest time, it had been just her and Hailey. She'd been in Redwood Ridge less than twenty-four hours and she'd had more offers of help and welcome than the span of Hailey's life combined.

That was a tough thing to get used to—ceding control. Hailey wasn't like other kids. Even leaving her with a sitter just to run to the store was a project. Plus, Avery feared she'd lost a lot of her social skills in the past few years, first with Richard being embarrassed by Hailey and wanting to keep her hidden, and then by the eighteen months it had taken for the divorce to go through. Rejected and emotionally drained, Avery hadn't had many friends during her marriage and had even less when she'd left Richard.

She pulled into a parking space in front of her mother's building and cut the engine. Pocketed among a row of other stores, it was similar in appearance. Small, brick, and two-story, it was square in design with a dark green awning over the front door. People milled about at café tables or strolled the cobblestone walk, chatting, despite the chill in the air.

Exiting the car, she inhaled pine and snow while getting Hailey unbuckled. A thick fog blanketed the mountains in the distance, bringing a slightly humid quality to the air. A tang of brine hinted from the nearby ocean. It was another world from what she'd been used to, but she found herself liking it, the freshness.

Hand in Hailey's, she strode into the store and sought out her mom at the front desk. Scarves and hats lined the back wall in front of ten or so round racks with vintage clothes. It smelled old, like musk and time. Two other women hovered near the register. The chatter died when she stepped over. "Oh, Avery." Mom pressed a hand to her chest. "We just heard. Are you okay?" She came around the counter and squeezed the breath from Avery's lungs, bathing her in patchouli.

"I'm fine. Heard what?"

"About you fainting, of course. Rosa tweeted about it and I was just about to call."

Her cheeks heated. She still couldn't believe she'd passed out right in front of everyone. And what did she mean Rosa had tweeted about it? Avery looked at the other two women close to her mother's age, a combination of curiosity and avid interest in their eyes.

One of them patted her arm as if to say, *poor dear.* "It's all over the thread. How are you feeling? I'd drop like a fly, too, if they made me watch a surgery."

The vets hadn't made her do anything, and Avery had no way of knowing she'd respond that way. Still, mortification scorched her cheeks. "Um, I'm fine. Why did Rosa tweet about me? I don't understand."

The woman laughed as if to say, *silly, silly girl.* "Why, everything is news around here. Rosa's my sister. She manages our Pinterest boards and Twitter account. I'm Marie, the mayor of Redwood Ridge. Welcome to our great town."

Crap on a cracker. Avery darted a glance at her mom, but no. She hadn't stepped into the Twilight Zone. She was really standing in her mother's store talking to the mayor about passing out not two hours before. Because it was on Twitter.

She cleared her throat. "Thank you."

The other woman extended her hand. "I'm Gayle, Rosa and Marie's sister. My sons are your new bosses."

Oh. Oh God. She saw the resemblance to Cade and Flynn now. Flynn had her coloring with reddish hair and pale skin. Cade had her blue eyes, gray flecks included, and her impossibly long eyelashes. "Very nice to meet you."

"What brings you by, honey?" Mom scooted back behind the counter.

Would this conversation go on Twitter, too? She eyed the other two women, but they seemed in no hurry to leave. Was nothing private in this town?

"I just got Hailey registered for school, but I need to figure out care afterward. I'll still be at the clinic when she gets out."

Mom fluffed her already wild brown hair. "That's easy enough. I can pick her up and bring her back here."

Avery opened her mouth to protest when Marie inserted, "Or you could have her attend the recreation center afterward. Some of the kids take the bus right there."

"Oh, I don't know." Avery glanced at Hailey. "She's…" Not like other kids. Different. She didn't want to say that aloud to strangers or make Hailey feel like an outcast. "Her needs are pretty particular. Everyone right now is unfamiliar to her."

Marie waved her hand. "Pah. Strangers are friends we've yet to meet. Miles and Anya have other special needs kids at the center, too. She'd be in good hands." She whipped out a cell phone from her Samsonite-sized purse and thumbed a text. Her dark brown bob didn't move as she bent her head. "There. All taken care of. They'll expect her on Monday after school. You should stop by today to introduce her, though."

Avery forced her jaw shut, teetering between anger and shock. A pounding thumped her temples. This was her life, her daughter, and she'd spent enough time under her ex's rules to ever go back to someone else running her life.

Both Marie and Gayle knelt in front of Hailey and started talking to her as if they were old friends. Even though Hailey didn't converse, the ladies weren't deterred. In honesty, Richard's family and friends ignored Hailey, so the fact that anyone acknowledged her took the anger right out of Avery's sails.

This wasn't the first time, either. Flynn and Brent had made it a point to address her. They all seemed to know Hailey was autistic, probably because of her mom—or Twitter—but they didn't act uncomfortable. They…*included*.

Hailey ate up the attention, flapping her hands and letting out one of her rare barks of laughter. Avery's chest swelled, her throat going tight.

"We'll…" Avery cleared her throat. "We'll stop by the rec center to check it out. Thank you."

Marie rose. "No problem at all. You pop by my office or drop me a call should you need anything. Ta, Justine."

"Bye-bye." Mom sighed dreamily as they disappeared down the walk. "I told you this place was great, didn't I?"

Avery shook her head, not sure if she was being Punk'd. "Twitter? I was on Twitter?"

Mom looked at her as if she were the crazy one. She tapped out a few keys on the computer and waved her over.

Avery made her way around the counter and looked at the screen. Sure enough, there was the @RedwoodRidge account. The banner was a wide pan of the main strip, and the profile picture was a sketch-drawn map with a tiny dot indicating the town. The most recent tweets were like that from a gossip rag.

Word is our sexy fire dept will be doing another car wash this spring. Rawr, ladies!

Dr. Cade says the PB butter cookies are his fave. Dr. Flynn says choc chip. Dr. Drake had no comment. Psst, it's snickerdoodles!

The RR marching band needs new uniforms. Buy candy bars, peeps!

Wildlife is so gorgeous!

Attached to that last tweet was a picture of what looked like a ranger leaning against a cypress and wiping his sweaty brow with his forearm. Lordy. Were all the men in Redwood Ridge hot? The veterinarians were.

New gal in town, Avery, fainted right in our OR. Poor thing!

Avery rubbed her forehead, her gut churning. There were fifty-three @ responses ranging from *oh no* to *the dear lass* to *hope she's okay*. She pulled out her phone, followed Redwood Ridge, and tweeted: *Doing great. Thanks for the concern!* Jeez. She had one hundred and twenty-one new followers.

This *was* The Twilight Zone. In Mayberry.

She needed to get out of here. Stimulation overload.

After giving her mom a hug good-bye, she drove to the rec center to check it out. It was everything the mayor said it would be. They had several after school programs, and the woman who ran the center, Anya, had special needs experience. Figuring she'd give it a try, Avery signed Hailey up and checked the time.

They only had an hour before Cade was supposed to pick them up to get pet supplies. They'd been living on fast food the past two days while driving, but there wasn't time to make a decent meal and still be ready.

She drove through a hamburger joint and parked outside an ice cream shop so they could eat in the car. Avery mentally added another twenty minutes to her yoga tomorrow morning to make up for the food. She'd always been just north of chubby, but it seemed after she'd delivered Hailey, the pounds just kept tacking on.

Richard hadn't wanted to have sex until she'd gotten back to her pre-pregnancy weight. He'd also attended all functions alone until the result of nearly starving herself and a rigorous workout routine got her back into a size twelve. Richard might be gone from her life, but the rejection and ugly feeling remained.

She longingly looked at the ice cream parlor and decided to go back to her healthy lifestyle tomorrow. A few days' setback wasn't going to kill her. Turning in her seat, she grinned at Hailey. "How about dessert, sweetie?"

Hailey squealed. *Sugar! Sugar, now!*

The kid at the counter was about sixteen and in that awkward stage of gangly limbs before his body filled out. He looked bored to be there, but welcomed them with a drone greeting.

"I'll have a scoop of..." Oh God. They had rocky road. Rocky road was kryptonite. "Uh, vanilla." Sigh. Cut at least a couple calories. "And do you have anything nondairy?"

The teenager rolled his eyes. "Dad!"

A portly man in his fifties strolled out of the back and wiped his hands on an apron. "Well, hello. I'm Hank. New in town? Just visiting?"

Avery went through the spiel about being Justine's daughter and just arriving.

He rubbed his bald head, a habit he seemed unaware of doing. "Heard you took a tumble at the animal doc. How are you?"

She resisted her own eye roll. Had anyone *not* heard about her embarrassing intro to her new job? "Great, thanks. I was wondering if you had anything nondairy? Hailey here gets rather sick from milk products."

The teenager walked to the freezer and scooped vanilla into a dish.

"Nothing frozen, I'm afraid, but I've got some cookies from Sweet Tooth down the road." He set a couple cookies in a bag and handed it to Hailey over the counter. "On the house."

"Oh no. I want—"

"Nonsense. On us. Next time, we'll have something she can eat. How's that?"

God. Everyone was so...*so nice*. "Thank you."

Still shell-shocked and contemplating whether the town was really inhabited by *Invasion of the Body Snatchers*, she edged her car to the outskirts. Dusk was descending, bringing a nip to the air and making the shadows longer. As she pulled up to the row of rental cabins, Cade unwound himself from the porch steps and rose.

"Crap on a cracker, that man is sexy." He had on a pair of well-worn jeans, snug in all the right areas, and a T-shirt under a waist-length leather jacket. His dark blond hair was windblown and brushed his brow. She shook her head. "He's your boss, you nutcase. Get a grip."

Hailey squealed. *I heard that, Mommy.*

As she unsnapped Hailey from the backseat and turned to face him, he...grinned. At Avery, then at Hailey. The breath left her lungs, and she got a little lightheaded again.

Chapter 4

Cade used his rearview mirror to glance at Hailey in her booster, then turned his attention back to the road. The pet supply place was forty minutes north, but Hailey seemed content with an iPad and headphones. It was odd seeing a little person in his backseat.

He cleared his throat. "If you don't mind me asking, where's her dad? You're from San Diego, right?"

"San Francisco." Avery turned to check on Hailey and resumed her spot in his passenger seat. "I got full custody in the divorce." She went quiet for a beat. "My ex didn't contest it."

"The divorce or custody?"

"Either." She turned her focus to the side window while Cade's head swam. Some people were too stupid to know good when they had it.

They drove alongside the Klamouth Mountains, heading toward the Southern Coast Range in a contented quiet. With the occasional curve, glimpses of the Pacific came into view, the shoreline and cliffs rocky. The fog was heavy near the bank in the late dusk, but not nearly as much as his thoughts. Her words slammed around in his skull.

Granted, he'd never been married, nor was he a father, but he couldn't see himself giving up rights to his kid. He'd probably learn more from Redwood Ridge's Twitter page than from Avery, but he was curious about her. "Was he a total prick, your ex? Pardon my language."

She breathed a laugh. "Doesn't matter. He's not in our lives anymore."

Good point. "What's his name?"

For that, she turned to study him with intense brown eyes. There was so much hiding in her gaze that he had to force his away or wreck the car trying to figure her out.

"Richard. That's his name."

He grunted. "So he *is* a dick."

Covering her face with her hand, she laughed. It sounded rusty at first, but it gained momentum. She had the kind of laugh that drifted into corners and made a person stop to listen. His chest did that funny twisty thing again at the sound, but damn, it felt good to make her laugh. He hadn't known her long, or at all, but it seemed to him she didn't do it often.

She sighed and laid her head against the seat. "I suppose it's no secret, anyway. Yeah, he's a jerk. I think he just wanted a trophy wife, which was fine, I guess, until he started treating Hailey like she wasn't there. I filed for divorce two years ago and just got it granted last month. He stretched out the proceedings that long." She tilted her head toward him. "Word to the wise, don't marry an attorney."

He fisted the wheel. She didn't strike him as a trophy wife, and the whole ignoring Hailey thing pissed him off. There was a wealth of information she wasn't telling him, but he let it go. "What do you call fifty lawyers chained together at the bottom of the ocean?"

Her grin stole his air. "A good start."

He laughed. "A woman who knows her lawyer jokes. Impressive."

"Why don't snakes bite lawyers?"

He shook his head. "Why?"

"Professional courtesy."

Laughing, he scratched his jaw and made a couple of turns before speaking again. "So you left the big city to come home to Redwood Ridge."

She appeared to mull that over. "I don't know if it's home, but my mom's here and I think it's a better environment for Hailey."

If he traveled a thousand places, Redwood Ridge would always be home. Crazy and annoying and irritating as it could be sometimes, it was home. "You'll settle in. Might take awhile to get used to things, but the people care about each other, take care of one another."

She nodded. "It only took an hour for half the town to know I'd passed out at the clinic."

"Only an hour?" he joked. "Aunt Rosa's usually faster than that."

She grinned, but it fell flat. "I met your mom today, and your other aunt. The mayor?"

He made a dismissive grunt. "Aunt Marie. My brothers and I call the three of them the Battleaxes. An impenetrable force of evil wrapped in good intentions. They meddle. A lot. Kind of frightening, actually."

Another laugh. He was on a roll, even if he was only half kidding.

"Your mom seems nice."

"She's certainly the tamest of the three. Still, don't stand too close or look in their eyes. It's a trick."

"Noted." She paused with a lazy smile. "What about your dad? What does he do?"

Dear old Dad. A pang of longing hit his gut. "He passed away from a heart attack nine years ago."

"Oh wow. So young. I'm sorry. That must've been hard."

No sugarcoating that. "Took us all by surprise. He started the clinic thirty years ago. My brothers and I never thought of doing anything else but following in his shoes."

She nodded. "Has Flynn always been deaf?" Her cheeks flamed. "Is that too personal?"

"Nothing's too personal around here. And yes, he was born deaf. Fluke of nature."

"And Drake? I didn't get to see much of him, what with my eyes closed and me on the floor."

He barked out a surprised laugh. "Drake. What to say about him?" Nothing she wouldn't find out via town gossip. "He's...mourning. He married Heather, his high school sweetheart, right out of vet school. She died from an aggressive form of ovarian cancer three and a half years ago."

Avery was silent as she stared out the window, rubbing circles over her collarbone. As he was about to ask if she was all right, she cleared her throat. "I would be devastated."

Drake had been beyond devastated. He'd been wrecked. He was getting better, but it had taken Cade and Flynn a year to even get him to go anywhere besides the clinic, and another year to pack up Heather's things to send for charity. Seeing his brother like that made Cade never want to fall that hard for someone, never sink that deep.

"He took it rough. You haven't met her yet, but Zoe was Heather's best friend. Zoe's our groomer. She has a little workshop attached to the back of our building."

She seemed lost in thought as he made the turnoff for the store. "Who did the murals in the clinic? They're wonderful."

He grinned, happy for the topic change. "That would be Zoe. She paints when she's not wrestling dogs into bathtime submission." He parked and cut the engine before turning to look at her head on, his arm on the back of her seat, hand inches from her soft brown waves.

"Are you really okay with hiring me?"

Something told him not to brush off her question too casually. And hmm. She had a light dusting of freckles on her nose he hadn't noticed before. Her berry scent rose to claim him. He never thought fruit could be such a turn on.

"I'm very okay with hiring you." Suddenly, he had the strongest urge to prove to her not all men were dicks. But he'd been an ass the night they'd met, so her opinion of him couldn't be that high. It didn't sit right in his gut.

"I'm sorry for the way I behaved when you brought in Seraph. Truly, I am." Her lips parted and her breathing grew deeper. "You said that."

Forcing his gaze to hers, and not dropping it to her mouth like he wanted, he swallowed. "Bears repeating. I'm sorry." He studied her another moment. "Can you do the job?"

She blinked. "Yes."

One corner of his mouth quirked in a grin, the one he knew drove women crazy. Charming her had just become his mission. Damned if he knew why. "Then stop worrying about it."

* * * *

Two hours into her new job on Monday, Avery knew she'd been handpicked for the position by the divinity himself. To use the term clusterfuck would be putting too much of a positive spin on the lack of organization.

They were going by a paper chart system, and there was no rhyme or reason to where they were stored. Some were in the back room, some on the front desk, others in the doctors' offices. It made her brain hurt. There was a small storage closet off the patient room hallway that wasn't in use.

After she'd finished her new employee paperwork, she turned to Rosa. "Can I do some organizing?" She didn't want to overstep her boundaries, especially on the first day, but to continue this Dr. Seuss system would waste patient time. Rosa would only be training her for two weeks before she retired, so now would be the best time to get anything done while someone was around to man the desk.

A slow grin spread over Rosa's face. "Organize, you say?"

"Um, yes." Why was she grinning like that?

Squawk. "Crazy."

Avery eyed the cockatoo on the perch by the window. She didn't know if the bird was calling Rosa crazy, Avery's attempt to organize crazy, or if it meant in a general sense. Either way, the feathered beauty was growing on her. It said the most random things and only spoke in song lyrics. She'd laugh if she could breathe among the clutter.

"You go right ahead, my dear. Organize to your heart's content." Rosa's grin was calculating, and after what Cade had told her a few days ago, Avery figured she'd best not ask.

Without a word, she made her way down the hall and propped open the storage closet, deciding to start in Cade's office. She eyed the two tall filing cabinets before chancing a peek inside the drawers. Empty. Shaking her head, she moved them into the storage closet along the wall, and proceeded to do the same thing with the empty filing cabinets from Drake and Flynn's offices.

She went back up front. "Which charts are for deceased patients?"

Rosa waved her hand behind her to the stack teetering by the printer.

Avery found a tote in the back room and dropped those charts inside before dragging it to the storage room in a corner. With one wall lined with filing cabinets, the other was bare, so she moved a few filing cabinets from the front desk area into the storage room and got to work putting charts away and labeling the drawers. By the time lunch rolled around, she was to the M's.

Cade walked past the room, stopped, and turned. He eyed her handiwork and put his hands on the top of the doorframe, stretching his light blue scrub top over his muscles. "Whatcha doing?"

Caught between filing cabinets and, well…a hard place, she pressed her lips together, trying not to stare at his yummy body. "Charting." She paused. She had asked Rosa first, but Animal Instincts belonged to Cade, Flynn, and Drake. "Are you mad I moved things?"

Humor infused his eyes, igniting all that blue. "Nope. Why don't you go to lunch? Or better yet, head over to the deli with me."

She bit her lip. "I was going to pop over to Hailey's school. You know, stalk her to see how she's doing."

His grin was slow and knowing. "Nervous, Mom? I'm sure she's doing fine."

She rubbed her forehead. "I know. It's just, she's…"

"Never been away from you this long?" He dropped his hands from the doorframe, still smiling. "Go on then, mama bear. We'll get lunch another time."

Mama bear? His tone was amused, low, raking over her skin. She shivered. *Shivered*, damn it! And why was he asking her to lunch? Before she could say more, he stepped away, leaving her to fan herself with a chart.

Brent walked past, chuckled as if the tech knew she was having a hot flash, and sashayed away.

Like it was her fault Cade was so lick-able.

Donning her coat, she walked the few blocks to Avery's school to get some air and chewed on a granola bar. It tasted like cardboard with chocolate chips, but she swallowed it to get something in her stomach.

Breathing deep, she inhaled humid air infused with pine and salt. The temperature remained in the upper thirties, but the stiff breeze was chilling. A low fog hovered in the distance, and Avery was learning it never really dissipated. Through rays of sun or storm-drenched clouds, it was always there, like a protective bubble for Redwood Ridge.

She passed many of the storefronts, figuring she'd make some time over the weekend to swing into them and check things out. The town square, set up more like an I-shape, was perhaps two miles long, with the vet office being near the southern end. The town catered to the tourism market with a café, bakery, bookstore, herbal cooking, and a candle shop, but there were also accounting offices, an attorney, and a dentist.

At the end of the street, she cut left and strode to the chain link fence encompassing the playground. She searched for Hailey, and found her off to the side with another little girl perhaps a year or two older. A teacher was helping Hailey bounce a rubber ball to the girl in a game of catch.

She stilled, fingers gripping the cold metal fence. Tears sprang to her eyes at the grin on Hailey's face and the bark of laughter that floated across the playground. Her chest swelled. Hailey had made a friend. On her first day! She wasn't distressed by the commotion of the other kids, but instead she…played.

"Is she yours?"

Avery turned to the woman next to her she hadn't noticed and swiped her eyes. She cleared the emotion from her throat. "Yes. We just moved here."

The woman nodded, tucking a stray piece of reddish hair behind her ear. Her gaze trained back to the girls. "That's my daughter, Jenny. Grew up my whole life here, but I still come by every day at recess to check on her. I can't help it. I work at the pharmacy. I'm April, by the way."

"Avery, and that's my daughter, Hailey." She glanced at the girls again, noticing the characteristics of Down syndrome in Jenny.

"Heard you fainted at the—"

Avery groaned, earning a laugh from April. "Who hasn't heard? I'm so embarrassed."

April's smile transformed her thin, regal face into something more approachable and friendly. "Did you faint because of the hot docs or something gory?"

She breathed a laugh. "Gory. I walked into the surgery room and down I went. Though the vets are attractive, aren't they?" She immediately bit her tongue at the unprofessionalism, her cheeks heating.

"Yep, all three of them. Smokin'. You'll learn soon enough the tactics some women will go to just to get their attention." April tilted her head.

"Not many single options here in Redwood Ridge, never mind selections that delicious. You're a lucky woman, getting to work with them."

She shook her head at the tease.

April shoulder bumped her. "Oh, come on. You wouldn't be admitting anything the rest of us don't know."

"True. So what tactics have you used?" If this wasn't the oddest conversation...

"Nah. I'm happily married. My husband's a truck driver, so he's gone a lot." April shifted on her feet. "You're staying up at the rental cabins, right?" When Avery nodded, April said, "We're right down the road in the apartments. We should get the girls together sometime. They seem to be clicking."

They pulled out their phones and exchanged numbers before April headed back to work. Avery needed to take off, too, but she glanced at Hailey one more time. Sighing in contentment, she walked to the clinic, her heart so happy it hurt.

Until she walked in the door and found Drake leaning against the front desk, arms crossed and a surgical cap covering most of his dark hair. Flynn and Cade stood off to the side, watching her entry.

Her steps slowed as she glanced at the clock, wondering if she was late. But no, she still had five more minutes. Dread pitted her stomach as she unbuttoned her coat with shaking fingers. "Is everything okay?"

"You," Drake said, pointing a finger at her, his face an unreadable mask. "Did you do this?" He jerked his chin at the lack of charts and newly available counter space.

There was still a lot to be done, but not if they were angry. She'd asked Rosa first.

Avery slowly walked to the desk and edged around Drake, the granola bar she'd eaten sitting heavy in her stomach. "The charts for today's appointments are here in this basket. When you're done with them, I figured you could just set them back here, and I'll file them away."

Cade dropped his chin to his chest, lips quirking as if fighting a grin. Flynn stood next to him, eyeing the ceiling. Both men's expressions were in direct conflict with Drake's.

Silence stretched, but she kept her chin up. She'd done nothing wrong, had asked permission first, and heck, the place needed organizing. How had they found anything before she came along? And it had only been one morning.

Drake straightened and stepped into her space. "You," he said, stretching the word out, "are a keeper. Well done." With that, he strode down the hall to his office.

Avery's jaw dropped. She forced it closed.

Cade chuckled and swiped a hand down his face.

Flynn signed, "*Thank you*," and followed Drake.

At Cade's silent laugh, his shoulders bouncing, Avery narrowed her eyes. "Was it necessary to freak me out like that? You guys just can't pat me on the back like normal people?"

Squawk. "Don't fear the reaper."

Cade laughed harder.

Brent and Gabby walked in from the back. Brent lifted his brows at Avery's irritation and Cade's hysterics. "What'd we miss? Dish, doll."

Squawk. "Laughing on the outside."

She eyed the bird. "Be quiet."

"Don't go breaking my heart." *Squawk.*

Apparently, that had been the last thread of composure for Cade. He wiped his eyes and groaned in distress when he couldn't stop laughing. Walking past her, lips pressed together, he patted her on the back and followed his brothers.

Avery rolled her eyes and went to finish charting.

Squawk. "Don't go away mad."

Chapter 5

After Cade and his brothers had mercilessly teased Avery for the systematic changes she'd made to the clinic, she'd stopped asking to do things and just did them. Her incentive was admirable, if not scary. It's not that the office was disorganized. It's just that it was…well, yeah. Disorganized. It had been so much easier just to succumb to the chaos than it had been to take the time to change.

Cade had dubbed Avery the Nazi but, damn, the clinic was running smoother than ever. So much so that Aunt Rosa decided not to finish out her two weeks, making today her last shift. Avery had hardly needed any training at all. She jumped right in with fervor and retained knowledge with frightening skill.

Once Avery had a chart system in place, she'd moved on to the storeroom. As in they had one now instead of boxes of supplies in various spots throughout the clinic. She'd cleaned out the janitor's closet, found some old shelving units, and unpacked. There were even—*gulp*—labels.

It actually had taken Brent twenty minutes to find twenty-two gauge syringes because they weren't buried in a box in the boarding room. They were on a shelf now. In a closet. With a label. Cade blew out a breath and shook his head in awe.

Finished with a round of patients, he headed up front where Aunt Rosa was reading a romance book and Avery was typing away on the computer. "Whatcha doing now?"

Avery didn't glance up from the screen. "Making a supply list in Excel."

Hell. Why was that hot? She wasn't his usual type.

Okay, to be honest, any female with too many brain cells wasn't his type. It wasn't out of a sense of shallowness he sought that variety, but preservation. Until he found someone who made his heart beat like Heather used to do for Drake, he'd stick with superficial. No point in getting hurt or hurting someone else. But ever since Heather died, Cade tried less and less to settle down or find that person. He was aware of it, aware he was doing it, and damn if he ever questioned his actions until now. People rarely recovered from that kind of love. Why search for it?

Perhaps it was Avery's long legs in those black leggings, or her pink sweater the same shade as her cheeks when she blushed, or her brown hair—more chestnut really in the sun—piled on top of her head and held in place with a pencil that seized his interest. He bit back a sigh. Nope. It was her brain, her humor, and her strength.

Hot.

Aunt Rosa glanced at him over the top of her book, a knowing smirk on her face.

Busted.

"A supply list?" Bully for him. His voice sounded normal. He still had no freaking clue why, but if he wasn't bumbling like a moron around Avery, he was saying moronic things. Where the hell was his swagger?

"Mmhm." *Type.* "So we don't over order things or run out. Gabby and Brent can just check off what they need and I can order from the supplier." *Type, type.* "Did you know you had ten cases of cat litter? Insane."

He scratched his jaw. "Uh. No."

"Putting Zoe's stuff on here, too. Her shampoos and whatnot for grooming." *Type.*

"She's making a supply list," Rosa beamed, waving her hand like this was an epiphany. *I told you I'm all-wise. I hired her!*

Cade frowned at his aunt. She'd been the office manager, for Christ's sake. She should've been doing this.

Flynn came up to the desk and tapped Avery's shoulder. *"Have you seen my backup bag? Gabby and I need to head out to Miller's farm."*

Avery nodded. "In the supply room, stocked for you. Your new bag should be here Monday."

At Cade's questioning glance, Flynn signed, *"A goat chewed my other one when Gabby was busy chasing a barn cat."*

And this was why he wasn't the house call vet.

Flynn tapped Avery's shoulder to get her attention again. *"Marry me?"*

She laughed. "Not today, but you're welcome. Shoo, now."

What. The. Hell.

As if sensing Cade's thought train and derailing it, Avery said, "He asks me to marry him daily. Hourly, depending on what I've done." *Type,*

type. "Relax, Dr. Cade. He's joking. Besides, I don't do office romance."
Right, Flynn? she signed.

Flynn grinned, the asshole, and strode into his office, only to emerge moments later with Gabby and his travel bag.

Cade flipped him off behind Avery's back as he was walking out the door. "Saw that." *Type.*

Of course she did. All moms had eyes in the backs of their heads. And that was the other thing. She had a kid. Not that he didn't like kids. He did. Maybe even wanted a couple of his own someday. But it wasn't just one person involved when dating someone like Avery. It was two.

And they weren't dating. Not even a little. He hadn't asked her out and, aside from that first day when her gaze had shown interest, she'd seemed immune to him.

That hadn't happened in…ever. He found it oddly refreshing.

With Flynn and Gabby gone, Cade glanced around. "Where's She-rah?" The cat was usually perched on top of the printer, plotting world domination.

"Avery put her on time-out. She's in the back room." Rosa's grin grew to *oh shit* size, and he figured his aunt had read all his previous thoughts. Like a Vulcan mind meld. Which was never a good thing.

Wait. A time-out? He looked at Avery. "You put a cat on time-out?" He didn't know whether that was cute or genius.

Avery never stopped typing, which was beginning to infuriate him. "Yes, she was scaring Thor."

Cade looked down, just noticing Thor's head in Avery's lap from the other side of her chair. The Great Dane looked at him as if to say, *Neener, neener.* "Dust bunnies scare that dog."

"Well, the cat needs manners. Plus, Thor and I are working on his courage. Aren't we, boy?"

Thor barked. And not in fear. *Yes, my liege.*

Unsure what to make of Avery, he scratched his jaw. She'd done more in one week on the job than Aunt Rosa had in twenty years. She was prettier to look at, too. Aunt Rosa caught him staring at Avery again, so he shook his head.

"Do I have any more patients this afternoon?"

"Drake has one more surgery and you have two patients—a terrier who chewed its way through a crate, thus cutting his gums, and strangely…" She trailed off and brought up her schedule. "A cat that's feeling 'off.'"

Cade groaned. He was so not in the mood for—

Rosa set her book down. "It's Jeffery Harrison's cat."

Well, that made no sense. Jeffrey had gone to high school with Cade, did not want to date Cade, and he didn't have a cat. Why make an appointment at all?

Rosa's brows lifted. "It's not just the pretty females worming their way in for appointments anymore. Avery's getting popular." She tilted her head, her expression saying, *whatcha gonna do about it, boy?*

So men were making fake visits to his clinic just to see his new office manager? Hell, did Jeffrey buy a damn cat just to ask her out? This wasn't a dating service. Had people never heard of a cell phone? When his temples started to throb, he closed his eyes and took a deep breath.

Type, type. "Maybe Jeffrey is batting for the other team now. Or the cat really is feeling off?"

Rosa laughed, high-fiving Avery, who never looked up from her computer. Screw this. Cade turned on his heels and went into his office.

* * * *

Avery looked over the front desk at her mom and Rosa—who were scrolling through Pinterest pictures on Rosa's phone—when they hemmed a third time. They'd been trying to goad her into looking, too, but Avery was on to them. They weren't even trying to be suave.

They were matchmaking, so she ignored them. Mostly. She did not need to be set up on a date. Especially not with her new boss. Any of them, for that matter. Avery had sworn off men, and besides, hello awkward? And Cade had more women hanging on his arm than the desert had sand granules. If she did date, it wouldn't be a man who loved women *that* much.

What had Cade called these ladies? The Battleaxes? Suiting. Seemed his mother and aunts were trying to recruit Avery's mother into their muah-ha-ha fold. The memory of one picture of Cade from last summer in board shorts and nothing else had her clenching her thighs together.

"Look at those biceps. Oh, he's cuddling a kitten. Avery, have you seen this?"

Avery closed her eyes and covered her ears. *Lead me not into temptation...*

Who was she kidding? She hadn't been in church since her wedding nine years before.

Finally, Cade's last patient of the day came out of an exam room. She blew out a breath.

Jeffrey seemed like a nice enough guy, if not a little obvious in stripping her naked with his eyes. He set the cat crate on the floor by his feet as Cade walked up front, followed by Brent.

Ready to cut Jeffrey off at the pass—literally, he'd made several passes at her—she pasted on a smile and stood. "That was so nice of you to bring your mother's cat in for her."

Cade snorted and handed her a list of services. *Depression?* Avery gave Jeffrey the total and he squared the bill. "You have a great weekend. Thanks for coming in."

Jeffrey shoved a baseball cap over his receding brown hair. "About that. What are you up to tonight? Maybe we could get some dinner?"

"Oh, that's so nice of you, but—"

"She's got plans."

No one moved for a fraction of a second. She was pretty sure the earth stopped rotating. They all slowly turned to face Cade. Yeah, that proverbial pin drop? They'd all heard it.

Cade froze, his eyes wide as if shocked he'd said anything, pen poised over the open chart in his hand.

Brent took in Cade's distressed face and straightened. "Um, yes. We're all headed to Shooters tonight. Avery's...spoken for?" He looked at her as if to confirm.

"I am?" Not that she was going to take Jeffrey up on the offer. She had no interest in dating, but still. Couldn't she just nicely turn him down? Why lie?

Brent fixed her with a *go with it* glare and then grinned at Jeffrey. "Sorry, big guy."

Rosa and her mom's head whipped back and forth between the patient, Cade, and Brent. Their avid interest in Pinterest was gone and replaced by the live floor show.

Cade muttered a quiet curse.

Jeffrey's confused gaze scanned the room. "Okay. Maybe I'll meet up with you later." He picked up the crate and left. Fast.

All eyes slid back to Cade. He opened and closed his mouth several times before tossing the chart aside, running a hand through his thick blond hair, and glancing heavenward. "Right."

Flynn and Gabby walked in the door at the same time Drake chose that moment to come up front from the back.

Drake's gaze swept over each of them in a millimeter of a second. "Are we having a moment of silence?"

Rosa's eyes narrowed. "Actually, we're trying to figure out why Cade just blocked Avery from accepting a date."

"I did not—"

"Ooh, a date?" Gabby stepped forward and set her bag down before adjusting her long, blond ponytail. "With who?"

"Jeffrey Harrison." Brent waved his hand dismissively. "Dodged a bullet with that one, doll. I'd thank Cade."

"I did not—"

"What time should I be over to watch Hailey?" Mom interrupted, earning a nod of approval from Rosa. "I'm glad you have plans to go out. You need to have a little fun."

Avery shook her head. "When did fake plans become real plans?" Flynn's eyebrows shot to his hairline.

"Does seven o'clock work for everyone?" Brent cocked a hip.

"I'm in," Gabby said. She picked up her bag and headed for the hall. "Shooters?"

Avery rubbed her forehead. "I didn't agree to—"

Rosa huffed. "Now, now. Cade asked you out, and you're new in town, so this'll be a good opportunity to meet a lot of people."

"I did not ask her—"

"Semantics," Rosa said. "Justine, dear, I'll see you tomorrow."

"I'll walk out with you. Avery, I'll be over at six thirty to watch Hailey." Flynn shrugged. "*I'm in.*" He looked at Avery. "*Drinks on me for your awesome first week.*" Deserting her, too, he went into his office.

Drake crossed his arms, looking like he wanted to kill Cade for some reason or erase the past five minutes from his memory. "Have fun tonight, kids."

"Wait." Brent pouted. "You have to come, too."

"I don't." Drake turned to go.

The tech was undeterred, using a teasing singsong voice. "Avery cleaned out and organized the surgical room."

Drake paused mid-step, back still to them, and sighed. "One drink and I'm out. And...thanks, Avery."

Brent clapped his hands like a giddy child and sauntered off, leaving Avery and Cade alone up front.

Silence stretched for one minute. Two.

Slowly, she turned in her chair to face him. "What just happened?"

He was leaning on the back counter with his chin down and fingers pinching the bridge of his nose. He didn't look up when he answered. "We just got railroaded."

Yeah, she got that part. "For the record, I didn't have any plans for tonight."

"Okay."

"I was going to take a hot bath and read."

He didn't move. "Got it."

"Now I do have plans."

"Yep," he said tightly.

"Because of you. I believe your exact words were, 'She has plans.'"

His shoulders tensed. "I remember."

She strummed her fingernails on the desk. "What if I wanted to go out with Jeffrey?"

For that, he lifted his head. "Do you?"

He pinned her with that blue gaze of his, rife with interest, curiosity, and something that made her belly heat…then her chest…and her cheeks. All flaming. There were some serious mixed signals or crossed wires in the two feet between them. Why would he step in like that if he wasn't… jealous? But that was ridiculous. He was a Trojan god, and she was a divorcee with a kid who'd gotten way too soft around the middle.

Except he was still staring, waiting for an answer as if it were of utmost importance. She hadn't done this dance in so long she was certain she was reading him wrong.

He shoved off the counter and made his way over. Backing her chair up to the desk, he leaned down, placed his palms on either side of her to cage her in, and brought his face within inches of hers. The scent of fabric softener and animal fur followed him as he looked in her eyes.

She stopped breathing. Was pretty sure he did, too.

"Do you want to go out with him?" he asked, his voice a low, dangerous rumble.

He had the start of a five o'clock shadow, which added to his devil-may-care attitude. The gray flecks in his eyes were more noticeable this close to him and the wide, almost bow shape of his mouth was only inches from hers. Sexual tension coiled in her gut, made drawing in air impossible. The heat from his body engulfed.

Crap on a cracker. "No."

He didn't move, but his lids lowered to half-mast when his gaze dipped to her mouth. Lazily, he brought it back up to her eyes. One corner of his lips quirked. "Good."

He straightened and headed toward his office. "I'll pick you up at seven."

He was halfway there before she blinked and recovered.

"I can drive myself."

"Never said you couldn't." He kept right on going.

She bit her lip. "This isn't a date."

"Never said it was." He stopped in his office doorway and turned to face her. His gaze leveled on her and held her captive. For a second, he seemed uncertain, but it was gone before she could react. Slowly, he drew in air and palmed the doorknob. "If we do ever go on a date, you'll know it's a date. And we'll be alone."

She shivered.

He shut his office door.

Chapter 6

"Just what in the hell do you think you're doing?"

Cade tore his gaze away from where Avery was playing darts with Brent, Zoe, and Gabby across the room to look at Drake. His older brother was in a mood. When wasn't he? "I don't know what you're talking about."

Except he did know. Playing dumb seemed like a better option.

The jukebox inside Shooters blared hard rock, the peanuts on their table were stale, and there wasn't a face in the crowd Cade didn't know. Same ole, same ole. Since when was he restless? Typically he rolled with the punches, let the night play out how fate intended. He shrugged, suddenly tired of the mirror scene, the same cheese-ass décor and come-on lines.

Christ. Was he getting…bored?

Flynn paused with his beer halfway to his mouth, watching them closely to read their lips. Normally Cade wouldn't exclude him from conversation and would use sign language, but the bar was busy and Cade had a suspicion this was a conversation he didn't want the gang listening to.

Drake crossed his arms and leaned back in the chair at their high-top table. "You cock-blocked Avery today when someone asked her out."

As if he didn't feel like a big enough ass. "I'm pretty sure she doesn't have a cock."

Flynn snorted.

Drake's brows lowered. "This isn't a game. Whatever you're thinking, unthink it. She's not your usual good time."

Translation: She's too good for you.

Cade ground his jaw and slammed the rest of his pint. Never mind he knew that. He didn't need his brother pointing it out. Besides, who said he couldn't offer someone more than a little fun? He was getting sick of people underestimating him and putting him in a box. The label was getting old quick.

And just when, exactly, had that happened?

Flynn must've picked up on Cade's tension. *"Maybe he really likes this one."*

Cade chanced a peek across the crowded bar, but the group wasn't paying attention and Flynn's back was to them.

Drake shot out a laugh that had little to do with humor. "He likes all of them. That's not the issue." He leaned forward, glare digging into Cade's patience. "She's the best thing to happen to our clinic since before Dad died. If your dick screws that up—"

Cade slammed his glass down. "I haven't done anything. And if I do, it wouldn't be before properly thinking it through." Except Avery had a way of shutting down thought.

Drake shook his head, a sound of disgust rolling from his throat.

"You know, I graduated from college, never miss a day of work, own my own home—"

"And never sleep with the same woman twice." Drake shifted his glass on the table, studying him. "There are levels and types of responsibilities, little brother. She has a kid. She doesn't need to date one."

He was sick of this conversation, too. Cade didn't know what more he needed to do to prove himself. What the hell difference did it make who got between his sheets? His sex life had nothing to do with his family or Animal Instincts.

Yet his gut twisted because he'd basically told himself the same thing Drake had not so charmingly spewed, and he was still thinking of making a play for Avery. She tied him up in knots. He wanted to dissect that, find out why.

"They're coming back to the table." Flynn sipped his beer.

Cade's gaze tracked Avery until she climbed onto the stool next to him. "So who won?"

Zoe grinned, the curve of her lips reminding him of her gypsy heritage, seductive and mysterious. "Gabby, of course. When doesn't she win?"

Zoe's once light brown hair was dyed blue this week. For more than a year, she'd colored it a different unnatural shade, changing it every week or two. No one knew why. She'd walked into the clinic one day with bright orange hair and never said a word as she'd set up in the back for her grooming appointments.

They'd all wondered. No one had asked.

Gabby took a healthy gulp of her ale. "Gotta be good at something. At least Brent didn't maim anyone."

Brent's aim was notoriously bad when it came to darts. Cade had a scar on his bicep as proof.

Brent waved off her comment. "Only because everyone scurried away, refusing to play with us." He turned in his seat and yelled to the bar over the noise. "All pussies!"

Gabby shoulder-bumped him. "How would you know a pussy if you saw one?"

Flynn choked on his beer.

Cade looked at Avery to see how she was taking the light banter at Brent's expense, but the curve of her lips said she was amused by the conversation. She was quiet, but comfortable. He guessed he just wasn't used to quiet women. Come to think of it, if not for Avery, he'd swear they didn't exist.

Avery dropped her chin in her hand. "I'll bet he's been with at least one woman."

Brent's eyes narrowed to catty, but he said nothing.

She shifted in her seat, crossing her long legs wrapped in skinny jeans that Cade would love nothing more than to peel off her. The knee-high black boots could stay.

"Are all of you from Redwood Ridge? You seem to know each other very well."

Most of them had grown up together. Brent was a recent Seattle transplant from five years ago. Gabby had been in Flynn's graduating class, Zoe in Drake's. Cade and his brothers were only a year and a half apart, Drake being the oldest, but they were close. At the clinic there was a respectful working relationship, but after hours it was like being back in the sandbox again. A guy couldn't ask for better friends.

Gabby readjusted her ponytail. "I can give you all the dirt."

Zoe laughed, a rich smoky sound that seemed to wind Drake tighter. His shoulders tensed as he swallowed the last of his whiskey neat and stood. "I'm out. Avery, thank you for everything. Seriously."

They all lifted their glasses. "To Avery!"

Her cheeks flushed as she stared at the table. "Thanks."

Gabby winced and set down her glass. "Damn, Cade. Cougar at twelve o'clock."

Judging by her gaze directed over his shoulder, he assumed she meant her twelve o'clock, not his. He turned in just enough time to catch Cynthia's perfume before she sidled up next to him, plastering her double D's in his face. Cynthia had been a lapse in judgment about four years back, but she didn't seem to take that personally.

He looked to Flynn for help, but his jerkface brother grinned. *"Just put her over your knee and she'll leave you alone."*

Why did he tell his brother anything? Yes, it was true Cynthia liked to be spanked, and yes, it was true she'd liked to scream out *Daddy* when in the throes. To each her own. It just wasn't his thing. In fact, he was pretty sure he was still traumatized.

Avery lifted her brows. "Do I want to know?" she signed to Flynn.

Gabby shook her head, eyes wide. "Not unless you've got daddy issues. Keep your eyes down. Don't engage."

Flynn laughed, wiping a hand down his face.

Cynthia shoved her tongue in Cade's ear and purred. Except she was so drunk it came out more like a tin drum roll. "Let's go back to my place."

He resisted a shudder and set his hands on her waist. "Ah, thanks for the offer, but I've got an early morning tomorrow. Besides, you know you're too much…woman for me to handle." Her curly red hair, courtesy of Clairol, tickled his face and barred him from seeing his friends laughing at his expense.

Cynthia licked his throat.

Avery made a strangled sound of shock.

Cade always found it difficult rejecting women. One would think he'd become a Master Jedi at by now, but alas, "no" was not in his Webster. He'd beaten around the word, teased at it, and siphoned his way out of messy breakups, but rarely had to hurt feelings in his diversionary tactics. On the off chance Cynthia would remember this moment after she sobered, he'd hate for her to be humiliated in front of everyone at Shooters because the town manwhore had turned her down.

Another freaking term he couldn't stand. It wasn't as if he'd slept with every woman. He was actually more selective than people gave him credit. His reputation had been embellished greatly through the years, through no fault of his own. Not that he'd minded much. Not until recently. Hell, he'd been on a dry streak long enough to briefly—perhaps punishingly—consider Cynthia again.

Nope. Scratch that. He'd stay celibate.

Brent, bless him, decided to save his ass from being swallowed whole. "Cynthia, honey, retract your claws. Cade's with someone else tonight."

Cade pinched his eyes shut as Cynthia stilled halfway into her climb up his body. He held his hands out, not touching her, hoping the lack of contact wouldn't set her off. She'd been known to be a hothead.

Slowly, she eased back to look at his face. Mascara smears shadowed the puffiness under her eyes, and her mouth hung open in shock, breathing stale beer in his face. She looked from him to Avery and back again. "Who's she?"

"Cynthia, meet Avery, our new office manager." Thinking fast, he tapped Cynthia's ass to cue her to get down. "I think I saw Jared staring at you from the pool tables earlier." Jared being the ex high school football star whose life peaked ten years ago. No harm, no foul sending her Jared's way. "I think he's interested. I'd hate to come between you two."

"Yeah?" Her unfocused gaze scanned the room. "Thanks, Cade. You're a helluva guy."

As she sauntered away, and the entirety of their table busted out into hysterics, he blew out a breath. "And you people call yourselves friends."

Gabby swiped her eyes. "I warned you she was coming."

Brent held out his hand, wiggling his fingers. "Zoe, hand over your purse. Quick." She passed it over and Brent dug through the contents, removed a small package of antibacterial wipes, and tossed it on the table in front of Cade. "Use them. Hurry, before infection sets in."

With air being in such short supply, Gabby thunked her head on the table and wheezed through a round of giggles.

Avery set her glass down. "You knew she had wipes in her purse?"

After what just went down over the past five minutes, that was what shocked her?

Zoe patted Gabby's back and slid a glass of water in front of her. "He's in my purse more than I am."

Brent nodded in mock seriousness. "True, dat."

Cade sighed and turned to Avery. "You ready to go?" He was so over this night.

Amusement still shone in her eyes as she nodded.

They drove back to her cabin in silence, but a comfortable one. He parked in front of the porch and got out to open her door. She looked up with round eyes as if no one had been so courteous before and then avoided his gaze. As they climbed the porch steps and he wondered how to end the night, Justine opened the front door, rushed past them, and headed for her car.

"Hailey's asleep. There were no issues. You two go on inside. Together. Alone. I'll see you tomorrow, Avery." With that, she got in her car, sped out of the drive, and disappeared onto the main road.

They stood staring after the taillights had faded and Avery pressed a hand to her forehead. "What is wrong with everybody?"

"Subtlety is not her strong suit, I take it?" He was used to his meddling family, but being the victim of matchmaking seemed new to her.

Her gaze landed on his chest and suddenly he was aware of her closeness, of the summer and berries scent of her rising over the pine and snow. Her breath hitched, her lips parted, and her lids grew heavy.

One step, one step and his body would be flush with hers and he'd know what she tasted like. He'd thought of little else this week, and he was starting to forget the reasons why he shouldn't make a move.

"Um…" She tucked a piece of hair behind her ear. "The woman at the bar, you're not…together?"

"No."

"But you used to be?"

"Yes. One night, years ago."

She nodded. "You were really nice about letting her down tonight."

"No sense in being an asshole about it." He shrugged.

Finally, her gaze lifted to his. Part shock, part admiration lit the brown depths. He couldn't recall when, if ever, someone had looked at him and seen respect. His chest swelled, giving him the false impression he could do anything.

The porch light caught the golden flecks in her irises to add to the punch of dark brown. She had clever eyes, expressive, with long lashes that framed all that pretty color. Avery wasn't a stunner, but she had an unmistakable natural beauty not found often anymore. The freckles lightly dusting her nose only added to her charm.

Her gaze dropped to his mouth and back up, telling him she was thinking of being naughty, too. "You should stop looking at me like that. I'm not dessert. I'm not even an appetizer."

He stepped into her space and cupped her cheek, cool from the air. "I disagree."

Cade wondered how long she'd been married to the dick who put those ideas in her head and how long it would take to undo the damage. She hadn't outright said anything, but he knew insecurity when he saw it. She was confident in work, with her daughter, in everything else, until he acted on impulse and got closer. Then her oh-shit meter went off.

She wasn't ready to be kissed, but he was going to pursue this chemistry to see just how combustible they were together. His mind was made up, if for no other reason than to show her just how desirable she was.

"I'll see you on Monday." Leaning in, he kissed her cheek, letting his lips drag across her smooth skin and graze a path to her temple. Her breath shuddered out, expelling puffs of air in the cool, damp night. "For the record," he said quietly into her hair, "I think you're sweeter than any dessert I've had."

And he'd had a lot of dessert.

* * * *

Squawk. "Highway to hell."

Cade muttered a curse.

Avery looked up from the billing statement she'd been going over with him, glancing first at the cockatoo and then Cade. The muscles in his forearms flexed as he leaned into his hands on the desk next to her. Large hands. They'd felt good cupping her cheeks the other night.

She shook her head. *Focus.* "What's wrong?"

"The Battleaxes are here." He jerked his chin at the front door. "All three of them at once. This can't be good."

Cade's mother and two aunts strode into the clinic. The three women couldn't be any more different. Rosa was in jeans and a T-shirt with a leather bomber jacket, her unnatural red hair plastered in place and not a stitch of makeup. Gayle's light blond bob moved freely as she walked. She was wearing a pair of khakis and a light blue sweater under a peacoat, sporting a natural look with a swipe of gloss and a little mascara. The mayor, Marie, was in professional mode in a tweed suit, her dark brown hair swept up in a twist and war paint in full operatus.

Avery's gut twisted. Cade turned to leave, but she grabbed his wrist. "Don't you dare leave me alone with them." She'd only met them a handful of times since moving, but they were intimidating as individuals. Together they could take down the Taliban.

"Mom, Aunties, what brings you out?" He leaned over the desk to kiss their cheeks. "Taking candy from babies? Solving the budget deficit and telling no one?"

Avery's pulse thrummed as heat pooled in her belly. There was nothing sexier than a good sense of humor.

"Har, har. Avery, dear. So good to see you." Marie took off her gloves and unbuttoned her coat.

"You, too, Mayor."

"Oh, please. Just Marie is fine."

Avery chanced a peek at Cade, but he was pretending to read the billing statement in his hands. Wimp. She cleared her throat and smiled. "What can I help you gals with today?"

"Well," Gayle started, but was interrupted by Gabby who walked up front with her attention on a chart.

"Avery, have you seen the…" Gabby's eyes rounded when they landed on the visitors. "Hey there." She moved around the desk, hugging each in turn, not the least bit afraid of the trio. "What a great surprise. Have you met Avery? Look at the wonderful job she's done in organizing us."

Cade tried to step behind Avery and leave, but she moved her chair back, blocking his exit. Stuck, he pasted on an affable grin. "I've got patients, so…"

He tried stepping in front of Avery. She stretched out her legs. "No, you don't. Your schedule's clear for twenty minutes."

"I have paperwork."

"You don't."

"I do. I'm sure of it." His jaw ground, but amusement lit his eyes. Obviously he was enjoying the game. His expression implored her to release him.

"Nope," she sang.

Rosa cleared her throat and looked at her sisters. "Told you."

Gayle's smile could've melted the arctic. "I do see. You were right."

Cade tensed. "See what? Right about what?"

The trio, complete with Gabby, stared between her and Cade, a mischievous gleam in their eyes over an inside joke.

Instead of answering, Marie nodded. "We've heard about the wonderful job you've been doing, Avery. That's why we're here, actually. We have a proposition for you."

Oh God. "Um…okay?"

Cade chuckled. She kicked him in the ankle.

Ever since last Friday night, when they'd all gone out to Shooters and Cade almost kissed her, there'd been a jovial atmosphere at work. Like crossing the line between strangers and friends. They'd bantered, joked, teased. Even Drake had cracked a smile or…well, just the one time. But it had been fun. She loved working here, and she was beginning to gain a sense of purpose again.

Gayle took the lead, leaning on the counter with her big doe eyes. "We're in need of someone with your organizational skills. You see, Jessica was put on bed rest and she normally runs the event committee—"

Cade barked out a laugh. Paused. Looked at each of the ladies. Held up a hand and laughed again. "You want Avery to head the Redwood Ridge event committee?"

Rosa nodded. "Exactly." She looked at Avery, who was too confused to move. "For now, it would just be the Valentine's dance, but we can see how that goes and then you could chair more things if all goes well."

Marie nodded. "The St. Patrick's pot luck, Easter egg hunt…"

Gabby bounced on her toes. "She'd be perfect. I mean, Avery's got great ideas, and you know she's super organized."

They kept chattering about her as if she wasn't there. She pressed a palm to her forehead.

Cade leaned down to whisper in her ear. "This is how Jessica got roped into the job. I'd run. Run far. Run fast."

"Who is Jessica?" She didn't even know this person and they were—

"Oh, Jessica runs the nursery." Marie waved her hand. "That's not important. She's stepped down and we need someone to replace her. We pick you."

"I...um." Avery sighed. God. "That's very flattering, but I don't know the town very well, and I've never done anything like that before." There. That should get them to—

"Nonsense. The meeting is tonight at the rec center. Be there at seven." Marie donned her gloves.

"Wait. I can't." Avery stood. "My mom has book club and there's no one to watch Hailey. Besides that, I'm just too busy."

Gayle smiled as if this had all gone according to their crazy plan. "The meetings are only ninety minutes once a week. Every two weeks if there's not an event coming up. Cade can watch Hailey while you're away."

Cade flinched. "I what?"

Avery's temples started to throb. "No. Hailey has special needs, and I'd need someone responsible who knows—"

"Are you saying I'm not responsible?" Cade crossed his arms, his brows lifting.

Dang it. "No, of course not. It's just—"

"I *am* responsible. And for your information, I could handle a kid for a couple of hours."

"Perfect." Marie moved to the door before Avery could even blink, her sisters following. "Cade will babysit Hailey, and we'll see you at the meeting. I knew this would work nicely."

They walked out with the same flair as when they'd strode in, leaving Avery's mouth agape. She stared at the door, trying to figure out if she was pissed off or freaked out.

Gabby grinned and slung an arm around her shoulders. "You'll do a great job." With that complete statement of non-help, she went back into Flynn's office.

Slowly, Avery turned to Cade.

"I walked right into that." He shook his head. "Twenty-eight years and you'd think I'd know when I was being trapped. Don't look at me like that. They're sneaky. Tricky. You were standing right here, too."

She sighed. "What did I just get myself into? And don't think you're off the hook. I can double book you on 'depressed' cats for the next three months."

Cade sprawled into the extra office chair and pinched the bridge of his nose. His dark blue scrubs stretched over the lean muscles of his thighs and biceps, momentarily distracting her.

He slapped his hand on his leg. "Redwood Ridge does several community events throughout the year. Mostly holidays, but the funds raised go to causes like the rec center, the fire department, the library. The event coordinator kinda oversees all of that."

Avery had spent a good amount of her time planning parties for Richard and his law firm. But it had been more than two years since they'd separated and she'd done nothing on this grand a scale. For a whole town? She was just beginning to get settled into the new job, new home. And Hailey wasn't accustomed to this many strangers around. She'd been doing really well in school and the rec center, but to leave her one-on-one with a man she barely knew was not something Avery was comfortable with, even if Cade was trustworthy.

Heck, none of this was what Avery was used to. For ten years, she'd been isolated from others in the Stowe mansion, raising Hailey with no assistance and little more than herself for company.

Avery sat in the chair across from Cade. She needed to give him an out. "About you babysitting, I'll just take Hailey with me, or find someone..."

She trailed off as his gaze met hers. Something like hurt flashed in his eyes, twisting his mouth, but then it was gone. He stared at her for a beat as if trying to calculate her reaction or his own. All she could think was, why didn't he want an out? Single, attractive man, Friday night—surely he didn't want to babysit.

It was hard to get a read on him. Usually he was charming and playful. A few times, he'd teetered on irritation, but always he was good with the animals. Patient. Kind.

Her breath caught. She could've sworn it was interest looking back at her, like the other night on her porch, but without the heat, the desire. Swallowing, she forced herself to look away when her cheeks flamed.

Scratching his jaw, he leaned forward, resting his forearms on his thighs. "I can stay with Hailey for a couple of hours." His gaze bore into hers, not a trace of humor in them. "I get the impression you don't lean on people often. It may seem like I got roped into it, and maybe I did, but that doesn't mean I don't want to do it." A moment passed, then two. "She's a great kid, Avery."

Cade had spent a few hours with Hailey and thought she was a great kid. Richard had been her father and never saw it. Coming from any other guy, it might've sounded like a line. But no. Cade was genuine, from the inflection in his low voice to his direct gaze to his actions when around Hailey. A person couldn't fake sincerity.

She closed her eyes and leaned her head back. "I'll drive you batshit with instructions. Blow up your phone with texts."

He rose and walked past her. "I can take it."

Chapter 7

Cade had just enough time to head home and shower after work before needing to be at Avery's. Figuring he'd bring along his black lab, Freeman, so he could play with Seraph, he snagged the extra leash from the kitchen on his way in.

Stripping off his scrub top, he turned to head upstairs to the bathroom and paused at the living room threshold. Cutin was hanging by all fours from the front bay window drapes.

Stoically sitting on the floor was Freeman, one eyebrow quirked as if to say, *it was your idea to bring home a cat.*

Cade cleared his throat.

Cutin squeaked out a meow and turned her head upside down to address him. *There was a wrinkle. I was just straightening it for you.*

Sighing, he picked up the kitten and set her on his shoulder—since that seemed to be her favorite spot when not clutching the drapes, shower curtain, or kitchen towel rack—and walked upstairs to the bathroom.

"You're getting declawed on Monday. Just so you know."

Meow.

"Don't take that tone with me."

Setting her on the vanity, he stripped the rest of the way and showered off the clinic aroma. After toweling dry, he put Cutin back on his shoulder and headed into his bedroom.

"I'm going to be gone for a bit tonight. You will not destroy anything in my absence. Got it?"

Meow.

"Don't be sassy." He set her on the bed, dressed, and went to fetch Freeman. "Who wants to go for a ride?"

Freeman, not one to bark, lifted his paw.

Twenty minutes later, Cade found himself leaning against Avery's kitchen counter with his arms crossed as the dogs got to know each other and Avery fluttered around like the end of days was looming. She'd been talking nonstop for fifteen minutes while making PB&J for dinner, and if Hailey weren't sitting at the kitchen table, he'd be tempted to shut Avery up. With his mouth.

She was adorable all worked up. Flushed cheeks, hands flailing. Admittedly, he'd only caught about half the things she'd said because he found looking at her much more interesting. Those jeans molding her perfect ass weren't helping matters any. She had a great body. Curves and soft edges, not a rail with nothing to hold.

She huffed a breath. "Are you listening?"

Not really. "I should only let Hailey play with matches after dark, feed her candy bars and soda for snack, and scary movies are acceptable if she won't go to sleep. Got it." He sat next to Hailey at the table and held up a fist for her to bump. "Oh, come on. You can't leave a guy hanging."

He was never really sure if Hailey was hearing him, as she never made eye contact and she always seemed to be deep in her head. Ducking his face close to hers, he grinned. "Make a fist, squirt." When she did after a brief delay, he gently bumped his fist with hers. "There you go. Don't leave me hanging again or no sugar high for you later."

Hailey whooped out a laugh, rough and short, but Cade's chest swelled at the small connection. The girl's round cheeks split in a smile as she glanced somewhere over his head. Sometimes she looked so much like Avery.

"Would you please be serious?"

Cade reined in his grin. Avery was worried about leaving her daughter and he got that. All attempts to pacify that anxiety hadn't worked, so he met her gaze from across the room. "She gets sick from dairy, she's prone to wandering, she's already in PJs, bedtime is eight, brush teeth first, cue her to potty, watch thirty minutes of her sleep video, and try not to touch her, especially on her head."

Avery's head whipped back, gorgeous brown eyes blinking rapidly. "Um…yes." She glanced around, clearly uneasy. "You have my cell number?"

"The first twenty times you asked. I got this. Go."

She sighed and looked down, where Seraph was doing his best to chase Freeman's tail. Finally, without anything else to nag about, she tapped Hailey's arm. "Pretty please be good for Cade. I'll be back after you go to sleep, but I'll check in on you. Okay?"

Hailey dug into her sandwich as an answer.

After Avery left, Cade eyed his own sandwich and glass of milk Avery had set out. Wiping a hand down his face, he ate in silence, watching the dogs. Seraph was still wearing the cone around his neck to keep him from chewing off the bandages from his amputation. He was due in Monday for suture removal and a follow-up. Figuring he'd save Avery a trip, he looked at Hailey.

"Hey, squirt. Wanna be my assistant? Seraph's all better now, so we can get all that junk off him. What do you do say?"

She squealed and flapped her hands, which he took as a yes.

"Awesome. Finish your…rice milk"—he shuddered—"and we'll hop to it."

Since she was prone to wandering, he brought Hailey outside with him to the car to get supplies and headed back in. After tossing their paper plates away, he rinsed out Hailey's empty cup and set his on the counter so he could put Seraph on the table.

"Okay, squirt. Just stand next to me and pet your puppy while I check his ouchie." He turned when she didn't move and found her drinking his milk. "Shoot, no. That's regular milk."

Taking the glass from her, he eyed the contents and tried to determine how much she drank, but it couldn't have been much. He dumped the rest, filled a cup of water, and gave it to her. "Just thirsty, eh? I hope that little bit didn't make you sick."

She seemed no worse for wear after a minute, so he pointed to the table and repeated his instructions. After a small delay, she did as he asked and petted Seraph's back while he removed the bandages.

The wound was closed and there were no signs of infection, so he opened a sterile disposable suture removal kit. "Doing a great job, squirt." He bent and quickly snipped the sutures before feeling around the area. The puppy wiggled at all the attention, but Cade got it done without too much headache. "I think we can take the cone off now."

Hailey squealed. Seraph barked.

He laughed and removed the cone, then tossed the stuff into the garbage. "How about we give this guy a bath?" Because of the injury, Cade had instructed Avery not to bathe Seraph, even though he needed one.

Freeman took off for parts unknown at the word "bath." For a lab, he hated water immensely. Hopefully Seraph was more cooperative than his own dog.

He rummaged around the bathroom until finding kid shampoo, then made his way back to the kitchen. He pulled a chair up to the counter, filled the sink with warm soapy water, and encouraged Hailey to climb on the chair before setting Seraph in the sink.

"I'm going to stand behind you, squirt. If I'm too close, just use your elbow on me." Straddling the chair, he caged Hailey in front of him and brought his arms around her. She didn't seem bothered, so he passed her a cup. "Go ahead and pour water over the doggy."

She didn't seem to understand, so he gently wrapped his fingers around where hers held the cup and dipped it into the water, then poured it over Seraph.

The puppy yipped and shook his head, flinging suds and water everywhere. Hailey whooped out another laugh, which pulled one of his own from deep in his chest.

By the time they were done there was more water on them and the floor than in the sink. He towel-dried Seraph and set him on the floor, then cleaned up the mess. His pocket buzzed with two incoming texts as he dropped the towels into the washing machine in the room off the kitchen. But Hailey needed to change, so he fished around her dresser drawers and came up with a new set of pajamas.

"Can you dress by yourself?" He made a show of covering his eyes and hoped the girl got the hint. When the rustle of clothing quieted, he peeked. "Good job, squirt."

Hailey settled on the couch with her sleepy-time show. He tossed her wet PJs into the washer and checked his cell.

Avery: Everything okay?

Avery: Why aren't u answering?

Grinning, he shook his head while thinking of how to answer. Deciding to goad her, he thumbed out his response.

Yep. Two corpses. Everything's fine.

Just as he wondered if she'd get the reference, her response came back.

Avery: Did you just quote the movie Clue to me?

Yes, ma'am. Impressed you knew that.

Avery: Love that movie. How's Hailey?

She's fine. Stop texting and pay attention to ur meeting.

Hailey grabbed the hem of his damp shirt and tugged. He pocketed his phone and realized she looked a little pale. "You all right, squirt? You—"

Without any preamble, she bent over and yakked down the front of him. Not just threw up—no-no—but projectile. White, milky vomit with chunks of PB&J. Oh, the stench. He'd never eat it again. Never.

He stilled, palms up, waiting to see if she was finished, unsure of how to handle this. He'd been yakked on a hundred times by animals, but never a tiny human. "Wow. So that just happened."

She wailed, flapping her hands and jumping in place. Completely unlike her happy-flapping, the distress from her had panic rising in his chest.

He squatted. "Hey, hey," he cooed. "No biggie. We'll just…uh." Hissing a breath, he stood. "Okay, wait right here."

He went to turn for the bathroom when he realized his clothes had to go or he'd drip the contents of Hailey's stomach all over the house. A quick survey showed she didn't get any on herself. At least there was that.

Setting his phone on the counter, he quickly stripped down to his boxers and tossed the soiled clothes into the washer, added extra detergent, then started a load. He used some disinfectant wipes he found under the sink to wipe down the floor. Hailey never moved, but at least she had her color back.

"This would look so bad if someone were to walk in right now." Grown man in his skivvies with an eight-year-old girl.

He washed his hands and walked Hailey to the living room to finish her show. "Be right back, squirt."

Hopping from foot to foot—because the temp had dropped to twenty degrees—he ran like a lunatic to his car, grabbed his extra set of scrubs, and thanked God that Avery didn't have neighbors. Once inside, he dressed and eased down next to Hailey on the couch.

Should he call his mom? She'd know what to do. Except it would be all over Twitter in under an hour. Or call Avery? But she'd freak.

The kid seemed okay now. Her complexion looked normal, at least.

"Hey, squirt. I know you don't like it, but I'm just gonna feel your forehead." Slowly, he lifted his hand and pressed his palm to her cheek, then her forehead. Didn't feel hot or anything.

Hailey shoved his hand away, never taking her gaze from the TV.

"Okay, okay. All done." He blew out a breath and closed his eyes for a moment. "You really do get sick on dairy, yeah?"

The dogs circled the floor and laid down next to each other. Seraph was getting around really well with just the three legs. He'd grown a bit in the week since his surgery and the tan cotton puppy fuzz was beginning to look more like fur. Another few weeks and he'd resemble more dog than puppy.

The credits rolled on Hailey's show. He cut the power and followed her into the bathroom, watching as she brushed her teeth.

"So, um… Your mom says to go potty, too, yeah? I'm just going to…you know…step out." He waited outside the door, back turned, while Hailey hopefully had peeing by herself mastered.

He breathed when the distinct tinkle hit water. Waiting a few moments until a flush sounded, he helped her wash her hands and nudged her toward her bedroom.

She climbed onto the bed and pulled the covers up. Cade realized he should've paid more attention to Avery because now he wasn't sure what to do. Turn on a nightlight? Kiss her on the forehead good night? He switched off the overhead light. Not finding a nightlight, he flicked on a lamp on the dresser in case she got scared and eyed Hailey's adorable little body, her heavy lids. She was an effing cutie. Dark hair just like Avery's and round cheeks. Hailey's eyes were blue, though, unlike Avery's brown.

Deciding to leave the door open, just in case, he lifted his hand. "Night, squirt. I'm right out here if you feel sick again or need anything."

Hailey sat up, the covers falling to her waist.

Cade stilled, wracking his brain for instructions he might've forgotten. "Want me to stay in here?"

She didn't move, so he turned off the lamp and sat next to her hip until she lay down again. The dogs came in, Freeman flopping on the floor by the foot of the bed and Seraph doing his damnedest to climb up by Hailey. Perhaps that was why she'd sat up. Used to sleeping with the dog?

Figuring it wouldn't hurt, he picked up Seraph and set him on the bed. Both puppy and child sighed, closing their eyes. Double damn. That was adorable.

Exhausted, he stretched out crossways on the foot of her bed, head and feet hanging off, but at least he was right next to her if she needed anything.

"This babysitting thing is a lot of work, yeah?"

No one answered, of course.

Along with complete muscle annihilation from tension, a fullness rose in his chest, a peace of sorts, at the night's events. A lot of work, yeah, but kind of rewarding in a way. The kid was pretty great when she wasn't puking on him, and getting her to laugh had felt damn good.

They didn't even burn the place down. Go them.

* * * *

Hating to admit it, Avery was glad she'd gone to the meeting. Once she got past the questions of how her date with Cade went—and repeatedly relaying it wasn't a date, just drinks with friends—the night wasn't so bad.

Besides Cade's mom and two aunts, there were five other women on the event committee. All of them were very nice and appreciative she'd taken the position. Not that she'd had a choice in the matter. Or a say.

Redwood Ridge apparently celebrated most holidays as a community. It was sweet in a small town way. Tonight's meeting had been to discuss the Valentine's dance next month. In year's past, they'd done it in the high school gym, but the other ladies claimed it had been just blah, not romantic, and wanted more pizzazz. Their words, not hers.

Avery had suggested a change of venue, easy enough, and they'd gone bonkers in glee. The dance would now be held at the botanical gardens, since they had a hall attached to the nursery dome. To boost interest and numbers, Avery had offered up the idea for a note exchange in the week before the dance.

Marie, having loved the idea, would use her mayoral power to have the rec center kids make heart-shaped notes and pass them to the post office for delivery. People would place an order, with phrasing, and the whole thing would go down like a secret admirer swap. Best of all, the money went to charity. Each event the town held would. The Valentine's dance funds were going to the art program at the high school.

Pulling up to the cabin, she grabbed her purse and went inside, anxious to see how Cade had done watching Hailey. After his teasing text, she hadn't heard anything from him. It had taken a lot of willpower not to call fifty times.

Pausing by the couch, she set her purse down on a table and glanced around. The kitchen light was on, the washing machine in spin cycle, and the house was quiet. Too quiet. Cade was nowhere in sight, nor were the dogs. Beginning to panic, she rushed down the hall to Hailey's room and stopped dead in her tracks.

Cade's dog, Freeman, lifted his head from where he was sleeping on the floor and set it back down, uninterested in her arrival. Hailey was tucked in, sound asleep, her dark lashes shadowing her round cheeks.

But Cade—God, her heart squeezed—was draped over the foot of the bed, face down, legs and head dangling off the mattress, lightly snoring with Seraph curled in a fuzzy ball on his butt.

She clutched her chest at the...*adorableness*. Her throat suddenly got tight.

Carefully stepping deeper into the room, she gingerly picked up Seraph off Cade's very tight, sexy backside and nuzzled the warm, sleepy puppy before setting him next to Hailey. Cade must've removed Seraph's cone, and the bandages were gone, too. He'd saved her an extra trip to his office by doing that.

Cade's head jerked up, his worried gaze falling on Hailey before relief filled his eyes. He rubbed his neck and spotted Avery. "Hey, you're home." The sleepy, hoarse baritone pulled a tiny shiver from her.

He rolled over and rose slowly, all sinew and grace, his gaze on Hailey to make sure he didn't wake her. Her chest pinched again. At full height, he stretched and scrubbed his hands through his hair, making it stand on end.

It seemed too intimate, standing and staring, but damn he was something to look at. And here she thought her libido had been permanently broken.

He wasn't wearing the same clothes from earlier. Instead he had on dark blue scrubs, his feet bare. Noticing her questioning glance, he tilted his head toward the doorway.

She nodded and bent down to kiss Hailey's cheek, taking a moment to run her fingers through the silkiness of her hair before following Cade into the kitchen.

He looked around as if confused, then glanced at the clock. "It's still early. Guess she wiped me out." He offered a nervous laugh.

Ignoring the urge to—she didn't know, but it would be stupid—she rubbed her arms. Scratch that. She knew exactly what she had in mind. She wanted to climb his body, kiss him to the point of breathlessness, and snuggle in his warmth.

She cleared her throat. "How did it go?"

"Uh...yeah." He scratched his jaw. "Don't get mad, but when my back was turned, Hailey took a sip of my milk. For future reference, I prefer beer. Anyway, it wasn't much, but she kinda got sick. All over me."

She pressed her lips together to try not to smile, but it was pointless. He was so flustered the grin escaped. Obviously Hailey was no worse for wear, so everything was fine. He'd handled it. "So those are your clothes in the washer?"

"Yeah. And some towels. We gave Seraph a bath after I took his stitches out." He looked behind him at the laundry room and then at her grin. "You can just give me back the clothes on Monday at work—" He crossed his arms suddenly. "Stop smiling like that. You're really not mad?"

She pressed a hand to her lips, shoulders shaking. "No, I'm not mad. I tried to tell you not to leave a cup around. She picks up anything—"

"I wasn't listening that closely. Lesson learned."

She sobered a little. "I'm sorry she got sick on you, though. Not fun. And thanks for doing all that for Seraph. It was really nice."

"Not a problem." He looked at her through blue eyes, humor gone and replaced with a soft affection. One corner of his mouth quirked as if undecided if his thoughts were funny or stupid.

Static charged the few feet between them. Pulling. His gaze never left hers as his throat worked a swallow. She'd kill to know what he was thinking, but something told her his thoughts weren't far from her own, that he was feeling the slow heat.

"Do you want something to drink?" she asked, and her voice came out more sultry than normal.

He cleared his throat twice before answering. "Yeah, sure. Whatever you have."

Starting a pot of coffee—decaf or she'd never sleep—she focused on her task so she wasn't tempted to look at him. Eye. Gasm. "Everything else went okay?"

"Kosher. How was the meeting?"

She turned. "You know, it was actually kind of fun. I don't know if it was the adult interaction or just getting away from the house on my own, but I liked it. The ladies were nice. Gossips, but nice. They acted as if everything I said was an epiphany. I think they just needed a fresh set of eyes and ears. Anyway, the committee isn't too demanding, so I think I can handle it. Don't tell them I said that."

He'd taken a seat at the table while she was gabbing, his chin now on his palm and a lazy grin tipping his lips. "Our secret."

Crap on a cracker, he was yummy. Her pulse sped. She turned away. "I'll have to get a sitter for Friday nights. Do you know anyone? One of the high school students, perhaps?"

"I can do it."

She gripped the counter. Hard. "An attractive single guy like you, occupied every Friday night? Can't ask you to do that." At the bar the other night, that woman had draped herself all over him. It wasn't the first instance, either. Since then, three new pictures with clingy females had all popped up on new boards.

"You think I'm attractive?"

Ordering her knees to lock and hold her upright, she faced him. "Coy is unbecoming." Not really, because her cheeks were flaming, but it seemed like a decent thing to say.

"I'm not fishing for compliments. I'm merely interested that you find me attractive." He leaned back in his chair, stretching his legs out. "And you didn't ask me to do anything. I offered. I'll watch Hailey during your meetings."

Unsure, she poured them each a cup of coffee and brought them to the table. Grabbing cream and sugar, she set those down, too. She took a chair next to him, her leg brushing his until she shifted. The intimacy wasn't lost on her. The two of them sitting in the dim kitchen, drinking coffee together. Richard, when they'd still been together, hadn't been home much, and when he had been, he certainly hadn't sat at the table and chatted. Back then, it was usually just her and Hailey eating meals together. It was odd having a man beside her, in her home.

"She's a great kid, Avery."

Her gaze shot to Cade's. And there he went again, being sincere and sweet. Most people had a hard time seeing past Hailey's disability to the girl inside. Cade didn't seem to see a handicap at all. He treated her like he did just about everyone else.

She took a sip of coffee before answering. "Thank you."

Leaning forward, he crossed his arms on the table. "Is it hard for you with her not being able to talk?"

Chewing her lip, she thought that over. No one had ever asked her before. "Sometimes. She uses sign language when really frustrated, and she has a speaking app on the iPad, which has pictures and such to show what she needs if she has to. I..."

She shook her head, her internal filter kicking in, not wanting to get too personal. He made it easy to talk to him, but he was still her boss and she didn't know what boundaries there were between them.

"You what?"

Staring at his large hands wrapped around his mug, she decided it didn't matter. Cade genuinely seemed interested. "I guess the only time her being nonverbal bothers me is...in the little things I miss out on. The inane chatter from normal little girls, hearing a giggle." She paused. "I'll never get to hear her say, 'I love you, Mommy,' like other parents take for granted."

He didn't say a word, but she could feel his gaze on her, quiet, intent, as she looked into her coffee. She closed her eyes briefly and shook her head, willing the flush to leave her cheeks.

"Anyway, I got used to the quiet a long time ago. At least I don't have to yell over noise, right?" She forced a breathless laugh. God, she'd give anything to have the normal sounds of kids playing, fighting. Most parents wanted quiet. She desired the opposite.

In the silence that hung, she couldn't take it anymore and lifted her gaze to his. What she found in his eyes she hadn't seen in too many years, if ever. Not pity, but sympathy. Respect. Understanding.

Awareness hummed. It had been years since someone had looked at her instead of through her. Her fingers tightened around her mug, and when he opened his mouth to speak, air trapped in her throat as she wondered if he'd shrug off the moment or embrace it.

She had no idea what she'd do if it was the latter.

Chapter 8

"Silence isn't always what it's cracked up to be," Cade said, and scratched his jaw at his witty, brilliant insight.

Hell, he'd rarely been shocked by anything. Growing up in Redwood Ridge, where everyone knew everything about you and secret was a word in the dictionary, he'd seen the best and worst people had to offer.

But sitting across from Avery at her kitchen table and listening to her share something so private his chest ached left him reeling like the floor had dropped out. He wondered how many times in his childhood he'd told his parents *I love you,* and then tried to imagine his own hypothetical kids and how he'd feel if he never got to hear those three words.

It was more than that. The way she'd brushed off the comment and claimed to be used to quiet had him guessing she wasn't just referring to Hailey. He didn't know anything about her ex, but if the guy had let Avery go, he couldn't be too right in the head.

Her cheeks were crimson. Even in the dim kitchen, he could make out the blush, and he was sorry to have embarrassed her. She met his gaze briefly, those cocoa eyes mixing with honey, and then skittered away.

And wasn't it a crazy bitch, but he had the urge to reach across the table and pull her into his lap. Talk to her until the night waned and sunrise peeked over the mountains. Suddenly, he wanted to know everything about her, and that sent a ripple of shock and need through his gut.

Mostly shock. Because unless he was referring to his friends, talking wasn't what he typically sought from females.

He took a sip of his cooling coffee. "Your ex, how is he with Hailey? I figure he's got holidays and every other weekend or something?" And if the guy showed up in Redwood Ridge, Cade might just rearrange his face on principle.

Avery shook her head, gaze trained on her cup, but weary exhaustion flitted in her eyes and was gone in a flash. "He hasn't seen her in two years, not since I filed for divorce." She looked up at him and sighed. "I have full custody. That was part of what took so long for the divorce to go through. The only thing I asked for was a small trust fund for Hailey, in case something happened to me. He didn't believe child support or a trust was pertinent if he signed parental rights away."

Forget rearranging his face. He'd break every bone in the guy's body. Instead of the plethora of choice terms that came to mind, Cade reined in his temper. "She's better off without him. So are you."

She nodded. "My sentiments exactly."

When he'd asked about her ex before, she'd been tactful. Not that she wasn't now, but she wasn't choosing her words as carefully. "You don't speak ill of him. Why?" She had every right to, by the sound of it.

"I don't like painting him in a terrible light in front of Hailey. He might change his mind one day about seeing her, and I wouldn't want to scare her off. He's her dad." She sipped her coffee. "The way I look at it, we both brought her into this world. By me bad-mouthing him, it gives her the impression half of her is bad, too."

Christ. Her selflessness knew no bounds. Had it been him, he didn't think he'd be so mature. Anger and betrayal and hurt did things to people. It was normal to lash out and react. But it was as if her feelings didn't matter, putting only her daughter first. He shook his head in wonder, his respect for her notching near pedestal height.

Since it seemed like she needed a topic change, he went back to his reason for being in her cabin in the first place. "So what else went down at the meeting tonight? They rope you into doing anything else?" He grinned to lighten the grief in her eyes, which he supposed was more for him than her.

She told him about moving the venue and the secret admirer exchange, which he found quite clever. "Online invitations and flyers will go out on Monday. I guess the dance was pretty casual before, but the ladies thought something formal would be more romantic. To be allowed inside, guests must dress in red or pink to attend. And it's suit and tie."

He laughed. "Like prom."

"Sort of." She shrugged, but her smile was back. "I think it'll be a nice change of pace, at least by the sound of it." She gestured to his cup. "You want me to heat that up?"

"No, thanks. I should get going." Not that he wanted to.

Disappointment settled in her smile, and he knew, right then and there, that she was feeling it, too. The attraction had been obvious, at least to him, from the minute she'd carried an injured Seraph into the clinic. It had only been amplifying since. He'd been taking things slow, biding his time for the moment to act instead of standing still.

She rose and rinsed their cups out in the sink. "Thanks so much again for watching Hailey. We'll see about next week—"

She stopped the pleasantries when he came up behind her and moved her soft brown waves off her neck to expose her nape. A breath shuddered out of her mouth, and then she seemed to stop breathing altogether.

Leaning in, he nuzzled the soft skin below her ear, keeping his body mere inches away, lest he jar her with his arousal. Her fruity scent encompassed him, filled him, and he fought the urge to nibble on her neck to find out if she tasted just as sweet. She didn't move, not away or closer, and he took that as a good sign.

He brought his lips to the shell of her ear. "You didn't ask me why I don't mind babysitting your daughter on Friday nights."

She shivered. He grinned in satisfaction. Oh yeah, she was right there with him. And unlike before, when he'd driven her home from Shooters, she was ready to be kissed.

"This isn't a good idea, Cade." Her voice, a breathy whisper so unlike her usual calm, was beginning to tear his composure to shreds.

"Good ideas are rarely fun." He knew it was the wrong thing to say when she turned to face him, and he found her walls back up, her spine stiff.

She wasn't the type of woman to go looking for fun, playful, or short-lived, but damn if he hadn't met anyone who needed fun more than Avery. And at the moment, he was feeling the opposite of playful. Not for one second did he think this was a game.

"You're my boss, and I'm not in the market for romance."

Yep. Walls. Funny, he usually respected them. He had some of his own, for that matter.

He placed his hands on the counter behind her, caging her in and taking a step deeper into her gravitational pull. "People don't usually shop for romance. It just happens." Like right now, for instance.

"You're still my boss. I need this job so I don't have to dip into Hailey's trust fund. People will think... It's not a good idea."

People were going to think whatever they wanted, regardless, and her job wasn't at stake. "Then how about we keep things just like this, until you're ready for more." He could do secret and he could do slow. Right? "No one has to know unless you want them to."

She started to shake her head—and damn, he'd never had to work this hard—but he leaned in until his mouth was a whisper from hers. Her eyes widened.

"Since you refuse to ask me why I don't mind the babysitting gig, I'll tell you. I like your kid and I really like you. Your organizational mind is so hot, and I've been itching to unwind the tension from you since you alphabetized the magazines in my office. Yes, I noticed that," he added when she opened her mouth. "I enjoy talking to you outside of work, like we did tonight, because you relax more and say things you normally wouldn't. Thus, the idea of seeing you every Friday night when you come home is a hell yes in my book."

The tiniest of wrinkles formed between her eyebrows as if she'd never heard something so ludicrous, but he could tell she was damn tempted to believe him. Wary hope and interest sparked in her eyes. "Um…"

"That. That right there nails home my point. You fluster the hell out of me." He'd put his foot in his mouth more times in the two weeks since she'd come to town than the whole of his teen years. "And it's too much fun watching your mind go blank when I say something you're not expecting. Such as, I find you very attractive."

She let out an uneven breath that skated across his jaw. He went from semi-hard to *down, boy.*

"Here's the part where you say you find me attractive, too." He grinned for good measure, and was rewarded with the clouding of her eyes.

"You know you're attractive. I could cut my teeth on your abs, but…"

Killing him dead. "You haven't seen my abs. Would you like to?"

There went the eyes again, wide. A sexy as hell blush tinged her cheeks. He could all but feel the heat.

Fun as this was, he was sweating with the resistance. "Going to kiss you now, Avery. Three, two, one…"

She sucked in a breath, dragging his with her. He brushed his lips across hers, testing, getting her used to him. He hovered there, barely touching, until she took the initiative and added more pressure. Letting her test the waters, he followed her command.

As if unsure, she fumbled, tensing against him. His gut clenched with the realization she probably hadn't been kissed since filing for divorce. And hadn't she said they'd been separated before that? From the little she spoke of her marriage and from what he'd gleaned, Cade doubted the ass had paid any attention to her needs.

Shoving the prick from his mind, Cade cupped her jaw and took over. Confidence was a fragile thing, and he wasn't going to be the one to break hers. He tilted his head, parting his lips to take more of her. Her lids drifted shut and he was lost.

One hand at the small of her back, he eased the other into her hair to gently hold her to him. After that, he lost track of what the hell was happening. His heart jacked against his ribs, his mind vanishing in a fog of sensation. She was soft. Everywhere. The crush of her breasts against his chest, the strands of her hair, her lips as they moved against his. So damn soft. In the space between newness and uncertainty, she found a rhythm and opened to him. Her hands fell to his shoulders and fisted. A holy shit female moan vibrated from her mouth to his. He was losing a battle with sanity.

Don't push her. Get a grip.

He eased his mouth away and brushed a kiss to her temple, keeping her body flush with his, struggling to draw air. Her breaths panted against his neck, hot and damp. Giving himself just a moment, he stilled until the spots before his vision cleared.

She muttered something that sounded like *crap on a cracker*, and he laughed. Looking in her lust-induced eyes, he fought the strange pleasure/pain in his chest.

"I need to get home." No, he really didn't, but staying any longer would kill him.

He kissed her forehead and stepped away, not missing in the slightest that she grabbed the counter behind her as if needing it to stay upright. He whistled for his dog while dropping into a chair to shove his shoes on. Freeman strode into the room and sat by the back door as Cade shrugged into his coat.

"Why'd you name him Freeman?"

He glanced at his dog and back to her. "He has light markings under his eyes and the stoicism of Morgan Freeman." He shrugged.

A slow smile spread over her face, and he had to remind himself he was leaving for a reason. "You named your dog after an actor?"

"Yep." He paused. "Why Seraph?" He jerked his chin toward the hallway where her puppy and child slept.

Her smile turned wistful. "When I saw Hailey snuggle up to him in the exam room, he was like an angel in that moment. I'd never seen her connect with something like she did with him." She rubbed her forehead and laughed. "It's a hassle getting her to leave him to go to school. And when we get home, the dog follows her everywhere, even to the bathroom."

The awed expression on her face did him in. She was the type of woman to appreciate the little things, accumulate moments instead of seeing the grand spectrum of it all. Rare, indeed.

He grabbed the knob and opened the door. "To him, you were the angels. 'Night, Avery."

* * * *

For some strange reason, Animal Instincts was hopping the next week, more so than typical. And then on Friday, Avery checked her Twitter phone app and discovered why.

Cade's Aunt Rosa had tweeted about Avery taking the event committee deal and that Cade had watched Hailey while she'd been out. One of Redwood Ridge's most eligible bachelors had shown he liked kids and he could do the responsible thing, which made him even more attractive. To women, it meant he had the potential to be tied down.

Which explained the sudden crush of female owners bringing in their pets for anything from "her coat isn't as shiny" to "it slept a lot yesterday" to "he looked at me funny."

She needed a bottle of wine and twelve hours of uninterrupted sleep. She'd barely tolerated the complaining clients when she'd had to shift some off of Cade's schedule to Flynn's. Even Drake had taken a couple, much to his dismay. People and Drake were not cozy bedfellows, which was why he mostly did surgeries. But she appreciated the help just the same. The patients? Not so much.

Flynn came in from the back, glanced at the waiting room, and shook his head. *"What the hell? They're still coming?"*

Instead of signing a response, she showed him her Twitter feed.

He leaned against the desk. *"That explains it. They're vying for Cade's attention and checking out the competition."*

"I'm not competition. There's nothing going on between us." Even though Cade had kissed her in her kitchen and her girly parts were still weeping with joy. The man knew how to kiss. But no one else knew that juicy tidbit.

"Liar, liar."

She shook her head. "Whatever. I'm just glad you're able to pick up some of the slack." Luckily, Flynn and Gabby didn't have many home visits this week, so they'd helped with most of the add-on appointments.

Now if she could just figure out what to do with the six casseroles in the break room fridge. Added to that, there were so many cookies and brownies that she'd gained twenty pounds just looking.

Cade and his recent appointment came out of an exam room. Avery couldn't remember the woman's name, but her white Persian was Fifi. No lie. Fifi. And Fifi's owner was a stacked blonde roughly in her mid-thirties who was severely underdressed for an Oregon winter.

When they stopped by the front desk to talk, Avery turned to Flynn and signed. "Watch this. Hair flip in point five seconds."

On cue, the woman let out a glass-shattering giggle and flipped her mane over her shoulder.

Flynn covered his face and tried not to laugh, but his shoulders shook and he emitted an awkward snort/groan combination.

Cade looked at them, narrowed his eyes, and tuned back into the senseless flirt.

"Wait for it," she signed. "Casual arm touch..."

Fifi's owner dropped her slender, manicured fingers to Cade's forearm and leaned in as if Cade were reciting Shakespeare naked.

Flynn hunched over, face red in hysterics.

Cade finished the chat, sent the woman on her way, and turned to them, shoulders tense. "What's so funny?" he signed and spoke simultaneously, pissy eyes narrowed.

Flynn sobered. Or tried to. *"Your harem is growing by the minute."*

"You're hilarious."

Avery sighed. "They're an embarrassment to my entire gender."

Cade glanced at Avery. "It's not like I ask for it. Seriously, what am I supposed to do with all that food? My freezer's full. So are Drake and Flynn's. And I don't encourage them, for the record."

He didn't discourage them, either. Which just gave her another reason not to get involved with him.

"Never said you did."

The look on his face dried her hilarity. He was irritated, edgy, and if she wasn't mistaken, embarrassed. His gaze dropped away from her and he closed his eyes, face tilted heavenward.

Guilt churned. She didn't realize it actually bothered him—her and his brother poking fun or the women treating him like a new toy. He was so affable and outgoing, letting things roll off his back. Not once, no matter how ridiculous the appointment or how busy they got, did he complain. His full charm had been cranked. Every patient was seen, and he didn't make them feel stupid for coming.

Flynn strode off as they stared at one another.

Cade sighed. "How's the afternoon looking? Is it just as crazy?" He eyed the semi-full waiting room.

"Hey," she said softly, and waited until he met her gaze. "Do you want me to handle this? The casseroles and desserts? I can screen the appointments better, too. Not book so full."

He opened his mouth as if to say something, but Brent strode up, handed him a chart, and took the next patient to exam. Cade scanned the file, breezed through what she figured was Brent's notes, and shook his head.

"Christ," he muttered. With his brow furrowed, he looked at her as if trying to formulate words, his gaze impenetrable. Frustration rolled off him in waves. Jaw locked, he glanced down the hallway, still making no attempt to move.

And something clicked into place. This was all her fault. The crazy week, the women, all due to a few tweets because he'd been nice enough to help her. Her stomach sank. "I'm sorry about all this. I'll get someone else to babysit Hailey for my meetings. It'll die down around here once the word gets out—"

He strode to her side of the desk so fast her breath seized. Gripping the arms of her chair, he put his face inches from hers. "Know what else will calm things down? Agreeing to go out with me."

Oh. Wow. Not expected.

They hadn't officially discussed the situation after their mind-melding kiss, but he'd offered to keep things under the radar if she said yes. She hadn't said yes. She hadn't been able to say much of anything after he'd knocked her into next week. With his lips.

Business and pleasure were not a good mix. Plus, people would think she'd gotten the job or preferential treatment because of their supposed romance. After Richard, she'd sworn off men. Two years strong. She'd been with him so long she didn't know how to do this anymore and, in honesty, Cade was way out of her league. They'd been flirty and cordial and mostly professional in the office. They hadn't seen each other out of the clinic. Things hadn't begun to get complicated yet.

Forcing back a shiver, she took in the perpetual shadow on his jaw, his direct blue eyes, and the scent of fabric softener. The muscles in his shoulders and forearms flexed, all predator-like. His full mouth was dialed to grim.

Wow. This alpha thing he had going on sometimes was just as earth-shattering as his sweet side. She forgot her own name. Her mouth dried to dust. Her heart pounded.

"Fine," he said at length. "Have it your way. Our secret. I can handle the fallout. I'll be over tonight to watch Hailey."

With that, he shoved off her chair, straightened, and headed into an exam room.

It took her a full five seconds to remember breathing was a requirement of life.

Squawk. "Blurred lines."

She eyed the cockatoo with a frown and jumped when someone cleared their throat to get her attention.

Thor startled underneath the desk, hauled ass to his feet, and rammed into the counter, knocking over a few charts. Before Avery could calm the giant Great Dane, he lunged at her for protection from the big bad five-foot blonde woman holding a…turtle. Yep, a turtle.

That was the last thing she saw as her chair tipped backward, hitting the floor with a thud, leaving one hundred and fifty pounds of trembling dog sprawled over her and her feet up in the air. Flat on her back, she calculated on a one to ten scale of how embarrassing this was, and came up with an eleven. She blinked at the florescent lights overhead.

She swore She-rah laughed at her from her cat perch on the printer.

Footsteps squeaked over the tile and moved closer, stopping beside her and Thor.

Drake's face appeared above hers. "He's not a lap dog."

He had a funny bone after all.

After two more grueling hours, she went to pick up Hailey at the rec center, finding April and her daughter, Jenny, talking to Miles at the front desk. They'd spoken nearly every day on her lunch break when she went to visit Hailey at school, but this was the first time she'd encountered her at the center.

"Oh, hey." April turned Avery's way. "I'm glad I caught you. How would you feel about getting the girls together for a sleepover at our place? They get along pretty great and it would give you a night off. I was thinking the night of the Valentine's dance, since we're not going. Plus, you'll be super busy with the event committee setting up things."

Joy hit her first, her chest swelling and her throat tight. Hailey had an honest to God friend. But apprehension soon followed, twisting in her stomach. The girls did get along well, not that Hailey engaged much on the surface, but Avery was hesitant to agree.

"She's never been to a sleepover before." Hailey had never been away from Avery for an entire evening, come to think of it. She also had a lot of quirks and special needs. April was trustworthy and Jenny was a sweet girl, though. Why not let her try? "I will be really busy that night. Could we test it out before then, that way if I need to come get her it won't be an issue?"

April waved her hand. "Sure. How about next Friday night? I could take them both home right from school."

Avery wouldn't get to see Cade that night, which should've warned her the sexy vet was on her mind too much. She shook her head. "That sounds great. I'll pack some overnight things in her schoolbag. If it goes well, you'll have to let Jenny stay with us next time."

They chatted for a couple minutes, and Avery collected Hailey to head home.

Later, when Cade arrived at the cabin at five-thirty on the dot, Avery was still staring off into space. She looked up at him, blinking furiously to hold back tears. "Hailey's having a sleepover next weekend. Can you believe it? She's made a friend."

Chapter 9

Cade stared at Hailey from the couch as she played a game of tic-tac-toe on her device. She'd been at it for fifteen minutes. At least she always won. "Can I play?"

In answer, she set the iPad down on the cushion between them and went first. Her hands flapped as her gaze darted over his shoulder.

He tapped the screen to place his X.

Without even seeming to look, she set her O.

This went on through three rounds, where she blocked his every move and won all three games. "You're ruthless. Good game, squirt."

She scrolled out of the app and swiped through others. The language one Avery mentioned popped up, and Cade remembered what she'd said last week about never hearing the words *I love you*. What he knew about autism could be put in a shoebox, but maybe he could… He didn't know. Maybe teach Hailey?

He rubbed the back of his neck and figured it wouldn't hurt to try. "What do you say we work on a project, just you and me?" He tapped the app and fished through some of the pictures. "Can you show me the I?"

She didn't seem to be listening, but after a few seconds she tapped the photo of the eye and a robotic voice said "eye."

"Rock on, squirt."

She flapped her hands and squealed.

He grinned. "Okay, show me a heart."

She repeated the process, taking her time, and tapped the picture, earning a voice that said "heart."

Not exactly "love," but close enough. "What about the letter U? Do you know your alphabet?" This one seemed to trip her up, so he swiped through the letters. "It's tricky, I know. Think of a smile. That's what the letter U looks like." When she didn't move, he hovered over the letter.

She pushed his hand away and tapped the U, the voice calling out her comment.

"You're a pretty smart cookie." He shifted a little closer, still respecting her space. "So that's how you tell your mom you love her. Eye, heart, you. Let's try it again."

Hailey backed out of the app and pulled up what looked like a neon coloring book. She dragged her finger over the screen, setting a bright pink line across the black background.

Clearly done with his lesson, he grinned and rolled with it. "You like to color?" He glanced at the fridge on the other side of the counter, but there were no pictures there. "Be right back."

He stepped down the hall into Hailey's bedroom, but after sifting through her toys, he couldn't find any crayons or paper. They'd just moved, so perhaps Avery hadn't unpacked them yet. Undeterred, he went to his car and fished in his glove box for the rainbow Sharpies he kept for charting and a legal pad he had in his trunk. Items in hand, he strode back into the cabin.

"Hey, squirt. Come in the kitchen for a sec."

Dutifully, she turned off her iPad after the slightest delay and seated herself at the table.

Setting the items in front of her, he pulled up a chair beside hers. "Want to color?"

She made no attempt to reach for the markers, so he grabbed one and uncapped it. She never glanced at him or the pad of paper as he drew a really terrible cartoon dog. When finished, he held it out for her, but she pushed it away.

"Not into coloring. Got it."

He glanced at the fridge again, remembering the one in his parents' kitchen growing up. It had been littered with drawings, report cards and, later, team schedules. Avery's was blank. Not even a grocery list.

Sighing, he eyed the girl again and her small hands planted on the table. "Can I trace your hands? Would you let me do that?" She didn't confirm nor deny. "I'm going to touch your wrist to move your hand, yeah? If you don't like it, let me know."

Watching her closely, he lifted her wrist, pushed the pad of paper over, and set her hand on top. When this didn't faze her, he bit the cap off a marker and leaned over. "Hold real still, squirt. I'm going to make a drawing of your hand."

Quickly, in case it bothered her, he traced an outline around her tiny fingers and sat back. To his utter shock, she set the other hand on the paper, too. He did that one as well.

"Should we have a look? Lift 'em up."

Hailey was neither ecstatic nor bored by what he'd done. She simply got up from the table unenthusiastically and went back into the living room, turning the device back on and settling on the couch.

"Right. Scratch coloring from the agenda."

He scrawled her name on the paper and the date. Since Avery didn't have any magnets, he'd hunted up some tape from a drawer and secured the drawing to the fridge. He glanced at the clock.

"Hey, squirt. Time to turn on your sleepy show."

After poking his head over the back of the couch to make sure she complied, he let the dogs out and sat next to her. No wonder this was a bedtime ritual. The video was dragging his eyes closed. Cartoon sketches danced and swirled to drone, soothing music until finally, blessedly, the credits rolled.

He cued her to go potty, covering his eyes while she did, and then waited for her to brush her teeth. Leaning against the doorway, he couldn't get his mind off how the kid was so well behaved. Unless she didn't understand his directions, she pretty much did whatever was asked.

Cade and his brothers had been hellions at her age, always getting into mischief, to which his parents only knew the half. Girls must be tamer by nature. He figured even if Hailey were verbal, she'd still be quiet and cooperative.

Like her mom.

There were pitfalls, too. He had to refrain from tucking her hair behind her ear when it fell in her face, since she didn't like touch, and more than once he'd had to fist his hands to avoid pulling her in for a hug. The lack of eye contact and seemingly distracted nature of her condition made her hard to read. He was beginning to catch on to her slight mannerisms, though.

After an hour of just one-on-one with the girl, he was beginning to get sick of the sound of his own voice. He wondered how Avery had done this for eight straight years. To never have a conversation, a verbal response most take for granted, could be disheartening. But when he could pull a laugh from Hailey, awkward as the sound was, or when she flapped her hands and squealed in delight, that was really something. He'd had to work hard at it, but it was all the more rewarding.

She dutifully went to her bedroom after rinsing her mouth. Tucking her in, he set Seraph on the bed beside her and called Freeman out with a whistle. Unlike last week, Hailey closed her eyes and didn't fight him.

"'Night, squirt." Leaving the door ajar, he made his way down the hall, grabbed some charts he brought in need of dictation, and plopped on the couch.

But after ten minutes, the words blurred in front of him as he kept remembering the expression on Avery's face when he'd first arrived. She looked like she'd been slapped upside the head, her pretty lips parted and her unfocused brown eyes wide. A sleepover for Hailey, a normal girly ritual, a right of passage, had put that awe on her face.

Giving up on the charts, he made his way into the kitchen to start a pot of decaf, since Avery would be back any minute. When it was brewing, he opened the fridge to grab creamer, and stilled.

She had a six-pack of beer in the door. He stared at the bottles of his favorite brand, trying to remember if she drank the stuff. The only time he'd seen her drink had been the one night at Shooters, and she'd had wine.

He closed the fridge and rubbed his neck. Jokingly last week, after discussing the Hailey milk incident, he'd told Avery he preferred beer. Had she taken him literally? His gaze landed on the door again, and he knew she had. Hell, she'd bought him beer.

Unsure what to make of this as it seemed such an intimate act, he went back to his charts until she came in the kitchen door and set her purse down on the table.

He rose from the couch and walked closer. "Hey. How was your meeting?"

She'd changed out of her professional work clothes before she left, but he got a better look now. Her jeans were faded at the stress points, molding her curves, and the plain blue tee barely skimmed below the waistband. He'd bet if he asked her to reach high for something, he'd catch a peek of bare skin.

She laughed, drawing him back to her face. "I'll give your aunt this, when she wants something, she's tenacious. Marie not only got the post office onboard for the admirer note exchange, she's got the rec center kids thinking it's a top secret mission."

Leaning against the counter, he crossed his arms. "Sounds like it was productive then."

She hummed in her throat and glanced at the coffeepot. After staring at it for a few moments, an unreadable expression on her face, she blinked. "How was Hailey?" She glanced down the length of him. "I see she didn't get sick this time."

"Ha. No, we survived. She kicked my ass in tic-tac-toe."

Her grin stopped his heart. "She's quite good at that game. Let me just peek in on her. I'll be right back."

As she disappeared, he poured them each a cup of coffee and settled at the table to wait. When she came back, she eyed the cups and turned for the fridge, freezing in place with her hand mid-air over the handle.

And he found himself holding his own breath.

* * * *

Avery swallowed hard, unable to tear her gaze from the paper on her fridge with the outline of her daughter's tiny hands. She recognized Cade's distinctive handwriting below them from his charts, the block letters and scratch.

"Tried to get her to color, but she wouldn't." The rough, quiet timbre of his voice held an edge of uncertainty.

"No," she breathed. "She doesn't like it. The therapists tried getting her to attempt it several times. She'll do it on the iPad sometimes."

He grunted. "Are you going to stare at that all night?"

Concern laced his tone, so she turned. He studied her with solemn eyes, his brow furrowed just enough to make out his uneasiness. Was he worried she'd be mad?

She pointed to the picture. "That's her first art project."

He opened and closed his mouth, but ultimately said nothing.

"I have a few stored away from teachers and therapists, but they were wielded with them holding her hand. Nothing just from her."

He shifted uncomfortably in his seat. "That's not original, either. I traced her hands."

Since he wouldn't understand this *was* unique, that he'd put her daughter's hands to something in the only way she'd allow, she opened the fridge and grabbed the creamer. She walked to the table and sat next to him, thinking first thing tomorrow, she'd buy a frame for that simple, endearing paper taped to her fridge.

Silence stretched as they sipped their coffee, until he finally cleared his throat. "So Hailey has a sleepover next Friday, yeah? Are you going to get a wink of sleep?"

This dragged a laugh from her, which she assumed was his goal. "Most likely not. She's never been away from home. I'll probably need a sedative not to call a hundred times."

His smile was sigh-worthy. "April is good people. Hailey will be safe with her." He leaned forward and scratched his jaw. "She and her husband moved here something like ten years ago. Nice family."

Avery got the same impression, but said nothing.

He shook his head, grin widening into swoon-worthy territory. "You'll still pace the floors with worry."

She nodded and looked away before she climbed over the table to lick him. "I'll still pace the floor with worry," she confirmed. Then, she placed her palm to her forehead and laughed at how well he knew her after such a short time. Crazy, that. Even more insane was how easy he was to be around.

"Avery."

She glanced up.

His smile slipped, his gaze falling to her mouth. He muttered something unintelligible, kicked his foot out, and wrapped his leg around the rung of her chair. Slowly, he dragged her chair in front of his until their knees bumped, his gaze never leaving hers. He leaned forward, not touching her, but the heated desire in his eyes was an instant bolt of contact.

She let out an uneven breath. "What are you doing?"

"Honest to God, I don't know." After his whispered confession, his gaze took her in—her hair, her eyes, her mouth—as if trying to figure it out. "I never know what the hell I'm doing around you." His lips parted like he wanted to say more, but he just shook his head and pressed his mouth to hers.

Like the first time he'd kissed her, he brushed her lips with a tender caress, cajoling her into joining him. The unfamiliar contact was a mere blink of uncertainty before fire flared in her belly. Spread. Consumed. She breathed in his scent of male and fabric softener, but it didn't ground her as she'd hoped.

"Been wanting to do that all week," he said against her mouth. "Kiss me back, Avery. Like you mean it. Give me some idea you're as—"

She sealed her lips to his, tilting her head to probe at a different angle. Parting her lips, she tentatively licked his lower lip, hoping he'd open. On a groan, he complied, and when their tongues finally met for the first time, something inside her snapped. Control and reason broke free of their leash and disappeared. Her hands fisted in the thick softness of his hair.

He sucked air through his nose and, never breaking the kiss, dropped his hands to her thighs and squeezed. A bolt of need shot straight to her core, causing an ache she hadn't experienced in too long, if ever.

Oh... His hands were on the move, sliding under her thighs. He lifted her from her chair as if she weighed nothing and deposited her in his lap to straddle him, bringing their chests flush. His hard to her soft.

He tore away to press his mouth to her throat, gulping air in tandem with her attempts to do the same. "Slow down," he murmured against her skin, even as his tongue darted out to lick her pounding pulse.

A shiver ripped through her body, his touch lighting her nerves, but she unclenched her fingers from his hair and eased back a smidgen to adhere to his request.

"Not you." He held her hips. "I was talking to myself."

He lifted his head to look in her eyes, his drugged with the same fever. Then his mouth was pressed to hers again, kissing her blind. Desperate. Her breasts grew heavy, aching to be touched, so she crushed them to the hard wall of his chest to alleviate the throbbing. But then other parts began to throb, and the urge to grind into the thick bulge between them was almost feral.

She whimpered into his mouth, needing...something. Him? He groaned in response, his hands moving north to play with the hem of her shirt. His warm fingers dipped beneath on their way to her ribs, and she tensed.

He stopped on a dime, sensing her shift. Slowly, he drew back far enough to look in her eyes. "Sorry. Too fast. Thought and reason aren't really processing just now." Though coarse with need, his voice was quiet, apologetic, making her fumble to formulate an explanation.

"It's just..." She hadn't been touched in God knew how long and the hard pecs below her palms were a direct contrast to her rounded curves. He was all edges and yum and she...wasn't.

"Just what?"

"I haven't had the time to do a lot of exercise or my usual yoga, and I might not be in the best shape, or what you're used to." She pinched her eyes closed as heat flared in her cheeks.

When he didn't say anything for several erratic beats, she peeked. His jaw was clenched and his blue eyes glacial. Her heart stuttered to a halt.

"I swear, if you tell me that asshole ex of yours called you fat, or so much as implied it, I'm driving to where he is to beat the shit out of him. Tonight."

Air seeped from her lungs. She'd had a hard time losing the baby fat after delivering Hailey, but she'd worked hard because the disgust in Richard's eyes had been palpable. But getting back to her target weight hadn't mattered in the long run because he'd sought someone much thinner and prettier from his office for his gratification. The betrayal and hurt, even after all this time, cut deep.

If she hadn't been enough to satisfy Richard, and they'd been college sweethearts bringing little experience to the relationship, how was she supposed to believe she could do so for Cade, who had worlds of knowledge and a trail of women in his wake?

"What's his address?" Cade ground, drawing her gaze back to his.

Her stomach rolled, and she looked away. "It wasn't him."

Richard wasn't to blame. No matter how he'd treated her, she was responsible for believing him or not. It was her old ghosts screwing with her head, and she thought she'd gotten over them.

Cade had been into it moments ago. His heart was still pounding beneath her palm, though she suspected that was in anger now and not lust. But his erection said he'd been turned on, too. Yet she'd doused that flame with reality, and the moment was lost.

"Avery—"

"No, it's okay." She climbed off his lap and he winced. From the loss of contact or something else, she couldn't tell. "It's getting late, anyway."

He stared at her a few more seconds and rose, whistling for Freeman. Cade stepped into his shoes and walked into the living room. The dog strode into the kitchen and waited by the back door while she made herself busy by rinsing out their cups at the sink.

She didn't turn when Cade came back, but his gaze bore holes into her. She gripped the counter as he sidled up behind her, setting a small stack of charts down by her hand.

"Look at me."

She shook her head, her stomach knotting. This was a bad idea to get involved with him. He was a playboy who probably just saw the challenge in her. If things at the clinic became uncomfortable because of this flash romance, she'd have a hard time finding another position. People already figured she got her current job by sleeping with Cade. Plus, she had enough on her plate, had been burned enough to know better.

Yet she couldn't deny the pull, the flutter in her stomach when she was around Cade. He managed to make her feel giddy again. Hopeful.

Cade ignored her denial and turned her to face him. His eyes sharpened in understanding, his mouth a thin line. "I'm not him."

She sighed. No, he wasn't anything like Richard, and to even compare the two was an insult to Cade. "I know. I think I just need time to get used to having someone interested again. Been a long time." She laughed nervously and tried to step away.

He put an arm out to stop her. "I'm interested. Make no mistake about that."

She lifted her gaze to his, and the breath punched from her chest. With dizzying absolution, she was positive no one had ever looked at her with the same desire and patience. And this thing between them had the potential to hurt her more than anything her ex had ever attempted.

Cade leaned in and kissed her. It was a gentle meeting, not passion-filled or hungry, and somehow that tripped her pulse more than what they'd done earlier.

Easing back, he looked into her eyes. "I wasn't going to take tonight any further than what we were doing. I'll go as slow as you want. Just do me a favor and push him from your head when we're together, yeah?"

Before an intelligent response could squeak past her lips, he grabbed his charts and was gone.

Chapter 10

Near lunchtime on Monday, Cade exited an exam room, sent Martha and her "depressed" hamster up front, rolled his eyes, and headed toward the break room to grab some water. He slammed into Flynn.

His brother grinned. *"I want to show you something."* He crooked his finger, so Cade followed, since he was headed in that direction, anyway.

Flynn paused at the fridge. *"Take a look inside."*

Sighing—because Cade knew there would be twenty more casseroles inside as they were back to back with mostly unnecessary appointments—he opened the fridge. And found it empty. Or almost empty. There was their usual bottled water, a few brown bag lunches, and Drake's pudding stash, but not a casserole in sight. He still wondered why the single women of Redwood Ridge found it necessary to supply him with a year's worth of home cooking.

Flynn lifted his brows. *"Avery is telling the patients we're no longer allowed to accept food because it's against health regulations."*

Cade opened and closed his mouth. "Why would she do that?"

Not that he was complaining. Half the time, Cade drove the stuff to the homeless shelter in the next town, since he couldn't eat it all. But it wasn't against health regulations as long as the food remained in the break room.

"You're an idiot." Flynn poked his chest. Hard. *"She's doing it for you. She knows it bothers you to get all this unwanted attention."*

That gave him pause. It was true. He wasn't fond of all the flirting or subtle lean-ins or any other form of vying for his heart, much preferring to let things progress normally without a shove. But he'd never said so. Not once. In fact, to spare hurt feelings, he went out of his way to be gracious.

"What did you have for dinner at her place on Friday?"

Cade blinked, sensing a trap. "Pizza." Hailey didn't react violently to white cheeses, so that was one of the few dairy items she could eat, in moderation. He narrowed his eyes. "Why?"

Flynn nodded knowingly. *"The way I see it, if she's funny, kind, eats pizza, likes your sorry ass, and is good in bed, you should marry her. Yesterday."*

Christ. "We've known each other a month, man. I haven't slept with her." The rest of his brother's statement he wouldn't touch with a ten-foot pole.

That only made Flynn's grin widen, the asshole. *"Thanks for proving my point. When's the last time you took a month to sleep with a woman?"*

Cade scrubbed his hands over his face and headed up front to see if it was safe to take lunch. Alone.

Avery was finishing up with Martha and the hamster as he approached. "Thanks so much for coming in today. Please take a goodie on your way out." She pointed to several plates of cookies on the counter, which usually wound up in Cade's office, since they were brought for him. "It's so nice of our patients to bring these for us, isn't it?"

Martha, a short brunette dental assistant from the office down the street, shoved a cookie into her mouth with a frown and left.

Cade would bet his right nut Martha had contributed to the sugar donation Avery was pawning off. Something pinched in his gut, which he attributed to hunger.

Squawk. "Sugar, sugar."

Avery laughed, having not seen Cade yet, and was typing something into the computer schedule. "Got that right, Gossip. She-rah, you leave that dog alone."

Cade glanced over, and sure enough, the cat had stretched from atop the printer and was eying a sleeping Thor by Avery's feet.

The cat paused, narrowed her evil eyes, and made to jump down.

"Ah-ah." Avery waggled her finger, never turning from the PC. "You go near that dog and you'll get it."

She-rah sniffed.

Avery reached over, snatched a spray bottle he hadn't noticed, and...squirted the cat in the face with a short stream of water. "I said leave Thor alone."

She-rah hissed, but remained on the printer, stopping her planned assault on the dog. She swiped her face with a paw, sent Avery a warning glare, and laid back down.

Cade stood there for several moments as the pinch in his stomach moved into his chest, and he had to remind himself he was at work. They were taking things slow. But the pounding of his heart against his ribs wouldn't cease. She was... She was so damn hot in her bossy mode. And very different from the vulnerable woman on Friday night.

"Do you need something, Dr. Cade?"

Hell. He wondered if he could get her to call him that when he kissed her again. Outside of the office.

Giving his head a violent shake to clear it, he tossed a chart down next to Avery and eyed the empty waiting room. "I'm taking twenty minutes for lunch."

She closed out her program and rose, preparing for her own break. "That doesn't go there."

He glanced at the chart she referred to and then her, the urge to kiss her so damn jolting he almost flinched. Grabbing the chart, he set it in Avery's file basket, never taking his gaze from hers. The electricity between them could supply the town for a week.

She smiled, turned on her heel, and headed down the hall.

He caught up to her and pinned her to the wall, earning a surprised squeak from her. After a quick glance to make sure no one saw, he stepped closer, shoving his thigh between her legs and crushing her breasts to his chest.

Her wide brown eyes didn't blink, and in this light, he could make out the honey flecks. "What are you doing?"

"This."

With his hands on her hips to hold her in place, he leaned in and kissed her. Not the careful enticement from her kitchen, but a full-on exploration to let her know how much she turned him on and just how much he appreciated what she'd done for him by micromanaging the plethora of female clients. And the cat. And damn it, the chickenshit dog.

She arched into him, fisting his scrubs, and moaned into his mouth like he made her forget their location, the day, and time space continuum, too. Her tongue stroked his, once, twice, rioting his thoughts right out of his head. Well, to the wrong head.

She smelled sweet, tasted sweeter, and if she kept grinding his thigh like that...

He tore away and rested his cheek to hers, breaths soughing. Holy hell, what she could do to him with a kiss. Her breathing wasn't stable either as she panted against his neck. His erection pressed into her hip, so he backed away, taking in her flushed cheeks and pert nipples.

Biting back a groan, he said, "Just wanted to tell you that. We can discuss it in great detail later, yeah?"

Her palms pressed to the wall behind her, those gorgeous eyes unfocused and her lips parted. "Yeah."

Nodding, he headed out the back door instead of into the break room because suddenly he needed to cool off. However, several gulps of crisp, damp air did nothing to steady his heart rate.

* * * *

Avery snuck out of the clinic at five on the dot. If she did so because Cade was occupied in his office and wouldn't see her leave, well that was a coincidence.

This non-dating dance they were doing was heating up, and she didn't know how to feel about that, so she shoved it from her mind. Almost. Her lips were still swollen from his kiss, and every time she thought about how he pinned her to the wall and devoured her mouth like he had no choice, a blush flamed her cheeks.

Richard had never pressed her up against the wall.

Straightening her shoulders, she got in her car and drove the mile to get Hailey. Maybe they'd go to the diner tonight for dinner. Get out of the cabin. After she parked in the rec center lot, she pulled out her cell to text her mom to see if she could meet them.

Anya manned the front desk and smiled as Avery opened the door. "Hello. How's dating the sexy vet going? You're breaking hearts all over the Ridge."

She sighed. "Cade and I aren't a thing." Despite what Twitter and the town's blog claimed. Despite the kissing. The really excellent kissing.

A lot of women in town were under the impression Cade was theirs. Every minute a new picture of him popped up on Pinterest with a willing female. It made it hard to figure out how seriously to take him.

"Oh, I don't know. People are talking. Cade doesn't date, as in at all, so this is pretty big news around here."

So was watching paint dry on the new park bench, but she kept her mouth shut until Miles brought Hailey up front.

"I missed you." Avery bent to zip her daughter's coat and squeezed her shoulder when she really wanted to kiss her. "How's she doing? Any problems?"

"Nope." Anya tucked a piece of strawberry blond hair behind her ear. "She's really great. The only thing that seems to upset her is the basketball games, so we keep her out of the gym."

Avery nodded. "Must be all the squeaky shoes."

She thanked them and led Hailey to the car. Once she had her belted in her booster, Avery checked her phone and noted her mom texted back with a confirmation of dinner.

They drove to the diner, which was surprisingly slow, but it was Monday. She noted a few men from the senior center were playing checkers at a table, but otherwise the place was empty. The fifties décor was retro-neat, she thought so when she first stopped in two weeks ago, but the neon signs and counter were under a layer of grease from years of fried food. The scent of French fries and hamburgers clung to the air, and Avery's stomach rumbled.

She spotted her mom in a booth and walked over, getting Hailey situated. "Glad you could come, Mom."

"Well, I don't want to take up your time with Cade, so I just wait for you to call. A woman needs private time with her guy."

Avery barely resisted an eye roll. "He's not my guy. He's my boss." Who kisses her a lot. Up against the wall.

Before her mother could respond, a waitress made her way over, a woman Avery recognized from around town, but had never spoken to. Avery quickly scanned the menu for something Hailey could eat while her mom and the waitress made small talk. In her late sixties, the woman had wrinkles around her mouth and a craggy voice that bespoke years of smoking.

Hailey shrugged her shoulders as if bothered by her voice.

"And what can I get the cutie pie?" The waitress, Mave, bent down at eye level with Hailey and ruffled her hair before Avery could stop her.

Hailey instantly stiffened and screeched, flailing her arms. Silverware and ice water went sailing. She slid to the floor under the table, earning gazes from the other customers, and continued the screeching at an insane decibel.

Mom laughed nervously and ducked her head.

Crap on a cracker.

Hailey didn't act out very often, and when she did, it could be quite embarrassing, but her mother's reaction had fury building in Avery's chest. People would see her response and take their cues from her, thinking it was okay to stare at Hailey like a freak.

Mave's eyes popped. "Oh dear. What's wrong with her?"

Avery tensed to the point of pain, her molars grinding. It always came down to that—what was wrong with Hailey. She was different, so that made it okay to act like ignorant imbeciles, right?

Instead of getting into it, Avery asked her for a few minutes and then slid out of the booth to squat by Hailey, who had stopped screeching. "Hey, sweetie. She's gone. All better. Can you come out?"

A few moments passed and Hailey crawled back into the booth to stare out the window, all signs of distress vanishing except her all too common rocking.

Avery reclaimed her seat, closed her eyes, and rubbed her forehead. "If you're embarrassed by us, we can leave." She drilled her mom with an unforgiving glare.

Mom's eyes widened from where they were watching Hailey and shifted to Avery. "I've never seen her do that. She's always so quiet."

Of course she hadn't seen an outburst. For years, it had just been Avery and Hailey against the world. Mom had moved to Redwood Ridge before Hailey was born, and had only come to San Francisco a handful of times. Regret filled her because Avery hadn't made any attempt to visit her mom, either. Between Richard's schedule and Hailey's therapy, years snuck out from under them.

"I'm not embarrassed." Mom took her hand and squeezed. "I'm sorry. I froze."

The tension drained from her shoulders. "It's fine." Mom didn't know any better. Most people didn't, so Avery would educate where she could and shrug off when she couldn't.

Mave tentatively returned, a wary smile twisting her already wrinkled face. "Everything okay?"

Avery forced a smile. "This is my daughter, Hailey. She has autism and doesn't care to be touched, especially on her head. It's an over-stimulant for her, which is why she responded that way."

"Oh, I'm so sorry. I'll make sure not to do it again."

Smiling, she tilted her head toward her daughter. "Hailey, this is Mave. Can you say hello?"

A few moments passed as Hailey seemed to process the command, and then she signed, "*Hello.*"

Once they finished eating and waited for the check, Zoe strode in looking harried with her blue hair at haphazard angles and her button-down shirt half tucked into her jeans. No coat. She moved to the register and dropped some bills, tapping her foot while waiting. Since she seemed to be in a hurry, Avery didn't stop to talk as the groomer from the clinic grabbed two to-go boxes and darted outside.

"She's had a rough go of things lately."

Avery glanced from Zoe's form disappearing in the fog back to her mom. "How so?"

Aside from her odd, unnatural choice in hair color, Zoe seemed okay. She'd gone out with them that one night at Shooters and she always came to work on time. Though not as chatty as Brent or Gabby, she was nice.

"Her mom was diagnosed with early onset dementia four years ago. Catherine's only fifty-one. There's no other family, so Zoe's taken it all on herself." Mom cleared her throat. "We try to get over there and help out when we can. Cat used to be in our book club, but now she barely recognizes Zoe."

God. How awful. She rubbed at the sudden ache in her chest, unable to imagine it. "That's rough."

After parting ways with her mom, dark had descended, bringing a salt-scented brine to the humid, cold air. The fog had let up, but was still hovering in the distance near the banks. Avery and Hailey walked across the street to the ice cream shop to get Avery a fix for later before heading home.

Hank, the owner who'd greeted them the last time, grinned broadly. "You've returned. Check it out." He pointed to the menu behind him. His round belly strained against a stained apron with the movement.

Avery scanned the board, her gaze stopping at the new addition. She stilled, torn between a sudden bout of useless tears and gratitude. Surely he hadn't...

He had. He'd given Hailey her own special on the menu. Orange sherbet topped with marshmallows, kindly named "The Hailey." He'd remembered she couldn't eat dairy. That was...dang. That was so nice.

Hank held up a Polaroid camera. She didn't even know those were still in existence.

"May I take a picture? For the board?"

Avery opened and closed her mouth. Swallowed hard. Her chest swelled, constricting her air. Dang it, she still couldn't talk, so she nodded.

As Hank took a shot of Hailey, her cheese face in place whenever someone said "smile," a man's voice resounded behind them. Deep and low, it skimmed across her skin like a caress and set her nerves on fire.

"The Hailey. Sounds good."

She didn't have to turn to know who belonged to the voice. It had been the focal point of many of her recent fantasies as of late. She couldn't escape him, even when she should.

"This calls for a fist bump." Cade crouched down by Hailey, his grin huge. "Remember what I said, you can't leave a guy hanging. Make a fist."

Hailey closed her fingers and awkwardly smacked Cade's fist, then squealed.

Avery's chest tightened more. Even her daughter was enamored.

Hank stuck the picture of Hailey on the menu board right next to her option and turned. "What'll it be, folks?"

Cade stepped up next to her, pointing to the picture. "We'll take three of those, Hank."

Chapter 11

Zoe leaned against the front desk near the end of the workday on Thursday where Brent and Gabby had congregated. "Everyone's all aflutter with this Valentine's dance."

Brent sighed dreamily. "You, doll, are a genius."

Avery's cheeks heated. "I'm just glad people are interested. Job done."

Gabby shook her head. "It's more than that. Seriously, you have no idea how boring the past years have been."

Avery closed out her program and shut down the system, since Cade was on his last patient of the day and Drake had finished with surgery. "You guys have a hot date picked out?"

They all shook their heads.

"I say we go as a group, like in high school." Brent waved his hand at his brilliance. "Power in numbers."

Squawk. "Rollin' with my homies."

Drake strode in and handed Avery his billing form. "We only did the front declaw, so don't charge for the back."

"You got it."

He went to leave, but Brent called his name. "You're going to the Valentine's dance, right? Our Avery did a bang-up job planning."

Drake paused and slowly turned, assessing Brent like he'd been dropped on his head one too many times as a child. "No."

Zoe tucked a piece of blue hair behind her ear and sat on the desk. "We're thinking of doing the group thing. No dates."

Drake shifted his gaze to her and slowly shook his head.

Avery recalled what Cade had told her awhile back about how hard it had been to get Drake out of the house and socializing since his wife had died. A dance was a huge social event. One nearly the whole town was planning to attend. She couldn't blame him for saying no.

Since he looked uncomfortable, she tried to come up with something to lighten the mood. "I could be your date, Drake. Platonic, of course. I'll beat the conversationalists off with a stick."

He tilted his head, studying her. And then it happened. He smiled. Not a full-on grin, but the corners of his lips quirked.

Zoe gasped. "Did you... Did you just smile?"

It fell, morphing into a scowl. "No."

"I saw it." Gabby nodded. "You did smile."

The frown deepened as he looked at Avery. "Thought you said you'd beat them off."

Zoe grabbed her chest, faking heart failure. "And he joked, too."

Poor Drake. This was what he got for his trouble.

Avery sighed. "You've got more than a week to think about it. Open invitation to join us. We'll try to make it painless."

Something in his gaze softened, almost like a thank-you, before he nodded and strode away.

A collective silence fell until Brent slapped her arm. "Look at you, playing up the brothers. I'm telling Cade you did that." A sly grin split his face.

Avery narrowed her eyes but, before she could retort, Cade and his last appointment came out of an exam room.

"Tell me what?" He handed Avery the chart and looked at Mr. Townsend. "Couple drops in each eye should clear it up. Give us a call if it doesn't." After the client left, he handed her the billing statement and glanced at the others. "Tell me what?" he repeated.

Brent cocked a hip. "Your girl just asked your brother to the Valentine's dance."

"I'm not his girl, and it was an invitation to join all of us." She stood. "Stop instigating."

Cade's gaze landed on her. "Which brother? I'll kill him." He grinned as if in afterthought.

"Yeah," Brent drolled. "Not his girl."

Avery shook her head and put the cockatoo back in his cage to cover him for the night. "Good night, Gossip."

Squawk. "Enter sandman."

Zoe hopped down from the desk. "Let's go dress shopping on Saturday. I can get someone to watch Mom." She looked at Gabby and then Avery.

"I'm in," Gabby said.

Cade deadpanned. "I wouldn't look good in a dress."

Gabby laughed. "Remember that Halloween in high school when you dressed as a cheerleader—"

"No. I don't remember, thus it never happened."

Avery rolled her eyes and nodded at Zoe. "I'll get my mom to watch Hailey. Barring a problem with that, I'm in, too." She didn't have a red or pink dress, so this solved her problem. She hadn't gone shopping with girlfriends since... Well, she couldn't remember when.

They made arrangements and the crew left for the day. All but Cade, who stood off to the side watching her. Since she couldn't read his expression, she called for Thor to put him away for the night.

Cade grabbed She-rah, much to the cat's dismay, and followed. "It was a joke, the cheerleader thing."

She grinned. "Okay."

"It was." He set the cat down and called Thor to follow. Once the animals were in the back room, he shut the door and eyed her.

The hallway suddenly seemed too small with her back pressed to the wall and him closing in like a predator, all fluid grace and delicious muscle.

He set his palms on either side of her head and leaned into them, his forearms flexing. "I suddenly find myself thinking of little else than you in a dress, wondering if you'll go with red or pink, if you'll choose something that shows a lot of skin—" He frowned as he cut himself off and jerked his gaze from her breasts to her face. "You asked my brother to the dance?"

A bubble of laughter rose in her throat, but she held it down. He made her feel young again. Between the kissing and his jokes and the giddy flutter in her belly. Whenever he was near, she wasn't a stressed out single mom with a disabled daughter and a useless ex-husband. Not with Cade. She was just...a woman again.

All of her reservations about them flittered away. She'd regret it later, but for now, this felt too good.

His blue-eyed gaze slid to her mouth and back up as if expecting an answer. The heat was unmistakable, but a flash of hurt twisted his mouth.

"Drake. I asked Drake to join us as a group, hoping he might say yes. You said it was hard to get him out since—"

He pressed a finger to her mouth and sucked in a harsh breath at the contact. "What did he say?"

"That he'd think about it." Or close enough, in Drake speak.

Something shifted in his expression as his eyebrows drew together, like he wasn't looking at her anymore. Grief warred with guilt. "He hasn't attended many community functions since Heather died. Just the ones Mom makes him go to, like the Christmas parties." His gaze met hers again, tender and hollow all at once. "He'll go. For you, he'll go."

She shook her head. It wasn't like that. Not how he was thinking.

Part of her understood his brother, what Drake was going through. Her husband hadn't died, but the loss of comfort, of having someone there and then suddenly not, could gut a person. It made it hard to trust, to hold on to anything, and being around others only amplified the feeling that everything was slipping through her fingers. For Drake, it had to be especially difficult. Not only had someone he loved died, but everything around him had a memory tied to that loss.

"He's got a lot of respect for you." Cade cupped her cheek, his thumb tracing her lower lip, his steady gaze watching the movement. "You're new. You don't remind him of her." He looked in her eyes, grateful and with relief, making her realize just how worried Cade had been for his brother. "Thank you for that. For trying."

His hand slid from her jaw to her throat, his fingers brushing her collarbone under her blouse. "The way he loved Heather, it was out of the storybooks. I used to watch them, wondering if anyone could live up to that. Then she got sick and..." He shook his head. "And I stopped dating altogether to avoid that kind of hurt. I did the random hook-ups and fun because there's no pain in not engaging."

They'd had quiet talks and they'd shared some heated kisses, but this was personal, on a different plane than where they'd ventured before. For the first time, it seemed like he was letting her see a piece of him no one else had, and it was costing him. Pleasure and pain lit his eyes, thinned his mouth. Whatever he was battling, he wasn't altogether happy about it.

Because her own heart was pounding, she cleared her throat and forced her lungs to take in air. "Red." At his questioning glance, she elaborated. "I'll probably pick a red dress for the dance. Pink's not a good shade on me." And since that admission wiped the regretful haze from his eyes, replacing it with something carnal, she kept flapping her mouth without the filter. "I'll see what I can do about finding something that shows...skin."

He closed his eyes, his jaw clenched tight. Resting his forehead to hers, he let out a ragged breath. "I can't wait to see you in it." He opened and closed his mouth several times before finally making up his mind. "Go with me. Be *my* date, Avery. No one has to know but us, as long as you..."

Her heart stuttered. "As long as I what?"

His breath skated across her cheek. He nuzzled her neck, behind her ear, sending shivers through her. The rasp of his growth echoed as it scraped her skin. "As long as you come home with me afterward."

He tensed, waiting for her answer, motionless against her as if her response would make or break him.

Their breathing was the only noise, so loud it ricocheted off the walls. The heat from his body wrapped around her. The expectation of what she'd say kept them both taut, ready to snap. His heart pounded, the thump hitting her chest. And then he stopped breathing altogether, and there was no doubt in her mind that he was, somehow, against all reason, as nervous as she was to be here.

There were other doubts, reservations that pushed against her skull from the inside. Like would she measure up to his other conquests? Richard had cheated on her, and that had killed her confidence. She'd lost so much of herself in their marriage and she swore she'd never do it again. And there was the fact that Cade was her boss. She had Hailey to think about...

He cupped her cheek unexpectedly, the only movement he offered as if silently begging her to give him a chance.

Some of the doubts were pushed aside. She wanted him. Wanted something just for herself that wasn't tainted or had ties to what she'd left behind. What would it hurt letting go for once? It didn't have to mean anything. Cade would make her feel good, could help her move past the stagnant halt her life had become.

She opened her mouth to agree to his request, but he kissed her forehead and stepped away. "Think about it. There's no rush."

She had a sickening sensation in her gut that she'd just hurt him, rejected him when he'd laid himself out there for her. But he was out the door without a backward glance before her mouth caught up to her brain.

All through the next day her suspicions were confirmed. Cade barely spoke to her, and he didn't find a quiet moment to back her against a wall to kiss her stupid like he'd done several times throughout the week.

The strangest part was, the town—aside from Cade's admirers—all seemed to be gunning for her and Cade as a couple. And she had made sure they had no public displays or anything to egg it on. She just didn't get it.

By the time she got to her meeting, her brain was fried and her chest hurt.

Hailey also had her sleepover at her friend Jessica's tonight, so Avery's nerves were raw, her stomach twisted in knots. She'd texted April several times with instructions for Hailey. April responded to every instance, not making fun of her or telling her to calm down. Which was nice, having someone understand.

The event committee met at the Botanical Gardens in the hall to go over placement of tables and decorations instead of convening at the rec center. All she could think about, besides whether Hailey was doing okay or not, was how she wouldn't get to see Cade when she got home.

She'd begun to look forward to that, to having his presence in her house. Having his scent lingering in the rooms or to discover what activity he'd done with Hailey. Their quiet talks around her kitchen table, and the bone-melting kisses weren't a hardship, either.

God, he was so good with Hailey, too. Patient, never dominant, never pressuring her to be normal like other kids. If Richard had shown a smidgen of that understanding, Avery might not have left him.

"What do you think, Avery?"

She shook her head and faced Marie. "I'm sorry, I didn't hear you."

The other members looked at her with varying degrees of knowing smirks, and she wasn't in on the joke.

"About the tables?" Marie pointed to the back wall, holding herself in complete professionalism. Being the mayor, Avery supposed she had to be, even though she was one of the Battleaxes and super sneaky. "Line both sides of the room with tables? Bar at the back. DJ up front. You haven't listened to a thing, have you?"

Heat flared in her cheeks. "I'm sorry. Hailey is having her first sleepover ever and my mind is elsewhere."

The women cooed, very sympathetic, which made Avery's face flame to scalding because Hailey had only been half of her distraction.

"I think that setup would be lovely." Avery glanced around, forcing herself to focus.

The room was long and open, with a rear wall of floor to ceiling glass that looked into the attached garden dome. Open wood beams slanted the rafters, giving a log cabin feel to the atmosphere. Two large chandeliers could be dimmed for mood lighting, and the floor was hardwood throughout.

"The streamers are going to be a pain to hang." Rosa directed her gaze up with a frown.

Avery dialed back her wince. "I think we should veto the streamers. The evening is for the adults, a romantic date night."

She eyed the tables along the wall, remembering Gayle had said they used this hall for a lot of weddings. "White tablecloths with flower petals. White lights strung from the beams to look like starlight. We'll turn off all the overheads, all but the chandelier up front for the dance floor, and let the soft glow illuminate the rest."

Really into the mood now, she glanced at Marie and did a double take. The other women were staring, slack-jawed.

Avery rubbed her forehead. "Or not. Whatever you think."

Marie nodded. "I think we were right to hire you."

Rosa slapped Avery's arm, nearly toppling her. "I love it. Let's do it."

By the time Avery drove home, she was swamped with fatigue and wondered if she'd manage to get any sleep with Hailey gone. Oh, look at that, she'd checked her phone. Again. She was pathetic. When was the last time she'd had a night to herself? Never. And she couldn't stop looking at her cell.

As she made the turnoff for the cabin, she started to fantasize about a hot bath, a hotter book, and a glass of wine. But as she pulled up to the cabin and parked, an entirely different fantasy came to mind.

One that involved a sexy animal doctor who slowly stood to full height and grinned from where he'd been waiting on her front steps, his trusty, good-natured dog by his side.

The pull of desire in her belly was fierce and, unaccustomed to it, she stared for a few beats, giving herself an internal pep talk on what it meant that she felt anything at all. Years, *for years*, she'd shut her needs down, and now it seemed they were making up for lost time.

With the worst possible candidate to snap the spell.

Then again, Cade couldn't break her heart. Not only had it been broken before, but he wasn't the type to reach deep enough to attach. A steady calm washed over her, settling her tension.

Nodding, she grabbed the door handle.

Chapter 12

Cade watched Avery emerge from her car with a questioning glance. Hell, he didn't know why he was here either, other than it felt like he had something to prove. To her, that he wasn't just some playboy who sought fun. To himself, that this thing between them was different and he was capable of trying.

By showing up tonight, he wanted her aware that this wasn't about Hailey, nor work. And that he wanted to be here. Truth was, he thought of little else but Avery when she wasn't around.

"Hi," she said, coming closer. "You get a Friday night free from babysitting and you come, anyway. Don't tell me we accidently domesticated you."

Her grin was teasing, a little nervous, but his gut twisted. She was one of the few people to treat him like he wasn't a joke, like he had more inside him than he allowed to show. Yet her comment sliced, eradicating that.

Or maybe she was just fishing.

She bent to pet Freeman, who ate up the attention.

He turned to retrieve the DVDs and microwave popcorn he'd brought, holding them up. "To distract you from pacing the floors." After witnessing how she'd freaked out leaving Hailey with him for a couple hours, he figured she'd go catatonic with her daughter gone a whole night.

She froze, still bent to pet the dog, her gaze sliding to the movies and then locking on him. It seemed to take great effort, but she straightened and swallowed. Her breath fogged before her face, masking her eyes, but he caught the wide wonder in them first.

That was the thing about Avery. No one looked at him with a cross between hero worship and affection. And she did each time he offered to help, whenever he said something kind, like she'd yet to experience either.

It made his chest expand with pride, made him want to do anything just to see it again.

And made him want to kill her ex all the more.

The admiration was probably underserving on his part. He had other, less honorable motives for being here. Like spending time alone with her. Because, yeah. The chemistry between them was a living thing. The heat in her eyes proved he wasn't alone.

He glanced at the movies in his hand just to break the intense moment. "Horror or rom-com?"

Her brown eyes did this kind of shining in the moonlight thing that made him step closer just to see if the honey flecks would be there. Her eyes said so much about her, radiating the emotions she tried to quash.

"You picked out a romance?"

The disbelieving tone had him shrugging. "Chicks like them. And it's a comedy, too, lest you forget that." Why did he have the urge to shuffle his feet under her gaze?

"I like scary movies," she said at last, walking up the porch steps. She held the door open for him. "Popcorn is my favorite food group."

He laughed and walked inside, calling Freeman. The dogs took turns sniffing each other's asses.

"I'm serious. Popcorn, chocolate, coffee, ice cream, and pizza. The five food groups. Health nuts are going to feel stupid one day, dying of nothing."

Okay, that was it. She might possibly be the perfect woman.

He reached out and snagged her around the waist, hauling her to his chest. "I have something I need to say." Leaning in, he kissed her soundly on the mouth and pulled away before things got too convoluted right off the bat.

Eyes wide, she reeled and pressed a hand to her forehead. "I'm not sure I heard you. Could you repeat that?"

Yep. The perfect woman.

"Maybe I should talk slower." Setting the movies aside, he wrapped both arms around her back, sliding his hands up the curve of her spine to tangle in her hair. "Communication is very important."

She gasped as he took her mouth, at leisure this time, exploring her taste and breathing in her sweet scent. She was everywhere, all the time. Invading his Friday nights, working at the clinic. In his head. Somehow, he didn't mind.

Despite their height difference, she fit against him, all soft and giving to his hard and unrelenting. And regardless of their other differences, they seemed to fit well in other areas, too. She was serious. He never tried to be. She was kind and generous. He typically gave what he got. She thought too much. He preferred action. But the oddity worked for them.

Wrapping her arms around his neck, she arched into him and raked her nails lightly against his scalp. Now he was hard. Painfully so. Hugest turn on? A woman who ran her fingers through his hair. Every time. He tore his mouth away before things went too far too fast and before she was ready. Not that she'd tried to tap the brakes.

"Grab the popcorn," he said against her lips, still holding her to him.

She reached behind him to the table. "What are you carrying?"

"You." Palming her ass, he lifted her and headed toward the kitchen, her toes dragging along the way. He set her on the counter and tossed the popcorn into the microwave. "Stop trying to hit on me, by the way. A guy likes to play hard to get."

She threw her head back and laughed. For once, carefree, she covered her face and let go. It was the single most sexiest and sweetest sound he'd heard. Just like that, the air evaporated from the room.

Pushing her hair back, she sobered. "I'll try to contain myself."

"Do that. Or don't." He stepped in front of her and set his hands on her hips. "You don't laugh often enough. It's very hot."

Her smile fell, but it stayed in her eyes. "I'm trying."

"Fresh start and all that?" She nodded, and he noticed her lack of tension. "You don't stiffen when I touch you anymore."

Setting her hands on his forearms, she stroked. "I'm working on that, too. Haven't done this in awhile. In fact, I swore I wouldn't ever again." She looked away and shrugged.

"Wouldn't ever date again?" She didn't respond, instead choosing to stare at his shirt, so he tilted her chin up until she met his gaze. "How long's it been?"

"Since I went out with someone? In secret or otherwise?"

He didn't have the heart to tell her they weren't a secret and never would be in a town like Redwood Ridge. It was obvious to anyone they came in contact with that they were into each other, even if their every move wasn't tweeted and hashtagged. Yeah, they had their own hashtag. Damn Aunt Rosa.

And Avery was deflecting. He couldn't have that. "Either."

She let out a sigh infused with a groan. "Richard is the only man I've been with. We met in college. He was two years ahead of me. We married right away. I think because he saw in me what he wanted from a wife, and he was laying the groundwork. He was on the fast track to partner in his dad's firm once he passed the bar."

He didn't care about what her ex did or didn't want, other than it directly resulted in how she saw herself. And she wasn't a house, damn it. "What did he want in a wife?"

"Arm candy. Quiet, not too pretty. Someone who was socially adept enough to carry conversation, but not challenge him." She set her hands on the counter behind her and leaned into them.

Aside from quiet, she was none of those things.

Her shoulder lifted in a shrug. She did that a lot, shrugged things off. "I lost too much of myself in him, until I didn't have a wish of my own or even trust my own tastes. He did it slowly. I didn't recognize what had happened and by then it was too late. Ten years too late. I won't ever get married again. Won't ever let someone break me down, mold me to their purpose."

Not that he was an expert in relationships, but he always figured there should be give and take. No breaking or bending, just respect for the other person. Like his parents' marriage, like Drake and Heather's. No one should ever have to be someone they're not, and by the sound of it, that's what had happened to her. No wonder she was wary.

"I think that's why I'm getting to be okay with what's happening between us." She straightened, looking over his shoulder to avoid his gaze. "There's no potential for more."

Temples throbbing, he narrowed his eyes. He didn't know why that pissed him off, but it did. They were already "more" or he wouldn't be thinking about her day and night and in between. Yet he understood what she meant. His reputation wasn't to stick, and she had no desire to do so again. Why did his chest ache then?

"I'll be your date for the dance."

His gaze whipped to hers. Held.

"And…the afterward part." She bit her lip, her expression more open than he'd seen yet, her eyes unguarded.

She was trusting him with something she hadn't with anyone else. Not for a long time, anyway. The courage it must've taken just to say that wasn't lost on him. He'd do everything he could not to make her regret it.

"I didn't offer to pressure you. When I said come home with me, I didn't necessarily mean it literally." His gaze swept over her face. "Not that I wouldn't love that, but I was serious when I said we don't need to rush."

A small smile ghosted her lips. "I wanted to tell you yes when you asked at the clinic, but…" She tucked her hair behind her ear. "You make me nervous."

"I make you nervous?" She had his heart pounding so hard it was cracking ribs and he made her nervous? "Likewise."

One of her perfectly arched brows rose, indicating she thought he was lying. "You're too experienced and charming to be nervous."

That was where she was wrong. Oh, so wrong. He had no clue what the fuck he was doing with her. He had no game, nothing to fall back on. The women and his previous encounters weren't even in the same realm as this, as her.

And this was...Not. Helping.

He pushed the button on the microwave, since he'd failed to do that before, and looked at her once more. She was grinning again, stopping his heart in the process as all his blood migrated south. "What?"

"You're cooking for me. It's sweet."

Kernels popped as the scent of butter wafted around the kitchen. She smelled better.

"I make a mean bag of popcorn. Nothing but the best for you. I make the finest mac and cheese this side of the fault line, too. Blue box, of course."

She patted her chest, her grin impish and adorable as hell. "Be still my heart."

No kidding. His, too. Except she *was* kidding.

He sighed. "Let's start the movie. And if you find yourself scared, feel free to climb on my lap. I can take it."

This earned another laugh. She moved off the counter and, since he was still in front of her, every inch of that soft, lithe body slid against his in her descent.

She tilted her head to look up at him. "What happens if you get scared?"

Already there. "You can hold me. With or without clothes."

* * * *

Avery put the movie into the disc player and checked her phone. Again. Cade served as a good distraction, but Hailey's bedtime had passed over an hour ago and April hadn't called. She hoped that meant Hailey was doing okay.

She sat next to Cade on the deep couch as the title screen popped up. "I haven't seen *The Exorcist* in years. Love this movie."

"Haven't seen it."

"What? Really? It's like a rite of passage."

"Will it frighten me?" He grinned and waggled his brows.

"It scared me to death when I was younger." She checked her phone again.

Cade took it from her and held it out of reach. "I will be the keeper of this until the movie's done."

"But—"

He shoved popcorn into her mouth and hit play. After setting the phone down on the table beside him, he threw his arm out, wrapped it around her waist, and pulled her closer until they were...snuggling.

For the first five minutes, she didn't move. Richard, even in their early years, didn't cuddle. She wasn't sure what to do. But eventually Cade turned off the lamp and she rested her head in the crook of his arm to tune into the film.

Seraph paced the floor between Hailey's bedroom and the couch, obviously missing his friend. She called him over and set him in her lap, absently petting his back. Freeman eyed them and laid down by Cade's feet.

It was all so cozy.

Cade smelled too good. Fabric softener and warm male. Resisting the urge to bury her face in his rock hard chest and sniff, she assessed every twitch he made, every breath he took. His solid thighs under his well-worn jeans kept snagging her attention, and she itched to drop her hands there to stroke. Every inhale had her shoulder brushing his pec.

Seraph moved to the floor by Freeman. Cade stretched his legs out, and she adjusted so she was reclining against his chest. His bulging, muscled bicep was right by her cheek, his thumb unconsciously caressing her shoulder.

This was crazy. A fire raged inside her, spreading and consuming. Her breasts ached. The apex of her thighs throbbed. She wanted...no, she *needed* him to kiss her, to press his weight down on her and run his large hands over her body. Something, *anything* to quell this fury of sudden lust.

She must've let out a frustrated moan because he laughed, gaze still on the screen.

"Yeah, I'll never eat pea soup again, either. Not that I cared for it much..." He trailed off when she looked up at him, finally sensing her mood.

He stilled as if trying to comprehend the shift. His eyes clouded, closing part way. His lips opened to draw in a shallow breath. Cupping her jaw, a question in his brow, his gaze raked over her face—her hair, her eyes, her cheeks...her mouth.

"Avery," he said quietly, but it sounded more like a prayer.

She was suddenly crawling out of her skin. If he didn't touch her soon, she was going to do something terribly embarrassing, like climb him and ride his thigh. Rip the T-shirt from his body so she could lick her way down to his jeans.

He gently brushed his nose with hers, the hesitation clearly costing him because the hand holding her jaw shook. Closing his eyes, he kissed her forehead, letting his lips linger on her temple. When he said her name again, she snapped.

Fisting her fingers in his thick, soft hair, she dragged his mouth to hers. A stunned beat passed before he became a willing participant and tilted his head. Taking the kiss deeper, he crushed her against him, stroking her tongue with his.

Yes. She all but heard the boom.

She moaned, and his hand traveled to her throat as if desiring proof the noise came from her. His shadow of a beard rasped her skin with the wild force of his mouth on hers, deliciously abrading.

He wrapped his arm around her back and eased her to the cushion, never breaking away. Lowering himself over her, he settled between her thighs and shoved his hands in her hair, holding her to his glorious assault as if he thought she'd evaporate. She wrapped her legs around his waist, and the hard bulge behind his fly ground into her heat, barely making a dent in her need.

Tearing his mouth away, he gulped air and made his way to her neck, licking and panting. She shivered from the nerve sensation overload and arched into him, his hard chest blocking the way, but her nipples cried *thank you.* He grabbed her hip, fingers clenching, before sliding his hand to her thigh to hold her leg in place.

He muttered something unintelligible and rocked his hips, pulling a feral sound from deep in her chest. Her breaths soughed until her lungs finally emptied. Cinching her shirt in his hands, he shoved the material past her breasts and stilled. His heated gaze swept over her blue bra, thumbs grazing the erect nipples straining against the lace.

"So beautiful," he murmured.

Doubt crept in, a sickening swirl to mix with the lust. She tensed, and he looked up, his gaze soft and understanding compared to the rest of him. His hair stood at odd angles from her fingers in the strands.

Trying to regulate her breathing, she fought to get the mood back, but it was lost. She didn't even know how to explain, but he deserved an answer. She pressed her hand to her forehead and swallowed. "He cheated on me."

Dang it. That…was not what she meant to say. She closed her eyes to block out whatever ounce of pity she'd find on his face.

Carefully, as if she might break, he tugged her shirt down and rose over her, bearing his weight on his arms. "Look at me."

She blew out a breath and opened her eyes, not finding pity, but patience. Somehow, that seemed worse. And if she wasn't mistaken, there was fury there, too.

"I'm doing this wrong if you keep thinking about him, yeah?" Frustration wrinkled his forehead, set a grim line to his mouth.

"What? No." She tried to sit up, but he didn't budge.

"Give me a second. I don't think I can walk." Tension stretched over his face when he finally looked back at her. "I don't know what else to say, except he was wrong. In case it escaped your attention, I'm harder than steel and that's all your doing. He has the defect, not you."

A rush of air whooshed from her lungs and the humiliation, the regret, seeped out of her pores. What was wrong with her? Hot guy making out with her on the couch, childfree for the night, and she couldn't get past first base. Or was petting second base? Didn't matter, she'd never score at this rate.

"I doubt it." He shook his head as if reading her mind.

"What?"

"The movie. I doubt it."

She turned her head at the part where the characters were heavy into an exorcism. The priest kept chanting, "The power of Christ compels you."

A giddy bubble of laugher caught in her throat. Erupted. No, this lust-induced frenzy whenever they were around one another was not religion inspired. Though if they ever got to the actual sex, she suspected he could make it just as inspiring. In seconds, her body shook with hysterics, him joining her.

The tension drained away and she was so, so grateful he wasn't mad. Any other guy would be pissed or pressuring for more. Cade, completely attuned to her every mood and nuance, simply rolled with it.

He dropped his forehead to her chest and sighed. "Such a shame. You really do have great breasts."

Chapter 13

After Avery picked up Hailey from April's, she scrolled through the Internet on her laptop while Hailey played tug of war with Seraph. The puppy seemed to be winning because Hailey kept dropping the rope toy. Most of the articles she found on dog training were pretty straightforward. Now that Seraph was healed, she really should start training him better, but never having a pet before left her fumbling. He seemed to have potty training down. He'd only had one accident in the house, but she let him out routinely every hour and a half. Plus her mom came by on the days Avery was working to let him out.

Maybe she should ask Cade, but she didn't want to bother him. Last night he'd gone home no doubt sore and seriously horny. She hadn't faired much better, spending half the night aching to finish what they started and too afraid to relax to get there. Eventually, his patience was going to wear thin.

Hailey whelped a laugh, which made Seraph yip in his puppy version of a bark.

Avery smiled, setting the laptop aside. Two peas in a pod, just like Cade had said. The dog followed Hailey everywhere, and Avery latched on to the joy it brought seeing Hailey connect to something. Really connecting.

"You like your doggy a lot, sweetie?"

Hailey squealed and flapped her hands. *Most entertaining, Mother!*

She laughed. "And what about your new friend, Jenny? April said you had a great time at your sleepover. Would you like to do it again?"

On repeat, she squealed and flapped her hands again.

Avery's chest filled to capacity, causing her eyes to moisten. Aside from a slip-up or two, Hailey hadn't had any outbursts or shown any signs of distress since they'd landed in Redwood Ridge. The quiet, remote town was doing wonders for both of them. There was still an adjustment period, but they were getting there. She couldn't expect ten years to vanish with the fog.

Mom walked into the cabin and removed her coat. She eyed Hailey and Seraph and grinned before suffocating Avery in a hug. "They're adorable. Look at them."

Mom had gone heavy on the patchouli today. Avery eased back before too much of the scent transferred.

She knelt down next to Hailey on the floor. "Sweetie, I have to go meet some friends, but you be good for Grandma, okay?"

Her mother patted Avery's arm. "What kind of dress are you going to get? Something sexy, I hope? You always dress too conservative."

Avery resisted an eye roll. Mom's version of fashion was out of a hippie catalogue. "I'll see what I can find. Thanks for watching her. She's not big into shopping, so she would've hated going."

She drove to the outer edge of town, past the mountains on her right and ocean to her left, navigating the winding roads. Zoe and Gabby said the outlet mall was in another county north of theirs, but right off the highway and easy to find. She hadn't ventured out much between work, Hailey, and the committee.

Finding the shopping center, she parked and strode in. Zoe and Gabby were already there, browsing through the racks. Brent was there, too, wagging his finger in disapproval of one of their choices.

He grinned when he spotted her and made his way over. "Let's find you something super sexy. Rawr."

Avery laughed. "Did your just rawr at me? And why is everyone so concerned about me finding a hot dress?" She accepted a hug from Gabby and nodded a greeting to Zoe. "Find anything good?"

Gabby held up a pink sequin number and rolled her eyes. "Didn't think finding pink and red would be so hard."

Zoe sighed. "Let's try next door."

As they walked out of the shop and to the next stop, Brent shoulder-bumped Avery. "Meant to offer before, doll. If you ever need a sitter, just call. My nephew's autistic, so I've got the basics down. Of course, I'm not a certain sexy animal doctor, but I've got a nice ass."

Gabby laughed and held the door open for them. "I don't think a babysitting requirement is to have a fabulous ass." She slapped his butt when he strode past. "It is nice, though."

Brent rolled his eyes with dramatic flair. "For reals, though. Just call."

Avery grinned. "I'd be afraid you'd turn Hailey into a diva."

He cocked a hip. "And what, pray tell, is wrong with that?"

"Got one," Zoe yelled from the back of the shop. She held up a short red spaghetti strap dress that darkened in color toward the hem.

"Love it." Brent fingered the satin material. "Go try it on."

When Zoe headed toward the dressing rooms, Gabby fished through a rack and sighed. "I don't know why it matters so much. It's not like anyone's going to notice me."

The comment was unlike Gabby's typical enthusiasm. Avery frowned. Gabby's natural champagne blond hair was long and sleek. Her blue eyes had a lot of gray in them, adding a certain allure. She had a cute bow mouth and a nice, curvy body. Why wouldn't people notice her?

When Avery said as much, Gabby shrugged. "I'm the girl next door, the buddy, not the one men want to date. Especially around here, growing up with most of the guys."

Brent and Avery shared a concerned look before Avery let the subject drop. She perused the rack and found a hideous dress with flowers sewn into the material. "Brent, I found your dress."

His gaze raked the item. He shuddered. "I'm here mainly to make sure you gals don't show up on Saturday looking hideous. Now put that back before someone sees you."

She laughed and moved on to another rack, spotting a light pink sheath dress with an empire waist. "Gabby, for you?" With her light complexion, the color would look great on her.

"Yes!" She grabbed the dress, checked the size, and bounced toward the dressing room.

A few minutes later, Brent made a noise of bottled excitement. "Oh, Avery, doll? Check it out."

The red dress was a slinky slip style that came to a V in the front and had a swoop scarf back. If she didn't eat between now and Saturday, she might fit into it.

She pursed her lips. "I'll try it on."

Moments later, in the dressing room, her stomach fluttered as she checked herself out in the mirror. It was a perfect fit, even having a built in bra because of the low back and coming to a stop just above the curve of her rear end. It was racier than what she usually wore, but why not? Slimming, too.

Hanging up the dress, she changed and headed back out. "Sold."

Brent clapped. "That was almost too easy. Let's grab some lunch and find shoes."

By the time Avery got home, she was exhausted but happy. She hadn't been shopping with girlfriends in ages, and the easy banter had lifted her spirits. It was nice for a change, not having to try so hard to say the perfect thing or act a certain way. And she was hereby taking Brent on all shopping excursions from now on.

On Monday, it snowed like the second coming. Eight inches by the time Avery was getting ready to leave for work and forcing a snow day from the school system. After dropping Hailey off at her mom's, Avery drove to the clinic, white-knuckling it the entire way.

Their little pocket between the ocean and the mountains didn't tend to get this much snow, so it was the topic of conversation. They'd gotten fourteen inches total by the end of the workday, and Avery stared at the accumulation through the front window. Everyone had taken off. All except Cade who was in his office finishing some charts. Avery's mom was keeping Hailey overnight, since school was cancelled tomorrow, too.

Hailey being away from home unnerved Avery, but Hailey had done well at Jenny's, and Avery needed to loosen her stranglehold on control. It took a lot of internal pep talk, but she conceded she wasn't alone anymore. She had help, she had friends, and letting them in was just one more step in moving on.

Earlier in the day, she'd found a box with several tablets equipped with an electronic medical record system. Gabby told her they'd invested in the software two years ago, but no one was willing or had the time to scan charts and get them off the ground.

Decision made, she went into the back room and grabbed the box with the tablets, figuring she'd get a jump on at least setting up a workstation to get the office digital ready. Maybe in an hour the roads would be clear and she wouldn't need heart medication to drive home. Until moving to Oregon, she'd only seen snow on TV.

Settling in at the front desk, she connected the scanner and installed the program into the clinic computer system. She'd been working at the cardiology office when they'd switched from paper to EMR, but that had been before Hailey was born, so she was rusty. This system was a little different in that it was targeted more for veterinarian medicine than healthcare, but the operating procedures were similar.

Glancing out the window, she noted the plows hadn't come through yet, so she checked next week's schedule and pulled the patient chart for first thing Monday to do a trial run on scanning the documents. After two attempts, she got the last few pages of dictation into the electronic chart. It would be a pain having to set up new accounts for the animals, and time consuming, but worth it.

She'd been so focused on her task that she hadn't heard Cade until he was right behind her. Jumping ten feet off her chair, she pressed a hand to her chest, heart thudding. "Crap on a cracker, Cade. You scared me to death."

He grinned. "Sorry. What are you still doing here? I thought I was alone."

She told him about Hailey and then the EMR project. Standing, she shut down the computer. "It's getting late. I'll do more tomorrow. I was just installing for now while waiting for the roads to clear."

The grin slid from his face as he stared at her, gaze roaming her face in that unnerving way that made her flush in embarrassment. Richard had never looked at her like that, even when things were going well with their relationship. She knew she needed to stop comparing, but she'd only been with one man prior to Cade and rarely did she know what to expect. God, how she hated that, hated having no solid ground to stand on.

He stepped closer and pulled the pencil from her hair she'd used to pin the strands off her face. One corner of his mouth quirked in amusement. "It's really hot when you do that, but I like your hair down." As if to emphasize his point, he combed his fingers through her hair and held the back of her head.

Hot. He'd just used her and hot in the same sentence.

She blinked, completely aware of him. Every single molecule and atom, aware. He made it impossible not to be. Cade filled a room, either with his laugh, his personality, or his blatant sex appeal. His hands were warm, almost as warm as his smile while he looked down at her, and she was helpless not to melt into him.

"I'm getting a few new fantasies about you and this desk." Leaning in, he brushed his lips over hers and sighed. "It could be so good between us, Avery."

He kept his eyes open, blue gaze tracking her response, and she was putty. "I want to."

"But?"

How could she put into words her reservations when she didn't fully comprehend them herself? She wanted him more than she craved anything in too long. Yet old habits died hard, and Cade wouldn't be easy to walk away from afterward. She'd have to see him daily at work, around town. There would be no escaping.

He closed his eyes and dropped his forehead to hers. "I hate what that prick did to you."

She wrapped her fingers around his wrists, him still cradling her head. "He didn't do anything I didn't allow. I'm not a victim."

He laughed without mirth. "You asked him to cheat on you? To ignore you and his own daughter? To kill your confidence one insult at a time?"

Her heart started to pound for an entirely different reason. They'd talked, but she hadn't delved that deeply into her past with Richard, not enough that Cade would know as much as he'd indicated. Which meant he'd read between the lines, he'd paid attention, and was figuring her out.

Ten plus years with Richard and he'd never remembered she hated peas. Six weeks and Cade could all but list her favorite foods. Angry at herself for comparing again, she shook it off.

"I didn't ask for him to do those things, but I allowed them. By not standing up for myself. For getting into a comfortable rut and not fighting, I allowed it." She sighed. "I know you're frustrated with our pace. I'm sorry. If you want to stop, if you want to see someone else, I understand."

Not that what they had was a relationship. She didn't know what label to slap on it, but relationship didn't fit. And the thought of ending things made her stomach twist in painful knots. But this would eventually end. His reputation proved he didn't have a long attention span.

He looked at her, a question in his eyes and fury closing ranks. "I haven't looked at another woman since you swept into town. I won't cheat on you or make you feel like shit or ignore you. If we decide to end things down the road, then that's what we'll do, but for now, I'm here because I want to be."

And there went the air from her lungs. He'd done nothing but prove himself, be completely honest with her, and she was acting like a skittish idiot. She just didn't know how to stop, to let go and…trust.

She threaded her fingers through his hair. He always initiated contact, and maybe by taking control of her actions she could take control of the doubt, too.

"I love it when you do that." His palms skimmed down her back and up again. "Your hands in my hair? Major turn on."

Empowered, she lightly fisted the strands, earning a sharp inhale from him. This was what she needed. To know what she was doing right. "What else do you like?"

He seemed to be concentrating hard on breathing as he paused a split second before every inhale and exhale. His gaze never wavered from hers, but his eyes darkened with arousal.

His throat worked a swallow. "I love it when your cheeks flush. It lets me know I've gotten under your skin."

Like now? Because their open discussion was fueling her internal temperature to critical. She had no control over that, though. That was biology. "What else?"

"You make a needy little whimper in your throat when I kiss you. That? Extremely hot. And anything having to do with your breasts is good in my book. Like that green top you wore last week. It was this side of clingy and displayed those babies nicely."

Note to self: wear more formfitting shirts. She could do that. The noise while kissing she'd been completely unaware she was doing, however.

He grabbed her hips, the motion seeming involuntary. "When you get into your bossy mode, I go instantly hard watching you organize things."

Interesting.

Just to be a brat, she picked up the pencil he'd pulled from her hair and meticulously set it in the cup with her other pens. She lifted her brows in challenge.

He groaned and narrowed his eyes. "Pushing your luck, sweetheart."

Sweetheart. He'd never called her an endearment before. Heat flooded her core and spread. Her heartbeat thundered in her ears. Guess she liked it.

Since it was fun watching him crack, she reached into his pocket and removed the paperclips he'd absently put there when she'd attach a note to his charts. Without taking her gaze from him, she dropped those into a tray with her other ones.

In the span of a second, she was pinned to his chest and held there by solid arms. His mouth crushed hers, needy, seeking. He shook against her, tension straining the muscles as he swept his tongue over hers. A mating. A claiming.

He backed her one step and lifted her onto the desk. She wrapped her legs around his waist and held him there. Driving her fingers into his hair—because he said he liked that and she did, too—she shifted to take the kiss deeper.

The phone rang.

They paused, still lip-locked. The machine kicked in, but no message was left. Cade patted his pockets out of habit, but she knew he didn't have the pager.

She tilted her head back. "Drake's on call this week."

His gaze lifted from her throat to her mouth to her eyes. Need shifted into tenderness, and she realized he was surprised she'd known what he was looking for with his movements.

"I should get going. Early morning tomorrow."

He nodded, tucking her hair behind her ear. "Drive careful, yeah? The roads look like a mess."

She smiled, pressed a quick kiss to his mouth, and hopped off the desk. He called her name when she was halfway to the break room to get her coat. She turned.

"Your laugh halts everything in my head. Forgot to mention that." He looked away as if...shy. He rubbed the back of his neck while she stood there, heart in her throat, tempted to jump his bones right there in the clinic.

He was good. Really good. A charmer without equal.

But he wasn't trying to persuade or lure or coax. He was being sincere, having picked up on her need to understand what he liked. He...saw her.

Saw. Her.

"Good night, Avery." He stepped into his office and kicked the door shut.

Chapter 14

"Hey, squirt. Can I see your iPad?"

Hailey pushed the device into Cade's hands and started to rock on the couch beside him. The action seemed restless and nervous to him.

"I'll give it right back. I promise."

He quickly connected the device to his laptop through an adaptor and pulled up Hailey's coloring app. After transferring several images she'd wielded, he unplugged and handed the device back to her.

"All done, squirt."

She didn't take it right away, leaving it to sit on the cushion between them. The rocking intensified and then worry slammed into his gut.

"What's wrong? Can you show me on your iPad? Or sign it to me?"

She didn't so much as turn her head, but the rocking slowed.

Maybe she needed space? He blew out a slow breath and walked to Avery's computer. After going into the control settings, he made her printer friendly with his laptop and ran off several of Hailey's pictures. Five should do it. They were nothing more than squiggly lines and mismatched shapes, but they were hers.

When Cade had first arrived to babysit, he'd noticed Avery had taken the handprints he'd traced and framed them above the fireplace mantle. Moved, he'd decided to add to the fridge drawings, but since Hailey didn't like coloring, he was forced to pull up the ones from her device.

He printed a couple for his own fridge and turned back to the kid. She seemed off tonight for some reason. Avery was going to be later than usual because of the Valentine's dance tomorrow and getting last minute details squared away. He was on his own.

Carefully, he sat next to Hailey and pulled up her language app. "Do you feel sick, squirt?" He'd watched her like a hawk, so he knew she hadn't gotten into anything. When she didn't respond right away, he guided her hand over the screen. "Yes or no? Do you feel sick? Have an ouchie?" She pulled her hand away.

At a loss, he turned off the device and switched on the TV. Going into the DVR, he brought up her sleepy time show. Perhaps she was just tired. Being a kid was exhausting, after all.

His estimation was confirmed when she yawned and tuned into the program. Afterward, she wasted no time going potty and brushing her teeth. He set Seraph in bed with her and cut the light. "'Night, squirt. I'm right out here, yeah?"

Making his way back into the living room, he put his printouts into his laptop bag and set it off to the side before heading into the kitchen and taping Hailey's pictures to the fridge. When he walked into the living room, Hailey was sitting on the couch.

Cade rubbed his neck. "Not tired after all?" He sighed, sitting next to her. How did Avery know what was up, since Hailey wasn't verbal? Something could really be wrong and he'd have no damn clue. "Don't get mad, squirt. I'm going to touch your forehead."

It wasn't hot but, strangely, she didn't push his hand away.

"I'm at a loss. Can you point me in the right direction? Show me what's on your mind?"

Just as he was about to give up and try to coax her back to bed, Seraph jumped up on the couch and Hailey dropped her head in Cade's lap. He froze, hands up like a criminal. Seraph settled into the crook of Hailey's arm and dozed off. Hailey's eyes drooped.

Hell. Now what?

He waited several beats until her breathing was deep and even, then snatched a quilt from the back of the couch and covered her. She'd never tried to cuddle with him before. She'd never so much as touched him. If he moved, he'd wake her, so he settled back and rested on the couch. The weight of her tiny head on his thigh and smell of her kid shampoo was oddly endearing. Gently, he set a hand on her shoulder and closed his eyes.

The next thing he knew, he was jerked awake by someone tapping his knee and Avery was in front of him. Rubbing a hand down his face, he looked at his lap. Hailey hadn't moved. "What time is it?"

"Almost nine." Her gaze darted between him and her daughter, confusion parting her lips and a tugging softness in her eyes. "What happened?"

"She was kinda off tonight." He shrugged. "Don't know what it was about. I tried to put her to bed, but she did...this."

Avery pressed her fingers to her lips and cleared her throat. Twice. "She missed you, I'll bet. She didn't see you last week because of her sleepover."

"You think?" His heart somersaulted in his chest. Or maybe he had indigestion. He liked the idea of Hailey missing him. He didn't know shit about kids, but he liked this one. A lot.

Her mom, too, if he was going there.

"I thought she didn't like touch."

Avery tucked a piece of chestnut hair behind her ear, not meeting his gaze. "She doesn't much. Sometimes she'll snuggle into my lap or play with my hair, but not often."

She closed her eyes and pulled in a breath as if centering herself. Slowly, she opened them and lifted Hailey from the couch. Since she seemed to need a minute, he didn't follow when she carried the girl into the bedroom.

He stood and stretched, then headed for the kitchen. Changing his mind about making coffee, he grabbed a beer and went back into the living room. He set the bottle aside and dropped onto the couch, head in his hands, wondering what the hell was going on. And why he didn't mind the new squishy feelings that seemed to be shoving around in his chest, taking up space.

The couch dipped beside him, but he didn't lift his head.

"Are you okay?"

"Yeah." He sighed and sat back, staring at the ceiling. "I guess it freaked me out a bit, her acting different. I thought something was wrong." He'd almost called Avery, but honestly, having Hailey fall asleep on him had been more jarring.

She studied him for a moment in that quiet, contemplative way of hers that made him want to crawl inside her head. Rattle out some words.

Setting her elbow on the back of the couch, she rested her head in her hand. "This one time, Hailey was maybe four years old, she wouldn't get out of bed. It scared me to death. She wouldn't use sign language, and she didn't have a device yet. This went on for two painful hours until a fever finally spiked and I realized she was sick. Nothing major, just the flu, but I was petrified."

He would've crawled out of his skin with worry. "How do you do it? How do you not go nuts without a way to know what's wrong?"

She shrugged. "You just do. That's parenting. She has some tells, nonverbal cues. I guess I just know her so well I watch for the signs."

He was starting to pick up on them, too, but it was more than that. Hailey wasn't just silent. She didn't offer affection, either. Not in the typical way anyhow. How did Avery get by with no hugs, no laughter, no chatter?

And then it dawned on him, a punch right in his gut, why Avery had such a hard time adapting to what was happening between them. She'd been separated from her dick of an ex for two years, which meant there were problems before that. She had a daughter who didn't speak, who she couldn't caress. She had a damn hard time trusting people and accepting help.

Because she'd been completely, irrevocably alone.

Had he been the first man to touch her, offer comfort or see her vulnerable side in all that time? The first to want to? Hell, no wonder she had walls. Quiet house, quiet kid, quiet mind. Like she'd shut it all down to exist.

He looked in her eyes, at the strength and composure in the cocoa depths, and for once in his life, he wanted to be the hero in someone's tale. Wanted to be the guy she'd fall into. His heart stuttered behind his ribs, and a trickle of sweat beaded down his spine, but he held out his hand in the space between them.

"Come over here."

She offered him a quizzical look, but scooted closer. He grabbed her thigh and slid it over his so she straddled him. Then he removed his T-shirt and tossed it to the floor. Her lips parted as her gaze drifted over his bare chest, his abs—too quick a perusal to really take him in—before meeting his gaze with wide eyes.

"Don't freak out on me." Grabbing the hem of her sweater, he lifted it to expose her belly. "We're just talking." With a couple swift flicks of his wrist, her shirt joined his on the floor.

She immediately covered herself, which was a crying shame. Those beautiful breasts were begging to be touched behind her yellow bra. But he set his hands on her thighs and left them there as he calmly looked in her eyes. It was the only idea he could conjure to get her used to him, comfortable in her own skin while in the same room with him. At some point, she had to stop living in her head and feel.

"How was the meeting?" he asked.

Her pink lips opened and closed. She cleared her throat. "You needed my shirt off to ask me that?"

Unable to help it, he grinned. "If I had my way, you'd do everything shirtless. Look at you. You're lovely." The subtle compliment wasn't lost on her as a disbelieving note traced her expression. He'd keep working her until that disappeared altogether. "But no, that's not why I took your shirt off. I'm trying to drop a barrier. Now, how was the committee meeting?"

"Um, good. We just…"

He drew lazy circles over her leg, working upward to distract her, but she broke off, so he prompted her to continue. "You just what?"

"Details. We just worked out the details." Her breathing hitched as his hands inched higher, tracing over her outer thigh and shifting closer to her hips.

He was seconds from needing to adjust his pants, but he held still for the sake of his cause. "What kind of details?"

"Who will set up what and where. That…" He brushed his fingertips up her sides, earning a shiver from her. "Kind of thing."

She stopped covering herself to drop her hands to his forearms. He skimmed the soft, warm skin beneath her breasts, wanting to lean forward and kiss her there. Hell, kiss her everywhere. Her eyes glazed and he knew he had her out of her head and into the just-feel-me zone.

"And what are you in charge of setting up, Avery?" He dipped his voice an octave, rumbling her name like a prayer. He'd need to start praying for patience soon. Watching her lose control, little by little, was the hottest thing he'd ever seen.

Her breath caught and her eyes shut as he traced the curve of her breast above her bra. Slowly, he brought his mouth there, kissing and licking. Damn, she tasted as sweet as she smelled.

"Answer the question," he said against her skin, bringing his hands around her back and splaying them low enough to dip his pinkies into her jeans. "What are you in charge of setting up?"

"Ah…the lighting. I'm making starlight."

"Starlight?" Her head rolled back and he kissed her exposed throat. Her pulse beat harder, faster beneath his lips. "How does one make starlight?"

She moaned. He nearly busted out of his inseam.

"I don't remember," she breathed, fisting her fingers on his shoulders as if unsure what to do with them.

"Touch me and tell me how you make lights into stars." He personally didn't give a shit how, but she was on the precipice of falling over the cliff of reason and, by God, he'd kill to get her there.

Without protest, her hands fell to his chest. Stroked. "It's all about placement." Her statement ended on a moan, vibrating from her chest to his and back. Her fingers moved lower, over his abs and stopping at his fly.

Jesus. "Placement?" Panting against her throat, he ran his hands up her back and cupped her shoulders from behind. He thrust against her core, just enough for her to feel the hard ridge of his reaction to her. "That kind of placement, sweetheart?"

"Yes. No." She gripped his waistband.

His eyes rolled back in his head hard enough to thunk his skull. His lips grazed her cheek in a path to her mouth. "Which is it? Yes or no?"

They weren't talking lighting placement anymore and they both knew it. For once, she didn't hesitate. She turned her head to hover over his lips, stealing all his oxygen. It didn't matter what she said. He wouldn't take things beyond this point. They had all night alone tomorrow to explore. Tonight was about preparation, about the learning curve, and teaching her how to be touched again. A reminder she had needs and he'd be more than willing to sate them. Tomorrow.

His dick wasn't getting the memo, though, and when she brought her mouth to his in answer, he forgot his own damn name or why they needed caution.

She crushed her mouth to his, her breasts to his chest, and cupped his jaw in the most shocking display of initiative. He'd always had to come to her, and her going after him as if there was no stopping it knocked any sense out.

His hands tangled in her hair, holding her to him while he plunged. Pillaged. A groan rumbled deep in his chest, laying claim and surrendering all at once. Her tongue stroked his as her hips rocked against his erection, and he had to break away or die from suffocation.

He stared at her, breaths rasping in and out of his chest, her dark eyes dialed to take-me and lips swollen from his kiss. And fuck it. He didn't need to breathe. He pulled her to him again. Teeth scraped. Tongues warred. Her nails raked his scalp and he almost came. Right there. In his damn jeans.

It was her who tore away this time, pressing her face into his neck and fighting for air as badly as he was. "Cade."

He closed his eyes to the breathy, needy tone of her usually calm voice and gripped her hips in an effort not to unzip her pants. "Yeah?"

Her hot breath skated across his neck. "This was a really good talk."

Tilting his head to look at her, he paused long enough to roll the words around until they sank in. He laughed and dropped his head back to the couch. "I keep telling you communication is very important." Tucking a piece of hair behind her ear, he took in her flushed cheeks and swallowed hard.

She was so goddamn beautiful like this.

"I was right about your abs. I could cut my teeth on them."

He laughed again. "A theory you can test another time." Like tomorrow, he hoped. He pressed his palms to his eyes to dispel the image of her nipping her way down his body. It didn't work. And he'd rather look at her, anyway.

"I'll meet you at the dance tomorrow instead of you picking me up. I have to be there early to set up."

He sighed, tracing his thumb over her bottom lip. "To make starlight?"

She smiled, and it hit her eyes like he hadn't seen often enough. "Yes. To make starlight."

If he was a more poetic man, he'd find a way to say something romantic, but he wasn't, so he'd just wait until the dregs of arousal cooled enough for him to walk out without limping. It might take awhile.

"What does your dress look like? I should've snooped around while you were gone."

"I'm picturing you snooping around my closet." She shook her head as if pitying him. "The dress isn't here. It's at Gabby's. Zoe and I are getting ready over there. Zoe's going to do my hair." She stopped and bit her lip. "This does feel like prom all over again."

He wrapped a strand of her wavy hair around his finger. "You're not going to let Zoe dye your hair blue like hers, are you?"

"I think she's changing it to red to match her dress, but no. I'm not that adventurous."

Before Avery came along, he'd always been the adventurous one in his family, willing to take risks, however calculated. Aside from buying his house and working the clinic, he didn't often tie himself to one thing or person, happy to whittle away at life until he found something that stuck.

He had a suspicion Avery was more than a sticking point. She was a glue factory. Instead of getting the itch to bolt, he wanted to know more. Something besides her ex or the shitstorm of a marriage. Her life before that, maybe, and he refocused on what they'd been talking about.

"Who did you go to your prom with?"

She bit her lip and narrowed her eyes. "A boy from the baseball team. He played right field and kissed like he'd never made it to first base."

He laughed. "Nice analogy. So no wild sex in the limo or after party?"

"No, thank goodness."

Nodding, he realized the topic change worked and he figured he could stand without pain. The Redwood Ridge Valentine's dance wasn't prom, but he hoped to make a better impression afterward than her right fielder. Ending the night with a home run wouldn't suck, either.

Chapter 15

Avery wrestled with a string of lights from the top rung of the ladder, blew a strand of hair out of her face, and cursed. The exposed beams in the botanical garden's hall were high. Too high for her to comfortably reach. Her and heights weren't exactly friends.

Now what?

Footsteps sounded from behind. She grabbed the ladder to turn, finding Drake and Flynn striding over. They tossed their coats by the front hall and made their way to the center of the room.

Flynn assessed her in a swift glance and grinned. *"I'm told you're making starlight. Need help?"*

Her conversation from last night with Cade came to mind and her cheeks heated. He'd obviously told his brothers some part of what had happened. Unsure how to feel about that, she resorted to sass to hide her embarrassment and grinned. "Are you a starlight expert?"

"I can be." Flynn winked.

Drake rolled his eyes. "Get down before you fall. Tell me what you need done."

Avery climbed down and handed Drake the strand. "What are you guys doing here, anyway?"

Flynn moved to the ladder and signed, *"Cade called. He was going to come help you, but he got roped into doing something for Aunt Marie."*

He'd asked his brothers to help her? How...considerate.

Drake looked down at her from the top rung. "Lights? How do you want them?"

Right. She straightened and gave Drake directions, watching his forearms flex as his white T-shirt stretched across the muscles of his back. How was it all three of the O'Grady men were single? Even Flynn was attractive with his dark strawberry blond hair and lean body. Like a runner. Wide shoulders, narrow waist.

By the time they were done with the first beam, Avery was thinking of setting up the tables herself. It was a little useless to have her stand around while the guys worked.

Flynn looked around. *"It looks nice in here."*

"I'm not done yet, but thanks." She'd still be fighting with the first strand of lights if they hadn't shown up. It was looking pretty great. She had Drake bunching the strings together so they draped in clusters, resembling falling stars. "How'd Cade talk you into this? And thank you, by the way."

Drake looked down at her from the ladder, dark eyes intent. "Help is around, Avery. You only need to ask."

Her chest constricted at the words she'd heard before. Somehow, coming from Drake, the meaning dawned clearer. He may still be trying to get over his wife's death, and he may prefer his own company, but he was a friend, too. He'd come if she needed him. "Thank you."

He nodded and went back to work.

She pulled out her cell and texted Rosa not to bother coming for the tables. She'd do them herself since she had time. She then texted the other ladies and told them the same thing with regards to their duties. Drake was nearly done, and she still had two hours before needing to be at Gabby's.

When Drake set the ladder aside, Flynn turned to her. *"So, you and my brother are a thing."*

Being new to Redwood Ridge and fresh off a divorce, the town gossip made her stomach twist. She'd led a sheltered, quiet life with Richard, and it was an adjustment having so many people interested in not only her love life, but everything else. She couldn't pass someone on the street without them asking how Hailey was or making idle chitchat about Cade. It was almost as if the whole town was trying to play matchmaker. Just this morning, the woman at the coffee shop had told her how Cade donated his time at a shelter every Thanksgiving before heading to his mom's. The woman followed this up by telling Avery what a "catch" he was.

Making friends and being social she could handle in moderation, but them delving into her personal life was hard to accept. She didn't know where this thing with Cade was headed. She wasn't interested in another long-term relationship or anything beyond what they were doing now. And he wasn't the husband and kids kind of guy. Why couldn't they just explore each other and have fun in private, without all the eyes?

Flynn lifted his brows in question.

She opted for smartass again and pretended he meant the other brother. "Drake might be shocked to learn we're a thing."

Flynn's grin was infectious. *"No, I think your type is someone a little younger, who's quicker to laugh. Am I right?"*

"Are we going to paint each other's nails next? I didn't bring my manicure bag." Drake frowned, eying Flynn through narrow slits as if pissed he'd brought up the subject. Was he upset she was—almost, kind of—dating Cade or had Flynn said something he shouldn't have?

Flynn shrugged. *"Just making conversation."*

"Well, stop." Drake's features smoothed out before turning back to her. "What else do you need done?"

She bit her lip. "I can get the rest."

"Or you could tell us what else needs to be done."

Right. Help was around. Maybe by the time Hailey got to high school she'd have that mastered. "The seating?" She phrased it as a question, unsure if they really were going to stay.

Both Flynn and Drake waved her aside once she'd told them where they were supposed to arrange the round tables. Sighing at her uselessness once again, she went into the storage room to retrieve the décor and get a jump on that. By the front door, she assembled and decorated the check in area. Back in the hall, she placed a white tablecloth on each table as the guys got them set up, adding the flower petals and votives. Then she dragged the chairs away from the wall and arranged ten at each table.

It was early afternoon by the time they finished. The staff at the facility was supposed to let the DJ in and were handling the bar. She needed a shower before heading to Gabby's.

Flynn waved. *"See you tonight."*

"Thank you so much for helping."

He nodded and strode out, leaving her and Drake alone. She sighed and leaned against the wall, studying Drake's tense posture. His hard gaze traveled over the room as he raked a hand through his black hair.

"Heather and I had our wedding reception here."

Her gaze flew to his as her heart squeezed. Being in the hall again had to be tough on him, yet he'd come to lend her a hand, anyway. Drake didn't talk much, but when he did, each word was infused with meaning. She didn't know why he'd mentioned it, but she was glad he had, glad he'd opened up a little.

"Cade showed me a few pictures of her. She was lovely."

He nodded. Slowly his gaze returned to her, pain and determination in his dark brown eyes. "Did you need anything else?"

"No, but thank you." She paused a beat. "I understand it's difficult for you to be here, so it meant a lot you came."

His face was stony reserve, but his voice was gentle. "We grew up together. Everywhere is hard to be. I make do. And you're welcome."

"Maybe one day you can tell me about her. I wish I could've met her." Her heart was breaking for what could have been. Drake obviously had loved Heather a whole lot.

His eyes glazed over as he stared at her feet. "She would've liked you." He crossed his arms and blew out a breath.

She took mercy on him. "Are you still coming tonight? I have my boxing gloves all ready to ward off any conversationalists."

A ghost of a smile traced his lips. "I think I'll pass. Appreciate the offer, though." He tucked his hands in his back pockets.

"It's because of the dress code, isn't it? You can tell me."

His smile widened. "You got me. I'm not fond of neckties."

She eyed his jeans and T-shirt. "How fond of that shirt are you?"

He glanced down. "I don't write it sonnets. Why?"

She took a permanent marker from her back pocket and uncapped it with her teeth. "Hold still." Securing the fabric in one hand, she drew a cartoon necktie on the front of the shirt, a couple buttons on the chest, and stepped back. "I'm not as artistic as Zoe, but it'll do."

He looked at the shirt and then at her. Shaking his head in amusement, the heavy sorrow lifted from his eyes, degree by degree. "You have me at a loss."

"Are we keeping tabs? I can write "Caution: Will bite" on your back."

The rusty sound of his short laugh echoed off the walls. "You win. I'll come. One hour, then I'm out."

She grabbed her coat and purse from the front hall, trying her best not to show her excitement he'd changed his mind. "I won't even make you dance with me. Brent, however, I can't control."

He shrugged into his coat and held the door, humor twisting his mouth. "He's not my type."

She grinned all the way home, pleased she'd gotten Drake to come to the dance. She could only hope his grief would lesson a little more with each venture out of the house, replace old memories with new ones.

Most of the snow had melted and the afternoon was mild, bringing in a thick fog. She breathed in the scent of pine and salt as she exited the car. Cade texted just as she unlocked the cabin door.

I have Seraph at my house. That way your mom doesn't have to come by to let him out.

A quick follow up came seconds later.

That wasn't meant to pressure you into staying. You can pick him up after the dance, if you like.

She smiled and shut the door. Cade hadn't pressured her at all, not even when most guys would've been pushed past the patience marker. She'd thought a lot about tonight and what might happen between them. Nerves pinged her belly, but it was mostly anticipation. Cade made her nervous, yet in a good way. It had just been so long since she'd had sex that she worried she'd let him down. Or embarrass herself. Richard hadn't exactly been experimental when it came to positions or trying new things.

Shaking her head, she thumbed a response. *Looking forward to tonight.*

Before heading to the bathroom, she called April to check on Hailey. Assured everything was fine, she stepped into the shower.

When she got to Gabby's house—a cute gingerbread tucked into the woods not far from Avery's rental—everyone was waiting for her in the cozy kitchen. Scarred birch cabinets and green laminate floors—very outdoorsy and rustic.

Brent handed her a champagne glass filled with mimosa.

She muttered a thank you as another text pinged her phone. Digging in her purse while following them into the living room, she pulled out her cell. She grinned at Cade's name on the display and the response to her looking forward to tonight.

Not as much as I am.

Brent peeked over her shoulder. "Oh, swoon. Doll, that man likes you bunches."

Zoe and Gabby started talking excitedly at once.

Avery lifted her hand. "Not talking about it, okay?"

She quickly glanced around the living room in an effort to mute the subject, taking in the hardwood floors and colorful furniture. The fireplace mantle had more than a dozen photos in mismatched frames. The space suited Gabby, cheerful and open. Tall windows and decorative bottles. Magazines and plants. A fat orange tabby was curled in a corner, ignoring their existence.

Zoe plopped onto the arm of the navy sofa. She had, in fact, dyed her hair a bright, circus-fearing red. "At least tell me you trimmed your naughty-zone. If you use the not-waxing excuse to back out of sex with Cade—"

"Not talking about it."

Her face heated to inferno. Some things were too personal, and she'd only known these people for six weeks. Besides, she was good in that regard. Richard had insisted she have laser hair removal not only under her arms and on her legs, but in the bikini area, too. She'd huffed at the time. Now she was just grateful she didn't have to shave daily. Not that she'd tell her friends.

Gabby flopped on the couch, blond hair in rollers. "Oh, come on. None of us have any juicy prospects. You could at least indulge us."

Avery slammed half her mimosa and swallowed. "Is nothing private?"

Brent laughed. "You're so innocent it's adorable. Now, seriously. Dish."

"We haven't…" She waved her hand and sighed. Giving in, she sat in a green armchair and rubbed her forehead. "God, I'm so nervous. The only man I've ever slept with was my ex, and that was so long ago I'm not sure my parts still work."

They cooed and offered comfort.

Brent squatted by her feet. "It's just like riding a bicycle. A vibrating, naked, muscled bicycle."

A giggle bubbled in her belly, morphing into a full-blown hysterical laugh. "You're a nutcase."

"No question." He rose and looked her up and down. "The first step is to make you look sexy. If you look sexy, you'll feel sexy. We need to get you some confidence."

"I'll do her hair," Zoe said.

"I'll apply makeup." Gabby stood. "Let's do this."

They dragged her to a small vanity in Gabby's bedroom and shoved her onto the bench. Zoe got to work on her hair, pinning the curls up in a loose knot behind her head. Gabby worked on her face, using a smoky charcoal to lightly accentuate her eyes and a deep red for her lips. It was more war paint than she was used to, but she had to admit, it looked nice. The evening called for formality, so she supposed going all out was okay.

What if Cade thought she was trying too hard? Would he like this look?

Richard hated a lot of makeup. He'd wanted her to dress and look sophisticated at all times. A wallflower. Once, she'd gone to the grocery store just to pick up milk, deciding not to bother with cosmetics, and she'd run into his partner's wife. Richard had gotten on the phone within the hour to ask if she was sick and why she'd go out looking unpresentable.

"What's wrong, doll?"

She glanced up at Brent and blinked the memory away. Cade wasn't Richard, and her ex no longer had a say in her life. She'd moved to Redwood Ridge to start fresh. Her plans never included getting mixed up in another romantic relationship, but she reminded herself Cade wasn't looking for one, either. This was just for fun until the attraction waned. No sense in freaking out over loss of control or worrying about someone trying to run her life.

She smiled. "Nothing. I'm fine." She glanced at the sleigh-style bed where the dresses were laid out over a thick pink duvet. "Should we get dressed now?"

Zoe's cell phone rang. She glanced at the screen and cursed. "That's Mrs. Tetherman. She's watching Mom for me." She took the call and walked into the hallway.

Gabby turned from the mirror. "I hope she doesn't have to cancel. She's been looking forward to this for weeks. She hardly gets out anymore."

Avery bit her lip, then remembered her lipstick and stopped. "Her mom's dementia is really bad?"

Gabby turned back to the mirror with a frown, applying eye shadow. "Worse every day. People keep telling her to put her in a home, but Zoe won't do it."

"I'll go over there if there's a problem. That way she can still attend." Brent sat on the edge of the mattress. "I don't have a date anyway, and her mother does better with men."

"That's strange, don't you think?" Avery moved to the bed and sat next to him. "I'd think females would be more comforting."

"Don't know, but Zoe's tried every female caregiver in three counties. None stick. I visit and her mom's fine."

Their conversation was cut short when Zoe came back into the room. "False alarm. Mrs. Tetherman just wanted to know where Mom's bedtime dose of medicine was. I had to move it to a locked cabinet…" She waved her hand. "Let's get you dressed, Avery, since you have to leave early."

She did have to arrive in under an hour to see to any last minute details and be sure the ladies running the entry table had everything they needed. Stepping into the bathroom, she put her clothes into a small bag to wear tomorrow and carefully took the dress off the hanger.

She zipped the back and then looked in the mirror, hardly recognizing her reflection. The dress made her breasts more full, her waist thinner. The bright red matched her lipstick and brought out the natural chestnut highlights in her hair.

Perhaps Brent was right. She looked good. Different, but good. Some of the nerves fled from her body. She was young, reasonably attractive, and had a man waiting for her tonight. She was going to have fun for once and not worry about the world closing in or controlling the outcome.

Chapter 16

Cade handed Aunt Rosa his coat in the entryway to the gardens and waited for his brothers to do the same. He endured a kiss from his mom, said hello to a few people, and headed toward the open ballroom.

Half the town was already in attendance, by the look of things. The lights were dimmed to nearly dark and candles flickered on the tables. To his right, the DJ played instrumental music while people mingled. To the left was the bar.

Bingo.

He ordered a beer and then turned to lean against the bar, his brothers flanking both sides. From here, he could take in the whole room. More importantly, scope out Avery. He knew she'd be fluttering about, and he wouldn't get to pin her down until the ball was rolling, so he'd wait here and hope to spot her in boss mode.

So hot.

Flynn nudged his shoulder and pointed to the ceiling.

A grin tugged at his lips. He'd be damned. It did look like starlight raining down from the rafters. In fact, the whole setup was so different from years past, he'd never know he wasn't at a wedding if not for all the pink and red.

Speaking of, Gabby and Zoe made their way over, Zoe decked out in a multi-tone red dress and Gabby in pale pink.

"You look lovely, ladies." Cade toasted them with his bottle.

Gabby lifted her champagne flute. "Thank you. Avery outdid herself. Isn't this great?"

Flynn nodded, eyes full of mischief. "*Drake hung the lights.*"

Zoe's eyes rounded on Drake. "You did?"

His older brother shrugged, not meeting her gaze. "Just did as Avery asked."

She stared at him a heartbeat too long and finally nodded. "I'm glad you came."

Drake cleared his throat. "Let's get a table."

The ladies had already snagged one near the dance floor in a corner before they'd arrived. Cade followed them through the crowd, craning his neck to check for Avery. He was dying to see her, to find out if this mysterious dress would drop his jaw. The way he figured it, she could wear a paper bag and he'd want her anyway.

"She'll be here in a minute." Brent smiled as they sat down, reading Cade's intentions. "She swore she'd stop working and have fun as soon as the music started."

Cade doubted it.

They made idle chitchat for a few minutes. Cade clenched his teeth and forced himself to sit still when all he wanted to do was prowl the room for Avery. His skin itched and his body tensed.

He didn't know if it was the anticipation for after the dance or just her not being within touching distance, but it wasn't like him to be so wound up over a woman. Sometime over the last six weeks, she'd crawled inside his head, his chest, and stayed there. Taking up space. Making him feel things. He rubbed the back of his neck and looked over the crowd.

And saw her.

The deep red of her gown matched the shade of her lips. The material dipped into a V at her breasts, clung to the curves of her waist and hips, and flowed in a slip to her ankles. A slit up one side hinted at the long legs beneath, allowing nothing more than a peek. Her hair was pinned up, exposing her regal neck, and she'd done something to her eyes to make them a warmer shade of milk chocolate.

With slow grace, she drifted over in—oh hell—fuck me red heels, and sat between him and Drake.

"Hey, guys. You all look great."

Since it was anatomically impossible to swallow his own tongue, he attributed the lump in his throat to nerves. Nerves? Him? He cleared his throat. "So do you. Beautiful."

The smile hit her eyes, and him somewhere below the belt. "Thank you."

When she turned to Drake, Cade forgot to breathe. The back of her dress was open, dipping all the way to the small of her back. The pale smooth skin begged to be stroked, kissed. Slowly.

Her calm voice brought his gaze up to his brother. "After I went to all that trouble to make you a tie, and you busted out a suit, anyway."

Drake ran a hand down his white shirt, necktie already loosened and first button undone. "I'll save it for my next formal occasion." One corner of his mouth quirked in...damn. Drake was smiling. Avery had gotten him to come to the dance *and* smile.

The rest of the table noticed, according to their wide eyes and parted lips, but no one said anything. Drake appeared oblivious to the attention. Cade met Flynn's gaze across the table. Flynn nodded in understanding.

Wait. She'd made his brother a tie?

He must've said the question aloud because Avery turned in her seat and breathed a laugh. "Not really. I—"

"Drew on my T-shirt with a permanent marker." The other corner of Drake's mouth lifted, transforming his half-cocked smile into a grin.

The breath seeped from Cade's lips. He was immediately thrown back into childhood, of playing baseball and throwing snowballs. To Drake and Heather's wedding, where that grin never once left his brother's face. It had been so long, so damn long since he'd seen any sign of life in Drake. Flashes here and there, gone too fast to note they'd even manifested.

There was obviously an inside story about the shirt, but Cade didn't give a shit what it was because the only thought taking up residence in his mind was getting his mouth on Avery, every inch of her. For making Drake smile again. For organizing the clinic and this event. For being a great mom. For having the courage to leave a comfortable, privileged life and start over.

For making Cade's heart pound, stop, and pound again.

The squeal of a mic echoed through the room and he jumped. Shaking his head to clear it, he took a long pull from his beer and forced his gaze to the interruption. Aunt Marie was on the DJ's stage in full mayor mode. In year's past, she'd always said a few words before kicking off the event. He sat back and pretended he'd heard what she said.

And then she called Avery's name.

Avery muttered an "oh crap" in response while standing. The room cheered as she walked to Marie and took the place beside her. His aunt put Avery on display, a position she obviously was uncomfortable with if her blush and clenched fingers were any indication. Yet she plastered a smile on her face and waved.

"Are you having fun?" Avery asked into the mic.

The patrons clapped and whistled.

"Good. I'm glad you all could make it. I'm getting a lot of compliments, but it wasn't just me who planned tonight. It was the effort of the committee, so please give them some love."

The room clapped. Avery rolled her eyes and waved her hand, indicating they weren't loud enough. The room erupted and she smiled.

"That's better. I'd also like to thank two special guys who helped me set up earlier and saved me from a fall off the ladder. Flynn O'Grady."

Gabby signed for Flynn, repeating Avery's words, and Flynn stood to take a mock bow, earning a laugh from Avery.

"And," she went on, dropping her voice to a conspiring tone, "whatever you do, please do not tell the other guy I said he helped me. Drake O'Grady would be totally embarrassed to know I said anything at all."

All eyes shifted to Drake. And hell. His brother was still grinning, eyes on Avery and slowly shaking his head in amusement.

Time seemed to stop as a collective pause filled the room. Then the applause erupted. Avery quickly quieted them down with a wave of her hand. She nodded to the DJ to go ahead and start, then bunched the front of her dress to walk down the stairs.

Cade couldn't testify to what song played or who did what as he tracked her hurrying back over to the table and reclaiming her seat.

"I can't believe Marie put me on the spot like that." Her cheeks were almost as red as her killer dress.

"Believe it, doll." Brent lifted his glass in mock toast. "You did good."

She turned to Drake. "Are you mad I called you out?"

Drake lifted one brow. "Do I look mad?"

Flynn grinned. *"How would she know the difference?"*

Brent rose from his seat and clasped Zoe's hand. "Ladies, we're dancing now." He claimed Gabby's hand with his other. "Avery?"

"In a minute," she said, settling back in her chair. "Go ahead."

And that was pretty much how the next hour went. Flynn got up for a song or two to dance with the others, but the three of them remained seated, virtually not talking and watching the crowd.

Finally, a slow song came on, and Cade shifted to Avery to ask her to dance, but she was conversing with Drake. Anyone who could get his brother to talk shouldn't be interrupted, so he draped his arm over the back of her chair and rubbed his thumb across the smooth, soft skin of her back.

She shivered. He grinned.

Flynn stood to dance with Gabby. Brent already had Zoe locked in, twirling her around the floor like only a gay man could pull off. He made the others look bad.

"Don't look now, but you might turn into a pumpkin. It's been ninety minutes since you arrived." Avery laughed and sipped her champagne.

Drake shrugged. "I think it's my car that would turn into a pumpkin, not me." His gaze traveled the room. "I'll take off in a bit."

"Is this bringing up bad memories?" She asked so softly, Cade almost hadn't heard over the music.

Drake swallowed, staring back at her with a blankness in his eyes. Just when Cade thought he wouldn't answer, Drake crossed his arms and shook his head. "Brings up good memories, which is bad."

Cade stilled. In the four years since Heather had died, he'd tried everything except strapping Drake to a chair to get him to open up, to say anything about the grief so he could move past it. Avery seemed to pull words from him with ease as if they'd known each other a lifetime. Or maybe because they hadn't was exactly why Drake could talk to Avery.

"Where did you and Heather meet?"

Humor filled Drake's eyes. "In the sandbox. I was four. She was three."

Avery laughed in the lilting, silky way that wound around Cade's chest. "Robbing the cradle. Was it love at first sight?"

Drake shook his head and looked down, but his lips were curved in an uncommitted version of a smile. "No, that came later." He sucked a shallow breath and eyed the dance floor.

Cade followed his gaze. The others were making their way back to the table. A ballad was still playing, but Cade remained seated. He'd get her to dance with him at the next set.

A wicked gleam lit Zoe's eyes when they sat down.

Brent narrowed his eyes at her. "What's that look about?"

Zoe shrugged. "Do you know how to do The Electric Slide, Avery?"

"Uh…yes. Who doesn't?"

Gabby threw her head back and laughed. "Good. Because Zoe just put in a request. We're getting you out of that chair."

Avery turned to Drake. "This goes both ways. I said I'd protect you if you came. Help a girl out."

Drake leaned his forearms on the table. "I have no defense against The Slide. Sorry."

The slow set ended and the opening to Zoe's request filled the room. Cheers went up as others made their way to the dance floor.

Brent gave Avery no warning. He stood, rounded the table, and wrapped an arm around her waist. "Let's go."

Avery shook her head.

Brent dragged her to her feet. Zoe and Gabby got in on the action, tugging on each hand until she had no choice but to follow. On the floor, she stood awkwardly for a beat as the others line danced around her until Brent hip-bumped her for encouragement.

The moment she gave in, Cade's heart drummed a hard, thumping beat against his chest, stealing his oxygen. Face flushed, she moved across the floor with fluid grace and a grin that encompassed the entire state. For once, she let go of those reservations she'd clung to and relaxed.

It was like watching a shell crack and fall away. A piece of her wall crumbling. He wondered if this was the real Avery, if she'd just buried her so deep she'd forgotten that part of her was there. If that were the case, the rare glimpse was enough to make him promise to move the moon to get this side fully exposed.

Because damn. He couldn't breathe. Couldn't take his eyes from her.

"Be careful, little brother. That looks like more than a good time on your face."

He blinked and forced his lungs to accept air. "So what if it is?" When Drake didn't respond, Cade dragged his gaze away from Avery to find a hard, determined set to his brother's jaw and something like murder in his eyes. "What?"

"She's a good person. I like her."

Cade was feeling a little homicidal himself. He reined it in and took a deep pull of oxygen to stop the pounding in his temples. "Maybe you should go out with her then."

Drake went rigid, eyes narrowed to slits.

What in the hell was wrong with him, to go after his brother like that? He knew that wasn't what Drake meant, and though Big Brother liked a lot of people, it had been too long since he'd remembered that fact.

"I'm sorry. That was uncalled for." Cade scratched his jaw and kicked his feet onto the chair beside him, crossing his ankles and his arms. "It's just..." Hell. Damned if he knew what the problem was, other than it involved a brunette about twenty feet away. "It's just her ex was a real asshole. As in, I'd leave nothing left of him if we ever crossed paths."

Drake's brows lifted. "And what? You're going to be the guy who proves not all men are assholes? You're going to be the one to make it all better?"

He scrubbed his hands over his face. "Maybe."

Except there was no maybe about it. From day one, all he'd done was kill himself with patience. Not rushing her. Waiting her out. Living for the moment when he dragged a laugh from her belly or got her eyes to lose focus from his touch. Wanting nothing more than to show her someone enjoyed her company, her self-depreciating wit, and her inane capability of caring for others, even those who'd hurt her deeply.

Christ. He'd been doing everything to get her to trust him, to fall into him. *Fall for him.* And he had a sinking suspicion he was getting way more out of his efforts than she was.

"I'll be damned."

He glared at Drake, at his quizzical brow and dropped jaw. "What?"

"You're into her. I mean, really into her."

No kidding. And to think he'd been happy Avery got his brother to talk again. "Where have you been? I told you that weeks ago. You know, if for once in my life you gave me a little credit—"

"Shut up." Drake shook his head as if unable to make heads or tails of the situation. "You're falling for her." When Cade opened his mouth, Drake lifted a finger. "I said shut up. You haven't rolled over and exposed your underbelly yet, but you're sure as shit halfway there. Puppy love."

"Have you lost your goddamn mind?" His heart started doing that jackhammer thing, and the edges of his vision grayed. That didn't mean his brother was right. Did it? "I never said love, never implied it. It's too soon. I like her, yeah, but—"

"Puppy love. The beginning stages before you fall so hard the rest of your life before her is a blur." Drake stood.

"Where are you going?"

"To see if my car's a pumpkin yet." The strangest smile twisted his mouth before he met Cade's eyes. "Godspeed. It's all downhill from here."

Cade opened his mouth, but Drake was already halfway to the door. He ground his jaw, unsure why he was so pissed. Or perhaps that was fear shoving around in his chest, causing a cold sweat to break out over his back.

He didn't know how long he sat there, fuming. Panicking. No, it was fuming. But when he looked up, the DJ had changed the set to a slow mix and his friends were back in their seats staring at him with a cross between curiosity and trepidation.

All but Avery, who was at the next table talking to the fire department. Ignoring him. Laughing. Tucking a stray piece of hair behind her ear. Laughing some more. Not noticing him at all. Laughing...

Flynn knocked on the table to get his attention. *"You okay?"*

"Define okay." Okay as in sunshine and rainbows? Was he still meandering through his life looking for the next good time? Was he still having fun and taking names?

Flynn's smile fell. *"Where's Drake? What's wrong?"*

Shit. He sighed. "He went home. Everything's fine. I'm fine." Or he would be as soon as he had Avery next to him again.

He shoved away from the table and walked over to where she was still talking to the firefighters. He used to like those guys.

Without giving her a chance to protest, he wrapped an arm around her waist, lifted her to the balls of her feet, and didn't deposit her again until they were in the middle of the dance floor. Then he put his arms around her and urged her closer, shifting into a slow glide. He breathed in her berry scent and closed his eyes.

Yes. That was much better.

Chapter 17

Avery burrowed deeper into Cade's embrace as they danced, absorbing his warmth and getting more than a little excited being against the solid wall of him. Her pulse tripped at the caveman way he'd dragged her onto the floor. Primal. Territorial.

Tilting her head back to look at him, she noted the tension around his eyes and mouth. "Something wrong?"

He looked down his nose at her. "Not anymore."

But there was something wrong before? "I was having a nice conversation with the fire department."

"I noticed."

Was he jealous? It was so absurd she almost laughed.

"Relax, Avery. I just wanted to dance with you. You spent most of the night talking to my brother, and we haven't had a second alone."

"I'm sorry. I was trying to make Drake more comfortable—"

"That's not what I meant." His chest expanded with an inhale. "He came tonight, which was a miracle in itself. Don't ever be sorry for whatever it is you do to get him to open up." Resting his forehead to hers, he sighed. "I just wanted to dance with you," he repeated.

"Well, I'm glad you almost asked me."

His grin turned her to mush. "Almost?"

"Actually, you didn't ask at all. You just kinda went all alpha."

"Alpha, huh?" He kissed the tip of her nose. "I'll show you how alpha I can be later."

God. Just...wow. Need and anticipation coursed through her veins. Her toes curled in her strappy shoes. "Promises, promises."

He growled and brought his lips to her ear, his breath hot. "I always keep my promises, sweetheart." His hands skimmed down her back and up again, making her shiver at his rough palms against her exposed skin.

Suddenly, everything was on fire. Thrumming, burning. The breath caught in her throat. Her pulse went crazy. Sliding her hands from his chest to his neck, the erratic beat of his heart pounded beneath her palm. The bulge behind his zipper pressed into her hip as they swayed.

He was just as turned on.

She had a suspicion every eye in the joint was on them. There had been gossip for weeks about the two of them, but they hadn't given the town anything to fuel the speculation. Until now. The way he held her, intimately close, and the way he was looking at her, all hunger, would leave no doubt.

"They're playing your song," he said, his voice all gravel.

Tilting her head, she focused on the music. "*Lady in Red* is my song?" She didn't know she had a song. Didn't know how to feel about him giving her one, either. That implied…more.

"You are wearing red, and last I checked, you are a lady." Humor blended with the heat in his eyes, turned the blue to a stormy gray. "And you're dancing with me. Facts are facts."

Shaking her head, she breathed a laugh. "Hard to argue with fact."

"I have more where that came from." He rested his cheek against hers. "Fact: You look so beautiful I can't breathe if I stare too long. Fact: I was jealous of a gay man because Brent spent more time on the dance floor with you tonight than me." He turned his head, rubbing his jaw along her cheek. "Fact: I want you so bad it hurts."

Her legs threatened to give out. She whimpered, hypersensitive to the press of his chest to her breasts, the throbbing between her legs, the moist heat of his breath, the light linen scent of him. Everything inside her went haywire.

"How long do we have to stay? Are you required to help clean up afterward?"

She blinked at his rapid topic change and stilled their motion. "No, the committee is coming back tomorrow. They gave me the rest of tonight off, since I set up and…"

He grabbed her hand and led her toward the back of the room, weaving through people at a clipped pace. In her heels, she struggled to keep up. He noticed and slowed his steps. A little.

Guiding her out of the ballroom and to the coat check, they waited side by side in silence for his Aunt Rosa to collect their things. He tapped his foot and thrummed his fingers on his thigh.

She focused on breathing so her face wouldn't connect with the floor from lack of oxygen. This was it. They were going back to his place. They were going to have sex. Was it odd she was more nervous now with Cade than she had been to lose her virginity to Richard?

With a knowing smirk, Rosa handed over Avery's purse and coat. Cade shrugged into his jacket and then held hers out for her to step into. Wasting no time, he nodded to his aunt, placed a hand low on Avery's back, and guided her to the door.

The cool breeze hit her face and she gulped air as they walked across the parking lot. They were at Cade's car, him holding the passenger door open before she realized where they were. If she left with him, he'd need to drive her back in the morning in order for her to pick up Hailey. Plus, if her car stayed in the lot overnight, everyone would know she'd gone home with him.

"Avery?"

Her gaze flicked to his. "My car's over there."

He stared at her a beat, a question in his open expression, hesitancy in his eyes. He opened his mouth as if to say something, but shut it again. Closing his eyes, he drew a slow breath, and her stomach twisted. He apparently interpreted her statement to mean she was turning him down.

"Can I follow you? So I have my car in the morning?" Or later tonight. Should she sleep over? Did he want her to go home once they were...done? She didn't know the rules.

His gaze leveled on her, the relief in his eyes contrasting the muscles working his jaw. He nodded and shut the door. "I live on a side street near Gabby's house."

"Okay. Just give me a minute and I'll follow."

On the short drive over, she checked her phone and was assured April hadn't called about Hailey. Relief filled her chest to mingle with nerves. She wove through town, passing the turn off for her cabins and made her way down Gabby's street. At the end of the road, she followed Cade onto a private drive that looped and curved through the dense woods. To the left was a modest two-story cabin, lights glowing from the interior to illuminate the pitch blackness.

Cade's car kept going another block until he turned onto a gravel driveway. She pulled in behind him and cut the engine, pausing for a moment to take in the house. Much like her rental, his home was a log cabin, but on a grander scale. Two stories and lots of windows. Pocketed between several pine, birch, and sequoia, it had a wraparound porch with bare wood rocking chairs.

When he opened his car door, she blew out a breath and did the same. He waited for her to come to him, muscles tense and jaw set. She didn't know if he was as anxious as her or if something else had him on edge, but neither did anything to calm the riot inside her head.

She glanced at the cabin. "I like your house."

He cleared his throat. "Thank you. I need to let the dogs out, but how about a tour after?"

She took the statement for what he'd intended—a way to distract her and make her more comfortable in the transition. It shocked her all over again how well he knew her, how well he understood her quirks and nuances. "Sure. I'd like that."

She followed him onto the porch and then stepped inside when he gestured for her to precede him. He'd left a few lamps on to guide her through a small foyer and into a wide open living room. Hardwood floors met a stone fireplace in the corner. Forest green leather couches made an L shape in the middle of the room, accompanied by bare wood accent tables. It was clean and tastefully decorated with forest prints on the walls and exposed beams.

"A man who knows how to decorate."

He laughed. "Gabby and Zoe helped with that. The layout design was mine, though. Dad owned all this property. He was going to build the clinic here, but chose town instead. We passed Mom's house on the way in. Drake and Flynn's houses are just down the road."

That was really nice they lived so close together. The location was ideal as well, tucked into the woods, but not far from town. Peaceful, serene, without total isolation.

"Make yourself comfortable. I'm just going to let the dogs out."

She glanced over the room, remembering he had picked up Seraph earlier, but the dogs weren't around.

"I have them in the mudroom out back."

She nodded. When he was gone, she walked around, finding a flat screen TV in a corner bureau and photos of his family on the mantle. She grinned at a picture of Cade and his brothers from when he was about seven years old, standing by a riverbed, arms around each other. A photo of Heather and Drake from their wedding was next to it beside a picture of Cade and an older gentleman. Their eyes were so similar she knew it must be his father. Drake got his dark hair, and Flynn his smile.

The clattering of toenails hitting hardwood sounded behind her and she turned just in time to catch Seraph mid-leap. Kneeling, she gave the puppy some love, showing equal attention to Freeman. They licked her face and she laughed, looking up at Cade in the entryway. She paused.

On his shoulder was a small gray kitten, nuzzling his neck. Cade seemed unaware of the adorable furball, his attention on her and a smile curving his lips. He blinked and must've noticed her distraction because his hand came up to pet the kitten.

"This is Cutin. She was a stray left out in the snow. The evening we met, actually. She was one of the reasons for my sour mood that night. Her siblings didn't make it."

Oh God. As if he wasn't sexy as heck enough, he had to stand there with his delicious body, stroking a kitten, and saying something like that. Swoon.

He shrugged. "She likes sitting on my shoulder for some reason. You want a tour?"

She wanted to rip his clothes off and lick him from head to toe, but she stood, somehow not passing out from the lightness in her head. "Yes."

They walked into a large kitchen off the living room, one she'd kill to have. About the only thing she missed about her time with Richard was their enormous kitchen. She'd loved sitting at the table early in the morning sipping coffee and watching the sunrise. When she'd gotten too lonely, she'd baked cookies or cooked a dinner he'd never seemed to make it home to eat. But the process had been the draw, the relaxation in the task.

Cade's design was much different, though. Black appliances, green marble countertops, and light oak cabinets. A patio door led to a deck next to a screened-in mudroom. An island had four stools tucked underneath, and off to the side, a nook held a table big enough to seat eight.

She imagined him and his brothers there sharing a beer. Or a gaggle of future kids fighting over the last drumstick while his wife laughed at something he said. Normal niceties, an everyday image. Things she'd never had because Richard had no interest in spending time with her and Hailey. A scene she'd never experience because she was done dreaming about such nonsense and had sworn off that kind of hurt again.

Still, her chest ached a little.

"Where did you go just now?" Cade stepped closer, running his fingers down one of her arms. "You look miles away."

She smiled and reached up to pet the kitten on his shoulder. "Nowhere. Just thinking." Cutin meowed and nuzzled her hand, making her smile widen. She was an adorable furball.

He nodded, looking like he didn't believe her, but he pointed toward the way they came. He gestured at a half bath near the base of the stairs and then started climbing.

She followed, her stomach flip-flopping with every step.

He led her to the right. "Bathroom." He stepped into a bedroom with a simple queen bed and dresser, depositing the cat. "Guest room. Though I never have guests, so I may need to rethink that." He scratched his jaw.

She laughed and trailed him past another bedroom.

"Room I don't know what to do with yet." He pivoted to the left, past the stairs, and into a tiny loft that held a computer desk and two bookshelves. "That's the master bedroom." He stopped outside a doorway and met her gaze, brows drawn together as if waiting for direction from her on what to do next. He cleared his throat. "My bedroom."

With more bravado than she felt, she walked into the room. Behind her, he let out a shallow breath that rasped between his teeth, and some of her uneasiness dissipated. If he was nervous, too, then she wasn't so alone.

His bedroom was amazing. Four poster mahogany bed in the middle of the room, with two matching dressers and two nightstands. The bedding was a slate gray pattern, complimenting the midnight blue walls. The colors might've made the space seem small if not for the patio doors letting in natural light and a window on the opposite wall. A porch had a grand view of the mountain base and forest.

She walked over to the sliding door and crossed her arms, taking in the moonlight hitting the trees and riverbed. A fog had rolled closer to the mountain base, thick and surreal as it hovered in the distance.

"This is really something, Cade."

He came up behind her, setting his hands on her shoulders and kissing her temple. "I don't hate the view." His voice was low and coarse, riddled with need. His hands drifted over her collarbone, heating her skin. "And I don't mean the view beyond the glass. I've pictured you here more times than I should admit."

When he dropped a kiss to her neck, his lips lingering, she closed her eyes and leaned into him, his warmth. He traced a slow sensual path from her neck to behind her ear, cupping her jaw with his hand. His arousal pressed into her backside. Her breasts grew heavy and a shiver tore through her.

But then the shiver morphed into trembling, and she couldn't seem to stop. Turning in his arms, she pressed her face to his neck, breathing in the now familiar scent of him and trying to draw calm through the desire. A mind of its own, her body didn't comply. The trembling became almost violent.

He ran his hands up and down her arms and kissed her cheek. "You're cold. I'll start a fire. Hang on a second."

He moved away from her, and it was all she could do to stay on her feet without his support. Tossing his suit coat on a chair, he loosened his tie, threw it aside, and rolled up his sleeves. He knelt in front of a small fireplace facing the foot of the bed and got to work building a fire, then he replaced the grate and disappeared into what she assumed was an adjoining bath to wash his hands.

She stood there like a nervous teenager, unsure of what to do. This was insane. She wanted him, wanted this, and she couldn't get her body to stop shaking. Her teeth gnashed, chin quivering. She fisted her hands, but that didn't cease the quaking, either.

He came back and stood in front of her, tenderness in his eyes, and reached up to hold her face. "It'll warm up in a minute."

Finding her voice, she blurted the first thing that came to mind. "I'm not cold."

He froze halfway to her mouth, hovering inches from her lips. Tension coiled in the space between them, and still, the trembling wouldn't stop. His eyes slammed closed as a muscle worked his jaw. He stayed that way, suspended, as he obviously tried to work something out. A myriad of thoughts must've swirled in his head because his face twisted with too many expressions for her to catch up.

Slowly, he straightened and opened his eyes, gaze blank and pinned to the glass behind her. She didn't know what conclusion he'd reached, but instinct said it wasn't in alignment with what she was thinking. Her stomach twisted into knots when he dropped his hands and backed away.

In her confusion, he moved to the dresser and pulled out a T-shirt, tossing it on the bed. After staring at it for a second, his chin dropped. "The bathroom's through there. You can wear the shirt to bed. Just…"

He sighed and finally met her gaze, patience and desire and guilt mirrored in his eyes. "Just please stay. We'll sleep. I'll hold you, nothing more."

And then she caught on. It took her a while, but she got it. Got him. Followed the dots to his conclusion. If she didn't set him straight, if she didn't make the move, they were never going to discover how explosive they could be together. He had too much honor to push, and she had little experience to guide her. But darn it, this was not how tonight was supposed to go.

His gaze never left hers. "Avery?" Barely whispered, her name was part question, part plea.

Forcing herself to move, she went to the bed and picked up the T-shirt, then walked to stand in front of him. His eyes tracked her movements, but he didn't seem to do so much as breathe. She passed him the shirt. He took it automatically, fisting it in his hands.

"I'm not cold and I'm not scared. Being with you doesn't frighten me, Cade." He seemed to need that reassurance, so she drove the point home. "I'm not scared. I'm nervous. That's all. Just…nervous. I don't have the experience you do, and it's been a long time—"

"Avery, sweetheart." He dropped the shirt on the floor and hauled her against him, wrapping his arms behind her back. "Don't you get it?"

No, she didn't. But it didn't matter because he crashed his mouth to hers.

Chapter 18

Cade hauled Avery to him and crushed his mouth to hers. Heart pounding, he ran his hands up the smooth skin of her back exposed by the dress and cupped her neck, holding her to him.

I'm not scared. I'm nervous.

That had been all he'd needed to hear. For a gut-dropping moment, he'd thought she'd put a stop to things. Thought she didn't want what he assumed was an inevitable progression. Didn't want him. He'd never forced himself on a woman, never would, and if he'd had any inkling she wasn't telling the truth, he would've been out the door and in his guest room.

Which reminded him how he was breaking his rules with Avery. With his previous lovers, if they hadn't done the deed at their place, they'd rarely made it past his living room. On the off chance that happened—and he could count on one hand the number of times that had occurred—they'd wound up in his guest room. Never his bedroom.

Avery was the first. He didn't know why, knew he shouldn't analyze it, but there it was. She was in his bedroom where he'd envisioned her too many times to recant.

Angling his head, he took the kiss deeper, gliding his hands into her hair and pulling the pins from her knot to release the silky brown strands. They fell around her shoulders, skimming her upper back, and he caught the unmistakable scent of her shampoo.

Need surged, but he kept his pace methodical, and he sensed the moment she let go. When she pressed her body to his, her trembling ceased, the muscles relaxing under his palms.

Never taking his lips from hers, he unbuttoned his shirt and took her hands in his, encouraging her to strip it off, wanting her to have as much control as possible. It was a power play, him undressing first to give her a modicum of reassurance. He could only hope it worked.

She hesitated a moment, but slid the material from his shoulders, down his arms, where it pooled at their feet. Guiding her hands to his chest, he pressed his palms over her fingers and nudged them down. Her thumbs brushed his nipples and he tore his mouth away to suck in a breath.

Her heavy lids lifted to stare at their joined hands, lips parting with a ragged inhale. On her own, her fingers descended past his pecs, down his abs to the button of his fly. Her knuckles brushed the skin below his naval, ripping a groan from his chest. There was something insanely arousing about her touching him with his hands covering hers. An intimacy, a joining.

That seemed to be all the encouragement she needed. Though her fingers trembled slightly, she unbuttoned his pants and eased his zipper down, her knuckles dragging along the underside of his straining erection.

He clenched his jaw to hold himself in check. Tonight was about her, not the end game, but restraint was nearing impossible with the scent of her in his orbit, with her touching him.

She tugged his pants down to his thighs, briefs along for the ride, and pressed a kiss to his chest. Emotion pinched behind his ribs, tenderness pulling at him from every direction. He kicked the clothing aside and wove his fingers through her hair. The satin from her dress caressed his shaft, silky, soft, and he pulsed against her.

Keeping one hand in her hair, he wrapped his other arm around her waist and stepped backward until the mattress hit his knees. He yanked the comforter and sheets aside, gripped her thighs, and lifted her until she straddled him. Holding her, he leaned against the headboard, sitting her in his lap.

The position hiked her dress past her thighs, and her gaze met his with a mix of desire and question. With both hands, he traced a path from her knees to her ankles, stopping at the straps of her shoes. He unbuckled the clasps, keeping his gaze locked to hers, and removed her shoes. Another time, he'd ask her to keep them on while he made love to her because those heels invoked more than one fantasy.

He leaned forward to unfasten her dress and remembered the back was exposed. "Where's the zipper?"

She smiled, warming her brown eyes and igniting the golden flecks. "On the side."

But before he could do the task himself, she brought her arm across her chest and slid the zipper down. The release of metal teeth mingled with their rapid breaths.

Cupping her elbows, he looked into her eyes. "I've wanted to get you out of this dress since I first saw you in it."

Her throat worked a swallow, but her gaze stayed on his, right there with him.

Sliding his hands up her arms, he slipped his fingers under the straps and slowly brought them down her slender shoulders. His gaze broke away to watch his movement, wanting to see how he exposed her inch by inch.

The dress bunched around her waist, baring her perfect breasts to him. She made an involuntary move to cover them, but he gripped her hands and kissed the inside of her wrists, meeting her gaze. "Beautiful, Avery. Never hide."

He leaned forward and took one rose-tinted nipple into his mouth, and groaned at her immediate response. She fisted her hands in his hair, holding him to her and arching her back, thrusting herself into his mouth. He swirled his tongue around the pebbled bud, his erection pulsing when she raked her nails over his scalp.

That. Damn, he loved that. He went from hard to holy shit in one second flat.

He moved to the other breast to give it equal attention and figured if he died right now, he'd go out a happy man. She tasted as sweet as she smelled, was as soft as the dress fisted in his hands.

Trailing kisses over her collarbone, he worked his way to her neck and licked the erratic pulse beating just for him. Her head fell back with a moan, and he grinned against her throat, inching her dress past her hips, up her body, and over her head.

Oh, hell. Black lace panties. He'd almost be sorry to see those go.

Her gaze met his, desperate, nervous, and her need slammed into him with the force of a wrecking ball. She liked things orderly, done in her own way, and at whatever speed she saw fit. Except when they were together. Like this, she was silently pleading for him to take over.

And that worked just fine. He'd give her anything she wanted, would enjoy it, and at the edges of his conscience, he feared that went beyond the bedroom, too.

Didn't matter. He cupped the back of her head and flipped her beneath him. Her chestnut brown waves spread over his pillow, the sight making his chest ache. To relieve the pinch, he kissed her, softly at first until her hands tangled in his hair again and he saw stars.

Slow down, O'Grady. She'd gone too long without a man. Taking her would be the equivalent of sinking into a virgin. God, he never wanted to cause her pain. He'd prepare her, get her ready so he wouldn't hurt her. If he could just get his damn body to read his head's memo, things would work out.

He kissed his way lower. Halfway down her soft, warm body, she called his name and he growled.

"Yes." *Me, not that asshole. Me.*

Dipping his tongue in her naval, he tugged her panties down her legs and tossed them over his shoulder. The breath stopped in his chest at finding her bare, just a small triangle of dark curls. So hot, so wet. Gently, he spread her legs and met resistance. She tensed under him and made a sound of protest.

He looked up and caught her wide gaze, hating the fucking apprehension he found in her eyes and the prick who'd put it there. He stilled, showing her he wouldn't do anything she didn't want him to, and gradually the hesitancy moved out. She bit her lip, clearly still uncertain, and he realized she may not have done this before. That perhaps in her entire short life, no one had thought to meet her needs.

Jesus.

He pressed his cheek to her inner thigh, biting back a sigh. "Trust me." Watching her carefully, he turned his head and kissed the spot where his cheek had just been. "Trust me."

Another moment passed before she nodded.

"Watch me, Avery." *See me, not him.*

Keeping his gaze locked with hers, he spread her legs and dipped his head, lightly kissing her mound, then her core. She didn't move, but some of the tension uncoiled from the muscles under his hands. He licked a path from her opening to her clit and a gale force wind expelled from her lips.

Her head flew back, her body bowing, breaking the spell. She was his again, in the room with him and not the uncertainty from before.

Cupping her bottom, he teased her clit with his tongue, working a fevered mewl from her throat before slipping a finger into her heat. Christ, she was tight. Her muscles clamped around him, urging more, so he inserted another finger and lightly bit her clit.

She cried out, her voice hoarse. Fisting the sheets at her hips, she chanted his name and, he swore to God, there was no sweeter sound on earth.

Blood roared through his veins. His pulse pounded in his neck. His vision grayed until he forced himself to blink in order to watch her, not willing to miss this for anything.

A few more strokes of his tongue, thrusts with his fingers, and she was there. Her mouth opened in a silent cry, brows drawn together in bliss.

She stilled around him a heartbeat before her body quaked. Her pale skin flushed, rosy nipples peaked, breasts rising and falling as she gulped air.

He eased her down slowly, fighting the need to string her orgasm out, have her crash a second time just so he could watch. But he was too hard, too close to the edge himself.

Next time. Next time, he'd expend more effort giving pleasure to them both. He needed her too much at the moment.

With her eyes closed, breaths rasping, he crawled up her body and reached into his nightstand for a condom. He rolled the sheath down his length, taking a second to stroke the ache before cupping her jaw.

He rubbed his thumb over her lower lip, swollen from his kiss and her biting. "Open your eyes, sweetheart."

* * * *

At his quiet command, Avery opened her eyes to his storm-tossed blue gaze looking intently down at her. Her body was still trembling in the aftershocks, the apex of her thighs pulsing.

No one had ever gone down on her before. Richard had been her only lover, and he didn't like oral. Once, he'd told her men didn't like the act. It was just something they did out of necessity.

But Cade hadn't made it seem like a hardship. He'd acted as if he'd wanted to, as if it pleasured him as much as it did her. And oh, pleasure her he had. Whatever nervousness she'd been feeling was gone, replaced with need and satisfaction. She stretched her languid muscles.

Cade shifted over her, settling his welcome weight between her thighs and crushing her breasts with his chest. The light dusting of his blond hair rubbed against her aching nipples, sending tingles through her, lighting her need anew.

"There you are," he whispered as if she'd gone somewhere else. As if that was even possible.

"Never left." She smiled and brushed her fingertips over the shadow on his jaw.

He swallowed, eyes darkening. A tiny wrinkle formed between his brows like he was trying to figure something out, but his features smoothed before she could question it.

Without taking his gaze from hers, he aligned his hips and reached between them to guide himself to her opening. His tip pushed against her, into her, and he stilled, staying just past the precipice of entering, waiting for permission.

Since she'd been dying to explore him, she ran her hands over the knotted muscles of his shoulders, down his sculpted biceps. His lids lowered as if liking what she was doing. Directing her perusal to his pecs, she grazed his nipples with her thumbs, earning a sharp exhale from him before moving her hands lower, reveling in each indentation of his defined abs.

Wow, his body was really gorgeous. Corded and beautiful without the bodybuilder bulge. A delicious combination of hard and soft. She skimmed her fingers up his sides, around his back, and leaned in to kiss his throat.

He'd held still in her exploration, strain shadowing his face, and she had a suspicion he was nearing a breaking point. Wanting him inside her, she wrapped her legs around his waist, nudging him a little deeper.

He inhaled, hard, and closed his eyes, brows twisted as if in a painful-pleasure state of his own paradise. "Avery." He kissed her forehead, her lips.

Easing his hips forward, he pushed deeper, going so slow she could feel every ridge of him against her sensitive walls. He was thick and long, yet not too big for her to accept. Because it had been a while, the stretch was a noticeable pressure, but there was no pain.

When she was full, so full, he stopped, completely rooted. She let out the breath she hadn't realized she'd been holding and wrapped her arms around his back, loving the shift of hard muscle under his skin.

He sighed against her lips, breath hot, body straining as he held himself motionless over her. "God, Avery. I can't..."

She hadn't been expecting tenderness, for desire to blend with sweet. The punch of her heart inside her chest was jarring. Her throat tightened, and she knew she'd underestimated this moment in her mind. There could be no casual with Cade, no simple act of fun and moving on. Somehow, she'd gotten invested. Not so deep she couldn't claw her way back out, but the cavern was there, calling from the depths.

He dropped his head and pressed his face into her neck. "I can't..." he said again, but she knew. She understood.

"Then don't wait."

As if that was all the permission he needed, he pulled out and thrust back inside, still so gentle, so careful. Remembering he liked her hands in his hair, she skimmed her fingers up his back and into his hair, fisting the strands.

He let out a low, guttural groan that rattled his chest. His breathing quickened, panting against her neck. Grabbing her thigh, he brought it higher on his hip, shifting the angle of his thrusts to go deeper, hitting her in a spot that made her eyes roll back in her skull. His other arm skated under her, lifting her hips.

He moved in earnest, their skin gliding against one another, their heartbeats pounding in unison. Her body hummed as she met him with every plunge. He held her tight, as if separating, as if allowing so much as air between them, would break the spell. They moved as a unit, as if they'd done this dance before, both new and old sensations taking hold.

They fit. Just...fit.

A sharp tingle low in her spine was the only warning an orgasm loomed. The shock of it, the sheer improbability, nearly had her losing focus. She never came during sex. Never. She grasped at the thin tether, holding on. Fighting.

"Let go, sweetheart." He lifted his head, bringing his mouth to hers and crushing her in a kiss of pure annihilation. His tongue stroked, matching the thrusting of his hips. "Let go," he said again, this time spoken through a groan as he dropped his forehead to hers. "Come with me."

Not *for me*, but *with me*. Together. He wanted them to fall together.

Even that one simple thing, a statement he probably didn't even realize the meaning for, demonstrated how different he was from anything she'd ever known. It wasn't about him or her, but them. He was selfless and giving. There was no defense against him.

"Avery, sweetheart." His tight, barely controlled voice filled her head.

And the fight fled, becoming irrelevant as sensations took hold. The tight ball of need exploded. She shook in his arms. Grabbed his shoulders. Arched. Found oblivion.

Died? Maybe. She couldn't tell.

A primal noise, part scream, all male, emitted from his lips as he grew rigid. He pumped twice more and stilled, pulsing inside her as he released.

Before the effect wore off, before he was even finished, his handsome face twisted in wonder and determination in the tailspin of his orgasm. His blue gaze collided with hers. Accusing, accepting. There and gone in a flash.

He collapsed onto her and she held him as their breathing soughed, both of them fighting for air. After a moment, when they'd caught their wind, he raised onto his forearms and pressed his face between her breasts as if unable to look at her.

He stayed that way so long worry fluttered in her belly. "Cade?"

Head down, he pulled out and rose from the bed, never meeting her gaze. "I'll be right back."

Then he went into the adjoining bathroom and shut the door.

Chapter 19

Cade tossed the condom in the bathroom trash and ran the faucet. Cold. Splashing water on his face, he looked at his reflection in the mirror, gritted his teeth, and threw more water on his cheeks.

He gripped the counter and leaned into his hands, forcing his lungs to take air before the black edging his vision had a chance to consume.

Damn Drake and his cryptic shit. Spouting nonsense about puppy love and...well, crap. That's what this was. A panic attack brought on by his brother. The frantic, erratic beat of his heart and the vise around his throat had nothing to do with Avery and the fantastic, mind-blowing, holy shit sex they'd just had.

Sex that didn't feel like sex at all. Thus his panic. Brought on by his brother. Or not.

It had never been like that before. Sex was a physical, extremely enjoyable act. But that's all it was. Physical. There had never been any kind of emotional element. Never. He enjoyed sex, enjoyed women. He could sense their needs and desires and be anything they needed him to be, in any position, at any random time. He got his jollies and moved on.

Except what had just gone down in there was no act. Her needs before his own was paramount, making her comfortable with him a given. But afterward, when she'd relented to her hunger, he'd...relented something else. Like a chunk of himself. He didn't think, didn't need to. He'd just... felt. And lost himself. In her.

He blew out a long, unsteady breath. Okay, he'd known Avery was different. Check. He'd gotten to know her better than other lovers before hopping into bed. Check. There'd been an insane amount of buildup and foreplay in the previous weeks. Check. He'd had to work damn hard to get her to trust him and herself before ever getting to this stage. Check.

Those things were rational. Explainable.

He was fine. Perfectly fine.

Yeah, he so wasn't. But he couldn't stay in his damn bathroom all night figuring it out and losing his shit in the process.

Straightening, he splashed another stream of cold water on his face, toweled off, and avoided his reflection on his way to the door.

When he emerged, Avery was on her knees on the floor, the bed sheet wrapped around her middle and her sweet round ass in the air as she looked under his bed.

He stopped and eyed her, not liking the tension building in his gut. But hell, she was such a sight if he ever saw one. Her hair was a tangled, wavy mess around her head, her cheeks were crimson, and her lips still swollen from his kiss. Her perfect breasts were playing peek-a-boo with the sheet and she looked adorable crawling around.

Speaking of…"What are you doing?"

She jerked up and blew a wayward strand of hair out of her face. "I can't find my panties." Her hold on the sheet tightened. "Or my other shoe. My extra set of clothes are in the car, and I can't go get them like this."

Because he had the violent urge to grip her by the shoulders and give her a firm shake, he leaned against the doorjamb and crossed his arms. "Why do you need your extra clothes?"

Oh, he knew. He wasn't an idiot, contrary to what his brothers seemed to think. But he'd be damned if he'd make this easy on her. He'd eaten the distance, had met her more than halfway, and she was still waiting for the other shoe to drop. Metaphorically speaking.

"To go home," she said slowly as if talking to a small child. "I guess I could just put the dress back on," she mumbled to herself.

Even that was adorable, which pissed him off to the point of no return. "I said I'd be right back. What happened in the two minutes I was in the bathroom to make you bolt?"

She sat on her haunches, confusion in her eyes, frustration wrinkling her brow. "Fifteen minutes. You were in there fifteen minutes. I may not have your experience, but I can take a hint."

"I wasn't issuing any hints. I was…" Freaking out. He sighed.

"Flipping out," she said, reading his mind. She went back to crawling around the floor. "Look, I get it. No hard feelings."

"No hard…" He pinched the bridge of his nose. "You were in that bed, too. You were into it." *Into me.*

It was as if she hadn't heard him. Her head ducked under the bed. "I warned you I wouldn't be any good. A husband doesn't cheat unless..." She emerged with her shoe. "There it is."

He remained where he was because if he moved he just might go postal. How many damn times did her ex need to whittle his way between them? "Now who's freaking out?"

"Cade." She sighed a weary moan and rested her head on the mattress, still on her knees. "I'm sorry it sucked."

"Were you even in the same room?" Yeah. Zero to postal. "Whatever has you hunting for your clothes has nothing to do with you sucking and everything to do with the crap he put in your head. And you didn't. Suck, I mean."

There were many, many adjectives to attribute to what they'd done together, but suck wasn't even in the vicinity. In fact, he was pretty sure Webster hadn't invented nearly half the words coming to mind.

"Then why did you hide in the bathroom?"

"I wasn't hiding." Much.

Her brows hit her hairline, sardonic disbelief twisting her mouth.

She shook her head and grabbed her panties off the bed. With some kind of crazy female maneuver, she managed to step into them while maintaining a hold on the bed sheet. As if he hadn't just seen her naked, hadn't kissed every inch of her sweet, soft skin.

Panic shoved at his chest. He crossed the room, tore the sheet out of her grasp, lifted her in his arms, and dropped her on the bed. Before she stopped bouncing, he crawled in after her and covered them with the blanket.

She turned on her side to face him, but blessedly made no attempt to leave.

He took in her mortified expression, the one she was obviously trying so damn hard to keep neutral, and struggled to find the right words. She could get him so rattled at the drop of a hat, he wound up eating crow more times than not.

He tucked a piece of hair behind her ear, letting his fingers linger by her jaw. "It takes two people to have sex. If one of them isn't into it, isn't open to the experience or isn't willing to give as much pleasure as they're getting, then it will suck. You were right here with me, Avery. *We* didn't suck." He swallowed hard. "And when a man cheats on a woman, that's *his* insecurity showing."

She wedged her hand under her cheek and stared at him. Her gaze softened, slipping back into the tender woman who he'd begun the night with and not the insecure person her ex had made of her. He was almost certain she didn't believe that dick's crap anymore, if she ever had. She was too strong in that regard. Yet he suspected no one had done anything to build up her confidence, either. The balance was askew.

Her teeth sank into her lower lip and released. "What happened in the bathroom?"

"I threw out the condom and splashed cold water on my face." Went a little batshit and had an internal pep talk. He closed his eyes for a moment. She'd been nothing but honest with him and deserved to know the lack of post-coital glow wasn't on her.

He traced his thumb across her lip. "I care about you. Sex has never been particularly emotional for me. I just needed a minute to get my head together. That's all." And if he could do it over differently, he would, if for no other reason than it made him sick he was another person to put doubt in her mind.

"This was just supposed to be fun." Concern showed in her eyes, but behind that he could've sworn there was hope.

He settled on humor as he didn't think either of them were ready for anything heavier. "I don't know about you, but I'm having fun."

A lazy smile curved her mouth. She brought her hand up to push away a strand of hair from his forehead, the move more maternal than sexual. "Me, too."

He shifted his pillow a little closer to hers so that they were sharing air. "Your marriage wasn't all bad, was it?" Irritation and something he couldn't name battled in his gut. Empathy maybe. He didn't know. But the idea of her spending ten years with a man who didn't care enough about her to hold on to a good thing didn't sit well.

Her smile fell a fraction. "No, there were a lot of good things. We weren't big into anniversaries or Christmas presents, but he always remembered my birthday. We met on campus on my birthday, and he would send a bouquet of flowers to the house every year."

Flowers weren't a gift. They were an accessory. And what kind of man wouldn't want to celebrate the day he got married?

He kept his thoughts to himself, though, as her expression drifted into memory. The moonlight streamed through the window at her back, casting her face mostly in shadow, but her scent mingled with his and settled his mood.

Her gaze flickered to his. "Richard was under a lot of pressure from his family even when we met. Rich relatives, big law firm. On paper, we fit. My mom was pretty flighty growing up. She loved me, does love me, but she's a dreamer. I saw in Richard the stability I'd been missing. At first, the friendship was enough to make up for the lack of chemistry. By the time we got married, it was like it was too late to back out. In time, his family changed him, made him cynical."

She sighed. "I know Richard cheating wasn't my fault. But in a way, I can't blame him, either. Neither of us got to experience being young or carefree." Her gaze took in his face like she was comparing again. "I guess I resorted back into the mind frame when you didn't say anything, when you...collected yourself in the bathroom."

What she said gave Cade a clearer understanding of the dynamics, but it didn't change his view an iota. The guy still didn't appreciate or recognize a good thing when he had it. The prick's loss, Cade's gain.

She'd never once used the term "love" when it came to her ex, and by her explanation of the marriage, love had never come into play. For either side. He thought about his own romantic encounters. Love had never blindsided him, but he wasn't immune. No one was.

Drake's words floated back to him, and he had to question whether his brother was right. His feelings for Avery, or the fact he had any at all, were unlike anything he'd come in contact with before. And what did it matter? Weeks ago, she'd told him she'd never lose herself in a relationship again.

He almost laughed. Denial aside, they were very much in a relationship.

Wrapping his arm around her waist, he tugged her closer, crushing her to his chest. He slid her panties down her legs and threw them over her shoulder. Then he settled on his back and drew her to his side, encouraging her to rest her cheek in the crook of his shoulder.

"Are you going to sleep?" Her warm breath fanned his skin.

With his eyes closed, he smiled. "Yep."

"Why did you take my panties off?"

His grin widened against her temple. "I'll demonstrate in a couple of hours after we recuperate."

She paused. He could all but hear the wheels turning in her head. Finally, she draped an arm over his chest and yawned. "Promises, promises."

He laughed and kissed her hair. "Oh, sweetheart. Challenge accepted."

When Cade next opened his eyes, a muted dawn was peeking through the window, and he was spooning a warm, soft female. Avery had his hand tucked into hers, clasped against her breasts, her breathing deep and even. His thigh was wedged between her legs, his happiness to see her poking into her backside.

Taking stock of the situation, he decided this sleeping with a woman thing wasn't half bad. The actual sleeping. Waking up to her scent and supple warmth could be quite addicting. Honestly, everything about Avery was an addiction.

She was all curves and no edges. He liked that, liked she wasn't a thin rail with nothing to hold on to. Both her body and her heart were giving, pliant—a direct contrast to a lot of women he'd been with. She wasn't perfection, he wouldn't want that, but even her flaws were cute, making her...perfect *for him*. Hell.

He bent his head and kissed the curve of her shoulder where tiny freckles sprinkled her pale skin. In the darkness last night, he hadn't been able to take all of her in. This morning, he'd make up for that. Burying his face in her hair, he inhaled, unable to resist. She smelled so damn good.

She began to stir, arching her back and emitting the sexiest little moan. Her long, dark lashes fluttered open and she turned her head, offering a sleepy smile. "Morning. What time is it?"

"Early." He looked over his shoulder at the alarm clock. "Not quite six." He pressed his face into her neck and licked her pulse, smiling when it kicked harder with his attention. "I believe I promised you something last night. Remind me what that was again."

She brought her arm up and behind her to sink her fingers in his hair. "I think it had something to do with missing panties."

His dick jumped. He swore to all that was holy, if she never took her fingers from his hair, he'd be a contented man. "It's coming back to me now."

He cupped her breast, settling the small weight in his hand and brushing his thumb over the nipple. She inhaled sharply, pressing her bottom in much closer proximity to his straining erection. Her nails raked his scalp.

That was the other thing. She was so responsive. Whether it was his pathetic attempt at humor, the endless array of questions he asked, or her body to his touch. Didn't matter the scenario, she responded. He thrust against her, earning another moan. Like that. Action, reaction.

Sexy. As. Hell.

Before he completely lost his mind, he reached behind him into the nightstand and pulled out a condom, ripping it open with his teeth. Once protection was in place, he pressed his hand to her belly, reveling in the quiver beneath his palm.

He licked the shell of her ear. "Place your hand over mine."

She did as he asked without issue, threading her fingers through his. He brought their joined hands lower, over her mound and between her folds. He groaned at how wet she was for him. Her head fell back as he spread her and dipped a finger inside. The motion was even more intimate with both their hands entwined as if they were stoking her pleasure together. He used his thumb to circle her clit and she bucked into his hand, emitting the hottest mewl from her throat.

Last night, she hadn't made much noise. Aside from a gasp or moan, she came quietly. He wondered if that was restraint on her part or just her sexual makeup. "You like that?"

"Yes," she breathed, writhing under his hand.

She was more than ready for him, and he was throbbing. Withdrawing his hand from her heat, he aligned himself and, from behind, slowly sank into her. He slammed his eyes shut and waited a beat for her to adjust. And damn, she was so tight in this position breathing was impossible.

When he could hold out no longer, he grabbed her thigh to lift it for a better angle and thrust. She cried out and buried her face in the pillow as if to smother the sound. He secured her leg in position with his own and cupped her cheek, finding it crimson. With embarrassment or desire, he wasn't sure.

"Don't hide from me. And be as loud as you want. We're alone." He didn't give her time to react. He thrust again, her inner walls like a glove milking his shaft. So hot, so tight. Perfection.

Her head whipped back, exposing her throat. "I don't... I'm not usually noisy. I'm sorry."

"Why the hell would you apologize for that? Let me hear you, sweetheart."

All she'd managed to do with her broken admission was prove she'd never been made love to properly. He was more than game for making it up to her. Repeatedly. He quickened his hips, pumping harder.

Brushing her hair aside, he latched his mouth onto her neck and nipped. Thrusting furiously, he licked the sting away.

A strangled moan tore from her again, and he knew she was close. He wouldn't hold out much longer, either. Sliding his hand between her legs, he circled her clit, working her into a fever.

She pressed back into him, tensing against his chest, her mouth open in a silent scream. Her hand fisted the sheet as her walls clenched him so tight he came undone. A tingle tracked from his lower back straight to his balls as she quaked in his arms.

He dropped his forehead to her neck, releasing hard and fast, until every last ounce of him had been wrenched dry.

He held her through the last of her aftershocks, depleted but determined to do better this morning than he had last night. The onslaught of foreign emotion was no different in the light of day. His chest cracked wide open and his throat seized. A painful, gratifying ache ripped through his gut and welled behind his lids, but he forced himself to breathe through it and figure out the cause later.

When she went limp, he pulled out and dropped the condom in the bedside trash before rolling over and dragging her on top of him. Their arms and limbs tangled. Her hair spread over his chest, her breath warm and uneven on his skin where she rested her cheek. He wrapped his arms around her back, slipping one hand into her hair to hold her to him.

Hell. Better than any blanket.

Chapter 20

Avery finger-combed her hair into what she hoped was submission, a little embarrassed she'd fallen back asleep. Especially since she woke up to find the bed beside her empty.

After she used the bathroom, she shrugged into the T-shirt Cade had offered last night and followed the scent of bacon and coffee downstairs. She stopped short in the kitchen doorway at the sight of him in a loose pair of sweat pants low on his hips and nothing else. His back to her, he was frying bacon in a skillet at the stove. The shifting muscles in his back was a thing of beauty. His blond hair stood at odd angles, total bed head and rocking it. And him barefoot? In the kitchen?

Crap on a cracker.

The dogs were sitting by his feet, tails wagging in a silent plea for food. Cade was having a conversation with them that entailed him saying "bacon" and the dogs tilting their heads, butts squirming in answer. The kitten was perched on his shoulder.

God. Clenching her thighs, she watched him another moment before the need for caffeine became astronomically pivotal.

He turned and grinned, his gaze sweeping down the length of her. His smile went from affectionate to predatory. Absently, he took Cutin from her perch and set her carefully on the floor, gaze trained on Avery. "I like the look of you first thing in the morning."

Really? She ran a hand through her hair. "Animal Kingdom? I can see the appeal."

He laughed. Moving away from the stove, he walked over and set his hands on her waist, lifting her onto the island as if she weighed nothing. "I'm instilling a new rule. If you're not naked, you can only wear my shirt."

She smiled as he stepped between her legs and wrapped his arms around her. "That will go over real well at the clinic."

Pressing a kiss to her neck, he groaned. "That reminds me of another fantasy." He licked her pulse and moved to the other side, nipping his way to her ear.

God, he was good at the nuzzling. Her nerves were on fire. Need zinged from where his mouth worked her over to straight between her thighs. No passing Go.

"What would it take to get you to call me Dr. Cade outside of work? Not all the time, mind you. Just once in a while. Something like, 'Oh, Dr. Cade, right there! Yes, that's so good.'"

Wrapping her arms around his neck, she laughed until her cheeks hurt. "Can I wear the white lab coat?"

He groaned again, a deep rumble. "Hell yes."

"I say the odds are good then."

"Definitely will remember that." He leaned back and kissed her forehead before stepping away. "Do you like bacon?" Back at the stove, he transferred the pieces to a plate to drain.

She reeled, the loss of his heat and arms a sudden vacancy. "Are there people in existence who don't?"

He laughed. "None I'd want to know."

"Agreed." Her gaze drifted out the patio doors, where a thick fog blanketed the damp grass. The sun was trying to unsuccessfully break through the cloud cover. At least a lot of the snow had melted with the milder temperatures the past few days, but spring was a ways off yet.

He poured a cup of coffee and brought it over to her, holding it out of reach. "Kiss and then coffee."

Blackmail of the lowest form. Not that she minded.

He grazed her lips with his, gently at first, but it quickly gained momentum. Increasing the pressure, he opened and stroked her tongue, lazy, seductive. She melted and wrapped her legs around his waist.

"Nimble minx." He took her coffee to the table, picked her up again, and deposited her in a chair. "We'll finish that thought after breakfast. Some brunette drained all my energy last night. And this morning. I need sustenance."

"Complain, complain."

He leaned close, brushed her nose with his, and busted out his panty-melting grin. "Oh, sweetheart. Not even in the slightest."

When his back was turned, she smiled at the easiness in being with him. Good conversation, humor, explosive in bed. He was good with Hailey and animals, cared about his family, and his attention to detail was staggering.

If she wasn't careful, she might break her rule of never getting involved again. She'd instilled it for a reason, good reasons, but Cade was slowly, increment by increment, wearing those rationales down to dust. Unsure what to think, or even if she should overanalyze what was intended to be simple, she sipped her coffee.

He brought the plate of bacon and a bowl of scrambled eggs to the table before digging into the fridge and removing a container of melon.

Her gaze locked on the drawings tacked to the fridge she hadn't noticed before. Hailey's drawings. The ones from her app he'd printed for Avery's fridge, too.

God. He...crap. He'd put her daughter's pictures on his own fridge. She swallowed hard, torn between the urge to wrap her arms around him and the need to distance herself from the emotions swirling.

Setting down two forks and plates, he took his seat next to her.

She shook her head to clear it.

Richard had never cooked for her, even something as simple as scrambled eggs. They'd never made love in the morning or enjoyed breakfast while half dressed. Looking back on the past decade with an eagle eye, she realized it had been more a marriage of convenience than one of mutual love.

She hadn't been with Cade long, and she wasn't sure she could even deem what they were doing as dating, but the differences kept hitting her like a blow. Hard. His compassion to Richard's indifference. Cade's humor to Richard's sarcasm. Cade's attention and affection to Richard's disregard.

Was this what it was like to matter to someone? Was her time with Cade and how they spent it normal? She swallowed with difficulty, wondering if she'd even recognize a regular relationship if it smacked her in the forehead.

He loaded eggs on her plate, looked up at her, and did a double take. "Avery?"

The concern in his blue eyes forced her to smile and shake her head. "I thought you only cooked microwave popcorn or mac and cheese." She dug in, even though her appetite waned.

Motionless for a moment, his gaze roamed her face as if trying to spot the lie. "I have other basic culinary skills." He dished eggs and melon onto his plate, closed his eyes, and sighed. His brows creased in frustration before he lifted his lids to pin her with a wary look bordering on helplessness. "One of these days, you'll be comfortable enough to tell me where your mind drifts off to. I can't stand not knowing what I did to cause such deep contemplation."

Damn. How could he think he'd done anything wrong? And the way he made it sound implied they were long-term.

Maybe she needed to be clear with him. Out of self-preservation and habit, she'd been holding a chunk of herself back. Openness wasn't something she was accustomed to, and for years she'd buried her thoughts and desires because the person she'd been with hadn't wanted to know them, hadn't cared.

After they'd made love last night, Cade had claimed to care about her, that the experience had been emotional for him. It wasn't in his moral code to lie or mislead, which left her with more questions than answers about what they were doing. But if they were to keep at it—and did she want to?—then she had to make him understand he wasn't the one not functioning at capacity.

"Eat, sweetheart." Gaze trained on his plate, he shoveled eggs into his mouth with what seemed like effort.

She managed the bacon and took a bite of melon, forcing a swallow. "If I told you it's me, not you, would you believe me?"

He didn't so much as turn his head. "No."

She rubbed her forehead. "When we're together, you..."

His body went rigid. "I what?"

God. She blew out an unsteady breath. "You're...not what I was expecting, I guess. You're different than—"

His fork clattered to his plate. He glared at her with a look of pure pissed off male. "Is that what this is about? Him?" He turned to face her. "I've got news for you, Avery. If you're waiting around for me to start acting like your dick of an ex, it's never going to happen."

"That's not what I—"

"At some point, you need to look at me and not see him." His voice steadily rose. "I don't know if you feel the need to torture yourself out of some twisted form of guilt or if you think he's all you deserve, but I'm not going to do a one-eighty. I refuse to treat you like you don't matter." He stood and walked his plate to the sink, spine stiff and mood posting back off warnings.

"Cade..."

He ran his hands through his hair and took more than a few ragged breaths before dropping his chin. He stood that way, back to her as if attempting to rein in his temper and get a hold of himself, while she could do little more than bite her lip trying to keep tears at bay. Not because he'd yelled at her and not because of the sudden distance between them, but because he was right.

She twisted her fingers together in her lap. "I don't compare you and him to make you angry or to make you feel inferior." He didn't move, and her stomach cramped in dread. "He's all I've ever known. So yes, I measure you against each other, to remind myself how different you are from him." She sighed and rubbed her forehead. "Every other second you surprise me with a sweet phrase or a kind gesture or..."

There was no point in explaining. He wouldn't understand. He didn't get that he was so much better a man than Richard could ever hope to be, and by her comparing, it forced her to allow their relationship to expand. Otherwise she'd never move past the hurt to see the good.

"Is that the truth?"

Her gaze landed on his tense back, and she wished so much she could rewind the past ten minutes and start this conversation over. "Yes."

He was silent another moment, but she thought some of the stress left his shoulders. He turned and leaned against the counter, arms crossed over his bare chest.

"I don't want fun." His voice came out hoarse and quiet, but his words were a scream in her ears. "You said you'd never let anyone break you like that again. I don't want to break you. I want to date you."

Damn it. Tears welled in her eyes. She tried to blink them away, but it was fruitless. They fell, tracking hot paths down her cheeks. Her throat closed, but she refused to look away, refused to hide from his honesty.

For a moment, she thought he might cross the room, his expression was that tormented, but he only gripped the counter behind him until his knuckles turned white.

"You've been in Redwood Ridge long enough to know my reputation." He held her gaze, a determined set to his jaw. "Ask me why a playboy like me is suddenly changing his tune."

Shaking, she wiped the wetness from her face with the back of her hands and crossed her arms. Unable to speak, she stared at him and shook her head, at a loss. The fact his admission had her in tears was answer enough in her book. She'd not shed one tear when her marriage ended. She suspected she felt way more intensely about Cade than she ever did her ex, which said a lot about her. And none of it good.

Her heart beat double-time when he crossed the room and claimed the chair in front of her. He dropped his forearms on his thighs and leaned forward, dipping his head to look directly in her eyes. In her personal space, but not touching. The sympathy, the understanding in his gaze, brought a fresh wave of tears.

His throat worked a swallow, gaze suddenly unsure. "None of my previous lovers made me want more." He offered a slight shake of his head, but it seemed unintentional, a battle waging in his mind. "More time, more mornings like this or nights like last night. Just…more."

Straightening, he cupped her cheeks with his warm, rough hands. "Give me more. That's all I ask. A chance to figure this out and where it might go." His voice was pleading, but insistent. Determined. His blue gaze was kind, not a hint of the mischief or hunger she was used to finding.

She'd been weak with Richard. And though she told herself not to be weak in this moment, the truth was, Cade only made her stronger. For once, why not let herself feel good? She'd never find true happiness if she based every experience on the past.

Sniffing, she whispered, "Okay."

His chin lifted in defiance. Or disbelief. "Okay?"

She dragged in a breath and smiled. "Yes."

His eyes narrowed as he swiped the remnants of tears from her cheeks with his thumbs. "That was almost too easy. And by almost, I mean you really know how to drag me across hot coals."

Breathing out a laugh, she placed her hands over his, still cradling her face. "There will be rules, though."

He groaned and closed his eyes, but he was smiling when he opened them. "I knew it. Lay 'em on me. What are these…rules?" His hands dropped to his lap and he gave a mock shudder.

Hailey had to come first. There was no one more important than her daughter. "No sleepovers when Hailey's in the house. It might confuse her or give her the wrong impression. She's adjusted well to the move, but she needs a routine." Her daughter was already attached to him. If she got the impression they were a couple, Hailey might never recover from another uproot in her life.

He tilted his head in agreement. "Not a problem. What else?"

"No PDAs at work."

For this, his mouth twisted. "Can I still sneak you off into a hallway and steal kisses?"

Cheeks hot, stomach fluttering, she bit her lip. "Yes."

"Then, I agree. Next." It was cute when he tried to maintain a serious face. He failed miserably, but his attempt was crushing her resolve.

"I'm not ready for the whole town to know about us." She loved the small community and the sense of home since moving here, but she needed privacy, space to breathe. At least for a little while longer.

"Are you ashamed to be with me?" His tone was light, but something in his eyes told her the question wasn't all games.

"No, of course not. I'd rather take the time to see what happens before we go broadcasting things."

He scratched his jaw, bristled with morning whiskers. "I don't know how to tell you this, but everyone knows about us. You can't hide anything around here."

That was one message she'd received loud and clear her first day. But there was a difference between rumor and truth. "I'm more comfortable with it being gossip for now."

A weary sigh fell from his lips. "You're not my dirty little secret, and I won't treat you like one. But fine. Mum's the word." His gaze swept over her face. "Anything else? Do I need to bark at the moon if I want to hold your hand or throw smoke signals if I want to see you?"

God, he was a charmer. She was sunk. "Nope."

"Excellent. I'm going to kiss you now, yeah?"

Sunk deep. She even loved it when he did that, threw the word 'yeah' after a statement as if turning it into permission.

He didn't say anything more, just cupped her neck and pulled her to him. She went willingly, laying her hands on his shoulders and slanting her lips over his. The kiss wasn't seductive or infused with heat. He explored her mouth as if telling a story, their story, full of tenderness and longing and affection.

By the time he pulled away, she was shaking with unresolved apprehension for how much he could invoke inside her. He was the tingle down her spine, a pressure in her chest, a flutter in her belly, a force in her head. Everywhere, at once. Consuming and devouring. Eradicating and destructive.

He kissed her temple, his lips lingering as his jaw stroked her cheek. "When do you have to pick up Hailey?"

She blinked at the invasion and cleared her throat. "Ten o'clock."

He glanced over his shoulder to the wall clock. "Not much time. What are you two doing later?"

Suspicion mounted. "Laundry."

He grunted. "Can I convince you to do something more fun?"

Needing some space, as they didn't have time to go at each other before she had to get Hailey, Avery collected her plate and brought it to the sink. "Laundry can be fun."

He made a sound of dismissal. "Do tell."

With her back to him, she grinned and rinsed off her plate. She wasn't flirty by nature, but he brought out her lighter side, the part that liked the teasing banter sometimes between them. "For starters, it means I'll be wearing my nightgown while I wash and fold. Without panties. Seems to me that might be easy access if—"

He was behind her with his arms banding her waist and mouth on her neck before she could so much as laugh. "I nominate laundry day every day. Twice on Sundays."

She laid her head back, the smile slipping as he worked his tongue and teeth over the sensitive spot on her neck. A tremble tore through her. Her legs gave out, but he caught her against his hard body.

"Hell." He lifted his head. Kissed her hair. "We don't have time." Turning her in his arms, he caged her against the counter. "I'd like to take you and Hailey somewhere this afternoon. A surprise," he amended before she could ask. "But we most definitely have to do laundry afterward. Many loads. I insist."

How he could take her from powerful, raging lust to laughing in the course of seconds she'd never know. "You insist? I guess I can't argue with that."

Chapter 21

Cade sucked in a cold blast of fresh air and glanced around the snow-covered hill. To the west was the steep incline of the Klamouth Mountains. To the east was the Pacific Ocean, which wasn't visible from their location, but the air was brine-scented and the crash of waves wasn't far off in the distance, reminding people it was there.

This was the perfect day weather-wise for their trip. The sky was a light gray overcast, so the reflection from the sun off the snow wouldn't be blinding and the temperature was in the lower thirties with heavy humidity.

His surprise was to drive Avery and Hailey an hour up the mountain to this sweet spot known mostly to the locals. The snow in Redwood Ridge had mostly melted, but up here this far north and seated next to the mountain there was powder aplenty. An inn catered to tourists was on the other side of the ridge, but this area was tucked away, semiprivate.

Kids were sledding the bunny slope at breakneck speed, and a shock of nostalgia hit him in the gut. "My dad used to bring me and my brothers here as boys. I haven't been up this way in years."

He remembered his dad, grinning while watching him and his brothers play, biding his time to nail them with the perfect snowball. He'd laugh in that rough, rustic way of his and grab his stomach.

Jesus, he missed him so damn bad. Nine years and the sudden assault of memories still hurt realizing Dad was really gone.

Avery smiled, cheeks pink from the wind. "How many broken bones came afterward? I typically don't participate in activities requiring an ambulance."

He laughed. "Such a mom thing to say."

People were off to the side near the crest of pines where a flat area held a hot cocoa stand and some tables. Taking advantage of the wet snow, many were building forts and snowmen.

He watched the families for a moment, struck by how deeply he wanted his own family one day. Content to enjoy things as they were, he hadn't thought a lot about marriage or children, only that he thought he wanted them. Someday.

Boys to play ball with like his dad used to, or girls to build a dollhouse for and pretend tea parties were the rage. Or the other way around, since he realized that was pretty sexist of him. Zoe would knock him upside the head for that, seeing as she was the best player on their summer baseball league.

But the warmth filling his chest meant the time to think about the future was present. He attributed the emotional shift to Avery and their new relationship. Perhaps because she already had a daughter, but he didn't think that was the reason. For the first time in his life, he didn't have the urge to move on, to find the next adventure or cheap thrill. He wasn't bored or itchy for action.

Avery settled something inside him. It didn't matter if they were watching a movie on her couch, making love in his bedroom, or cooking dinner at her place. None of it was tedious. Hell, he couldn't stop thinking about her or when he could next see her. Couldn't stop wondering when he'd get to do the simple, mundane things with her again.

When Mom lost Dad, and so suddenly, he'd had to witness just how hard it was for her to survive without him. They'd been a solid unit all his life. It was as if she suddenly didn't know how to function. And when Drake had lost Heather, well... Drake still wasn't himself almost four years later. It had gutted him. It made Cade wonder, and not for the first time, if getting this deep in a relationship was wise. All that pain awaited. But he couldn't live his life expecting the worst, could he?

A small hand latched on to his and he glanced down. Hailey swung their arms while looking everywhere at once in that adorable, distracted way of hers.

That was the other thing. Children didn't typically frighten him, but they didn't give him the warm fuzzies, either. This one? This one brought out protective instincts he didn't know existed and made his throat close when she reached across the barriers of her handicap to form a connection.

Like holding his hand. Or cuddling on the couch.

"I don't know if she'll like snow," Avery said, glancing over the horizon and back to him. "Might be a sensory overload for her, like sand. She can't stand it." If she noticed what Hailey had done, she didn't say so. Her smile was warm, lighting her eyes as she shrugged. "We can try."

He looked down at the tiny person next to him. "Whatcha think, squirt? Want to try sledding or building a snowman?" He knew she wouldn't answer, but sometimes she gave off subtle signals to tell him what she wanted. Nada this time.

Undeterred, he led them closer to the pine trees to a quieter area and scooped up a handful of snow. He turned Hailey's hand over and set the fresh powder in her palm. She immediately dropped it and started rocking. Not good.

Avery pulled the girl's mittens from her pockets and put them on Hailey. "Try now."

He repeated the process with the same result. "Guess not."

Plopping his ass in the snow, he gathered enough powder to compact together for a snowman base, watching Hailey out of the corner of his eye. She didn't appear interested, but she didn't wander off, either. By the time he got to the head, Hailey had moved closer and Avery was snapping pictures on her phone.

Cade made a tiny snowball and set it in Hailey's hand. "Don't drop it this time. Throw it." When she did neither, he gently grabbed her wrist and made the motion for her. The snow hit Avery square in the cheek.

Phone poised in her outstretched hand, she froze and narrowed her eyes at him. "Not funny."

He disagreed. Gathering another snowball, he helped Hailey throw again. This time, the girl barked a laugh. "She thinks it's funny."

Avery didn't retaliate, but her smile was reward enough.

They tried sledding, but Hailey never made it past sitting down. After an hour, they called it quits and packed it in.

On the drive back, Avery turned to him. "I'm sorry she wasn't into it."

He shrugged. "No worries." He had fun, nonetheless.

His cell went off in his pocket and he cursed for forgetting to attach Bluetooth. He dug the phone out and answered without glancing at the ID, keeping his eyes on the road.

Drake's voice filled his ear. "Family dinner has been bumped up an hour."

Cade glanced at the dashboard. "We're on our way back now. We'll make it."

He glanced at Avery, but she was looking out the side window. He hadn't told her about dinner plans, figuring he'd work up to it. Every other Sunday, he and his brothers went over to Mom's. This would be the first time he'd brought someone along.

Drake grunted his acknowledgement and disconnected.

Cade set the phone in his lap and wound his way over the curvy highway, wondering if she'd flip out about having dinner with his family. It wasn't as if she didn't know them, but working together or hanging out at the bar was different than sharing a meal in someone's home. The last thing he wanted to do was scare her off after they'd finally seemed to break ground this morning.

He drummed his thumbs on the steering wheel. "We're heading to my mom's house. For family dinner. If that's okay with you." He ground his jaw at his brilliance in blurting it out in rapid-fire succession. "Mom invited you. Hailey, too. It's just us and my brothers. Nothing fancy or anything."

Jesus, O'Grady. Shut it.

She looked at him, brows arched and lips hinting at a smile. "Nervous?"

Hell yes. Seemed like gnomes were doing cartwheels in his stomach, and he didn't like the foreign feeling one bit. Why he was nervous, he had no clue. This was Avery. She fit in anywhere and his brothers already loved her. His mom took a liking to her the first time they'd met and brought her up in conversation too often to ignore the hint.

He shrugged. "A little."

She grinned.

"Fine. A lot." He sighed. "Are you upset I didn't talk to you beforehand? We can do it another time, yeah?"

"I prefer you ask me first next time, but I'm good with it."

They were on the steeper decline off the mountain road. One patch of black ice or a curve too fast and it would be lights out. He had precious cargo to think about. He couldn't chance a look to verify she really was okay. The inflection in her tone, one he was growing to know quite well, indicated she was fine. He, however, was not.

"You're the first woman I've brought home. Not including my prom date." Which had been Zoe on a friends-only basis, so that didn't count. "Technically, you know my family, so this is more of a formality, yeah? I mean, it's just dinner."

Christ. He'd need a straightjacket in about ninety seconds.

"Breathe," she said in her calm voice, amusement tinting her tone.

"I'm breathing." For the most part.

Her hand came down on his thigh, and even through his jeans, her heat seeped into him, calming him in an instant. She stroked his leg with her thumb, meant to be a soothing action, but it was having the opposite effect with a certain part of his anatomy.

"Just remember, we can do laundry later."

His gaze whipped to hers and back to the road, long enough to catch a glance of her hand covering her mouth, attempting to contain a grin.

He was nervous and she threw humor at him. *At him.* The guy who typically made light of everything. Who didn't do the dating thing or bring home a date.

Yet Avery, who'd been burned by exactly what he was trying to attempt, opened herself to him and had the strength to go for it, no matter how much a relationship probably scared her. If anyone deserved to be cynical, it was her. Tenfold. But she wasn't. She was kind and giving and funny and quirky and organized and…

Perfect.

Just like that, every emotion he'd been battling with regards to her slammed into his chest with full seismic force.

Surprise…happiness…nerves…worry…protectiveness… compassion…respect… lust.

Utterly blinding. Deafening. Excruciating.

One after another after another until he thought he'd need to pull over or risk crashing the car. His hands shook against the wheel, forcing him to clench his fingers in a death grip. He was pretty sure this was what a heart attack felt like. No air. Crippling pain in his chest.

The worst of it all was, Drake had been right. At the forefront of the emotional upheaval and shoving its way to the surface was love. Yeah. *Love.* And not the cuddly puppy kind.

He should've seen this coming. And what in the hell was he supposed to do about it?

Focusing on the road, on her soothing touch, he forced oxygen into and out of his lungs. By the time they'd pulled up to his mother's house, the answer hadn't been forthcoming, but he was measurably calmer. Figuring he'd corner Drake later, he slapped on his game face.

She didn't attempt to exit the car, instead shifting in her seat to face him. One look and he knew she saw right through him. Her eyebrows rose and her eyes took on a serious, compassionate softness that pummeled him.

Slowly, she nodded in an ah-ha. "If you're this upset, we don't have to go in. We don't have to do laundry, either. We can just call it a day."

He was wrong. She didn't get it. Or she was giving him an out.

Screw that. He didn't want an out. "I want to go inside and enjoy the time with my family. With you and Hailey right there."

She stared at him for an unnervingly long beat. He couldn't read her expression to save his life, but he suspected she was doing more of her mind juju. Then, without a word, she opened the door and slipped out of the car. Taking Hailey's hand, she walked up the porch steps.

He followed and nodded at Flynn when his brother opened the door. Cade hung up their coats in the hall closet, breathing in the scent of Mom's home cooking, hoping his Spidey senses were right and that was meatloaf he smelled.

As Avery and Hailey walked deeper into the house and said hello to Drake, Flynn turned to Cade.

"Bringing home a girl to meet the family," the asshole signed. *"How the mighty have fallen. When's the wedding?"*

In answer, Cade showed his brother his favorite digit, the one between his pointer and ring finger.

Stepping into the family room, he half expected to see Dad there. His father's medical journals were on the bookshelves right where he'd left them and his favorite chair was in the corner, empty. Nostalgia lanced through Cade's gut and he shook it off.

Besides Avery and Hailey, Drake was the only one present, sitting on one of the plaid couches his parents had since 'Nam, and watching a nature show on Discovery Channel. Closed captioning was on for Flynn and a fire was roaring in the corner hearth. Drake's German Shepherd, Moses, and Flynn's golden retriever, Fetch, were sleeping on the thick beige carpet under the bay window. Neither moved to acknowledge the newcomers.

"Cade? Is that you?" A clattering followed Mom's question and Cade imagined her fluttering around the kitchen, mashing potatoes and taking the meatloaf from the oven. Mom, the multi-tasker.

"Yeah," he hollered back. "Avery and Hailey, too."

"Oh good. Avery, dear. Come in here with me. There's too much testosterone in there."

Seeing her in his parents' house caused a cozy warmth to fill his core. He stayed in the doorway to take the moment in, but she was on her feet and motioning for Hailey to follow her.

"We're needed in the kitchen."

Flynn shook his head. *"I've got her. Go ahead."*

Cade looked down at Hailey, who hadn't moved too far from him and was watching Flynn's hands with more focus than he'd seen from her to date.

"Are you sure?" Avery bit her lip, and he had to wonder when the day would come she'd realize her and her daughter weren't a hardship.

Flynn nodded, redirecting his attention on the girl. *"Remember me?"*

Hailey didn't respond, but she was watching his brother intently, as was Avery with a worried wrinkle between her brows.

Flynn squatted in front of Hailey. *"I don't talk, either."* He looked at Avery. *"Does she play checkers?"*

Avery nodded. "She prefers tic-tac-toe, though."

Flynn grinned at the girl. *"Think you can beat me?"* He didn't wait for an answer. Rising, he headed down the hallway toward their old bedrooms, Hailey in his wake.

After a moment, Avery walked around the corner and disappeared into the kitchen. When his mother's voice drifted into the room, he knew Avery would be occupied for a while.

Cade looked at Drake and jerked his chin toward the door. "Take a ride with me to get the dogs." They needed to be let out and Freeman usually came with him to Mom's.

It wasn't a request, and Drake didn't take it as one. He rose from the couch and slipped into his coat, then held the door open for Cade.

In silence, they drove the short distance to Cade's cabin and parked. He didn't have much time and wanted to get back before Avery knew he was gone. Yet he fisted the wheel and made no attempt to exit the vehicle. He wished his head could make sense of the emotional riot.

Drake gave him an assessing side-glance. "Are we going to make out?"

Cade couldn't help it. He dropped his forehead to the steering wheel and laughed. The entire day, if not the past few weeks, had been surreal. "Hell, Drake. It's good to have you back. One more thing I can thank her for."

His brother didn't respond, but tension filled the car, crackled in the air. Cade lifted his head and stared out the windshield, unsure what to do or say.

After several long, awkward minutes, Drake sighed. "I never went anywhere."

Not physically, but ever since Heather died, his big brother had mentally and emotionally checked out. Maybe it was Avery's doing or maybe enough time had passed since Heather's death for Drake to move on. Perhaps a combination. Either way, his brother was acting less like a ghost and more like part of the human race again.

Drake crossed his arms. "Since we're not here for incestuous reasons, and thanks for that, I can only assume this is about a certain woman?"

He leaned his head back and closed his eyes. "All the great tragedies start with the phrase 'There's this girl...'"

"As do the epic love stories. Not all end in tragedy."

Cade opened his eyes and stared at his brother. "You look like Drake, sound like Drake, but—"

"You brought me out here. If you didn't want my opinion, you should've brooded in silence." One corner of his mouth quirked. "It has its merits. Silence."

He returned his focus to the windshield, rubbing the back of his neck. "How did you know it was love with Heather?"

Drake laughed without mirth. "You just know. And the fact you're asking means you're there."

Cade had pretty much reached the same conclusion, but what he really wanted to say was wedged in his throat. Words that, if spoken aloud, couldn't be taken back, and he wasn't sure he wanted the truth.

He'd watched Drake grieve for his wife, stood there as his brother's life had crashed down around him, and he'd been powerless to do a thing. All that pain, all that misery. Cade was only hovering on the outskirts of that kind of love, and he couldn't fathom how Drake put one foot in front of the other after his world had been stolen.

"I don't..." Cade blew out a ragged breath. "I never wanted to fall for her, for anyone. Why set yourself up for pain when you can see it coming?"

Drake's gaze pinned him to the seat. Direct, swift, and more than a little irritated. "So this man-to-man isn't about advice or confirmation. You're asking for permission to walk away. Because what? You could get hurt?"

Cade shook his head, his unfocused gaze drifting off. He didn't think he could walk away from Avery, even if he should.

Honestly, he didn't know why he'd brought Drake out here, other than his brother might very well be the only one who understood what he was dealing with. And the only person who could get him past his reservations about plunging altogether. When push came to shove, if Heather hadn't died, Cade didn't think they'd be having this conversation. Love would just be another grand adventure and not something to fear.

"You're not asking the right question, little brother." Drake's solemn gaze met his, his tone mild, but not brooking argument. "You need to ask if it's worth it, if I'd do it again knowing the result." He leaned closer. "Hell yes. I would."

Drake grabbed the handle and opened the door, sliding one foot down to the ground. "I'll get the dogs. You get your shit together."

Chapter 22

Avery and Gayle had just brought the food out to the large kitchen table when Drake and Cade strode in, the dogs at their heels. Drake seemed no different, but Cade's gaze wouldn't meet hers and his mouth twisted in what seemed like unpleasant thoughts. She had no clue why it had taken thirty minutes to drive a block to get the dogs, but her stomach cranked in worry.

Cade rubbed the back of his neck and came deeper into the room, eying the table. "Looks good, Mom."

"Thank you. Sit down, everyone."

She liked Gayle's home. Unlike Cade's two-story, his mom's was a ranch and not nearly as updated. The place had a lived-in feel. Photos were everywhere she turned—the mantle, the walls, the fridge—and went as far as his parents' wedding. The furniture and appliances seemed dated to the boys' youth. Even the kitchen table had nicks and scars. The house was simple and friendly, like Gayle.

Avery hung back, waiting for everyone to take a seat in order to assess where they wanted her to sit. In the end, she wound up next to Flynn and across from Cade. Instead of taking the open spot by Cade, Hailey plopped down at the head of the table where no place setting had been laid out.

Avery tapped Hailey's arm. "Sweetie, there's a plate by Cade for you."

Hailey didn't move, and nerves pinged in Avery's belly, especially when everyone seemed to be sharing uncertain glances with each other.

"She's fine," Cade said at length, eyes on Hailey. "Only someone as awesome as my dad gets to sit in his spot."

Oh God. That had been his dad's place at the head of the table. She rose. "Hailey, please move to the other chair."

Drake cleared his throat. "Sit, Avery. Like Cade said, she's fine."

Avery looked at Gayle just to be certain, still uneasy.

She smiled and nodded her agreement with her sons, waving her hand in dismissal of the situation.

Blowing out a breath, Avery reclaimed her seat. She leveled a smile in Drake's direction. "You're so bossy."

He grinned right back. "This from the woman who alphabetized my surgical vials. Twice."

"Well, I don't know how you found anything in that mess of a cabinet. Besides, that's organizing, not bossing."

His brows lifted, grin widening. Who knew Drake had dimples? "Okay, you told Missy Hamilton not to come back to the clinic unless she was wearing a bra. That's bossy."

Flynn choked on his drink. "*You did not. Really?*"

She huffed. "I did so. You can't walk into a place of business with all your...goodies hanging out. And who brings a goldfish in for a checkup? Come on."

Flynn shook his head. "*Dump my brother and marry me.*"

She laughed. "I'll consider it." Glancing around, she realized heads were pivoting between the conversation and she was holding up dinner. Her cheeks heated. "Um... This looks really delicious, Gayle. Thanks for having us."

Gayle picked up a bowl of peas and passed it to Drake with a motherly smile. "Oh no, dear. The pleasure is all mine."

Avery went to load Hailey's plate only to find Cade had already done it. He also had a cup of milk in front of him, having switched out his lemonade with Hailey's glass.

Flynn zeroed in on that, too. "*Stealing milk from kids? Not nice.*"

"She can't have dairy, jerkface."

"Language, Cade." Gayle tsked and forked a slice of meatloaf onto her plate. She looked at Avery. "I'll remember the no-dairy for next time."

Cade's brows lowered. "Jerkface is not a curse." He turned to Hailey. "Right, squirt? Just don't go repeating it at school. Deal?" He held up his fist and, after her typical delay, Hailey bumped it back.

When he looked up at Avery, a half grin cranked in satisfaction, her heart outright stopped pumping. She couldn't look away from that intense shade of blue—a force of nature when combined with amusement and a clear case of love. He wasn't trying to win her over with her daughter's affection or spending time with Hailey to get to Avery. He did all these sweet, simple things because he...legitimately loved Hailey.

It was blatantly apparent in the care he took, his patience, and the way he looked at her. He pushed her boundaries, but only to get a read on her, and never so far as to upset her mood. Able to read her mannerisms, he headed off problems before they began and was learning her likes.

Most of all, he spent time with Hailey. Today's snow adventure was the truest test of his character. Instead of getting angry or disappointed Hailey hadn't been an excited participant, he'd shrugged it off.

Avery's heart lodged in her throat, her eyes suspiciously close to watering. She stared down at her plate to get a hold of herself.

Richard had never tried to bond with their daughter. Not truly, and definitely not after her autism diagnosis. He hadn't seen the point. He thought she was broken. In his eyes, Hailey had a major defect and since she didn't respond in the normal way to situations, he'd stopped trying at all. And though Avery swore to herself she'd strive to quit comparing Richard and Cade, in this one blaring instance, she couldn't help it.

Richard was Hailey's father, but love never came into play. Cade had no blood tie, no familial connection, yet he adored Hailey. There was no question. That was the kind of man he was. Real. Genuine.

She wasn't sure if she should be jealous someone else was in Hailey's life. Stupid as it sounded, Avery had never needed to vie for her daughter's love. And as much as her head told her to wave a caution flag that Hailey was attached, she just couldn't. Hailey deserved to be adored.

Cade swallowed, his eyebrows drawn in a silent question, asking her what was wrong. That right there got her every time. His intuition.

She offered a smile and broke the potent contact to take a bite of mashed potatoes. Now was not the time to dissect feelings. Not surrounded by his family. She'd analyze her thoughts later and figure out what to do, if anything.

By the time they made it back to the cabin, it was pushing Hailey's bedtime. She seemed tired anyway, so Avery skipped the usual sleepy time show and had Hailey brush her teeth. Her eyes were drooping before her head hit the pillow.

Avery sat on the edge of the mattress and tucked the sheet up to Hailey's chin. Seraph bounded into the room with his three-legged hobble and sat at Avery's feet to be picked up. He was getting bigger everyday, but the little pup hadn't mastered jumping quite yet.

She bent to pick him up, scratched behind his ears, and settled him next to an out cold Hailey. He circled the mattress twice before curling up to her chest. Since she was asleep, Avery took a moment to run her fingers through Hailey's dark hair. She let Avery hold her hand and occasionally cuddle, but sometimes Avery just craved touch. She loved these stolen moments, held them close to her chest when Hailey's limitations went against Avery's needs.

Cade was waiting in the other room. She pressed a kiss to Hailey's forehead and made her way out, finding him in the kitchen, leaning against the counter and staring off into space. That introspective expression was on his face, but he smiled when he noticed her walk in. Affection lit his eyes, warming his smile as she drew closer.

He kissed her temple as she stepped into his arms. "Aunt Marie called your cell while you were in with Hailey."

She glanced over his shoulder to the counter. "Probably wants to discuss the St. Patrick's Day potluck. She's been hinting about new ideas since we finalized the Valentine's dance."

He laughed. "Luring you to the dark side, one event at a time." His grin was in full charm mode. "The O'Gradys are the biggest contributors to the potluck, being Irish on Dad's side and all. You haven't tasted anything until you try his beef stew recipe."

Settling closer, she wrapped her arms around his waist and got a little thrill having his hard body aligned perfectly to hers. "Your dad cooked?"

He made a sound of agreement. "Sometimes. When he did, he was damn good." His gaze swept her face. "My mom likes you."

She pressed her face to his neck, enjoying their few minutes alone. She didn't realize how much she'd liked to be held, to snuggle, until Cade. "The feeling's mutual. Even if she is one of the... What do you call them? The Battleaxes?"

His chest shook in a laugh. "Yes. She's tame compared to her sisters, but she can be just as conniving if she's invested. Aunt Rosa's the instigator and Aunt Marie's the enforcer."

"They seem harmless." Mostly. Avery had been the target of their focus a few times, but none of it had been malicious.

"They're not. They're capable of mass manipulation of epic proportions. Match making, swaying public opinion to their cause, butting into personal business." He wrapped his arms tighter, giving her a squeeze. "You're right, though. They mean well."

She let out a contented sigh as her muscles relaxed. His linen scent mixed with husky male was becoming her new drug. They stayed like that for a few minutes as if satisfied by nothing more than holding each other.

The washing machine went into spin cycle, the whirring sound filling the room, and she lifted her head. "You started laundry?" How...domestic.

He brushed a strand of hair away from her face. "Hailey's load. And speaking of, you're not wearing the aforementioned laundry outfit."

God, he could melt the panties off with just one heated look, one word in that rough timbre tone. "I guess we should remedy that." She went to step away, but he grabbed her waist and lifted her onto the counter.

Hands on her hips, he moved between her thighs. "I like you best in nothing at all." Leaning in, he brought his mouth to hers, kissing her lower lip and sliding his tongue across it for entry.

When she opened, he stroked her in a sensual, languid exploration that had her pulse tripping and her breasts heavy. Too soon, he eased back a margin to look in her eyes, and what stared back at her made her heartbeat speed for an entirely different reason. Behind the need, the heat, was adoration. She recognized the expression from movies, books, or other couples she'd been near, but not once had she ever been the recipient.

Maybe she was reading too much into the moment. It was just a look after all, but her skin flushed under his study and, as they stared at each other, sharing air, the need in his eyes moved out to make room for...

No. Now she knew she was crazy. After less than two months, Cade couldn't possibly love her. Would he even know romantic love if it parachuted down in front of him?

Heck, would she?

Though he never abused his charm, he had every single woman in the county eating out of his palm. They sashayed into the clinic, assaulted him in the bar, and came on to him just walking the street. By her observation, he didn't lead them on and was always up front with them. But the fact remained, he'd never fallen for any of them.

Perhaps he felt more deeply about her, but this wasn't love. He was confusing affection and caring for the real deal. Had to be.

His jaw clenched in what she'd come to understand was a nervous or angry gesture as he cupped her cheek. But his touch was a caress, stroking her with his thumb, his gaze tender. Total surrender. That's what his expression relayed.

Total surrender.

"Avery..." His low, hoarse voice washed over her. A plea. An admission.

She couldn't do this, didn't want to. No, he wasn't Richard. Yes, Cade was a good man. But she'd done this merry-go-round before and it had been disastrous. Love stole everything—personality, will, reason. Independence. She'd fought too hard to fall again. She was growing to depend on his attention, his kiss, his kindness, his sweet words. Hailey was already attached.

He tensed against her, and she opened her eyes to look into his. Infused in all that amazing blue was distressed alarm. Desperation.

"Don't," he said through gritted teeth. He sucked in a breath, speaking again in a softer voice. "Don't put the wall back up."

Before she could wrap her head around the situation, he reached behind his neck and pulled off his shirt, revealing his ripped muscles and smooth skin lightly dusted with hair. He fumbled in his pocket, then withdrew a condom and set it next to her. Keeping his gaze locked to hers, he unbuttoned his fly and shucked his pants, standing before her in all his naked, yummy glory.

The man was built. Beautiful. Already hard, he stroked his length once, twice, his gaze open and devastatingly revealing. Hunger and heart.

Mouth watering, she remained still, welcoming the throb between her legs and the ache which followed. This she could do, and he seemed to sense that, like he always did. He'd closed the door on emotion to keep her grounded, keep her with him.

But at what cost? In time, maybe panic wouldn't clutch her chest, and she could grow to accept another pass at something more. But not now. And she would only hurt him in the process if his heart was engaged.

"I said don't." He closed the distance and yanked her shirt over her head. Unfastening her pants, he encouraged her to lift her hips, then tossed those aside, too. He ripped the condom wrapper with his teeth and rolled it down his length.

All the while, he kept her gaze held captive, unable to look away.

Then his arms were around her and he was lifting her from the counter. She gasped, wrapping her legs around his hips and grabbing his shoulders as he backed them to the table. Her spine pressed against the cool, smooth surface, and he followed her down. His length rocked against her folds, testing her readiness as his mouth latched on to her neck.

The sensation stimulus was blinding. Her nipples rasped his chest hair, the contrast a burn. His erection teased her clit, sending sparks through her body. His tongue and teeth on her neck lit her nerves, drew a violent tremble from deep within.

Oh God. They were going to have sex in the kitchen, right there on her kitchen table.

His finger trailed from her mound to her opening, and at discovering how wet she was, he groaned. Fisting his base, he aligned his shaft and eased inside.

She moaned as he stretched her walls, filled her with hard heat, and kept going until he was rooted and she could do no more than pant against his neck. Every time they came together it was old and new, familiar and fresh, comforting and energizing. A collision of contrast and need and sensation.

He laced his fingers with hers and brought them over her head, his forearms on the table caging her in. The new position nudged him deeper, had more skin to skin than ever before. He looked into her eyes, not only trapping her with his body, but his gaze.

Trapping her to him. All of him.

"Do you see how good we are, sweetheart?" His throat worked a swallow. "Do you feel it?"

That was the problem in a nutshell, wasn't it? It was too good. And things that were too good to be true usually were. It just made the crash more painful.

Despite the warning in her head and the lump in her throat, she nodded.

He brought his mouth to hers and kissed her so thoroughly she couldn't remember what planet she was on and didn't care. She just wanted him, for however long it lasted.

Reading her need, he began to move inside her, shallow thrusts at first and then with deeper strokes. She dug her heels into his backside, urging more, her body straining for the oblivion only he could give her. He rolled his hips with each drive, his pelvis grinding over her clit and bringing her closer to shattering.

His fingers squeezed hers, silently telling her he was close, asking her to let go. He kissed her again, frantic, searching. He must've found what he was seeking because his groan vibrated her chest and his pace quickened.

She threw her head back. Arched. Already so close, she tumbled over. Wave after wave, the force hit. She quaked underneath him, her breath trapped in her chest and her head reeling.

He pressed his cheek to hers and rasped her name as he came. Rigid, he dropped his forehead to her brow, eyes pinched tight, his handsome face twisted in desire. He let out the breath he'd been holding, his hips still thrusting with shallow strokes as if seeking to prolong the orgasm.

Slowly, he opened his eyes, released her fingers and wrapped his arms around her back, providing a cushion from the hard table. So many emotions traveled in and out of his eyes, passing too quickly for her to read.

Mouth open, brows drawn together, he seemed like he wanted to say something and changed his mind. He eased out and dropped the condom in the trash, coming right back to pick her up.

It stopped being awkward after the first couple times, and she still had to bite back the urge to inform him she could walk, but he seemed to enjoy carting her places. Not often. A boost out of the car, a lift from one room to the next. Like a Cade O'Grady version of sweeping her off her feet. She could do without the shyness that rose or the damsel-in-distress impression, but Cade obviously got enjoyment from it, so she rested her head on his chest and went with it.

Carrying her down the hall, he walked into her bedroom and gently set her on the bed, climbing in beside her.

It dawned on her as she turned on her side to face him that he'd always made it a point to care for her after making love. Even that first time, once he'd eventually emerged from the bathroom, he'd found a way to pull himself together. Whether it was cuddling, skimming a reassuring hand over her back, or just lying next to her, he'd find something touching to do to ride out the aftereffects.

In all her life, from her mom to her ex to Hailey, she'd always been the one taking care of others. Part of that was her need for control and order. But mostly, she'd been playing the hand she was dealt and had done what was needed. The role reversal with Cade only served to add another element to the heady mix.

He took her hand in his and kissed her palm. "Relax. I know rule numero uno is no sleepovers with Hailey in the house. I'll leave in a little while." His thumb stroked her inner wrist. "I'm not taking off seconds after being with you, though. Get used to it."

God. He was killing her. As Brent would say…swoon, doll, swoon.

Cade brushed her nose with his. "Not that I'm complaining, but what's that smile for?"

She made a sleepy noise in her throat. "Just thought of a Brent-ism for this exact moment."

"Brent-ism? Should I be concerned you're thinking of my tech right now?"

"Nope." Letting out a sigh, her lids drooped as exhaustion claimed her. What was she going to do with him?

Chapter 23

It was barely lunchtime and this was quickly turning into the day from hell. In the clinic hallway, Cade swiped the device screen to pull up his next patient's chart, hoping to hell for a depressed hamster or routine vaccination.

He'd had to euthanize Mrs. Frederick's eighteen-year-old cat when she'd brought it in for weight loss and he'd discovered a pancreatic tumor. Shit way to start the day. Especially because Mrs. Frederick was pushing ninety and was recently widowed. She loved that damn cat more than her deceased husband. Not that Cade blamed her. Mr. Frederick had been a crotchety old fart who spent most of Cade's youth bitching they played ball too loud. Like it was Cade's problem the Frederick's lived across the street from the little league park.

Then they had to put down a German short hair for age-related issues, and Christ if watching ten-year-old Andy Diedry cry buckets over his dog didn't nearly kill Cade. Brent was still misty over that one.

Between those appointments, he'd had to pry two blondes and one brunette off him when the three of them cornered him in an exam room. The two blondes were retrievers in heat and their brunette owner was… well, in heat, too, he guessed.

To add insult to injury, something was off about Avery today. She'd barely spoken three words to him all morning and, judging by her expression, she was teetering between livid female and basket case, depending on when he caught her amid patients. He hadn't had five seconds to himself to ask her what was wrong, but he hoped to hell he hadn't done something.

For the past couple weeks, ever since he realized he was batshit crazy in love with her, things had been pretty good between them. They'd settled into a routine of complete denial where he didn't tell her his feelings and she pretended she didn't know he had any. No L words had been exchanged, but the look in her eyes that night after dinner with his mom had been like a billboard pronouncing her holy-hell-in-a-handbasket reaction.

He'd been dodging proposals and willing females for years who hadn't taken the hint when he'd ended things for getting too serious. And Avery wasn't ready to hear him say the three words. Oh, the irony.

Whatever. He'd do denial for as long as it took for her be comfortable with the idea. He was in no hurry. He'd continue watching Hailey on Friday nights for Avery's committee meetings, have dinner at her house a couple times a week as they'd been doing, and sneak out her door after making love.

Hell, though. Would it kill anyone if they knew about their relationship? Why couldn't he take her out to dinner? Just once. Or hold her hand in public and not have her pull away as if he had leprosy. And though he understood the no sleepover thing, it was gutting him how badly he wanted to wake up next to her.

Focusing on his workload, he skimmed through his next patient's chart in Avery's recently installed EMR system. Thank Almighty. A routine appointment. Knocking on exam room two's door, he strode in to shake Mr. Weaver's hand.

A three-year-old Westie immediately attacked Cade's shoelaces with reckless abandon. Cade ignored mini-Cujo and looked into Mr. Weaver's rheumy eyes. "What can I do for you today, sir?"

"Well, Snowball here has something wrong with him." Mr. Weaver shook his head. "He rubs himself all over the floor and does this shaking thing like he's got the devil in him."

Without even looking at the dog, Cade knew the issue, but he picked up the Westie and set him on the table. He took out an otoscope and checked Snowball's ears. "Any change in diet?"

"No, I feed him that expensive crap you told me to."

Biting back a grin, Cade felt the dog's abdomen. "He's sleeping okay? Playing normally?"

"Yes."

Cade listened to the lungs and heart. "He's getting the heartworm medication monthly?" He checked the dog's gums and teeth, cooing to the terrier breed before it could get snippy. As a pup, Snowball had taken a good chunk out of Brent's finger. In the dog's defense, Brent had been taking a rectal temperature at the time.

"Yes. He gets that tick stuff, too."

Cade found the telltale skin irritation on the dog's back and paws, but chose his words carefully. Mr. Weaver was a Vietnam vet who never married and was pretty set in his ways. Though he only made appointments when necessary, he was pretty needy when he came in. Cade figured it was loneliness.

He rubbed Snowball's ears and gave him a treat for being good. "He's got some skin allergies, I'm afraid. It's fairly common, but treatable. We can start him off on an oral medication, and if that doesn't work, we can combine meds or try injections."

"No. That's not the problem. He shakes. It has to be seizures." Mr. Weaver crossed his arms, and Cade mentally checked himself in for the long haul.

"Dogs often roll on the floor to scratch an itch and when they use their hind legs, it can appear as if they're shaking. I can completely understand where you got the notion."

"Then it's his heart. There's something wrong."

After twenty minutes, Cade couldn't spare any more time and not piss off the other patients waiting, so he reiterated the allergy diagnosis, handed Mr. Weaver the pills, and chatted with him about the weather to distract him as they strode out.

The rest of the day was more shit. By the time he'd seen the last appointment of the day, he was ready for a hot shower and to sink into a hotter woman.

Closing his office door, he made his way to the lobby to see if Avery was up for Chinese tonight when he found her leaning against the front desk staring at her phone. That had to be the fifth time he'd caught her today with the color drained from her face.

Heart pounding and worry eating away the lining of his gut, he dipped his head to put his face level with hers. "What's going on? Is Hailey all right?"

She glanced up with wide eyes as if not realizing he was there. The hand holding her phone shook as she pocketed the cell. "She's fine."

He opened his mouth to bombard her with more questions because something wasn't right, but Brent chose that moment to make an appearance.

"Hey, doll." His tech glanced between the two of them, brows steadily moving north. "Ruh roh. Trouble in paradise?"

Avery quickly shook her head and straightened. "Everything's fine. Something's come up, though. Would you mind closing shop for me?"

Screw all. That was the straw that broke the veterinarian's back. Avery didn't ask for help often, and she took her responsibilities very seriously. Not that he gave a rat's ass she'd asked Brent to close the clinic. Why she had asked bothered him. He took a step forward, but Brent was there again.

"You got it, doll. See you tomorrow."

She surged forward and kissed his cheek. "Thank you."

"No problemo. Get your cute rear outta here." To put a period to his point, Brent swatted her "cute rear" as she passed him.

Squawk. "I like big butts."

She pointed a warning finger at the cockatoo and disappeared down the hall to retrieve her things.

Cade shifted his attention to Brent. "Did you just smack my woman's ass?"

He didn't know whether to be pissed or amused, but he was crawling out of his skin to find out Avery's issues and needed a distraction. He wouldn't get anything out of her until she was at home and had time to process. He was in for at least a couple more hours of worry.

Frustrating woman. Frustrating, beautiful woman.

Brent cocked a hip. "Aw. Jealous much?"

"I'm not jealous. Your door doesn't swing her way." Otherwise Cade might introduce Brent to his fist.

"I meant that I'm smacking her ass and not yours." Brent tsked and covered Gossip's cage.

Squawk. "Enter Sandman."

"That's right. Night, night." Brent turned to face Cade, picking up She-rah from the printer. "What's up with our girl, anyway? She's been pouty all day." He stroked the cat's back like an evil lord, one pinky up in the air.

Cade didn't think Avery was pouty so much as...rattled. He had no clue what or who could do that. "Hell if I know. I'll head over to her place later and find out."

Avery rushed in from the back, waved to them, and used her hip to open the door. "Night, guys. Thanks again, Brent."

Cade fisted his hands on the counter. "I'll be over in an hour."

Her gaze whipped to his, wide and alarmed. She ran a shaking hand over her forehead and looked down. "Not tonight, okay? I'll call you later."

Then she was gone, leaving Cade to stand there like an idiot. A confused, pissed off, scared to death idiot.

"Ouch. Dismissed. What did you do?"

Cade raked a hand through his hair, staring after her. The urge to follow her and demand she tell him what the fuck was going on was so fierce his head pounded. Nauseous, he closed his eyes for a beat.

He could either respect her wishes and pace his house in worry tonight, or he could ignore her request and try to offer the comfort she needed. Despite her walls and roadblocks, she did need him. Not in a clingy, suffocating way, and not because she was weak. When they were alone, her eyes told him she was falling for him right back. So, yeah. She needed him.

Together, they had trust and respect and mutual admiration. They talked and laughed. And had really, really hot sex.

Together, they were stronger.

Hell. Decision made.

* * * *

Avery had forced herself to sit at the kitchen table after work and eat the stuffed peppers she'd put in the Crockpot this morning. It exhausted what little energy she had left. Time with Hailey was precious. Between Hailey's school and Avery's work schedule, she only had a couple hours at the end of the day to spend with her little girl.

But she hadn't been able to eat much, and instead of chattering to Hailey about her day, Avery kept replaying the events in her head. Eventually, she'd directed Hailey to the couch to play on her iPad so Avery could do the dishes.

What she needed was a monster glass of wine and to forget today ever happened. A pint of Ben & Jerry's would have to suffice. And the day wasn't over yet.

The morning had started with the woman at the coffee counter badgering Avery about her relationship with Cade. It seemed innocent enough, and the woman probably meant no harm, but she wouldn't take the hint. Her parting shot had been telling Avery to check the town's Pinterest boards.

Not liking the sound of that, she'd headed for the safety of her car to scroll the site on her phone. There had been an entire board created just for her and Cade. Pictures from the Valentine's dance, a couple from the ice cream shop, and the kicker—a photo of Cade kissing her in the clinic's hallway. She had no clue when it was taken or by whom, but she knew it was not someone from Animal Instincts. They'd never do that. Yet it was a blatant disregard for her privacy and had her stomach cramping.

Then she'd stumbled upon two clients outside the bathroom discussing none other than her. Avery flinched as she washed a plate and set it in the dish rack, remembering the hushed conversation between the two young women.

"She's not even that pretty. What's he doing with her?"

"He'll get bored and move on to greener pastures in under a month."

The cattiness had stung and played on her insecurities. Though the barbs had hurt, she tried not to let them bother her. She was secure in the fact that Cade wanted her. Only her. She saw it in his eyes, felt it in his touch. For now, anyway.

Plus, there were new pictures of Cade with different women on the Pinterest boards. Some as recent as two days ago. They were obviously non-sexual in nature and mostly selfies on the fly, but it made her question, all over again, if she could trust what was between them. How long could his interest last when he was used to…choices?

Yet it was just another thing to screw with her head today.

Turning off the sink, she dried her hands and checked the clock again. Twenty minutes and she could put Hailey to bed. Normally, Avery cherished every minute with Hailey. Loneliness seeped through the fissures once her little girl was asleep, and in those quiet hours, Avery found herself hoping.

For someone. For normal. For an end to having to do it all alone.

Dangerous thinking, that. And yet something told her she had, in fact, found what she'd secretly been wanting, even if she couldn't admit it aloud. A heart's desire. Cade was coming hazardously close to proving he was The One, and she feared, more than anything, that it was all an illusion.

She blew out a breath and shook her head.

Yes. Bedtime was dangerous to her heart. Too much time to think. But tonight was different. The queasiness turning her stomach and abject uncertainty squeezing her chest wouldn't abate until she could be alone.

Because she needed to find out why Richard had called her today. Three times. He'd left a general message the first instance, claiming he needed to speak with her, but he hadn't bothered with voicemail after that.

Thousands of scenarios shoved around in her head. Did her ex suddenly want visitation rights? Did he want to fight custody? Had she left something when they'd moved? Was there an issue with the trust fund?

The acid in her stomach burned a path to her chest. She was going mad with anxiety. Fisting her shaking hands, she took a calming breath.

She sat next to Hailey on the couch and was glad her sleepy time show was almost through. "I'm sorry I wasn't very with it today, sweetie. Mommy just had a bad day. But that's not your fault. You didn't do anything wrong."

When the program was over, Avery shut off the TV and was about to direct Hailey to the bathroom when a knock sounded on the front door. Cade strode in without waiting for an answer.

Her first reaction was how glad she was to see him. Her pulse fluttered and her belly quivered. Having no idea when she'd grown to rely on him, on looking forward to their time together, relief deflated her chest that he was here. Nothing sounded better than curling up on the couch with him, leaning on him for the support he was so willing to give. When had her happiness become so dependent on someone else?

But she'd asked him not to come tonight and he ignored that request. He didn't typically disregard her feelings, and on the day she really needed him to listen, he hadn't.

His gaze seemed tentative as he looked at her. He hadn't moved from just inside the doorway. Shoving his hands in his pockets, he implored her to say something with a pleading intensity to his eyes.

"Hailey, go brush your teeth. I'll be right there." Avery waited until the water ran in the faucet before addressing Cade. "I asked you not to come tonight."

Not one muscle moved. "I know. I…"

"What?"

He sighed, his shoulders sagging. "I was worried. You've been off all day and—"

Her cell rang, reminding her why she was so "off" today, as he put it. She pulled it from her pocket and tensed at Richard's name on the screen. Sending the call to voicemail, she pressed a hand to her stomach to keep the contents inside and closed her eyes.

"Do you need to get that? I can put Hailey to bed."

Irritation—for Richard, for the bitchy clients talking about her in the hallway, for Pinterest—surged in her chest until she nearly exploded. Her head pounding, her breathing short, she pinned Cade with a glare. "She's my daughter. I got this."

He flinched as if she'd slapped him. His lips parted while he stepped forward. "Avery."

Damn. Regret added to the churn in her stomach. Her mood wasn't his fault. "I'm sorry. I didn't mean that." She sighed. "You should go. I'll talk to you tomorrow."

"Like hell. Talk to me now."

She was nearing the end of her rope. "Damn it, Cade. I can't tonight."

Undeterred, he jerked his chin toward the hallway. "Do what you need to. I'll wait."

She was too darn exhausted to argue. Deciding this battle wasn't worth winning, she nodded and stepped out of the room.

But by the time she got Hailey settled in bed, Avery was shaking with fury. She was directing it at the wrong person. The events of her day weren't Cade's responsibility, but she didn't want him around for this. To see her cracked open and…exposed, two minutes from falling apart.

He hadn't moved from the spot she'd left him, hands in his pockets and standing in the middle of the living room. His shoulders were tense beneath his coat, his jaw working a grind.

His anger was masking concern, and something about him losing his cool was sexy beyond measure. Fierce blue eyes met hers, and all she could think about was closing the distance and letting him fix the mess. Kiss away the uncertainty and fear.

For the first time in her life, someone wanted to hold *her* up. It was so damn tempting. Against her ingrained nature and experiences, yet tempting nonetheless.

But Richard needed a call back, and she'd never settle down until she found out what he wanted.

She pulled out her phone. "I have to make a call. Wait if you want."

He made a motion like he was unhinging his jaw. "I want." In emphasis, he shrugged out of his coat and tossed it on the couch.

With more bravado than she felt, she walked through the kitchen to the back door and stepped outside. Letting the cool, humid air wash over her heated skin, she squared her shoulders and connected the call.

Chapter 24

Cade swallowed past the boulder in his throat and rubbed a hand over his stomach. Acid was slowly burning a hole through his gut as he peeked around the living room corner a third time.

Avery was still standing just outside her back door, illuminated in moonlight and motionless. With the phone pressed to her ear, she occasionally nodded or responded to the other person, seemingly as calm as the shallow riverbed snaking through the yard. But her body language screamed with tension. From the wrinkle on her forehead to the stiff way she held her shoulders, she was wrung tight.

He ran a hand over his neck and resisted the urge to storm through the door and find out who was making his sweet Avery a wreck. And why. All day, she'd been killing him. Her mood, the distance, was so unlike her, and it was still assembling. She'd always been reserved, a little aloof, but she'd never been abrasive. Hell, she'd actually snapped at him when he'd tried to help earlier.

Something was wrong, and the walls he'd meticulously torn down were rebuilding around her as he watched, helpless to do a damn thing. The urge to howl rose in his chest. He paced instead, wearing her hardwood floors to dust.

Fifteen grueling minutes later, the door latch clicked as she stepped through. Face pale, hands shaking, she walked into the living room, her gaze dazedly staring at her cell phone. She stopped near the couch and looked around as if unaware of her surroundings.

Shit, shit, shit. More shit. "Avery, sweetheart. What is it? Talk to me." At this point, he wouldn't put it against him to shake an answer out of her.

She dropped to the couch and rubbed her forehead. "My…" She cleared her throat. "My ex is getting remarried."

He stilled. The hurricane force of air he'd been holding demanded an escape from his lungs. Was he the biggest asshole in existence to be relieved? This wasn't exactly bad news, at least not to him, but the shell-shock in Avery's eyes wouldn't allow his pulse to settle.

Not sure what to do, to say, he walked to the coffee table in front of her and perched at the edge. She wouldn't look him in the eye. An entirely different kind of anxiety raked his chest.

She shook her head and laughed without mirth. "I was worried he was going to try to take Hailey away from me, and he called to say he's headed down the aisle." She looked at him with a bite in her eyes. "He's not even marrying the assistant he cheated on me with. It's a socialite friend of the family." She rose so fast he got whiplash. "He didn't ask about his daughter once. Never gave any indication he wanted her there for the nuptials. Can you believe him?"

Cade stood and faced her. She had every right to be angry, and he understood her behavior now, but the fact she didn't lean on him, or attempt to tell him what had been going on, had his own fury battling for dominance. They'd been together long enough he should've been the one she went to when scared.

She still didn't get she wasn't alone anymore.

Maybe he was itching for a fight, or perhaps he'd just reached the end of his patience, but his brain disconnected from his mouth. "I'm more interested in why you didn't tell me he'd called."

She whirled to face him, brows arched. "Excuse me?"

"I was with you all day. Hell, I've been with you all along, trying my damnedest to get you to let me in." He paused. Did he just…Yes. He did.

The other side of the fence wasn't looking too great. Always careful, he'd never led his previous lovers on and was out the door the minute things even tilted in this particular direction. And though he'd never promised them anything, had been brutally honest, he was getting a glimpse of how they must've felt.

It sucked.

Regardless, he slammed the door on his past and every other woman who'd tried to do this exact thing to him. Because Avery was it for him. He'd met his match. And she couldn't even open her mouth to tell him something was wrong.

To make this shitstorm complete, he had the worst sensation that it didn't matter how much time he gave her. She would never meet him halfway.

He closed his eyes and sucked in some much needed oxygen. The denial of not admitting how deep he'd sunk threatened to disintegrate. Words he'd never said to another woman, never wanted to. This was unchartered territory for him, and he didn't know what the hell he was doing. For once, he was pretty damn sure he wasn't the one fucking this up.

Slowly, he opened his eyes to meet her unapologetic chocolate gaze. Eyes he'd gladly get lost in, and had. She had no idea how much she said with one look. If he were locked in a room with two terrorists, her ex, and a gun, and only had two bullets, he'd shoot her ex twice. He loved the guy that much. And she was still letting him control her life.

"Do you still love him?"

"What kind of question is that?" She crossed her arms over her chest with defiance, but the look in her eyes told him the bravado was false. She was just as scared.

"An honest one." He stepped closer until he was a heartbeat away and could breathe in her berry scent, which did nothing to calm him. "Answer me."

The edges of anger in her eyes gradually softened to understanding. She clenched her fingers as if restraining herself from reaching out. "No. I don't still love him."

Okay. Hell. That was good. "Then why couldn't you lean on me? Have I ever given you the impression I wouldn't understand?"

Instead of answering, she pulled out her phone, swiped the screen, and held it out to show him. "I don't love my ex, but do you still love this lifestyle? Because these pictures indicate you do."

Pinterest. He fucking hated the site. And most of those pictures were taken out of context. A woman in Shooters who'd climbed in his lap. Etcetera. He ground his teeth. "I—"

Something tugged at his shirt. He glanced down to find Hailey out of bed, holding out her iPad for him. "Just a second, squirt." He looked back at Avery, but her focus was on her daughter, and Cade had lost his train of thought. A common occurrence these days.

Hailey tugged again.

He pinched the bridge of his nose. "I said just a minute, Hailey."

Avery gasped.

At his own harsh tone, he winced. Dropping to his knees in front of the girl, he barely resisted the urge to pull her in for a hug for being an asshole. "I'm so sorry, squirt. I shouldn't have raised my voice. What do you need?"

"I think you should leave."

His gaze cut to Avery's. Tension knotted his shoulders. Fear clawed his stomach. "Don't do this." He rose.

She let out a long-winded sigh and closed her eyes. When she opened them again, his Avery was back. A tired, beaten version of her, but Avery just the same. "It's been a really long, really bad day. Too much for me to take in. Please understand. The fighting is upsetting her. Just go, Cade."

"That's it?" Just go. As if it were easy as that?

"No." She stepped closer and cupped his jaw, her touch tender. "I just need some time to acclimate."

He understood she was used to doing things all by herself, and changing that pattern would take time, but he wanted to be around when she... acclimated. Stepping back, he dropped his hands on his hips, fighting the need to roar. Again. Head pounding, the pressure in his chest grew to unbearable.

He stared at her for he didn't know how long, attempting to get past her armor and remembering how to breathe. It was no use. She was trying, but she'd shut herself off. Not that she'd ever really opened in the first place. Not completely.

He should walk away. Cut his losses and move on. She obviously didn't give a good goddamn about the potential between them. At the very least, she wasn't as invested as him. Except he couldn't walk. She was in his head and heart and blood. In his every thought and action.

Agony. Bliss.

And no one had ever shown her she mattered, had put her first. He sure wasn't going to cement that proof in her mind by doing the same. Because...shit. He loved her even when she was trying not to do the same.

Avery broke the epic stare down when a chill raced through the room and she shivered. She glanced toward the kitchen and froze. "Oh God. *No.*"

Ice crystallized in his gut as he followed her to the open back door. The room was chilly enough to indicate it had been open at least a few minutes.

She ran outside and screamed for Hailey, eyes wide, wind whipping her chestnut strands. "I got distracted by Richard's call. I didn't lock the door after I came in." She stumbled down the back deck stairs. "Hailey?"

The hair on his nape stood erect. Abject terror, unlike anything he'd ever known, shoved through him, stealing the beat from his heart. He ran inside and down the hall, but the girl wasn't in her room. Seraph was gone, too. Pulling his cell from his pocket, he dialed Drake.

"It's almost ten o'clock—"

Cade grabbed his coat and walked back outside as he spoke. "Hailey's missing. Get Flynn and meet me at Avery's. First rental cabin in the row on Justine's property. I'm going out to look for her. Have Flynn wait with Avery."

"On it."

He disconnected and gripped Avery's shoulders before she could take off alone into the night. "Call 911 and wait here. My brothers are on their way."

"No, I need to go—"

"Stay here in case she comes back." He gave her a little shake to ensure she'd heard him.

Her watery, panicked gaze met his. Her breath hitched. "Cade?"

"I'll find her. I promise." He didn't give her time to argue. He took off for the cluster of trees and didn't stop. Hailey couldn't be that far ahead of him, but he had no idea which way she'd gone.

Engaging the flashlight app on his phone, he shone the beam on the ground as he ran. Most of the snow had melted, but after a few yards, he spotted footprints in the mud heading east. Shit. The closer Hailey got to the mountain base the more danger of encountering a wild animal.

His phone rang and he connected before looking at the screen.

Drake's voice was short. "Which direction did you take?"

"East. I found footprints. Is Flynn with Avery?" She needed someone with her, and Flynn wouldn't be able to hear anything if he was involved with the search.

"Yes. The sheriff is one minute out. I'm two minutes from you."

"Break northeast. I'm heading southeast." He went to disconnect, but thought of something. "Call for the dog. Hailey won't answer, but Seraph might bark."

"Got it."

The foliage crunched under his boots as he wove through braches and over exposed roots. Every few seconds, he whistled for Seraph and called Hailey's name, stopping only long enough to listen for sounds. The wind was humid, but biting, and his fear notched to cataclysmic when he realized Hailey probably didn't have her coat.

Footsteps pounded to his left, but they were too heavy to be Hailey's. Drake's voice rang through the still night, yards from his location. "Hailey? Seraph? Come on, boy. Where are you?"

Cade glanced down, but he couldn't make out her tracks with the dried leaves. Tears stung his eyes and clogged his throat. "Hailey! Seraph!"

This was all his goddamn fault. If he hadn't started the fight with Avery, if he'd just kept his mouth shut, he wouldn't have scared the girl and she wouldn't have bolted. He swore to all that was holy, if something happened to her, he didn't think he'd survive it. Would never forgive himself. Just like Avery, Hailey had woven herself around his heart. So embedded, they were an extension of him.

"Hailey! Seraph!" He tried to whistle, but his jaw trembled too much to form the motion.

Helpless, he stopped and tugged at his hair in frustration.

A whine pierced the air, so faint he thought it might be himself making the noise out of desperation. He froze, eyes scanning, breath clouding in front of his face. It was too damn dark.

There. It came again. Due east.

He ran in that direction. "Hailey! Seraph!" He broke through a cluster of trees and came to a dead stop near a hollowed log.

Seraph sat on his hind legs, tail wagging. He barked, and Cade could've sworn the damn puppy smiled.

Hailey was next to him on the ground, rocking in place, staring heavenward.

Relief sagged his shoulders as he knelt in front of her, gaze scanning for injuries. His heart nearly cracked ribs with the force of each beat.

"Hey, squirt. Are you hurt?" His voice was unsteady, but he did his best to keep it calm, not illustrating the sheer panic when he couldn't find her. He'd freaked her out enough for one night.

Hailey, of course, didn't respond, didn't so much as look at him, but she was rocking, indicating she was unnerved. Her face was pale, aside from her bright pink cheeks. Her dark hair was windblown and knotted, but otherwise she seemed all right.

Alive. Thank Christ in heaven.

"I'm going to touch you just to be sure you have no ouchies, yeah?" He didn't give her time to react. He ran his shaking hands over her head, down her arms, across her torso, and finished with her legs, carefully watching her face. She didn't flinch or show distress.

Shrugging out of his coat, he wrapped Hailey inside and dialed Drake. "I've got her. She's okay." His voice broke. He bit his tongue and cleared his throat. "Head back and tell Avery. I'm on my way."

Disconnecting, he slammed his eyes closed as hot tears leaked down his cheeks. He attempted to draw in a steady breath, but damn it… His chest cracked open, spilling the fear and guilt. His shoulders shook as he swiped a hand down his face, hunched over, and gave himself a minute to collect his shit.

Hailey might not be his own, but this glimpse into fatherhood, into what it was like to love someone more than anything else, was gutting. The determination to protect her surged deep, a call unlike anything he'd known. Hell, he'd do anything not to go through something like this again.

No. She wasn't his daughter. Not by blood. But somewhere in the space of a couple months, she'd become his in every way that mattered.

He shook his head, noticing her tiny pink socks were wet and soiled. He plopped on his ass to remove his shoes. "I'm so sorry I scared you, squirt. We weren't fighting about you. Sometimes… Sometimes adults fight. But everything's all right now."

Removing her socks, he put them in his pockets and worked his own on over her little feet. The sight of her swimming in his coat and wearing his socks brought a fresh wave of tears. Shoving his bare feet back into his shoes, he stood.

"Please, *please,* don't ever scare me like this again." He picked up Seraph and set him in her lap, then lifted both the dog and the girl into his arms. He stared down at her a moment, caught between affection and apprehension. "I love you, squirt. Just so you know." He sighed. "Let's get you home."

She didn't fight him, and most of her shivering had stopped by the time he reached the clearing near the cabin.

Red and blue lights from the police cruiser were a beacon in the black inkiness. Drake and Flynn stood with Avery on the back deck, the sheriff off to the side talking to Justine and Gabby. They all looked up when he approached.

Avery wailed and ran toward him, launching into his arms. Fresh tears trekked down her pale cheeks as she wrapped her arms around his neck, squeezing Hailey between them. She took the girl from him, leaving his arms unbearably empty, and fell to her knees.

Seraph loped off toward Gabby.

Cade glanced away and eyed his brothers, the relief evident in their eyes. If only Avery could see just how much these people, his family, loved her, too.

The energy drained out of him in a blink.

Glancing back at her, he breathed for what felt like the first time in hours and cleared his throat. "She's okay, sweetheart."

He wasn't okay, but at least Hailey was home safe. Everything else was a clusterfuck, but all's well and all that.

Avery nodded repeatedly, running her hands over Hailey to check for injuries. Hailey was unusually complacent with the touch.

Needing a finger of whiskey and a hot shower, perhaps some bleach to scrub this night from his memory, he nodded to his brothers and walked around the cabin to his SUV. He was seconds from the worst adrenaline crash of his life. Hell if he was sticking around here for that.

He didn't answer the knock on his door at home an hour later when his brothers came calling. And he didn't respond to Avery's text, which only read: *Thank you.* He'd never made it to the liquor cabinet to pour whiskey, nor had he showered. Instead, he sat in his dark living room for hours, with Freeman lying across his feet and Cutin perched on his shoulder, while he tried to embrace the numbness.

He found himself missing his dad with a burning agony as if the loss was a fresh wound, and wishing the old man were here to tell him what to do. About Avery. About Hailey. About his feelings and future and how to handle this overwhelming need to take care of them both. Because Cade had no fucking clue.

All he did know was that despite all the crap that could go wrong, all the ways he could lose them, taking the risk was worth it. No matter the outcome.

He just had to prove that to Avery.

Chapter 25

From the back deck steps, Avery smiled at Brent's attempts to play with Hailey by the riverbank. They were sitting on a log, Brent making girly sounds on behalf of the doll in his hand, and Hailey not taking the bait. She did laugh at Brent's antics a time or two, though. He'd come by after his shift at the clinic with the excuse to share his niece's Barbies with Hailey, but Avery suspected it was really a ploy to check up on her.

Which was fine. She'd needed the distraction from her heart-stopping scare. After the medics had checked out Hailey and Avery had gotten her settled in bed last night, she'd walked down the hall to find only Drake had remained behind. He'd insisted she take the rest of the week off, sat with her for an hour in quiet reassurance, and then left without another word.

She sighed. Strong, silent Drake. Flynn had been a godsend while the men were out searching. He'd paced with her, rubbed her back, paced some more. Both were so unlike their brother Cade it was hard to imagine they were related. They all had different degrees of humor and protectiveness, but Cade just…well, was different.

Cade hadn't responded to her text. She'd tried to call him today during his lunch hour, but it had gone right to voicemail. Their argument sat like lead in her belly. The fear in his eyes when they'd discovered Hailey gone tore at her heart. He loved her daughter. And he'd found her when Avery had been frozen in shock, too numb to move.

For years, it had just been her and Hailey. Even when Richard had still been in the picture, it was just them against the world. Cade had broken through the barrier she'd created to protect them both. He hadn't been afraid to let them in, to love her daughter, and she'd pushed him away with both hands.

Before Hailey had gone missing, Avery had intended to hash out their issues later, in the light of day and with a fresh mind. She was too raw from Richard's call, too overwhelmed at the time to think straight. When Cade had gotten short with Hailey, something inside her snapped.

Had she been thinking rationally, she would have recognized Cade's apology immediately after he'd realized what he'd done. And he hadn't said sorry to Avery. He'd addressed Hailey himself. Something Richard would never have done.

Heck, he was getting married and never thought to include his daughter.

She blinked and brought her surroundings into focus. The late afternoon sun was dipping west behind the tree line, creating long shadows and a chill in the air. The pink and purple hues of sunset reflected off the river behind Brent and Hailey. An owl hooted from that direction, and she loved the inquisitive noise. It beat the woodpecker driving her nuts in the mornings.

Despite her initial reservations, and Camp Crystal Lake aside, it really was quite beautiful out here. It was getting to be peak season for tourism, though. Her mom would need the cabin back soon. Avery needed to amp up her apartment search. She'd sure miss this view.

As if reading her thoughts, her mom moved from a deck chair to sit beside Avery on the stairs. Her scent of patchouli rose over the pine and rain-dampened grass. She bumped Avery's shoulder with her own. "I'm so glad you both are making friends. I knew transferring here would be good for you."

Avery watched Brent and Hailey, unable to argue that point. Hailey was forming attachments in her own way, and was having fewer tantrums. In fact, Avery could count on one hand the number of fits since they'd moved to Redwood Ridge. Hailey also seemed more content, more…happy.

She sighed. "Cade loves her an awful lot. You only have to look in his eyes to see it." Or note his actions when he thought no one was watching. That was the true test, the greatest illustration of his character. Heck, even his brothers were good with her.

"She's pretty hard not to love. You did a great job with her, honey." She paused a beat. "I'm pretty sure Cade loves you as well."

Avery closed her eyes. She knew that, too. "I wasn't looking for love, Mom." She didn't want it, at least not initially. She'd barely survived the first time, and she hadn't loved Richard half as much or in the same way as she'd grown to love Cade.

"Well, take it from someone who knows. Whether you look for it or not, love finds you."

Since Mom had been married four times before, Avery figured her mother was an expert in all things romance. Or was really, really bad at it. "I don't know how you do it. How do you leave yourself vulnerable time and time again?"

Her mother looked out over the expanse of land and breathed deep. "There's no greater feeling. The flutters when you first kiss, the putter of your heart when you know it's real. I live for that."

Avery tried to remember a time when she'd felt those things with Richard, and came up blank. Being with Cade, on the other hand, was like riding a rollercoaster set for derailment.

"I've been chasing that feeling for almost twenty-eight years." Mom looked at her, and missing from her gaze was her typical airiness. "I've loved other men since your father, but not as hard. So, I keep chasing it, hoping I'll find it again."

They never talked about her dad. Growing up, Avery had rarely asked and her mom wasn't forthcoming. Most of the time, she figured her mom didn't know who Avery's real father had been. "What was he like?"

Her mother's smile grew wistful and distant. "Like you, actually. You got my physical characteristics, but you inherited a lot of his personality." She leaned back on her elbows. "He was…cautious. He never met a problem he couldn't solve or an emotion he couldn't master. Until I swept into his life. We had one wild, wonderful summer, and you were the result."

Pain filled her eyes, wrinkling her brow. "I regretted not telling him about you, but he was destined for great things, and I didn't want to weigh him down. Then, this one day, you must've been three or four years old, I burned your grilled cheese sandwich. You put your little hands on your little hips and looked over your nose at me. I swear, you looked just like him." She sat forward, dropping her gaze. "I decided to get in touch with him, only to find out he'd died in a boating accident the spring before."

Tears threatened, not for her own grief, she'd obviously never known her dad, but for her mother who clearly loved him even after all these years. Avery swallowed the tears and took her mother's hand. "I'm so sorry, Mom."

"That's okay, honey." She kissed Avery's temple. "I get a piece of him every day in you." She sighed, her breath fogging in the chilly air before her face.

Suddenly, her mother looked her age. Years of life and laugh lines fanned around her eyes and mouth, punctuating the no-holds-barred way she lived. Not present on her face was regret, which made Avery wonder if, in twenty years, she'd have the same to say for herself.

Mom patted her hand. "I don't want you to end up like me, loving too many people in a vain search for the one. But I don't want you to wind up like him either, so guarded about opening your heart that you miss love when it comes around."

Avery inhaled slowly, filling her lungs. She had been doing that very thing her whole life, and she had to wonder now if it was genetic or taught. From day one, she'd been comparing Richard and Cade, weighing the similarities and differences. Not to measure them, but because the person she'd been with Richard was a vast cry from the person Cade brought out in her.

"You never loved Richard. I think you know that now since real love has entered your life." Mom grinned. "He wears blue scrubs and a stethoscope, in case you were wondering who I meant."

Avery laughed and dropped her head to her mom's shoulder. Maybe she should've taken more cues from her growing up. Sure, Mom forgot to charge her cell phone most days and she couldn't make a lasagna to save the homeless, but she was wiser than Avery had given her credit. "Love you."

"Love you more."

* * * *

By the time Friday rolled around, Avery was sick to death of her own company. She appreciated Drake giving her the time off, but she was crawling out of her skin. Which was interesting because before moving to Redwood Ridge, all she'd had was silence and Hailey. No friends, no job, no life.

Cade had texted this morning before his shift, letting her know he'd be over tonight to watch Hailey during her meeting. That's all the contact she'd had with him. In five days. One text. She was doing her best to give him space and let him think things through, but how was he supposed to do that without all the facts? The way they'd left things seemed like…an end.

She forced herself not to pick up the phone and call him, or snatch her keys to drive to the clinic. He said he'd be over tonight. She'd talk to him then.

What other choice was there? Despite her protective stance and determination not to shift into her old pattern, she'd gone and fallen in love with Cade. Fallen hard for his humor and heart and heat. And because he was who he was, she knew she wouldn't regret it, even if they were over.

Until now, she hadn't been close to love. Not the real kind that hollowed her core when they weren't together, or made every stray thought drift to him, or made her laugh and cry and worry and hope.

Her mother was right. She hadn't loved Richard. He had been a safety net. Settlement. The easy route she'd been too weak not to take.

There was no settling for Cade and no safety. With him, she didn't need those things. Because true security came from not being able to live without him and knowing, without any doubt, he felt the same. He'd put her first and do anything to make her happy. Without conditions and obligations. He'd been selflessly putting her back together from the beginning, and he hadn't been the one to break her in the first place. Men like Cade loved because they wanted to, because they had no choice. He was capable of the unguarded emotion in ways she'd never encountered or fully allowed of herself.

He'd catch her. Every time.

It made her sick to her stomach that he thought she didn't feel the same. In the past, she hadn't loved with bone-deep intensity, but she was smart enough to recognize it when it slammed into her chest.

Blowing out a breath, she donned her coat and picked up Hailey from school. Back at the cabin, she settled Hailey at the table with her device and kept herself busy by making chili, lest she go insane waiting for Cade to arrive.

He walked in the front door just as Avery set two bowls on the table with a basket of rolls. Without glancing up, he stripped off his coat and hung it neatly on the peg. His boots were next, which he set by the door. He stepped into the kitchen and all the air evaporated.

Still wearing his scrubs, the muscles of his arms and chest filled the dark blue material. Her heart fluttered and desire pooled in her belly. Her mom had been right about that, too. Any lingering doubt about loving him was erased. No wonder Mom chased this feeling. There was nothing like it.

Taking a seat next to Hailey, Cade peeked over her shoulder at the device. "What's up, squirt? Can I play?"

Hailey squealed and flapped her hands.

A grin split his face and he tapped the screen, placing an X on the tic-tac-toe app.

Avery's stomach twisted into knots, her throat tight. He hadn't looked at her once. He smiled at Hailey, but there were shadows under his eyes as if he hadn't slept, and his shoulders sagged.

"Hi," she breathed. "I made chili." She pinched her eyes closed at her lame attempt to start conversation.

His glance darted to the bowls. "Smells good. We'll finish this game and dig in."

Still no eye contact and his tone was as flat as the table.

"Can we talk?" She twisted her fingers together and fisted them to stop. All she wanted was to run her hands through his hair and force him to look at her. Pull him in for a kiss and tell him how stupid she'd been.

His back tensed as he ran his hand over his neck. Several beats passed before he turned his head in her direction, but the blue of his eyes didn't lift to hers. "Later, when you get home."

Did he say that because he didn't want to discuss things in front of Hailey? Worried he'd raise his voice again and scare her? Did he not want to dump Avery with her daughter around?

Heck, for all she knew, he was concerned about global warming or crop circles for all the indication he was giving.

Her stomach threatened to revolt. This shielded, defensive man before her wasn't her Cade, wasn't the man she fell in love with.

"Cade…"

His eyes closed for a moment, brows pinched as if in pain before he shook his head. When he spoke, his voice was weary and soft. "Later, sweetheart. Go to your meeting."

Sweetheart. If he used his endearment, that had to be a good sign, right?

They were going to be discussing the St. Patrick's potluck at the meeting. Mostly groundwork and ideas. The sooner she got there, the sooner she could get back and put herself out of this limbo misery. Perhaps she could even feign exhaustion and cut the pow-wow short a half hour early.

Shrugging into her coat, she kissed Hailey and said good-bye.

She couldn't attest to anything discussed at the meeting because she'd spent the entire time fidgeting in her seat, checking her phone, and dissecting every syllable that had escaped Cade's mouth. Since he'd only said a grand total of three sentences to her, the reliving was brief. Yet she'd scrutinized and dismembered those three sentences, analyzing the inflection of his voice until she'd nearly pulled her hair out with frustration.

Blessedly, no one stopped her to chat on the way out, and she was able to drive home without wrapping the car around a tree. A miracle, considering her distracted state.

Cade's car wasn't parked out front when she arrived.

Panic squeezed her throat as she fumbled with the seatbelt and exited the car. The lights were on, casting a warm, yellow glow from the cabin as she barreled up the porch steps. She was about to shove through the door when she noticed a small piece of paper taped to the glass above the knob.

We're at my house. Meet you there. ~Cade

His house? What were they doing there? It was past Hailey's bedtime. Plus, he'd never taken her anywhere while he'd watched her in the past. She checked her phone, but she hadn't missed a call.

She froze. Something was wrong.

Trembling, she raced back to the car and sped down the tree-lined road toward Cade's place.

Chapter 26

Cade sat across from Hailey on the bed and practiced their project one last time on her iPad before Avery arrived. He suspected this was what the girl had been trying to show him on the device the night she'd found him and Avery in an argument, which only made him love Hailey even more.

Checking his watch again, the acid in his gut became volcanic. Avery would be here any minute.

All week it had been a battle not to go over to her house, not to call or answer her texts. He missed her so damn much he'd gotten a collective eight hours of sleep between the time he'd walked out of her cabin and last night. He'd forced food down and went through the motions at work, all to bide his time to get to tonight.

He'd wanted her to have time to think, to get settled after their argument and reach her own conclusions without his interference. He could only hope she missed him half as much as he did her. If she didn't, all his plans and arrangements would be for naught.

Truth was, he could wait her out. Yeah, he'd been impatient as of late, but when he picked apart her actions, her reactions, he knew their relationship would eventually lead where he wanted. She loved him. She might not know it yet or trust herself with the knowledge, but she loved him.

Except sitting on his hands and abiding by patience was not what she'd walk into any minute, nor was it working. And what he'd done would either throw her into his arms or have her bolting. He couldn't be sure which, but he had to do something. This holding pattern was killing him dead.

The front door slammed and Cade's heart tripped at the thud.

"Cade?" Avery's voice floated up to him.

He sucked a harsh inhale and looked at Hailey. "Showtime, squirt. You ready?"

She squealed and flapped her hands.

"Cade?"

Avery's tone was panicked, so he rose quickly. "Wait here. Be right back."

Leaving the bedroom, he rounded the corner and stopped at the top of the stairs. "Up here."

She darted to the base of the steps and stopped. "What's wrong? Where's Hailey?"

Damn. Scaring her to death wasn't in the plan. "She's upstairs. She's fine."

Hunching over, she grabbed her chest and exhaled.

He met her halfway up the steps and ran his hands down her arms. "I'm sorry. I didn't mean to worry you."

She closed her eyes and nodded, her shoulders deflating.

Completely unprepared for what seeing her would do to him, he drank in the sight of her. It had only been a few days, but it had been the longest few days of his damn life. Before she'd left for her meeting, he couldn't look at her or he would've lost it.

His chest filled to capacity, and his throat suddenly grew tight. She had on a minimal amount of makeup, her chestnut hair was up in a hazard ponytail, and she wore nothing more fancy than jeans with a T-shirt under her coat, but she was the most beautiful thing he'd ever laid eyes on.

That was the thing that tugged at his gut the most. She didn't have to do or be anything but herself and he wanted her. No frills or fluff. She didn't cling or pretend or coax. Avery was real and genuine and simple.

Her chocolate gaze met his, flecks of honey swimming in all that brown, and he pretty much stopped breathing. If eyes were the window to the soul, as the saying went, then her windows had just been wiped clean. Finally, there was no hesitation or restraint. She was wide open, looking at him as if her heart was there for the taking.

Lifting his arms, he stripped her coat off and tossed it down the stairs, then cupped her cheeks in his hands. "I missed you."

Relief filled her eyes. When, *when* would she stop doubting him?

"I missed you, too. About what I said earlier this week, I'm sorry." A pained expression twisted her face. "I don't want to hurt you for anything. You should know, I don't think I ever loved him, and I'm done letting the past cloud the present. I—"

He kissed her softly, not to shut her up, but to stop the excuse. He didn't need an explanation. He just needed her. He got why she'd said those things. Honestly, he did. He couldn't even blame her, but if it was the last thing he ever did, he was going to make her understand that he'd never treat her the way that bastard had.

She sighed when he pulled away, her warm breath skating across his jaw. Slowly, her heavy lids lifted and her gaze darted around. The hazy seduction began to clear. "Why are you guys at your place, anyway? You've never taken Hailey to your—"

Her gaze landed on the pictures he'd hung on the wall in alignment with the slope of the staircase. Five in total. One of him with both his parents after graduation. Another with him and his brothers outside the clinic last fall. A cute shot of Avery and Hailey he'd snapped on his phone during their snow excursion. Hailey and Seraph on the floor in front of the fireplace, playing tug-of-war, was closest to his favorite.

That honor belonged to the photo he'd stolen off Pinterest…him and Avery dancing. In her knockout red dress and him in his suit, she was smiling up at him. One of his hands cradled her face and the other was low on her back. Lights twinkled behind them. Cade had no idea who'd taken the picture, but he was grateful. One look at them and it was obvious she was his whole world.

Maybe she'd finally get that.

Her voice was thick when she broke the silence. "When did you hang these?" She was still staring at the pictures, so he couldn't read her reaction, but her body didn't stiffen against his.

"This week."

Her gaze darted to his, and something battled in her eyes. Hope? "After our fight?"

Understanding dawned. The frustrating woman thought he was done with their relationship and hanging pictures meant he wasn't. "Yes, after our fight." He pulled her closer and kissed her forehead, the knot in his chest loosening as he inhaled her scent and touched her soft skin. "I have something to show you. Come upstairs."

She nodded and he took her hand, leading her to what was once an empty bedroom he'd had no clue what to do with. He knew now, though.

Swallowing hard, he pushed the door open and stepped inside, dropping Avery's hand to give her breathing room. She halted over the threshold and gasped.

The dogs were sitting on the bed, battling for Hailey's attention. She was busy playing on her device, paying them no mind.

"Oh, my God." Avery pressed a hand to her forehead.

Was that a *this-is-awesome* Oh my God or a *holy-shit* Oh my God? He couldn't tell and, at the moment, she only offered her profile.

Deciding that keeping his mouth shut was the best recourse until she gave him some direction to her thoughts, he took in the bedroom again as if trying to see it through her eyes.

The room was painted a light pink with a mural of a life-sized dollhouse on one wall. The lacey curtains over the bay window were white to match the new furniture—a full-sized bed and dresser. There were throw pillows all over the floor because Hailey liked pillows, and a small table in the corner.

Avery made a choking sound, and he feared he'd gone too far.

Needing to explain, he rubbed his neck. "You said you needed to move out of the cabin before tourist season started. Instead of getting an apartment, I thought maybe you could move in here. With me."

Her wide gaze whipped to his, and he snapped his jaw closed. Why the hell could he never say the right thing when it concerned her? The point was to try and ease her into things, and he was mucking it up.

"This would be Hailey's room. Obviously. Zoe painted the mural for her. Gabby picked out the furniture. The pillows were all me." Hell. He pinched the bridge of his nose and closed his eyes.

When he opened them, she hadn't moved one iota and looked like he could knock her over with a feather. Then—*damn it*—tears started pooling in her eyes and panic took on a new name.

"You don't have to decide right away. Or do anything now. The offer's there, if you want it. Open for as long as you need." *Christ. Shut it, O'Grady.*

Silence hung.

Hailey squealed, drawing their attention to her. She bounced on the mattress, gaze trained up and hands flapping, making the dogs bark. At least one of his girls liked the idea of staying with him.

He couldn't take the silence. Walking to the bed, he sat on the edge and turned on the iPad. If he looked at Avery and found her closed up tight, he'd lose it, so he kept his gaze down.

"Cade…"

He shook his head at her quivering, quiet voice. *Don't say no, sweetheart. Please.*

Scrolling through the apps, he attempted one more time to explain. "I know we haven't been together long, and I know you're scared. But this thing between us? It's real. I think about you all the time, and I want you in my life. Both of you."

Hell. He wanted to be a family.

Finding the app he needed, he called Hailey to him and had her stand between his knees. "Ready, squirt? Show your mom what we've been working on."

Hailey's finger hovered over the button a few seconds before she tapped the icon and a robotic voice said, "Eye." Moving on to the next key, she tapped "Heart" with no hesitation.

Cade's gut clenched. This next one always stumped Hailey when they'd worked on their project.

Hailey paused, but after a moment, she tapped… "U."

Cade threw his hands up and barked a laugh. "Yeah! That's my girl. Knuckles." He held out his hand and she bumped her fist to his. "She kept getting stuck on that last part, but…" He looked up at Avery and did a double take.

Tears streamed down her pale cheeks, eyes red-rimmed and puffy. Her forehead was scrunched, her lips parted, and her breathing labored like she was on the verge of hyperventilating. With her hand fisting her shirt over her chest, she uttered some form of a startled noise as her gaze darted between him and Hailey.

"You…" She pressed her lips together and wheezed. "You taught her to say *I love you*?"

"Uh…not exactly." He shot to his feet, worried she was going to collapse and wanting to be ready to catch her. "We couldn't find a "love" button, so we had to go with heart." He shrugged.

Damn if her breathing didn't grow more labored.

Shit. It dawned on him he hadn't said the words to her. He'd planned to start off this whole crazy tirade with that and got lost in his frayed nerves instead.

Grabbing the device from the bed, he tapped out, "Eye. Heart. You." Then he added his own ending. "Two."

There it was. She could take it or leave it. He should probably warn her that if she chose the latter, he'd chase her to the ends of the earth and back.

Or maybe she knew because finally—thank Almighty, *finally*—a grin broke out on her face and she sucked in an uneven breath.

Just in case he wasn't clear enough…"I love you. Move in with me today, or next week, or next year. I don't care when, as long as you promise to do it eventually. When you get used to the idea of us living together, and my socks on the floor or my snoring doesn't bother you, then I'll ask you to marry me. I think it might be too soon for a proposal today, but you're it for me. Just know it's coming. Baby steps."

He had point five seconds to take in her watery, ragged laugh before she launched herself at him and pressed her lips to his. He stumbled backward and grabbed her ass, righting them before they fell.

Hell. Yes. Right where she belonged.

Sliding one hand into her hair, he deepened the kiss, stroking his tongue with hers, tasting the salty saline of her tears. She kissed him with no restraint, meeting him in the middle and pouring so much emotion into the act he almost got weepy himself. His heart was so happy it turned over behind his ribs.

When oxygen became vital again, he eased back to look in her eyes. "I'll have you know, this is very inappropriate behavior to do in front of a child."

She grinned and glanced at the bed. "She's asleep."

With Avery still in his arms, he turned. Sure enough, Hailey was out cold. "My plan worked. You have to spend the night with me." He pointed to the dogs. "Stay."

Then he cinched Avery higher so she could wrap her legs around his waist. He shut off the light before heading down the hallway to his bedroom. *Their* bedroom.

"I heart you, too, Cade."

He came to an abrupt halt beside the bed. "Is that a yes?"

"To which part?"

"Any of it. All of it. Take your pick. In fact—"

She laughed, the smoky sound sealing all the empty spaces in his soul. "Never mind. I love you. A yes to everything. Now say it back and then take me to bed."

"*It back*," he teased, then laid her out on the sheets and followed her down. He pressed a kiss to her cheek. "I do love you back." He kissed her other cheek. "And front." Kissing her forehead, he whispered, "And top." His lips trailed to her chin. "And bottom. I love you everywhere in between."

Wrapping her arms around his neck, she laughed and nuzzled his jaw. "Okay, okay. I get it."

He stared down at her, at everything he never knew he wanted but somehow got anyway. "There was never a doubt in my mind, sweetheart."

Check out a preview for the next Redwood Ridge book,

Tracking You...

Chapter 1

Gabby Cosette smoothed her hand down the simple baby blue sundress she meticulously picked out for this evening and tried not to look too eager. Or throw up. That wouldn't do, either.

From a back booth, she glanced around the only Italian restaurant in Redwood Ridge, comforted by the fact it was still early yet for the dinner rush. The place was a good choice. Right? Not as casual as Shooters—the bar her and her friends frequented—but not as formal as one of the seafood restaurants that dotted their Oregon coastal town. A step above grabbing coffee or a beer, yet it didn't scream desperation.

Was a booth in the back too obvious? Had she overdone it with her makeup? Maybe she should've put her hair up instead of down?

No, no. She went for light and natural on purpose. The patrons of Redwood Ridge had known her all her life. It wasn't far out of the realm of ordinary for her to wear a dress and light cosmetics. She was being a basket case.

It's just… Well, she hadn't had a date in a year. A year!

To calm her nerves, she drew in a deep breath and focused on the red checkered tablecloth. A votive candle flickered on the windowsill to her right, the flame reflecting off the tinted glass. The parking lot stretched beyond, where her date's car was not in one of the available spots.

It was silly to get this worked up over a first date, especially with Tom. She'd gone to elementary and high school with him. His parents still lived down the street from hers. Strange how he'd never shown any interest in her romantically, yet out of the blue, he'd asked her out this week.

Then again, most everyone in town viewed her as the sweet Cosette girl, everyone's friend. Thus the no date in a year. It was hard to get a guy to think about kissing her, never mind imagining her naked, when she had platonic all but tattooed on her forehead.

The waitress strolled over in her apron, holding a notepad in her hand. "Are you waiting on someone, sweetie pie?"

"Yes." She smiled and grabbed her cell on the table. Tom was five minutes late. "He should be here any minute."

"Ooh. Is it a date?" Mavis planted a hand on her plump waist and grinned, the wrinkles around her eyes growing to crevices. Gabby wasn't sure how old Mavis was, no one really knew, but she never seemed to age past the state from when Gabby was a child.

Gabby opened her mouth to answer, but Tom strode toward her, weaving around tables and plopping in the seat across the booth.

"Couldn't find ya at the bar. I wasn't expecting a table."

It was still early, and Le Italy didn't get that crowded even on a Friday night. How hard could it possibly have been to locate her? "Give us a sec," she told Mavis and waited for her to step away.

Tom had blond hair too short for her preference and a thin mouth. His unremarkable brown gaze darted around the restaurant and back to her. He made no attempt to apologize for being late, and it appeared as if he'd just come from work. His jeans and T-shirt were paint-splattered. The hazard of working for his dad's commercial painting and roofing company.

"Thanks for meeting me." He took off his ball cap and scratched his head.

Why did that sound un-date-like? "Um…sure thing. How's work going?" Her gaze dipped to his hands, no better off than his clothes. Maybe she should've picked Shooters after all.

Something felt very, very off as her belly twisted. Not with nerves this time. Confused, Gabby's mind scrolled through their conversation from earlier in the week when he'd brought his dog into the vet clinic where she worked. As he was checking out, he'd anxiously spun around to face her and asked if she could meet him tonight.

"Good. Work's good." He put his hat back on and glanced outside. "Getting to be warmer out, so the jobs are picking up."

Perhaps he was just nervous, too. Her tension drained a degree.

Mavis returned and asked for a drink order.

Tom lifted his hand to wave her off. "Nothing for me, thanks. I can't stay long. Got a poker game with the guys tonight. I need to shower before they show up."

The forced smile Gabby had plastered on her face began to wilt like her mom's petunias in August. What did he mean he couldn't stay long? And why would he ask her out and schedule a card game on the same night? Plus, he could shower for his friends, but not her?

Mavis divided her gaze between them, a mix of bewilderment and irritation lifting her brows. She tapped her pen to her pad as the silence hung. "Can I get *you* something?" She focused on Gabby, her tone indicating she should order something.

"I'll have a sweet tea. Thank you." When the waitress walked away, Gabby looked at Tom. He'd thrown his arm over the back of the booth and had stretched his legs out. The aroma of Ode de Paint Thinner wafted across the table. "So…?"

"Right, right." Tom leaned forward and crossed his arms. "I appreciate you letting me do this in person."

She stilled. "Do what?" Because she was definitely getting the this-is-not-a-date vibe now.

A warring shift in contradiction took over her body. Everything inside grew rapidly chilly while her skin heated in what she hoped wasn't a blush. Her pale complexion always gave away her emotions, and she hated that more than she'd hated freshman algebra. Math was evil.

He let out a tense laugh, which sounded more like a guffaw, and drew several heads from other diners. "Not exactly a conversation you want to have over the phone or somethin', ya know?"

No. She didn't know. "Maybe if you just tell me?"

He played with the parmesan shaker, not meeting her gaze. "Well, the whole town's buzzing about Rachel and Jeff's split."

She frowned, not connecting the dots on his crazy pattern. Her older sister had only dated Jeff for a few weeks which, per Rachel standards, might as well have been marriage. Rachel liked to keep her options—and legs—open.

Guilt immediately consumed her for the crass thought, but it didn't make it any less true. She and Rachel couldn't be any more different. Rachel was aloof and sexy. Gabby was the girl next door. Men desired Rachel. The only thing they desired from Gabby was a shoulder to cry on after her sister shot them down.

She twirled a strand of hair around her finger to keep from fidgeting. "I don't understand what Rachel and Jeff have to do with…" Unable to finish the sentence—because she had no idea anymore what "this" was—she waved her hand between them.

"Well," he said in an aw-shucks kind of way that made her want to grind her teeth, "now that Rachel's available, I thought maybe you could put in a good word for me?" He blinked up at her hopefully.

She stared at him for several stunned beats.

The reality of the situation slowly crept into her head and shoved around her skull. Her stomach dropped somewhere near her ankles. When he'd asked her out at the clinic earlier this week, she supposed he hadn't actually asked her "out." The phrasing he'd used had been something more like, *Can you meet up with me on Friday?*

And stupid, stupid her had taken that to mean he wanted a date.

As if. Like anyone would ever be interested in her when her sister had gotten all the good genes and didn't have the reputation of being everyone's pal. Good ole Gabby.

"This wasn't a date," she muttered to herself, more to ground herself to the situation than for confirmation.

"Huh?"

Closing her eyes, she shook her head to let Tom know her utterance wasn't important. To him, it wasn't. Because she wasn't the one he wanted, and there was no sense in amplifying her mortification. It wasn't his fault she'd brainlessly gotten excited.

God, she was an idiot.

Her heart sank a little as hope withered a painful death. She shouldn't be surprised, really. It wasn't like this was the first time someone had tried to use her as a go-between. If not with her sister, then her friends. Still, she'd been looking forward to tonight, had thought it was a blessed break in her dry spell.

A lump formed in her throat as tears threatened. She looked around the room until she could get the pathetic emotions under control. Many of the tables had filled since she'd arrived. Man, if she started crying now...

"So what do you say?" Tom set the shaker aside. "Could you help a friend out?"

Friend. She nearly choked on the word. Instead, she cleared her throat and forced a smile. Who was she to stand in the way of potential true love? "Of course. I'll talk to her tomorrow."

His nervous grin widened into something more genuine, drawing attention to the slight crookedness of his two front teeth. "You're the best, Gabby."

Yep. That was her. She resisted patting her own back in a sarcastic response.

Did she really want a relationship with him, anyway? Probably not. He wasn't classically handsome, but he had his charms. His looks didn't matter to her as long as he had a good heart or sense of humor. It was more the idea of having someone that appealed.

Which was not going to happen. Not tonight.

Tom rose from his seat and tipped his ball cap as if it were a Stetson. "Thanks so much. I gotta go."

Of course. Alone again. Maybe she should become a poet. It had worked for Hemmingway.

She nodded. Her gaze followed him to the front door, and then over to the bar where she was thinking of doing a little Cuervo therapy.

Flynn was leaning against the bar, his direct sights on her. Still wearing his dark blue scrubs, his posture resonated his typical laid-back demeanor. Now there was an attractive man. Tall enough for the top of her head to reach his chin and ropey muscle on an athletic build. Wide shoulders, narrow waist.

All three of the O'Grady brothers were sexy in their own unique way. But they'd grown up together, and there had never been any chemistry between her and them. Cade, the youngest brother, was engaged to their office manager as of a couple months ago, and Drake, the eldest brother, was a widow. Gabby couldn't envision him dating again, at least not anytime soon. Flynn wasn't seeing anyone.

Not that it mattered. She worked for Flynn and his brothers at their vet clinic, so that was an automatic hand-slap.

From across the room, Flynn's eyes narrowed as he tilted his head in question toward the door. *Where'd your date go?*

Flynn was deaf, and through the years she'd grown to read him easily. They always had a strong connection, being able to understand one another without words. Part of that was being good friends and part was due to working closely together for many years.

She shrugged in answer, keeping her disappointed expression open for him. Sucked to be her.

His brows lowered and he straightened from the bar, poised to head over until the bartender tapped his shoulder. Flynn signed for his takeout and carried it over to her booth, setting the bag down on the table before sitting.

His hazel eyes, framed by criminally long lashes, swept her face. *"What happened?"* he signed with his hands. *"I thought you had a date?"*

Per their routine, she signed and spoke simultaneously. "Me, too. Turns out he wanted my help getting in with my sister." At his scowl, she shrugged, embarrassed enough without the urge to discuss it. "My own fault. I read too much into the initial conversation."

He stared at her with disbelief and shook his head. His handsome, angular face was dialed to irritated and his full lips were twisted. He ran a hand through dark strawberry blond hair just this side of wavy. Flynn had a tendency to forget routine trims.

Mavis made her way back to the booth. Her gaze zeroed in on Flynn. "Decided to eat in?"

Habit had him turning to Gabby. He could read lips, but sometimes people spoke too quickly or didn't face him fully so he couldn't see what they were saying. Gabby signed Mavis' question.

He grinned, back to his usual glower-free self, and nodded.

Well, it wasn't a date, but Flynn was better company, anyway. Gabby looked at the waitress. "He'll have a beer, whatever's on tap, and can I get the largest piece of tiramisu you can find?"

"You got it, sweetie pie."

Gabby watched her walk away before letting out a sigh, chest deflating. When she looked at Flynn, his expression indicated he was patiently waiting for her attention again.

He leaned forward as if to punctuate a point. *"He's an asshole."*

She laughed. "Aren't they all?"

"Not all." He pulled a Styrofoam container of lasagna from the to-go bag, opened it, and grabbed her fork from her place setting. He waited for her to take it from him before signing, *"Dig in."*

He picked up his fork and took a bite, then did a double take when she just poked at his lasagna. *"Hey. You all right?"*

"I'll be okay. Just not today. Today, I mope." He was one of the few people she'd admit that to, and since his gaze had softened and worry wrinkled his brow, she forced herself to take a bite. "Thanks, Flynn."

He nodded, watching her intently. *"Movie night. My house. I'll even let you pick."*

Why the hell wasn't he dating someone? Seriously.

Sad truth was, women tended to overlook Flynn because of his disability, just like they overlooked her for being in the friend zone. People sucked. "Maybe we should make one of those pacts. You know, the one where if neither of us is married by the time we're thirty we marry each other."

One eyebrow quirked in his custom you-done-gone-crazy. *"I'm thirty-one and you turn the same in a couple weeks. That ship has sailed."*

Yeah. "Fine. Throw logic into my delusions."

His shoulders bounced in a silent laugh.

She smiled. "Okay, hot date. What if I pick a sappy movie?"

He shrugged. *"I'll hide my man card. Tell no one."*

Covering her face, she laughed until her chest ached. When she sobered, her mood was irrevocably lighter. Praise God for good friends. "Just for that, I'll share my tiramisu."

"Deal." He ate a few more forkfuls before his smile slipped a fraction, the hint of seriousness reflecting in his eyes. *"For the record, I would've taken the pact."*

She dropped her chin in her hand before moving to sign. "We would've had such cute babies, too."

"Word. Now eat or I'll make you watch Die Hard *again."*

She scooped a bite of cheesy carb goodness. Calories didn't count on crappy days. "Which one?"

He whipped her a "duh" look. *"All of them."*

Death by Bruce Willis. Could be worse things.

Meet the Author

Bestselling author Kelly Moran says she gets her ideas from everyone and everything around her and there's always a book playing out in her head. No one who knows her bats an eyelash when she talks to herself, and no one is safe from becoming her next fictional character. She is a Catherine Award winner, Readers Choice finalist, Holt Medallion Finalist, and earned one of the 10 Best Reads by *USA Today's* HEA. She is also a Romance Writers of America member. Her interests include: sappy movies, MLB, NFL, driving others insane, and sleeping when she can. She is a closet caffeine junkie and chocoholic, but don't tell anyone. She resides in Wisconsin with her husband, three sons, and two dogs. Most of her family lives in the Carolinas, so she spends a lot of time there as well. She loves hearing from her readers. Please visit her at authorkellymoran. com, twitter.com/authorkmoran, or facebook.com/authorkellymoran.

Made in the USA
Middletown, DE
01 May 2017